I0787978

SERENITY RAYNE & CASSANDRA FEATHERSTONE

NEW MOON RISING

CHILDREN OF THE MOON: BOOK ONE

Ebook Cover: Covers by Christian
Alternate PB Cover: Pretty in Ink Creations
Editing & Formatting: Little Tailfeather Publishing
Alphas/Betas/Arc Teams: Cassandra's claws, Serenity's Den & BCATs teams
Sensitivity Readers: Brit Mason, Gail Jericho
Cassandra's logo: Pretty in Ink Creations
Serenity's logo: Pretty in Ink Creations
Translation Consultant: Mo Jacobs
Legal Services: Joshua Farley, esq.
Images/Fonts: Creative Fabrica, Depositphotos & Photoshop
PR Services: Sam o'Neill

CONTENT INFORMATION

Content warnings are important and we don't ever want to harm a reader, so if you'd like more comprehensive warnings for any of my books visit: https://cassandrafeatherstone.com/series-by-cassandra-featherstone/

(This does get updated as I write, so it changes.)

This is a *paranormal whychoose romance with poly elements.*

There are many situations included that are intended for <u>mature audiences (18+).</u>

In this book, there may be instances/references that could trigger some individuals such as:

BDSM, *violence outside of the families, bullying outside of the families, PTSD, body dysmorphia, bad language, impact play, body modifications, casual sex, mention of self-harm, masturbation, voyeurism, objects used as toys, bondage, shifted sex, rough sex, biting, marking, mating, orgasm control, submission, blood play, death (outside of family group), drug and alcohol use, slow family group build, tails/horns/ wings during sex, body modification, primal play, knotting, parental death, unusual genitalia, multiple harems and FMCs, piercings, tattoos, brands, threats of violence, injury to FMCs friend, jealousy, possessive alpha holes, murder, injury by knife (not MCs), magical sex, raw sex, talk of heat cycles, abusive relatives (emotional), asshole fathers, asshole uncles, elitist jack holes, fangs, multiple partners, copious caffeine consumption, unhealthy coping strategies, and more.*

Everything is <u>consensual</u>, except death.

Consent is ALWAYS sexy, and our MCs will always seek it.

STALK SERENITY EVERYWHERE

Facebook: Serenity Rayne Readers Group
Twitter: Author Serenity Rayne
Instagram: Author Serenity Rayne
Goodreads: Serenity Rayne
BookBub: Serenity Rayne
Amazon: Serenity Rayne
Website: https://www.serenityrayne.com

Join her Pack Updates:
Bi-weekly updates on new releases, snippets, and contests.
https://www.subscribepage.com/o0b9s4

STALK CASSANDRA FEATHERSTONE IN THE DARK CORNERS OF THE WEB

JOIN MY FACEBOOK GROUP AND FOLLOW ME EVERYWHERE!

WANT MORE?

SIGN UP FOR MY BI-WEEKLY MANIFESTO FOR A FREE SERIES SAMPLER:

AUTHOR RAMBLINGS

Readers,

I come to you with a book that I am intensely proud of. Not only because I believe it's a fabulous beginning to the series, but because writing it was a personal and professional triumph.

When we announced this series last February, I was completely jazzed to be working with an amazing author. But due to other circumstances, I'm sad to say I almost didn't follow through with it.

There were issues I was dealing with in both aspects of my life that were difficult, but Serenity's support and friendship over the next few months as a co-author and friend were integral to surviving the miasma of other problems. I spent much of the spring and early summer mired in an abusive situation that damaged my mental, emotional, and physical health in ways that took the latter half of 2021 to address and resolve. But every time a horrible missive or vague taunt appeared, Serenity was there.

I considered a lot of options during that time, but allowing an emotional terrorist to win wasn't one of them and she helped me sort through that and find strength.

The road to healing has not been easy—I had to fight a continuous battle on many fronts to not allow this behavior to affect me in public, but also to make sure I don't allow the same abusive, controlling machinations and insults to cause me harm. That's difficult when you have a connection not easily severed, but I can now say that I responded with as much grace, class, and kindness as possible while not always having access to the awful lies being propagated.

My doctor suggested adopting a dog and Tilly has been one of the best decisions I could have made. I wasn't prepared to increase my anxiety medication to a level where I'd have trouble working simply because I had this bullshit in the background. But also, I pulled away from most public open spaces little by little, limiting the amount of exposure I had to vague insults and slurs designed to be seen but not understood.

Let me tell you… finishing *Bloodthirtsy, Rejected in the Hollow, Hoist the Flag,* and now, *New Moon Rising,* was more than just a challenge based on length, timeframes, or ability. It also is a testament to my determination and the amount of true friendship I was shown by my co-author and a few good colleagues. There were times when I was sinking deep enough into the muck that it seemed impossible to achieve anything—and it didn't matter if I did because I was as worthless as the abuser continually suggested.

It's hard enough to deal with imposter syndrome as an author without another person telling the world you're riding their coattails and wouldn't be a success without them. Trust me.

This note is not a commentary on that individual or even that erroneous, narcissistic sentiment.

What's it about is *freedom.*

Because while I was suffering through all of this nonsense, Serenity was ridding herself of a similar problem in her life. And together, we helped one another through the doubt, pain, shame, and hurt inflicted by those who claimed to care about us.

Much like the relationship Fiadh and Feray have, it was forged in shared pain and betrayal, determination, strength, and fire.

That's why this book is a testament to the belief women can and should truly support each other, even if they aren't actually blood. It's a demand for people to treat others, no matter how different, as people deserving of love and kindness rather than using your position of power to abuse them to make yourself feel better. And it's a love note to two women finding their inner power after being shunned and abused by those they trusted only to rise up and find their happiness despite the obstacles thrown at them.

That's the gift we give to our readers who love and support us—the promise that we will not allow petty dictators to prevent us from sharing our characters and worlds.

We will not be broken.

Blood and guts,

Cass & Serenity

NOTES FOR READERS

A few things you should know...

This is multi-book series, so *everything will not be revealed in the first book*. Some plot lines will continue through series in a larger arc and not get resolved in the first or even the next book. We promise it will all get tied up and have a HEA; don't worry!

Children of the Moon is set up to have both FMCS and their men in the *first* and *last* books. Books 2 and 4 will feature Feray and her men (with cameos!) and Books 3 and 5 star Fiadh and her man. They will all come together again in the last book!

New Moon Rising is a whychoose/poly romance, which means neither of our FMCs will have to choose. It may start a slow burn because, let's face it, eight dicks and two vaginas are a *lot* to deal with and that's not even counting all the holes involved.

It will get spicier towards the end of the book and *definitely* in the following books. If you're looking for porn with little to no plot, no judgement, but this isn't the series for you. It's also not closed door or FTB, so we believe the spice will be worth the wait. We realize spice scales are subjective and everyone has different opinions on it, so forgive us if ours and yours aren't totally aligned.

There are some characters and creatures that speak in other languages. We have made the *translations clickable end of chapter notes* to help.

There are some words that are slang, jargon, or foreign that may seem to be spelled wrong—*please email the authors or find them on social media rather than report to Amazon* if you think something is wrong. It may not be and we want to make sure it doesn't get taken down so everyone can read!

If you see this book *anywhere besides Amazon in e-book format,* please reach out to us via social media. Pirating kills our ability to write full time and we are so grateful for your help.

Contact Cass for issues or to report piracy: cassandrafeather stonepa@gmail.com

A NOTE TO CASS'S FAMILY MEMBERS AND FRIENDS...

THANK YOU FOR SUPPORTING ME BY BUYING MY NEW CO-WRITE.

<u>FOR THE LOVE OF EVERYTHING THAT'S UNHOLY</u>, PLEASE DO NOT READ THIS BOOK IF YOU INTEND TO ASK ME ABOUT THE CONTENTS.

THE LAST TIME ONE OF YOU READ MY BOOKS, IT WAS THE TOPIC AT A WEDDING SHOWER.

THERE IS NO AMOUNT OF ALCOHOL THAT WILL HELP ME FORGET HAVING TO EXPLAIN THIS STUFF TO GRANDPARENTS, ESPECIALLY WHEN YOU MADE ME DIAGRAM IT ON *COCKTAIL NAPKINS WITH LIPSTICK*.

STAHP. PLZ.

They want to eat your dreams and feed you the crumbs.

Make sure you dream so big they fucking choke.

— KALEN DION

DEDICATION

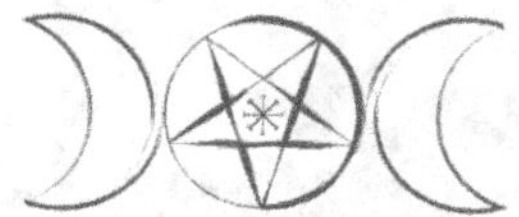

Just a reminder:
You're allowed to talk about what they did to you and how it hurt you.
It doesn't matter how they feel about you discussing it.
If they wanted people to think they're nice, they should have been nicer.
We only take payment in changed behavior.

PROLOGUE

A powerful wave of apprehension hits me as we approach Claridon's house. Pausing at the edge of the forest, I wait until we can see what awaits us. The silence is deafening as we take in the wreckage of what was once the home of our dear friends.

They splintered the heavy cabin door in pieces littered around their yard like an explosion sent the shards flying. When the wind shifts, the foul stench of death and rot slams into us, making my wife gag. Lights are flickering ominously in the shattered windows and another scent—burnt food—catches the breeze as we approach.

"Cast protection before we reach the porch," I murmur.

"Ego invoco deus ab mihi. Protego mihi ab hostili et malum.¹"

I nod solemnly, repeating her words to invoke our Goddess' watchful eyes on me as well. The scene in front of the house does not inspire confidence about what we will find inside.

The air is thick as we step onto the porch and another smell wafts towards us—blood. Its metallic tang invades our senses almost to the point of tasting copper on my tongue. Climbing over the debris, I look at the once cozy living area. Shredded cushions, torn drapes, stuffing, and other destroyed furnishings lie scattered around the room. When I bend to examine the destruction, I find coarse animal hairs embedded in the remnants. I pick some up to sense the aura of the creature it came from, but all I feel is death.

The bloody hoof prints puzzle me—I do not recognize them as belonging to any creature I'm familiar with. Whatever came to this house was not a normal shifter, nor was it a common magic user. The level of malice and lack of emotion concerns me. Its aura is like that of a necromancer or one of their creations.

I follow a set of heavy prints to the hallway leading to the dining area and kitchen. Swallowing hard, I prepare myself for the carnage I know will appear. The rotten food and decomposition scents are so bad I have to raise my shirt to cover my nose before I vomit.

It is certain our friends are dead; no one can lose the amount of blood that coats the surfaces and walls while staying alive.

"What made those claw marks? I've never seen such deep furrows," my wife whispers.

I shake my head, holding a finger to my lips to keep her quiet. I've never seen that type of mark, either, but we don't know if there's anyone still here. We must stay silent while we explore. The food on the stovetop is burned and has flies on it—that's the rotting smell. Wood is barely burning in the oven, just a few embers remaining, but it tells me our friends were caught unaware.

It means the malevolent being that attacked the wolves did it within the past few hours.

My heart stops when I remember their baby girl. Feray had to be here when it happened; it's the New Moon and both of her parents stay home during the start of the new lunar cycle.

"Freya, forgive me. I almost forgot the baby," I hiss at my wife.

Her eyes widen and her hand flies to her mouth. I see the tears forming as she thinks about what the condition of this place means for a defenseless infant. Together, we leave the kitchen, intent on heading back through the outer room to the stairs.

Just beyond the landing, we stumble over the body of Claridon. His corpse is mutilated, but I recognize those battered hands anywhere. He clearly put up a hell of a fight to keep the intruder from making it past him. Despite that, it ripped his chest open and his intestines are hanging out. Blood spatter decorates the once lovingly decorated walls, painting them vermillion and signaling his desperation to protect his family.

Swallowing again as I look at Imogen, I tilt my head at the trail of bloody hoof prints that lead to the nursery. We were here when they found out they were expecting, when they assembled the room, and even after Feray was born. Now the beauty of that memory has been sullied by the scene before us.

We have to be strong...

Once we're both ready, we follow the prints to the door of the baby wolf's room. The sight that greets us is horrific: it splayed Lyra out as if nailed to a cross and impaled her head on a post of the baby's crib. Blood is dripping down the whitewashed wood, making its way to the pink carpet. Dead eyes stare sightlessly at us as we hold our breath and enter. The injuries to our friend are a testament to how hard she fought to protect her child, though in the end, she also failed.

I don't want to see what this monster did to the baby we considered a sister to our child. Forcing myself to approach, I stare at the empty crib in astonishment. There's no sign of Feray, nor that it harmed her in this room. I whip my head around to look at my wife in shock.

Was this a kidnapping? Why would they kill everyone so brutally instead of simply sneaking in to snatch the baby?

My eyes dart around the room until I reach the closet. I stalk over, throwing the door wide. There's a pile of dirty linens and blankets in the bottom, which is unlike Lyra. She always kept everything tidy, so much so that we all teased her about it. Tossing the clothes over my shoulder, I dig down until I reach the floor. I call for light and my magic brightens the dark space enough for me to see a tiny seam at the baseboard.

Claridon was always paranoid, and I never understood why. We both lived simple lives in a small town of magic users and shifters, well outside the dangers of the big city. He was a master craftsman and Lyra ran a bakery; there was nothing to worry about. Humans were far away from our little town and the stench of corruption from the gangs and Councils doesn't exist in Silver Falls.

But I recognize a bolt hole when I see one, so I search frantically until I find the lever that will spring the door open. It takes several tries to successfully open the door—Claridon was top-notch at his trade—but when it swings out, I gasp.

There, wrapped in her father's shirt and Lyra's clothing, is Feray. She has the warding amulet Imogen made for her on her chest, and I realize that even while scared for their lives, Lyra and Claridon ensured the beast wouldn't find their child. Between the magic of our amulet and their scent swaddling her, the baby is hungry and tired, but safe.

I lift the tiny infant out of the hole gently, my eyes filling with tears. Her baby scent makes my heart hurt for my fallen friends and I clutch her to me tightly. It's our responsibility to take care of her now; I know that. Imogen nods when I look at her with a sad expression, then walks over to the dresser, opening a drawer. When she hands me the baby sling, I know she feels the same.

Once I secure Feray to my body, we make our way back to the stairs and head out of the house. It will need to be burned to keep that creature or anyone else from following the scent trail to our home. We don't want anyone to know Feray is alive; she will be safe with us as long as we continue to have her wear the amulet that suppresses her wolf.

Raising her with our daughter, in a new town, is the only way to keep her alive.

I didn't wake up this morning knowing I'd have to abandon my entire life and our home, but I know as surely as the sun will rise tomorrow what we must do to protect this baby. Looking down at her curiously, I ponder the situation again. A magical beast used as an assassin seems like overkill if their target was the infant. Slaughtering her family was also unnecessary—that thing could have slipped into her room and killed her before anyone knew it was there.

Lifting the magic on her amulet for a moment, I wait until Feray opens her eyes. That's when I realize why my friends put it on her. My wife walks up beside me and runs a finger over her cheek. Her red hair looks very much like mine and as long as we keep the magic refreshed for the spell, she will look as though she is our natural daughter.

"We must pack up and move immediately," Imogen says as we walk out. "The capital city is vast, and no one knows us there. That will allow us to raise her as our own—a sister to Fiadh."

"Yes," I murmur. "I will send a message to the local council to inform them we are moving. The death of our friends and their daughter are too much for us to bear here. You simply need to keep her secret in our home until we leave."

She nods. "What about the monster who did this? Who would send it to kill a baby, and why?"

"Someone who scared Claridon enough to make a secret bolt hole in the nursery and forced Lyra to ask us for that amulet. I don't know what they were up to, but obviously, it was much bigger than our tiny town."

Imogen frowns. "We made three amulets, love. Why weren't Lyra and Claridon wearing theirs?"

"I don't know, Gen. Whatever the reason was, they took theirs off and someone powerful hunted down their daughter. Nothing is what it seems here, but we must protect Feray. We will keep her wolf suppressed for as long as possible—up to her Ascension if we can. She'll grow up and if she's destined for something bigger, she'll be able to assume that mantle when she's ready."

Taking this baby on and keeping her secret violates our coven laws; we both know it. Hiding her means we will always be on the run—we need completely new identities when we flee to the capital. It's a lifetime commitment, but the look on my wife's face tells me she's certain this is the right thing to do.

I know without a doubt that being was pure evil, and it came with one purpose: *assassination.*

Tomorrow, we begin our lives on the lam with two babies—there is no other option .

---

1. I call on the gods. I protect myself from enemies and evil

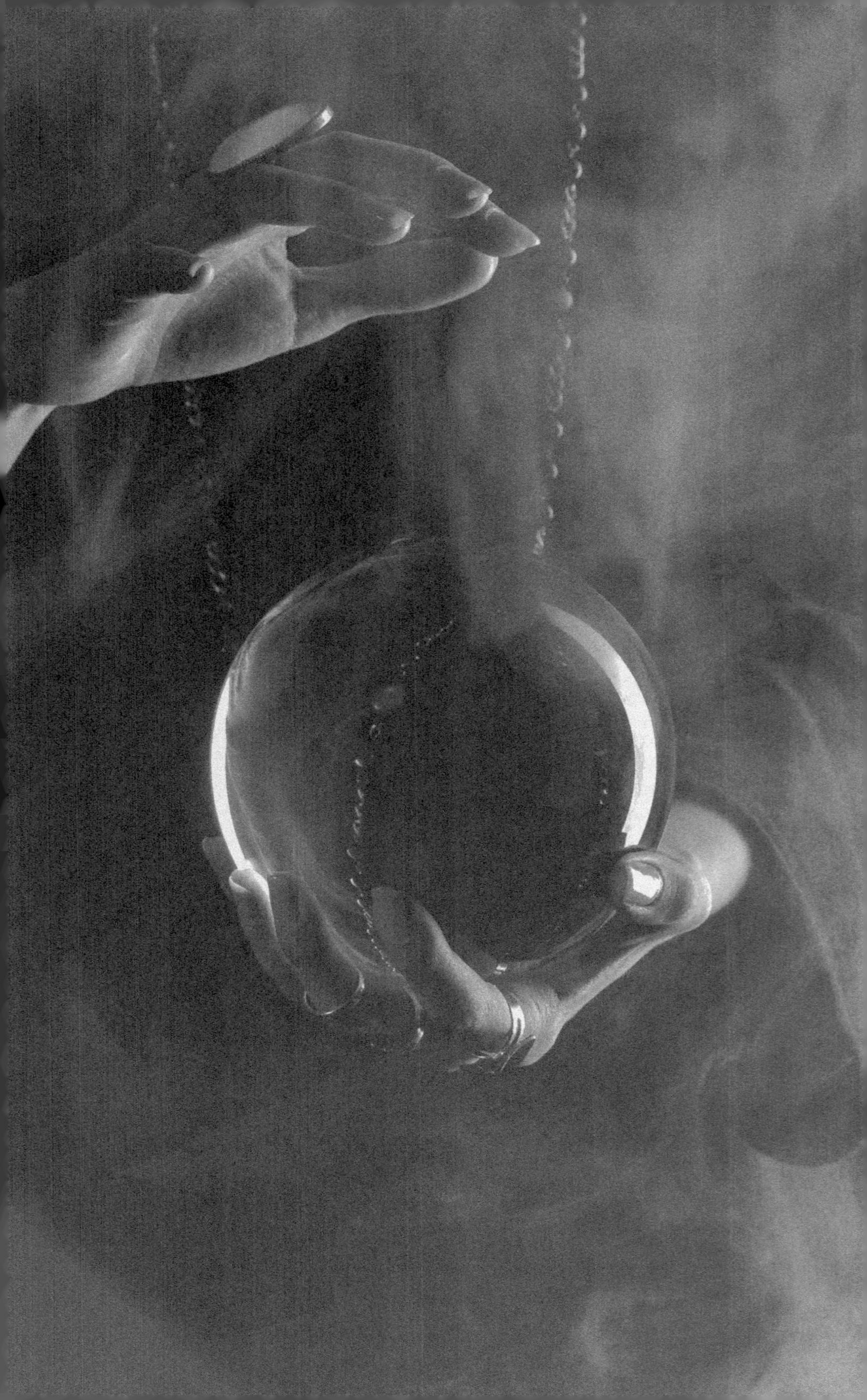

1

FIADH

The crowd in the bar is rowdy as fuck because it's two days from the Ascension. Major moon phases make the shifters in town go wild and even the magic users get extra when something as big as Ascension draws near. Philly's clientele doesn't include a lot of the snootier supernaturals in Briarvale—vamps, demons, and ancient creatures prefer the fancy clubs and bars in the upscale neighborhoods.

That means my sister and I are his only helpers, even when it comes to chop blocking a salivating gator shifter or strong arming a drunken centaur that's pissing himself with a four foot fucking horse cock.

We live a glamorous life, Feray and I.

Sighing, I wipe down the scratched and scarred wood of the bar while my sister hauls buckets of ice to the big freezer. We'll need a lot of it tonight—the moon is waning, and the air feels heavy with impending magic. Of course, I can't do much of it myself; hopefully, ascending will finally change that. I shouldn't complain, I know, and I try not to because what tiny bits of sorcery I can manage is one hundred percent more than what my poor sister can do. The Morgenstern twins had the reputation in school of being different in every way *except* their lack of any magical abilities.

At least we're long past having to suffer that particular humiliation daily.

"Are you brooding again?" Feray asks as she passes me with a stack of pint glasses. "You know, standing around grumbling to yourself won't change the fact that this place is going to be insane tonight."

I roll my eyes at her. "I know that. But I hate having to fight this shit with nothing but grit and rage. After the Ascension, maybe we can really help Philly keep this place from getting wrecked all the time."

She snorts and sits the beer glasses on the counter. We'll need three or four times what she's brought to start, but the *Dionysian Delights* bar doesn't have fancy racks for transporting large amounts of glassware. It's elbow grease and arm muscles all the way. "I'm not sure *anything* can keep this place from the drunken antics of its customers, sis."

"We'll see once I get my full magic," I say stubbornly. Blinking, I turn back to Feray with a sheepish grin. "And you, too, of course."

"For the love of the Horned God, Fiadh. We both know I'm destined to be a novice for the rest of my life. I can't get flowers to wilt, much less work on anything complicated. I'm a dud and there's no use pretending tomorrow night will change that."

Frowning, I walk over and put my hand on my sister's shoulder. Our parents never made her feel bad for struggling in school with her magical aptitude. She was a rockstar in every other kind of course, but if it involved practical application, Feray flunked out. She's probably right about tomorrow, but since this is the biggest birthday since the car crash that killed our parents, I refuse to let her feel down about herself.

"I believe in you, Fer."

"Thanks, Fi," she mumbles, ducking her head. "I'm going to get more glasses. We have little time before the doors fly open and we're ass deep in alligators."

"Literally," I reply wryly and she grins as she jogs back to the kitchen.

Hopefully, we don't get eaten before we gain our powers.

"Do you see those two groups?"

Looking in the direction Feray is pointing, I stop rinsing the shaker when I see it. On opposite sides of the bar, there are groups of shifters that aren't dressed like gang members, but they're definitely glaring at one another like beefing criminals. "Yeah, I see them."

One side of the staring contest is lithe and slick looking, wearing expensive Supreme jeans and various designer clothes with fat gym shoes. If I were to guess, at least one of them is dealing. They're all probably members of some outfit that provides any number of mind-altering substances that people in Briarvale are eager to imbibe. With so many species in town, cross-selling to one another leads to immense profits, so it's a well known, but ignored illegal enterprise.

The Species Councils are easily bought and the High Council is even less scrupulous.

The group pretending to play pool while they size up the dealers are sporting feathered mohawks, and that tells me exactly who they are. The *Flaming Cocks* work the auto theft and racing rings in Briarvale. They're low rent gangsters, not powerful enough to go up against the drug ring they have eyes on, but I get the sense something is going to pop off, eventually.

"Philly," I call out.

Our dearest friend, employer, and landlord, Philly, comes tottering out of the kitchen with a sweaty grin. "Ayyy, Fi-Fi. I'm cookin' here. What's the story, mornin' glory?"

His usual grumpy schtick makes me smile and I wait for the chubby satyr to make his way over and hop on his self-titled 'lookin' stool' before I respond. "There's gonna be a rumble in Brighton tonight."

"Ya know, your knowledge of rockabilly is one of my favorite things about ya, kiddo. But yer right, those idiots are dancin' on a knife blade. Won't take much." He takes a clean towel from the stack and wipes his face and neck. "You two can handle it, right? I got food to cook and oysters to serve."

Gee, thanks, Philly. Way to be a hero.

"I have my brass knuckles," I reply and Feray reaches into her pocket to pull out the taser she carries. "And it looks like Fer is armed."

"Good, good. You girls are the best thing to ever walk the boards in this joint, ya know? Don't know what I'd do without ya." That said, he hops off the stool and waddles his way back to the kitchen.

"I love Philly, but he's *got* to be part chicken," Fer grumbles under her breath. "I've never met a goat so scared of everything in my life."

"You've never met another goat in your life," I counter. She giggles and I give her a serious look. "Make sure that fucking thing is in your apron, not a deep pocket. I don't want you struggling to get it out when this bullshit starts."

She moves the weapon and gives me a mock salute. "Yes, Captain, my Captain!"

"Oh, please… just take these beers to the group of mermen over there and I'll take the whiskey to the leaders of the Sharks. Or the Jets. Whatever the hell they're in charge of."

"On it!" she replies as she balances the five beers on her hands and takes off.

My sister may be freakishly strong, but she's so much kinder and gentler than I am.

That's why I'm carrying the tray of rye whiskey and Coke chasers over to the group of guys who, despite being not much older than us, definitely have life experiences I don't want her to know about. When I approach, the crowd parts to reveal their leader. His stormy gray eyes pin me with an assessing glare and I pretend not to notice his sharp cheekbones and messy raven curls. Carefully unloading my tray onto the tall tabletop, I avoid his gaze until I see a mirror image of him giving me an encouraging smile.

Bad boy has a nice guy twin—some stereotypes are *true.*

"Bring the bottle," a deep voice commands and I turn to look at the leather wearing asshole. He's looking at me with barely contained disdain and it takes everything in me not to punch him in the dick.

"You know, 'please' is a universally accepted addition to requests, asshat."

Hot guy snorts, and his crew follows suit. I can tell his twin isn't comfortable with their behavior, but he also doesn't stop them. Finally, Mr. Smooth Criminal stalks over and stands a hair's breadth away from me. "If you want begging, I have much more amusing ways to get it that aren't so… public."

Smiling prettily, I purposefully whack him with my tray as I tuck it under my arm. "Oops. Sorry about that. I'm just so clumsy."

Doucheface holds up his hands, giving me a dark smile as he backs up into his snarling gang of stooges. "I hate to see you go, but I love to watch you leave, Sassy."

Gross. The hotter the guy is, the more objectionable his personality is—it's a reverse corollary or something.

"Hey Fer! Pull a fresh bottle of Turkey so I can grab it!" I call as I twist through the crowd towards the bar.

My sister gives me a thumbs up and I skillfully avoid ass slaps from drunken idiots until I get to the brass rails of the bar. Pushing my dark hair out of my eyes, I look at my fiery haired twin with an irritated expression. She hands me the bottle, then waves a fifty at me.

"The mermen were generous. We can order dinner after shift," she grins broadly. "Late night Chinese here we come."

Not only did she get tipped while I got hit on, but she isn't getting groped, either.

"I should try the innocent waif look," I grumble. "Maybe I could doe-eye people and my ass would be less sore at the end of the night."

"Then you couldn't punch them and you seem to enjoy it," Fer says with a smirk.

I blink. She's got me there. "Well, fuck. That would take *all* the fun out of working in this dump."

"Right?"

A loud whistle interrupts our conversation and I roll my eyes. "To be continued. I have to take this to the criminals in the corner. Just keep an eye on their friends, will you? Those feathered fuckwits are nothing but trouble on a good day."

"I'll let Philly know."

As if that's going to help anything. His furry ass will hide in the back all night if he knows there's a gang war brewing out here.

"Good luck with that," I mutter.

Sighing, I head back over to the hooting morons with the bottle and slam it on the table with a dark look. Nice guy dips his head with a smile and dickface smirks before tossing a hundred at me.

Normally, I'd shove it down someone's throat if they tossed money at me like a stripper, but even my pride won't let me turn down a Benjamin for doing almost nothing.

"Keep us happy and you'll see more, Sassy."

Okay, that's it.

"Look, you slimy cartel chaser... My name is Fiadh Morgenstern. Not honey, baby, darlin' or even *sassy*. Cut the crap or I'll shove my boot so far up your ass you'll be tasting my tread for months." I slip my hands into my pockets, sliding my fingers into the shiny knuckle dusters quickly. If I need them, I want to be ready.

A chorus of 'ooooh' comes from his minions and the rich twatwaffle actually laughs. "I think I'd actually enjoy experiencing your tantrum."

Huffing, I turn on my heel and head for the bar, done with sexy pouting asswads who need to be taken down a peg. Unfortunately, my whirl of anger puts me right in the path of a pool stick and when I knock into it, one of the mohawked car thieves blows his shot. His friends squawk with laughter and he spins around, eyes full of fury as he stalks toward me.

His stride and size aren't the part that has me backing away. No, even if he's one of the leaders, he won't be muscled and fit under that vest. The scary part of these guys is what happens when they unleash the fire within—the *Flaming Cocks* is literal. They're cockatrices and they won't hesitate to set anyone who crosses them ablaze.

"Shit, shit, shit..."

Suddenly, the shy twin appears beside me, glaring at the fiery asshole as he stalks toward me. "It was an accident, man. Leave her be and go back to your game."

His answer is a fire dancing on his palms as he holds them up at the nice guy. "Bitch just cost me a grand. She's gotta pay."

Rage fills my veins and red is all I can see when he shoots a line of fire at my would-be savior. Pulling my hands out of my pockets, I haul off and clock the overgrown chicken as hard as I can. He drops to the ground like a bag of laundry and I shake my hand as it throbs. "Goddamn, that always hurts like a motherfucker."

"But it was hot as fuck, Sassy." Asshole leather guy comes up, grinning wickedly as he taps the nice twin on the shoulder. "Time to go, bro. We should scram before these fuckers start something we have to finish."

"Got it, Khol." Sweet guy turns to me with a sheepish smile. "Thanks. And sorry for… all this shit."

I follow his gesture, groaning internally as I see knocked out cock's friends tearing the tables they were at to pieces.

"Gee, thanks. I'm sure this was totally worth it."

He bites his lip, smiling a little before he follows his brother and the rest of the dealers to the exit. I watch the doorway they left through until a chair flies past me, breaking on the wall next to the door. The fury grips me again and I turn around, dropping into a fighting stance.

"Alright, boys. Let's get dangerous."

2

―――――

FERAY

This cold winter morning differs from every morning before it. Tonight, Goddess willing, my sister and I will finally be able to access our powers. I'm excited, but what sets the hairs on my neck on end is knowing we will meet our mate or mates. A soft squeal of anticipation escapes my lips as I jump in place, trying to calm my nerves. An unexpected feeling creeps up my spine. *What if he is mean? What if he has poor hygiene?* My greatest fear rises as I walk through our apartment and I swallow hard.

What if I'm still a dud, and no one wants me?

Fi is grumbling at the kitchen table while sipping at her coffee. I swear, that girl has a permanent resting bitch face. I love my sister to death, but even I'm not brave enough to mess with her until her second cup of coffee. Her favorite mug is in her hand—the one with the middle finger on the bottom. I picked her infamous black mug up at a solstice festival last year as a gag gift. *Who knew she would fall in love with the blasted thing?* I can't help but laugh when she raises the mug to her lips, giving the world a big 'fuck you. The stark white skeleton hand with its digits curled and the middle finger extended cracks me up every time I see it.

"What's got you laughing?"

Trying to stop laughing is proving to be a more arduous task than expected. I attempt to get my laughter under control as I grip my dark blue and white ceremonial gown. Shaking my head, I finish folding the gown for tonight. "Your favorite mug is basically telling the world to fuck off for you. It's funny."

Fi nods and looks back down at her list. "We need to head out soon and pick up a few things. I'm out of several oils and herbs."

"Got it. I'll be ready when you are." Grabbing my mug and sipping at the last of the high octane caffeine, I get back to work organizing the crystals, herbs, and oils we have in stock.

"I hope we don't fuck up in front of everyone," Fi mutters to herself as she heads to her room to get dressed.

"Yeah, that would be horrible," I murmur softly.

I honestly don't know what she's worried about—at least her magic works. Exhaling roughly, I think about how tough school was for me. I barely passed my witch classes. If it wasn't for all the other basic education classes, I would have failed epically. A weight rests over my heart when I think about our parents' disappointment that I couldn't perform basic spells. The tightness in my chest makes it difficult for me to catch my breath because I feel like I'm walking into the dreaded conjuring exam again. The cold sweat, clammy palms, and heart beating out of my chest are familiar sensations. My only comfort is that Fi will be with me if I get too anxious.

Running my fingers through my hair in frustration, I change to go to the store. Jeans and a tee shirt are my outfit of choice and, paired with my favorite boots, I know I'll at least be comfortable. Goddess knows I'm uncomfortable trying to conjure in front of others since I'm an absolute failure, so I definitely want to be relaxed now.

Strolling through town gives me time to watch people. Several shopkeepers are closing early to prepare for the Ascension ceremony tonight. Fi and I have attended several over the years. We've always loved watching mates find each other and people gain their magic. My sister says I'm a hopeless romantic. The way people's faces light up with recognition and they close the distance between each other is so magical. Seeing their expressions when they know they've found 'the one' is *everything*.

"Feray, where did you go just now?" Fi smirks; I guess the lovesick look on my face gave me away.

"I was remembering last year's matches. I hope we're that lucky."

"Ah, sappy shit again." Fi pulls me in for a hug and kisses my temple. "Be as sappy as you want—if it makes you happy, then go for it."

A fond chuckle escapes my lips. "Someones gotta be the sunshine to your grumpy." Poking her side, I scoot away before she can retaliate by tickling me.

"Yeah, well, boring women rarely make history." Fi winks, then heads into the herb shop with a sassy sway in her hips.

THANKFULLY, the trip to the herbalist was uneventful. I always worry that my reputation for being unskilled will precede me when we go to the places magic users frequent. It was a common theme in school for the popular kids to taunt me every time I entered a magic skills class and their families were all involved in the Council and all the major businesses that provide magical supplies in town. I can't step foot into the witch district without setting off the 'dud alarm', it seems.

Fi had to haggle over the exorbitant prices, and I'm sure that has less to do with what we bought and more to do with who we are.

Nothing in these shops is priced; you bring it up to the counter to be informed how much it will cost based on market demand—supposedly. I think it has more to do with the person buying than the demand or scarcity of the items; we've never visited a shop or market where Fi didn't scoff at the sticker price we've been quoted.

I don't know what I would do without her. She bulldogs her way through everything and wins every time.

Next, we hit the crystal shop to stock up on what we were told to purchase for tonight. Fi will need them to brew the tea we're supposed to drink before the Ascension, so this stop was vitally important. Leather satchels line one wall, and the glimmer of their embedded protection crystals catches my attention. I pick out two new ones for us, though, deep down, I know I shouldn't spend my money so frivolously. I justify the expense as necessary for a 'one-time, special event' because it will make for a great surprise for Fiadh's birthday.

Stuffing my purchases into my bag, I rejoin my sister at the counter. Once she's done berating the snooty salesperson, we exit and head back towards the bar. Townspeople are rushing around, getting final preparations ready for the city-wide celebration. Some are hustling bags of supplies, while others are carrying decorations towards the town square. Pre-constructed platform pieces are being hauled by the burly bear shifters who run the construction operations in town. They'll help build the ritual circle and all the special seating for the High Mage and Council to observe.

"Come on, Feray! We don't have time to fuck around if we're going to get ready."

The wind shifts suddenly, and I sniff as a warm cinnamon-caramel scent drifts to me. It smells so good that it makes my mouth water. I can't help stopping to stare at the scene before me as I search for the source of the delicious scent. Something niggles in the back of my mind, whispering to me I should follow the scent. My sister's voice breaks through the haze, and I sigh, giving up on pursuit. "I know; I was just curious. Something smelled really good, and I needed to figure out what it was." I stay still for several beats, fighting the urge to chase it regardless before following my sister.

Once we get to the bar, we make a beeline for a table towards the back. Spreading out our haul from today, Fi and I examine everything to make sure we didn't forget anything. Surprisingly, Philly is cleaning and setting the tables—it's an Ascension miracle. The pool table in the corner is finally getting re-felted after the bar fight the other night and the dart boards are getting re-corked. My eyes drift around the interior of the *Dionysian Delights*—the bar we both work and live above. Taking in the improvements, I realize Philly must be hoping for an influx of drunks after the celebration tonight.

Turning back to my sister after I study the work, I notice she took it upon herself to separate the additional herbs and stones we acquired. "Fi?"

"Yeah?"

Fiddling with the stones in front of me, I try to quell the anxiety settled in my chest. Deflection away from my actual concern about my lack of magic seems safer; Fi will only reassure me I'll be fine even if she doesn't believe it. "What do you think our mates will be like?"

Scoffing, Fiadh rolls her eyes. "Anyone who ends up with one of us is a lucky bastard. We are strong independent women that don't need to be babysat or coddled. How many of the others who ascend tonight can say that?"

"I would like to be coddled and snuggled," I mumble with a pout. When she snorts, I suck in a deep breath. "Whoever gets you better be strong or you'll eat them alive."

"Damn straight!" she exclaims with a laugh. "And whoever you get better be good to you, or I'll castrate him with a rusty butter knife." Fi pulls a dagger from Goddess knows where and brandishes it, spinning it on her palm to make her point.

Blinking, I stare at my sister, amazed she can still shock me after all these years. Deep down, I know she's not joking—which is what surprises me. There is not a doubt in my mind she would stab a bitch if needed and not give a single fuck about the consequences. That's not my style, so I can only appreciate that she's so protective of me. I nod quietly before I look down at the crystals, grouping them before placing them into our bags.

The clicking of hooves on the wood floor of the bar announces Philly's approach. "That damn Ascension taking away my only workers. I'm going to have to run this joint solo on one of the busiest nights of the year. Stupid mages and their fancy ass parties." Slamming the rack down on the bar top, he stomps behind it and starts stacking the pint glasses with an irritated bleat.

I love when he gets all goat-y and pissed. It's adorable.

"It's only one night, Philly; don't get your tail in a bunch!"

I look up at my sister as she yells at our boss from across the bar. Rolling my eyes when he grumps again, I get up and walk over to the bar to help. Philly and I work in silence, stocking the bar while my sister puts the rest of the oils and crystals together. I don't mind helping our gruff landlord and boss—he saved us by taking us in after our parents died. Besides, I didn't want to fuck any of this up anyway, so it gives me an excuse to let Fi handle it.

Fi finally pauses for a moment, walking over to pour herself a whiskey. Snickers of disbelief escape her lips first, then she erupts into a full-on belly laugh when she picks up one of the new coasters Philly ordered. "You gotta be shitting me!"

Tilting my head to the side, I pick up a coaster and inspect it. There's a caricature of a satyr that looks like he's dancing in the grass. The font he chose looks childish, but it absolutely fits my boss and the way he runs his establishment. I think it looks friendly and happy, so I don't see why my sister is laughing so hard.

"Seriously, Philly? This thing is ridiculous!" Fi snarks as she packs up our belongings. Her face is rife with amusement; ragging on him is one of her favorite pastimes and she's the only person I know who can get away with it unscathed. Most people get two hooves to the ass out the door for giving him guff.

"Who owns this place: me or you?" Philly crosses his arms, trying to look imposing, though he's on the short side for a satyr. His tail flicks left to right violently, reminding me of a cat that's going to attack.

"You may own it, but we run the floor," Fi says as she looks down at the satyr with an arched brow.

"You may run the floor, young witch, but I own the joint. And I'm in charge of your rent." Philly smirks, at Fi, knowing he's got her.

Of course, we all know he'd never raise our rent or toss us out—we're a family and this is his way of teasing us.

"Son of a bitch," Fiadh mutters. "You win this round, Philly."

"Damn straight I do!" He winks and waddles back to the kitchen with his head held high.

Shaking my head, I can't help smiling as I think about my sister and her favorite hobby: 'poke the satyr.' The two of them have a unique relationship—he's almost like an older brother. One pokes fun at the other until they finally have to admit who wins and afterward, everything is fine again..

Sometimes, I feel like an odd person out. My magic hates me, my sister excels at everything she does, and I don't have any other friends besides Fi and my boss. I don't know why; I've always been kind and accepting of others. Even Philly, short and ill-tempered as he is, is never alone; he has friends all over town. And he's as cuddly as a cactus. Fi is trouble waiting to happen and a dick magnet, but I swear, she could sell the ocean to merpeople. As long as they don't piss her off, men and women alike love her party girl personality.

Me, on the other hand? I love watching people from a distance. I like to stalk the room more than I like to be involved in group activities. It's not that I don't like people; my experiences in school have taught me to be wary of large groups. It's always been a trap in the past—I feel like I'm having fun and safe, then days later, I find out my gut was right. Gossip, rumors, and catty behavior seem to be the only goal of the girls I meet and it's burned me more than once. That's why the huge group spell casting, in public, tonight has me on edge. It's two of my least favorite things: spell casting and a huge group of judgy mages and wanna-bes who will likely humiliate me for their own amusement.

I look at the ornate clock Philly has above the bar. My heart sinks when I realize that in less than three hours, we will be a part of that terrifying circle of sharks. Hopefully, they don't expect my sister and I to suddenly join their little cliques because our magic appears. We've been each other's strength and support from day one, especially when they treated us like garbage. No mage or mate will tear us apart, that's for sure.

Reluctantly, I get my sister's attention. "Fi, we gotta get moving. We still have to brew the tea, and then get into our gowns." As much as I dread the crowd, I'm excited to see what my sister will become. Fiadh is sure to have amazing powers; she's always been gifted.

She comes over, hugging me to her side. Her grin is lop-sided as she drags me to the stairs to head upstairs to our apartment. "Night, Philly. Don't wait up!"

I stay quiet as we head up the slanted steps, winging a prayer to the Goddess that this will be, as promised, the best night of our entire lives.

After all, we're due for a little good luck after all the bullshit we've been through. It's not too much to ask.

3

FIADH

I know Feray is worried about the ceremony.

She's been off all day, but at first, I thought it was because we had to go places where we're treated like shit in order to prepare our supplies. Then she started asking questions about our potential mates and I realized that she's not only scared about the magic portion but also about the mate identification process. Her fears aren't unfounded—our pseudo-exile hasn't made us untouchable, but it will not please any mates who have well-known families or high-profile reputations. There's a genuine possibility they could even reject us in public, and I've thought about it every day for the past couple of months as this date approached.

Goddess, help the asshole who shuns one of us if I get my powers. Prison doesn't scare me in the slightest.

Shaking my head as we gather our basket of spell supplies that every ascending witch has to donate to the ceremony, I mentally run through the checklist again.

We're wearing our ceremonial gowns, though ours are likely the most basic ones we'll see. I couldn't justify spending a small fortune on something that might get ripped off during the mating rut. Fer wheedled with me about it, but I held firm. Dresses that will get destroyed should not have to be saved up for that kind of dough needs to be conserved for emergencies. The basket Feray is gripping in her hands is filled with oils, incense, herbs, and candles. I tucked our crystals in the pockets of our gowns for quick access. I refused to sew them in the hems because I want to retrieve them for later.

As much as I hate being the bean counter, it's how we've been able to stay comfortable since our parents' death. The suspicious circumstances of their accident made it easy for their insurance company to fight paying for their policies, and the Seelie Fae who dominate the police force refused to investigate further to help us. We've been on our own since the house sold and we paid off all the debts. My romantic, soft-hearted sister would love to have fancy clothes and tools and an apartment furnished with luxurious furniture, but it's just not in the cards for us. At least, not for now.

Maybe we'll get rich mates and our powers. One can hope, right?

"Is everything good?"

I smile at Feray. She's trying so hard to look excited despite her fears. "Yes, we're good. Let's hit the bricks, sis."

Together, we head down the stairs and through the back hallway of the bar to the exit in the alleyway. Avoiding the pre-Ascension drunks is high on my list, so I motion for Fer to follow me through the smelly, garbage lined path until we hit the main street. Even in our part of town, people are out and about, buzzing with excitement. Philly's bar is wedged against the nicest tier of the Night District where it meets the shifter quarter. Feray and I don't belong in either section of our neighborhood, but the people there aren't much for community building, anyway. Living there means we have a bit of a hike to the business section where we were earlier in the day, but that's where the big event is happening.

"What powers do you *want* to get?" Feray asks suddenly. "I'd like invisibility, I think."

Snorting, I roll my eyes. "Of course you'd want to make sure no one can see you. Though, it's probably not a surprise that I'd dig something bad-ass like elemental control or psychokinesis or even precognition."

Her nose wrinkles as she looks at me. "Knowing everything about the future would ruin all the surprises, Fi."

"It would keep us from getting hurt, too, Fer. Think about what life would be like if we'd known to stop Mom and Dad from going on that store run that night. Everything would be different."

"I don't know. Movies and TV and books say that the notion is inaccurate. If we'd stopped them, it would have... you know, like butterfly wings in China."

My smile widens as I see the tension slip out of her a little. Theoretical discussions always get Fer going, and if this one helps her relax before we arrive, I'm all for it. "Chaos theory. Well, it's possible. Telling what we knew might have set a whole different ribbon off of our current timeline. Like DC 52 and shit."

"Yep. Or maybe it would have caused the event to keep repeating as it tried to force Fate—like in *Final Destination*."

"That wasn't Fate; it was death. But I get where you're going— unavoidable tragedy, no matter what paths split off, right?"

She pauses as we approach the edge of the town square, looking around with a frown on her face. "Yeah. Something like that."

"ON THIS, one of our most glorious nights in the Wheel of the Year, we give thanks to all the gods and goddesses who bless our people with their bounties. The initiates, the members of our coven, our honored guests from other Councils and species, and of course, myself as High Mage, welcome you to the Ascension!"

The applause is deafening as the sharp-featured old jackass pontificates from his spot on the raised dais. Looking around, I see leaders from the other supernatural councils looking smug as he defers to them one by one. Briarvale is a city rife with corrupt leaders and crooked citizens—the most influential politicians are all bought and sold by sources both legal and illegal. Everyone on the stage has their fingers in every pie in town and they're eager to receive the adoration of their unwitting public.

Like I said, living in the rough part of town means you witness many things you'll never speak of, especially when it involves these bozos.

"Is that the Chairman of Scaleon Pharmaceuticals?" Feray whispers in my ear.

I nod, noting the evil looking old man eyeing initiates hungrily. The fucker is known for having disgusting proclivities and the pharmaceuticals part of his business is a front for being the biggest drug lord on the Eastern seaboard. Next to him is the one of the Seelie royals, shining in their Daybreak Court glory, and after that, a darkly handsome Unseelie Fae who must be part of the Midnight Court contingent. Further down, several alphas of shifter packs are muttering to one another, a demon prince is chatting with a vampire duchess, and a dragon lord. Smaller communities like orcs, dwarves, nymphs, elves, and phoenixes are at the very far end of stage right. On the opposite side, all the various magic users like wizards, warlocks, mages, and elementals watch the crowd with judgmental eyes.

The supernaturals with the most human left in them are always looking at those below them with disdain.

All these people are here because, though it is preferred to find your fated mate within your own species, over the years, that has become less and less common. The mixing of clans and covens has become so normal that every ceremony like this has council reps from the others, so the mating rituals can be witnessed and accepted within their communities without question. Even the crowd of onlookers in the bleachers and elite seating sections are filled with unmated males and females from all walks of life hoping to make matches with higher tier initiates in the magic user society.

Feray and I are not *in the category anyone is hoping to be mated with, unfortunately.*

"Fellow wielders of the power of Nature and the Dark, take your places in the circle around the cauldron. The Ascension is about to begin!"

My sister's hand grasps mine, squeezing nervously as we follow the instructions of the priestess. While the High Mage presides over the ceremony, he never does a damn thing himself, so his acolytes organize everything while he watches from his self-assigned pedestal. It's a fitting metaphor for how our society works and until tonight, it made me smirk. Now, with the fate of my sister and I hanging in the balance, I resent the hierarchy that will either grant us a new life or sentence us to the bottom of the barrel forever.

Darksome night and shining moon,
Harken to our joyous tune.
North, East, South, and West,
We call ye forth to this circle blest!
Body, Mind, Spirit, and Heart,
Make sacred this space, a world apart.
Gentle Mother of Earth, powerful Father of Sky,
Join with us—the time is nigh.
Great Spirits, Divine Ones, Creators of All,
Answer our most reverent call.

> *The circle is cast, the light unbroken,*
> *So mote it be—our magick has spoken.*

As the power in our circle hums with the charge of the Gods and Goddesses, I close my eyes. This is only the beginning of the ritual—consecrating our space and drawing down the moon to invoke the deities who grant us the blessing of our full potential. A glance at Feray tells me that as usual, this isn't affecting her like it is me, and I try not to let it wilt my hopes. She's never connected with magic the way I do and my concern for her status distracts me for a moment. Witches are *always* affected by spells worked by this many people in this proximity—I don't understand why it never works for her.

Our priestesses are lighting candles of various colors as they walk past, tossing herbs on us before painting symbols on our foreheads with fragrant oils. I know this ceremony is incredibly complex, but the anticipation of gaining real magic is thrumming in my veins. I barely hear the words they are chanting, nor do I see anything past the fire and bubbling iron pot in the center of the circle. The air is heavy with their auras and everything else is silent as they work their spell.

The High Mage stands, giving the initiates an imperious glare as his acolytes work to bring the elements and deities to our ritual. I don't know why, but something about the way he looks at all of us makes my skin crawl. It's not just that he's an elitist old fool; no, there's something sinister about the glee in his expression as he watches from above. I don't know if it's because he sees something he likes or if it's because he doesn't see anyone powerful enough to challenge him, but it makes me wonder if the Ascension ceremony is part of his scheme to stay in control of magic users.

> *Here we stand, hand in hand,*
> *Forming an impenetrable band*
> *Let their powers fuel my own.*
> *With these words, our powers shall GROW!*

A column of hot brew shoots into the air from the cauldron in the middle of our circle, bubbling like a fountain as the combined abilities of everyone present sparks the change in the air. A feeling like a punch in the gut rocks me and I drop to my knees, barely able to crack my eyes open to see others doing the same across the circle. Magic is sparkling in the air like a rain of glitter, coating everyone in a freaky aura like a UV powder at a rave. I lost Feray's hand when I dropped, but I can't seem to move to find it again.

All I can do is kneel and let the fire in my veins rage through me as I shriek into the night.

The excitement I felt about finally feeling the connection to the Universe and the core of my being fades as pain takes over. No one told me this would feel like being burned from the inside out while needles stab every inch of you repeatedly. It's hard not to choke on every breath and I finally give in, placing my head on the cool ground to find some relief.

That launches my mind into a dark black space, taking away conscious thought in a blink.

I hope my sister is okay...

4

FERAY

SO MANY PEOPLE...

Mages, vampires, bears, and many other supernaturals are gathered in the stands and outside of the circle. My nerves are on edge and everything is making me want to jump out of my skin. All the extra noises and scents surrounding me are sending my anxiety off the deep end. I was okay until the priestess started tossing the herbs around. My allergies kicked into overdrive, and there's not much I can do about it. Between itchy eyes and a runny nose, I swear to the Goddess, I hope this is worth it.

I glance briefly at Fi—she's in her glory. She looks positively radiant, smiling as she takes in everything around her. Pure, unadulterated joy ebbs from her every pore. We're such opposites; I feel like I want to rip my skin off and she's basking.

The Priestess is moving around the circle with her acolyte, greeting and anointing each initiate with whatever the fuck is in her bowls. She finally gets to Fi and I, smiling when we curtsey to her as we were taught in school.

"Sisters, welcome to the circle. May the Goddess bless and keep you safe always." Her smile is painted on and there's a distinct lack of sincerity in her tone. That slight change in vocal tone is something I've never picked up on before—it's an odd development.

Fi is the first to get painted. Her excitement is palpable and I'm happy for her. This may be my greatest fear, but it's her deepest wish.

When it's my turn, they brush their oils on my skin and I start to itch profusely. My hands twitch, making me fight the urge to scratch off the top layer of my flesh. *What the actual fuck did they put in that oil?* My skin feels like it's going to melt off my bones. The pain is quickly getting past the point of tolerable. I'm trying to be strong, but I don't know how much more I can take.

I have a deep-seated urge to run, but where would I go and why?

"I feel so amped up!" Fi is bouncing around like she's hopped up on too many bottles of energy tonic.

"My skin is melting off," I snap as I rub at my forearms vigorously.

"You must be allergic to something in the oil." Fi grips my wrist, looking at the red blotches popping up.

Everywhere the oil touched feels like it's on fire. I can barely force myself to focus on my sister's face. Her happiness means the world to me, and I would do anything to make sure she gets the happily ever after she deserves, but this reaction is painful and distracting. I don't know what else to do besides tell the one person who listens to me.

"I'll be okay, sis; I promise."

I force a smile as we return our focus to the High Mage and Priestess. Whatever they're doing is making the scents in the area stronger, and my poor ears are ringing because of the rise in the crowd's noise level.

What is happening to me? Why are my senses overloaded?

It feels like I can sense everyone here and the weight of them is crushing. The sensation of touching everything in the vicinity makes my life force feel smothered and heavy. Hairs on my arms and the back of my neck are standing on edge as I take in the people closest to us.

Something is not right with me and it's not an allergic reaction.

The High Mage chants something about fueling his power, and a slight tug towards him prickles over my body. Planting my feet, I resist the pull. I don't know what this jerk's game is, but I will not be part of it. I grit my teeth, standing firmly in place when the other witches sway with his chanting. Part of me is raging against the shackles of this circle and its protective barrier. Something inside is urging me to run like hell from this ceremony before it harms me further. My skin is burning and my lungs are struggling to adequately take in the much needed oxygen. My fight-or-flight instincts are set on ten and my brain is screaming that I should have gotten out of here ten minutes ago.

The Priestess comes by with more incense and herbs; I swear, they are trying to kill me. "Damn these herbs. Is this amount truly necessary?"

I practically growl when the column of brew shoots up from the caldron like an eruption of jizz on a good Friday night. Its contents rain down on us in technicolor brew spew, making me cough and choke—the magical substance is hot, wet, and sticky. Everywhere the fluid hits itches and burns like crazy. I don't know what in the hell is going on, but *none* of this is like what we were taught in school. This shit is fucked up.

Fi releases my hand, falling to her knees and letting out the most guttural scream I've ever heard.

The area around the cauldron is lit up like a Fae Summer Solstice party, with sparks and flashing colors illuminating everyone. It's as if a drunken dwarf ran around flinging neon paints on every available surface. Nothing is free of these annoying splashes of bright colors that are making my eyes ache as badly as my skin and limbs.

Tink tink tink...

Bone chilling fear fills me as I look down and see what is making the odd sound like cracking ice. Cracks appear in the amulet Mom gave me as a baby and the crystal shatters in its copper wire. It fills me with dread—it's like a bad omen on top of a bad omen tonight.

"Feray, you must never take this off."

Mom's last words echo in my mind as I watch the crystal fall away in small shards. My abject horror only grows when the last shard falls to the ground and excruciating pain electrifies every nerve ending in my body. It's worse when I electrocuted myself, tinkering with the frayed wire in the bar's lights last summer.

"Fi..."

My sister is lost in the thrall of the magic, so she doesn't respond. Instead of sparkling with new magic like her, I feel like I'm being torn asunder from the inside out. My temperature spikes radically and my internal nerd brain attempts to comfort me by thinking about the laws of quantum biology in relation to chemical changes.

Heat is energy, and that means part of me is changing; the laws of thermodynamics relate to energy conversion and I must be converting energy. If the pain I feel and the fire in me translate to power, I could end up stronger than the High Mage. That petty revenge would make this entire miserable experience completely worth it—he's a douchebag extraordinaire.

Power thrums through my body until I finally drop to my hands and knees as I struggle to breathe. My muscles spasm, making it difficult to do anything other than kneel here like a shivering lump. I sneak a glance at Fi, noting her body is lit up like a broken glow stick. Her face is frozen in a silent scream and suddenly, she drops to the hard ground. Since I cannot move, I watch her ribcage closely to see it rise and fall. Thank the Goddess, it seems my sister will survive whatever the hell this debacle is.

Why am I in pain? Why am I not glowing like Fi?

The questions haunt me until a tearing sensation races through my muscles. I turn my head in supplication to the sky where Hecate's moon shines bright like a beacon. Her glow soothes the primal urge within me briefly. My eyes remain locked on the moon, feeling like a fucked up Rubik's cube being manipulated by a twisted sadist. The snapping of tendons and sinew is almost deafening when it sends a pain worse than I've ever experienced through my frame. I scream through the next burst of agony ricochets through me. My throat feels like sandpaper when air finally escapes my mouth. The deep, raspy howl vibrating in my throat and chest scares the hell out of me. My heart pounds erratically in my chest as I try to endure what-ever the Goddess has decided my fate is.

Am I being punished for something?

Falling to the ground, I double over as the torture increases tenfold. Slamming my eyes shut, I pray I can survive this wave of torment without blacking out.

Several heart-stopping moments pass, and when the latest surge of pain abates, I crack an eye open. There's light gray fur racing down my arm to my hand—this can't be. Slowly, my fingers shrink until they are the toes on an animal's paw: large black toe-beans attach to a broad, black pad.

My head whips to the side as my jaw drops in shock. Fi is standing up now, a glowing halo surrounding her. Her hands cover her mouth as she stares at me with wide eyes. She attempts to speak several times, but no words escape her lips. Her hand reaches out to me twice, only to withdraw each time.

What kind of monster do I look like for my sister to be so distraught?

Arching my back as the next bolt of pain electrifies my body, I remain stiff as more popping, tearing, and burning rips through every fiber of my being. Whatever is possessing me tosses me forward, and my eyes open as my hands hit the dirt hard.

Paws? I have paws?!

I hoped the power surges made me hallucinate, but obviously not. Panting, I stare at myself, then look around in wonderment. My vision has changed—the colors look different, as do my surroundings. Everything has infinitely more detail; I can see every part of the tiny fuzzies Fi hates all over her gown. Sparkles float through the air and I can see *every. single. one.*

Were they there all along?

Everything is so different now. My senses are in overdrive, and I have no idea how to control any of it.

It seems like I'm some sort of canine with light colored fur. Turning my head, I examine my new body as best as I can.

Shit. I have a fucking tail. How the bloody hell does that damn thing work?

Mages and other supes are running around the circle chasing their mates and each other, but all I can do is lie here in shock

Wait! Mates. We should have...

I turn my furry head to look at Fi and the pain in her eyes tells me all I need to know.

Not only am I not a witch, neither of us have mates.

I attempt to stand when it hits me. Trying to coordinate four legs instead of two is *hard.* The fucking things seem to have a mind of their own.

Newborn horses can figure this shit out—it can't be that difficult, right?

By my sixth attempt, I finally stand and walk a little. I'm still wobbling as I try to keep my paws under me, but once I gain some semblance of balance, I look up at my sister again. Sadness and a tiny bit of pity mar her beautiful features.

Today, I've finally taken the cake as the biggest loser—I can't even get being a witch right.

5

FIADH

When I come back to my senses, Feray's problem is apparent—she's *not* a witch. I have absolutely no idea how the sister born on the same day as me, raised as my fraternal twin, is not a magic user, but a wolf shifter.

Neither of our parents have shifters in their family tree; I know it for a fact.

But now is not the time to show my fear of her heritage. After the magical hold expired, I should have had powers fritzing out. I don't, and we haven't had a single eligible mate even look in our direction. Even the skeeziest idiots in the stands aren't coming towards us.

I'm powerless, Feray isn't a witch, and we don't have mates.

The enormity of that statement hits me and I turn, shielding myself from the chaos around me as I throw up the stupid tea we drank on the ground. Once the High Mage figures out we're lower than low, we'll be outcast even further than we are now. Growing up in a middle class family with no special powers or influential connections already marked us, but now… we're doomed to living in the apartment over the bar forever.

A whimper comes from the wolf next to me and I look down at her with tears shimmering in my eyes. If only I had been granted powers or found a mate, I would have been able to protect Fer better. Since I turned out to be an ugly dud, we're both screwed.

Suddenly, Feray growls. Her hackles stand on end and her head lowers, ears flat and canines bared as she looks past me. I turn to face what's become a crowd of the elite supes from the stage—all of them glaring at us with imperious expressions. My eyes narrow as I feel the magic struggle to ignite within me and fail to accomplish anything. It only makes the crowds of asswads laugh and the High Mage look even more furious than before.

"Like their mother and father, these girls are unable and unwilling to contribute to our species. Indeed, this witch and wolf are worthless; they have no mates or powers to speak of. They will remain in the lower echelon."

His decree actually stops all grunting and moaning from fated mates fucking around us, and everyone goes silent. I've attended Ascension ceremonies for years to prepare for this and never has this asshole made a public decree like this. He's put a giant target on our backs and that of anyone who associates with us from the magical community. We won't even be able to get laid by a witch, mage, wizard or warlock with his declaration.

He basically cast us out of our society. Why?

Feray throws her head back and howls mournfully. My fists tighten and I look at the smug old bastard with renewed hatred. There was no reason to make this announcement; he could have allowed us to slink off with our literal and figurative tails between our legs, but he chose abject humiliation.

One of the other supernatural leaders snickers and it's followed by a chorus of whispers amongst the group standing with the pompous dick that's supposed to be our leader. He doesn't chastise them; in fact, he smiles wider when his brethren point at Feray. I get the sense that he's enjoying this and I have no idea why; did our parents offend him somehow? If so, how the fuck is that *our* fault? My gaze narrows on the people surrounding him, waiting for one brave person to stop this bullshit.

But it doesn't happen.

Instead, the murmured barbs get louder and the laughter spreads. My nerves are already frayed and I wing a prayer to the Goddess that is making me suffer to at least keep me from getting into a brawl. I take a breath and close my eyes, gathering my thoughts as best I can before I look the flaming asshole in the eyes.

"Dishonoring the dead is not befitting of someone of your stature, High Mage. We are not responsible for our parents or our genetics. I would like to file a formal complaint with the City Council, the state and national coven leaders, and any other applicable authorities regarding your behavior."

His eyes widen, clearly not expecting me to stand up to his dismissive bullying. "Are you sure, little witch? It will mean an investigation into your family and your... mongrel sister's lineage. If your mother or father cheated on their fated partner, we will take action based on coven laws."

Fuck me.

Feray tosses her head, growling low before she howls again, and I pause my tirade. Even I know my people are the least accepting of mixed matings, much less polyamorous couplings within that dynamic. Magic laws mean she will be exiled and shunned by *all* supernatural communities for our parents' mistakes, even lenient wolf packs. She'll have no one; I won't be permitted to leave with her.

The tiny spark inside of me flashes again, but nothing makes it past my curled fingertips, so I spit at the High Mage's feet. My voice drips with disdain as I finally grind out, "I withdraw the complaint

—for now. However, I reserve the right to revisit your vile behavior at a later date."

"I thought you might," he says smugly. Waving his hand at us dismissively, he turns to leave with his cadre of ass-kissing royals and leaders without another word.

I watch them, fury burning in my veins as I memorize every single face and name for a list of who I'll be taking my vengeance out on if my powers eventually appear. Every single one of those nasty worms will reap the consequences of their inaction if I'm able; I don't care if it takes my entire life.

Leaning down, I rub my hand over my whimpering sister's furry head. "Come on, Fer. We'll go home and see if we can get you cleaned up. I don't know how to help exactly, but maybe Philly does. These fucking pricks don't deserve another minute of our time."

She tosses her head in what I assume is agreement and I wait for her to take slow steps forward. Her legs aren't quite steady yet, but she gets better as we head to the edge of the drunken, sexed-up crowd. By the time I lead her to the darkened streets behind the Ascension revelry area, she seems to have gotten walking under control.

"Don't worry, Feray. Our life won't change—not really. You didn't have powers before and I only had a little. The assholes in our community treated us like shit and that won't change. Philly loves us and we love him. We'll go back to the same life we had before except with fur; I promise."

The wolf lets out a short yip, and I smile to myself. I know my sister is hurting and confused, but in her new form, she has limited ability to deal with the trauma. She may understand me and she can think, but there's no outlet for the sadness I feel coming off of her in waves.

"I mean, we both shed a lot already, right? All that long hair gets everywhere, so this won't be *that* much worse. And maybe Philly can talk to some of his shifter friends, so we get tips on how to help you learn to use your new abilities. We'll get books at the library and online if we have to. I've always been your pack, so it doesn't matter if you don't get one. Hell, I could probably use the exercise if you need to run on full moon nights…"

My voice trails off when she howls in that haunting, sorrow-filled tone again. I'm trying so hard to be positive and it's not my wheelhouse. The truth is, I'm better suited to don my knuckles and knock the teeth clear out of that old pervert's head. At least then Feray would know he experienced as much pain as his words are causing her.

Unfortunately, taking care of her means I'm not able to grieve my own losses, but since my parents died, I've always been the caretaker.

I don't begrudge my soft, squishy sibling for needing me. She provides an equal balance when I'm about to rage out and get myself arrested—again. That's what best friends do and no one on this planet is going to convince me that the lanky, cream-colored canine next to me isn't my real sister. Genetics be damned.

As we walk, I self-soothe by muttering, "High Mage. High Priestess. Alpha Knox, Bright Moon Pack. Leona, Pride Maxwell. Antares and Andromeda, Seelie Fae. Lucarius, Demon Court. Xander, Angel Court." Repeating their names until I burned them into my mind helps me quell my anger enough to get us most of the way home.

A loud, rumbling sound comes from the wolf at my side, and for a brief second, I smile. "Shit, Fer. We'll have to get some food when we get home. I mean, I don't know as much about shifters as I should, but I remember that shifting takes a lot of energy. I bet you're hungry as a… well, a wolf. You need to eat soon."

Feray barks her response and I chuckle. I don't know if this will make our budget tighter, but she'll get what she needs if I have to take another job on the side to pay for it. It's the least I can do.

When we reach the corner closest to the bar, loud sirens and shouting, paired with a sickening scent, fill my senses. Feray barks, hurrying toward the emergency personnel in the street, and I have to chase after her for a block until we both come to a dead stop.

Flames jump and flicker over the building that Philly's bar and our apartment are in, and the shock almost knocks me to my knees for the second time tonight. There are aquatic shifters and water elementals everywhere, using their powers to try to douse the fire as it continues to burn with a dank, rotten smell that makes me want to hurl again.

"What in the *fuck* is going on?" I shout at the running firefighters. Panic is making my heart race and I'm clutching at the scruff of Fer's neck to keep her from bounding into the fray. "Where is Philly? Someone *answer* me!"

A burly shifter with a name patch that says 'Chief' stalks up to me. He looks down at my sister and then back at me with a dour expression. "Who are you and why are you inside of the perimeter? No civilians allowed!"

"We *live here*, dickwad! Tell me what the hell happened!"

I can't help screaming at him; it's all too much. The failed Ascension, the shitty leaders' smirks, and now our home going up in flames? With no sign of Philly anywhere, my world is crashing down around my feet, and I don't know if I can take much more.

What the fuck did we do to piss the Goddess off?

"I'm sorry to hear that, ma'am, but it doesn't mean you can be this close to the blaze. We're working to put it out, but the source has to be something magical 'cause my guys are having a bitch of a time getting it quashed."

"Where is our landlord? He lives here, too!"

The face he makes stops my heart for a second and after he wipes his brow, the Chief shakes his head. "They carted the owner of this place off to the hospital, Miss. He's in an awful bad way; the healers weren't sure if he'd make it."

His words pull another howl out of Feray and stars appear in front of my eyes right before I drop to the ground with a primal scream that echoes off the buildings.

In one night, our entire world has crumbled beneath our feet and I don't know if I can pick up the pieces.

FERAY

WHAT WAS SUPPOSED TO BE THE BEST DAY OF OUR LIVES TURNED INTO MY worst nightmare.

My poor sister didn't get her powers. I got a new form instead of magic—four paws, big teeth, and a shedding problem. As if we don't laugh daily about finding long hair everywhere around the house, now we have fur to contend with. Trying to learn to control my new body isn't easy; I'm no better than a newborn calf at this point.

Who knew this would be so difficult?

My heart's breaking as I watch my sister stare at me with intense pain in her eyes. Our total rejection in the mate department only compounded our failure to level up our magic. Nothing tonight happened the way we hoped it would and yet our life has changed completely—and not for the better.

My breaths are labored like someone is strangling me as I watch Fi go toe to toe with the High Mage and his cronies. I make little wolfy noises, but it doesn't help. My sister says it's time to leave and I follow without question, struggling to walk without toppling over. Looking at the shops as we walk home makes my heart ache more.

Fond memories of shopping together in the witch district—even though we aren't favored—are likely the last time we'll be allowed in those places. At least before the Ascension, we were treated with disdain but not outright disgust; it will be much, much worse now.

The scent of burned embers, flesh magic, and something I can't put a name to fills the air with a disgusting tang. The wind shifts several times, making it difficult for me to figure out where it's coming from.

Damn these new senses.

My head is spinning from the loud noises and pungent smells. I feel like my eyes, ears, and nose are so overstimulated that they're going to bleed. The pain behind my eyes is throbbing so hard I want to smash my head against something until I pass out.

It's not until we round the corner that I see where the odd smell is coming from.

Our home—our safe haven—is going up in hot, flickering flames.

A mournful howl wants to rip free of my muzzle, but I squash it. I don't want to draw further attention to myself. I've already painted a big bullseye on our heads for eternity. Watching the different shifters and the elementals working to get the blaze under control, all I can think about is Philly.

I hope that stubborn old goat is okay. I don't know what we'd do without him.

Fi finally gets a firefighter to stop long enough to ask him where Philly is. The way his hard expression changes makes my chest feel like someone pushing hard on it. He says that they rushed him to the hospital and a lead weight drops on my heart. That feeling only increases when he murmurs the EMT isn't sure he'll make it.

Throwing my head back, I howl the most woeful cry I can muster. Mid-howl, an excruciating pain overtakes me—just like earlier at the ceremony. My body feels like it's being ripped apart from the inside as things start to pop and snap to realign themselves. The sound immediately turns into a blood-curdling scream—the most distressed one I've ever let out in my life. My sister screams along with me as she falls to her knees. When I finish shifting to human form, I dive at her. Wrapping my arms tightly around my prone sibling, I hold on to the last thing from my old life I have left. Fi holds on to me tightly, burying her face against my neck.

I feel so broken—not only in body, but in spirit.

Suddenly, I realize I'm naked in front of a bunch of guys I've never met before.

The firefighter returns with a blanket, and I could kiss him. He gives me a knowing smile as he explains it's not the first time he's seen a shifter lose control and shift suddenly. To be honest, I don't know how any of this works, so it's probably not the last time I'll flash my ass in public. Fi wraps me up in the blanket and looks me over to make certain I'm okay.

"Are you hurt? I've never heard a sound like that before," Fi asks without taking a breath.

"Yeah, I'm okay." My voice is raw with emotion and I can't stop the deluge of tears streaming down my face as I stare at what's left of our home.

"Don't cry," she says, trying to wipe away my tears. "We can't do anything here. However, we can go sit with him until the goddess decides if he'll survive."

Listening to my sister's words, I shake my head and swallow the pain within me. My nose clogs, making my voice turn nasal and croaky. "I'm sorry. I'm not a witch like you. You might not have a mate because of my… minor problem. If it wasn't for me, you could be happy right now." I turn away, not wanting to look at her and see the sadness etched on her face as my words ring true.

Fi yanks me back quickly, an angry fire burning brightly in her eyes. "This is not your fault—you can't control who you are anymore than we can control our parents keeping secrets from us." She looks at the fire and then back at me. "We will figure this out. Don't worry about it; for now, we need to go to Philly."

As she finishes her sentence, a firefighter motions to a second rig sitting near the building. "If you ladies want, you can take a ride with the EMT back to the hospital to see your friend." His tone is kind and I can tell by the tattoo on his forearm he's a shifter.

I nod silently, acknowledging his words, then without warning, I hug him before I follow my sister to the ambulance. Once we get ourselves situated, a different fireman offers me a business card, explaining his cousin owns a construction company. He might fix the bar once everything settles down for a good price, depending on what kind of insurance Philly has. That's the only good news I've heard in hours, so I nod. Thanking him, I force myself to be braver than I normally am. The EMT pokes his head in, saying it's time to go before he closes up the back of the rig.

With that, we're on our way to the hospital. I stare at Fi as she scrolls through things on her phone. "Fi?"

"Yeah?" She doesn't look up at me; instead, she focuses on the screen in front of her.

"What are we going to do? We've lost our home, our clothes, everything..." Fi has both of our bags we packed for the ceremony, which means my phone is safe, but that's all we have left.

Fi's eyes soften and she puts her phone away. "I'm working on that. We have enough in our account to stay in a hotel for a week, plus buy some clothes and feed ourselves. But until Philly gets the bar repaired, we need to find another job."

My sister has always been the planner, so it doesn't surprise me she's already thought of everything. She's much better with money than I am—she has spreadsheets detailing where our money has to go over the course of the month and how much we need to make to be comfortable. Fi always knows how many hours of work it will take between the two of us to get us there with a little extra leftover.

Shaking my head, I imagine having to interview somewhere new. I'm not painfully shy, but given tonight's events, I'm going to have a very hard time convincing someone to hire me. Fiadh gets up, moving to sit next to me. She wraps her arm around me and I lay my head on her shoulder. We've learned to lean on one another since our parents' death, but we also let Philly in. Now he's hurt and there's nothing either of us can do to help without magic.

"I'm scared, Fi. You say we'll be okay, but a lot can happen between today and tomorrow." I close my eyes, trying not to think about how our day has gone to hell in a handbasket.

"We've been in worse spots than this. It seems worse because we're starting over from scratch. Maybe that's a good thing, though?" My sister gives me another squeeze and kisses the crown of my head before moving back across the ambulance to sit in front of me. She reaches out and pulls my hands from hers. "We've always taken care of each other and this won't be any different. I'll sort out the finances and you'll help me admit I have actual feelings besides rage." She stares at me, waiting for me to acknowledge her words. "You could even say we're our *own pack*."

Something inside of me settles when she says she's my pack; I'm not as anxious as I was before. Suddenly, it occurs to me why that helped: wolves are pack animals. Rogue males can be solitary, but females are never without a pack. For me to be without one would drive my wolf crazy. "Okay, Fi. What are we going to do about jobs"

"It won't be easy, but we have options." She picks her phone up and opens the screen. Turning it to face me, she shows me the page she was on. Fi was cruising job boards and several of the vampire-owned bars are hiring night shifts. I blink when I see they are paying much better than Philly ever could afford to.

"It's not ideal, but we need to build up savings. We have to support ourselves until they reopen the bar—if it reopens at all. We don't know how long it will take Philly to rehab… if he even survives." Fi laughs wryly, her face pained as she mutters, "Good thing I was the one who took out the insurance on the bar in Philly's name. Without it, he wouldn't be able to afford to rebuild."

Taking my sister's phone from her, I scan through the help wanted ads. Unfortunately, the most common one is from the vampires— that means we'll work in a sex club or a blood bar. A chill runs down my spine as I think about it. Fi will love every minute, but I'll want to disappear. Bartenders can't hide, though, and I'm not comfortable serving. The only upside is the vamps could give a shit less about the witch council's decrees, so they aren't likely to be discriminatory.

After all, blood is blood, right?

I sigh heavily, handing her back the phone in defeat. "Alright, sis. I guess we will go see Philly, then find a place to sleep tonight. Tomorrow, we can interview with the vampires." Despite my honor, I know it's going to be hard once the word gets around town about my heritage. People will stare even more and everywhere we go, we'll be watched.

I hate it already.

"That sums it up. We'll check in with the doctors to see how bad Philly is and adjust our plans from there. I looked for a hotel close to the hospital that would be equidistant to the clubs hiring. If we stay there, we can monitor Philly, while we look for some place to work."

Fi always has a plan—I don't know how she does it. It doesn't matter how bad our situation is; she's always cool, calm, and collected. She even pulls off miracles when we absolutely need one because she's the best sister a girl could ask for.

I frown to myself as I watch her continuing to make arrangements on her phone. Hopefully, Philly's not as bad as they originally thought. I suspect my hope is misplaced, but I'm trying to be positive. The furrow in Fi's brow tells me she's worried, too, but at least she's comforting herself by making plan after plan.

Ascension night will forever be the second worst night of my entire life—right behind the night our parents died on that lonely stretch of road.

7

FIADH

When we get to the hospital, our ride drops us at the ER. Considering I'm covered in magical Ascension dust and my sister is naked under a blanket, you'd think we would stand out. Apparently, this night is worse than All Hallows Eve for humans, so we don't.

The waiting room is full of drunken, drugged, passed out, bruised, cut, and half-shifted people groaning in chairs or on the floor. Feray's eyes are as wide as saucers and I know she's worried someone will recognize us. It would be our luck to have a reveler from the ceremony start a mob out for our blood. Patting her shoulder, I use my eyes to communicate that she should stay close as we approach the administrative desk.

"How may I triage you: alcohol, narcotics, magic, fire, ice, bullets, penetrative objects, dangerous shift, sexual misadventure, or other?"

I blink at the monotone of the nurse in front of me. She sounds almost resigned and definitely exhausted. It may not be as helpful as I thought to go through the channels rather than sneaking our way in.

"Centaur," Feray whispers as she sniffs. "I smell the hay."

An enhanced sense of smell could be very handy if it develops further.

The woman glares at her, not moving from her spot at what must be a custom-made workstation. "It's rude to do that without permission, young lady."

"We apologize, ma'am. It's been a rough night. My sister and I had unexpected news at the Ascension and when we got home, our building was on fire. The emergency personnel dropped us off so we can see our friend—he was badly burned."

Her eyes widen and I don't know if it's because she's heard about us or she knows who Philly is. All her irritability turns to compassion within seconds and she adjusts her glasses, peering at us more closely. "Oh, dear. Are you… naked under that blanket?"

Feray turns as red as her hair, hiding as she nods and grips the sides of it tightly.

Clucking her tongue, the centaur shakes her head. "The first shift is rough, especially for some in your unique situation. I'm not a gossip, mind, but the stories are here already."

Damn. She knows who we are.

My gaze is sharp as I watch her click a few buttons on her computer. "Thank you for saying that, but we'll be fine. We need to see our friend; it sounded bad."

"It is bad, dearie, but since I'm one of the species those snooty assholes in the magic community shun, I want to help the two of you first. Your friend isn't going anywhere at the moment and you can't talk to him while he's in a coma."

"Oh, noooo," Feray says softly. Her head leans against my shoulder, and I know she's crying again.

I have to close my eyes for a moment as I take the rage and humiliation inside of me, then shove them into a box. Feray needs me to be strong and so does Philly—I cannot break down right now. There will be time for me to deal with my emotions later. This woman is offering to help and we don't have a choice but to take it, though I'll be very cautious. "What kind of help?"

Her lips curve and she nods. "Good for you. You should suspect everyone until this blows over; it will keep you safe. However, I'm simply going to escort you to a restroom and give your sister some scrubs to wear before taking you to the ICU. I'd prefer to make sure you arrive in better condition than when you showed up."

She seems genuine and Fer needs clothes before her damn ass freezes. I'll have to trust her—a little.

"Okay," I say as I nod. "Take us there. We'd appreciate your time and consideration."

"Definitely the clothes," Feray murmurs, pulling the blanket tighter as we wait for the nurse to unfold herself from the odd chair. "I haven't been naked in public like this since I was born."

ONCE THE NURSE—NAMED Stella—gets Feray set up with scrubs, we head upstairs to the burn unit. Philly stabilized and could be moved from the ICU to that ward while we were getting cleaned up. The thought makes my heart squeeze a little and I wing a prayer towards the Goddess for his recovery. She's been cruel tonight, but I have to believe I earned some grace by not getting violent with the fuck-heads who mocked us at the Ascension. I left with what meager dignity we had in order to protect my sister, and that has to count for something in her eyes.

"The doctor on duty tonight is one of our best. He's so gifted that other hospitals attempt to lure him away constantly. Your friend is in excellent hands," Stella says as she swipes her card at the double doors.

I nod, still numb when I think about how close we came to losing the one person we have left in our family. Blood or not, Philly is the big brother we never had and losing him at the same time as this major disappointment would have destroyed me. "That's good to hear, but um... Philly's not... I mean, he isn't wealthy. I'm worried..."

Her laugh is much like a perky 'neigh' and she shakes her head. "Do not worry. There is a well-funded grant program in the burn unit. Many fire-wielding species' families have been contributing to it for a long time. I suppose they do it out of guilt—not every fire wielder who gets their powers does so without damage—but it is quite useful for those injured in this situation."

"All the fire wielders? Like dragons and elementals and phoenixes and everyone else?" Feray asks curiously.

It's the first time she's spoken since we got her dressed, so I'm grateful for the distraction.

"Yes," the centaur says simply. "We have similar programs for ice and disasters and other things that might occur when new super-naturals gain powers they cannot get control of. Fire is one of the most contributed to because so many creatures and magic users can access its destructive ability."

This must have been set-up many years ago because the current leaders of Briarvale and the Councils don't have a generous bone in their bodies.

"That's good. Hell, he only has most of the required shit for codes and insurance and licenses because I make sure they get filed and paid for. He's an amazing person, but his business sense is not the best." I give Stella a crooked smile and she chuckles.

"Dr. Bennu will be back in a few minutes," she says as she leads us into the room. "You can't go beyond the sheeting yet because of the risk of infection, but you can see your friend. I'll make sure your names get on the visitor list at the desk before I head back downstairs."

Fer and I walked closer to the bed. It's blocked by a sterile barrier, but we can see inside. Poor Philly is as red as a cherry tomato—I can only assume it's because they're working on the burns little by little. His eyes are closed and his chest is rising with the whirr of the machines he's hooked up to. The satyr has never looked so small or weak as he does now and it's terrifying. I suck in a deep breath, pushing my emotions into the tiny ball inside of me again so I can soothe my sister.

"He's going to be okay, sis. They could move him, and that *has* to be good news. It doesn't look good because these things are helping him, but he's not dead. We have to be strong so we can help him until he gets better." My words are braver than I feel, but since the Ascension, I can *feel* the fragile tethers my sister is holding by. She needs me to be in control and make plans.

Feray turns to me with red eyes. "How can you keep *saying that?* Our whole life has gone to hell on a sled and you are the least optimistic person I know. You don't have to pretend for me, Fi. I can handle your anger or grief, but I can't handle you shutting me out because you want to protect me. Our friend is gravely injured. You have no powers, we have no mates, I'm not a witch, our home is in ashes, and we need new jobs. There is *nothing* about today that is okay!"

I blink, digesting her outburst quietly. She's not wrong; all those things are our reality now and she is an adult. I'm so used to being the responsible one that I assume she's unable to deal with anything. Now that we flunked our fucking Ascension, we both need to take control of our lives. "Okay. You're right. That's all true and today is a fucking shitshow. Philly might get better or he might get worse— we don't know. But the only thing we can do right now is put our heads down and work hard. Hope is a thing that floats and all that garbage."

A cough behind me stops my flow and I whip my head around. The handsome man gives me a rueful smile as he waves a clipboard. He appears older than us—thirties, maybe—and his brunette hair is ruffled like he's been running his hand through it. His doctor's coat says Dr. Easton Bennu and underneath, *Head Phoenix Healer, Briarvale General Burn Unit.* "Hello, ladies. Sorry to interrupt."

Feray tilts her head, sniffing the air for a second and then scratches her forearms. I'm not used to the weird tics that seem to be plaguing her since she shifted tonight, but I assume it will eventually calm down. "Thank you for coming to see us. I'm sure it's really busy in the hospital with the… ceremony."

Something in the air makes my fingers twitch at my sides, but I have no idea why. Everything is topsy-turvy right now and I have no baseline with which to judge my reactions—physical or emotional. But I can tell this guy is making my sister nervous, so I need to step in. "What's the prognosis, Doc?"

"I won't lie to you; it's not good. He's stable and if we can keep him comfortable as we debride the tissue without him coding or stroking out, then his chances improve a lot. Part of my job is to work on the charred skin while one of our dreamweaving nurses attempts to keep his mind in a place that will control his blood pressure. Once we get through all that, your friend will have a long road ahead, but he's less likely to die." The serious look on his face tells me he's trying to be gentle but there isn't much he can say that is positive.

My sister walks closer, wringing her hands. "This has been the worst day of our lives, Dr. Bennu. I appreciate you being so careful. It's really hard to focus on everything because so much has happened since we left for the ceremony earlier, as you just heard."

His gaze narrows and he watches Feray for a moment, then shakes his head. "I can't help with many of your unfortunate issues, but I will be here to watch over him until we get past the worst of the procedure. He won't be alone and he will have someone dedicated to his survival."

I frown. "Of course he will. We're not going anywhere."

The doctor continues looking at Fer, despite answering me. "Oh, not a good idea. This is horrifying for those of us who do it to save our patients. You cannot stay while we do this—the screams alone will haunt your sleep for the rest of your life. I can't allow it in good conscience."

"I believe you," Fer says before I can respond. "Maybe we should find a place to stay for tonight, Fi?"

"That would be a very good idea. I don't want to traumatize you further."

Looking at Philly, then Dr. Hottie, and then my sister, I sigh. There's no way I'm going to win this argument. I don't know what's going with Feray and this guy, but she's too vulnerable to be smiling at him like this. Every bit of this situation feels like it's a powder keg and I do not have the spoons left to clean up the blast. So I finally give in and nod at them both. "Okay. We'll be back tomorrow, though."

"Yes. We will definitely come back tomorrow," Feray says as she picks up her bag.

Just fucking great—no mates, no powers, no home, and my sister's finally decided to get a sex life with our injured friend's doctor.

What the hell else does the Universe have in store for us?

8

FERAY

My head is pounding. Between all the unfamiliar noises and the intensity of the smells, it leaves me in a constant state of over-stimulation. These new heightened senses are a nightmare. *How do shifters deal with this daily for their entire lives?* I think about it and it occurs to me that without my amulet, I probably would have shifted when I was much younger. My parents would have taught me how to control this and I wouldn't be so confused by all the changes coming at once.

There had to be a very important reason our parents kept me in the dark our whole lives.

Staring at my hand in the morning light, I have flashbacks to seeing a paw instead of a hand.

How is that even possible?

My parents are witches; Fi is a witch. *Is she powerless because she's part wolf like me?* That would mean our mother was unfaithful—which I highly doubt—or one of them had a secret ancestor they didn't tell anyone about. That also seems unlikely because the witch council has everyone's lineage traced back for centuries. I've seen the documents and the family tree painting that lived in our childhood home.

I push the thought aside and slide out of the bed, trying to not disturb my sister. She has the weight of the world on her shoulders and I don't know what to do to help her. I'm probably the reason we don't have mates, and definitely why the council has their beady eyes focused on us. All of our problems lie squarely at my feet and I have to figure out a way to make up for that. Fi can't be forced to suffer and also has to clean up after me as well.

Silently, I pull on the borrowed scrubs and grab the room key off the dresser. Once I'm dressed, I leave the room and head to the lobby to grab some of the free continental breakfast. Thankfully, it's empty, so I don't have to engage with anyone. I just want food and not to have a bunch of people staring at me. Loading up two plates with the late morning leftovers, I frown at how little there is. A staffer finally takes pity on me and hands me a coffee carafe to take the rest of the coffee with me.

As I gather more food, he keeps eyeing me and finally, I give in and confirm who I am.

To my surprise, he tells me he was kicked out of his pack because he couldn't shift. I'm surprised, but it's sort of nice to hear that he's also packless. He gives me a quick rundown of some important social conventions as I continue piling things on my plates. When his boss isn't looking, he hands me a bag of pastries and left over bagels to take back with me. I'm overcome with gratitude and an instinct I've never felt before takes over. Pressing my cheek to his, I thank him for his kindness, then scurry off with my haul.

The moment I pop the door open, Fi wakes up. Once she stretches and sits up, she gives me a curious look. "What did you do? It looks like you robbed the place."

My sister closes the distance between us and takes the coffee out of my hands. I smile—she's a caffeine and adrenaline junkie. "There was a nice man working downstairs. He gave me extra because he has a sad story like us." I sit the food on the dresser, avoiding eye contact with her. "He could smell that I'm a wolf and told me he never got his. It was nice to know someone else had problems and didn't stay broken forever. After that, he gave me the leftover bagels and pastries. He said he remembered what it was like to be shunned and wanted to help."

Fi takes her plate before heading to the bed, digesting that information quietly. I know she wishes she could help more, and it's eating her up inside. She's always felt like I'm her responsibility to protect and she can't fix this for me. After she takes a few bites, she looks up at me with a serious expression. "We need to get clothes and find a job. You should call the bears since the witches treat the shifters like shit. Being a wolf, you might get us a better deal on the repairs."

I want to question why she thinks witches are mean to the shifters, but then the harsh words of the High Mage replay in my head. Despite having some leaders from shifter groups with him, he still acted like I was lower than dirt. Closing my eyes, I feel the wolf within me stirring angrily. A wave of sensation runs over my skin and when I open my eyes, fur is rippling along my arm down to my hand. My nails elongate, displaying black claws briefly before shrinking immediately.

"Fuck! I can't even do the wolf thing right!" Angry about being such a fuckup, I snarl under my breath.

"Feray, calm down. We don't need your wolf busting loose and destroying the place." My sister scoots closer and runs her hands through my hair soothingly, just like she did when we were little kids.

Normally it works, but now I feel like she's babying me and it irritates my wolf. An unrestrained growl escapes my lips as I move away, putting space between us while I work to get my inner beast under control. "I'm trying—honestly, I'm really trying."

Drawing in a deep breath, I focus on centering myself, as they taught us in every spell casting class. It never helped me find magic, but somehow, it makes my wolf stop pacing inside. Letting out a sigh of relief, I shove the first danish I find into my mouth. I'm hungry as hell, and that can't be good for maintaining control over the animal within me.

Fi takes my silence as a cue to continue with her organization for the day. As I chew on my pastry, I listen to her go over the list of essential items. She decides what path we need to take from here to get there, along with any potential problems we might face. Half her words sound like they're underwater as I get distracted by staring at the sharpened details of the room I know my human eyes never would have noticed.

The snapping of Fi's fingers draws me out of my examination of the comforter. "We need to get going. The stores open soon and I'd like to get in and out before they get busy."

I know it's because of me; she doesn't want anyone to say nasty things.

Lowering my head, I nod. It's not as if I can do much else. A new shifter is the most out of control after their first change. Add to that the edict from the High Mage and being around during the busy times is a powder keg waiting to explode.

As if she knows what I'm thinking, Fi grabs her bag and ushers me out the door. The elevator feels like a cage this time, and I don't know why, but I'm glad when we make it downstairs. The shifter from earlier gives me a small wave as he ducks down the service hallway. Last night was too much of an emotional blur for me to pay much attention to our surroundings, so stepping outside of the Archmoor Hotel, I finally take in our surroundings.

I see the tower of the hospital down the north end of the main drag; it's about six blocks away, which is helpful for visiting Philly. At the other end, they lined the road with different shops and, from the smell of it, food vendors. Fi grabs my hand and starts dragging me down the sidewalk. Everything looks, smells, and feels so different from before. Things I'd taken for granted before now are so much more interesting.

It's obvious the moment that we cross from the upper crust part of town into the Elvish District. The soft scent of spices, honeysuckle, and jasmine fill the air. They're not overpowering; instead, the blend is soothing to my nerves. The calming scent of lavender wafts from a particular shop and Fi walks into it, tilting her head for me to follow her. It's one of the elvish run thrift stores I've heard so much about.

"We should find some decent items here. Well, at least enough to tide us over until we get back on our feet." Fi gives me a weak smile, clearly forcing it for my benefit.

Kissing her cheek, I head down the racks of clothing to find something to fit me. I'm not as thick as my sister—she's curvy enough that, combined with her height, it's hard to find trendy stuff. For me, my long legs give me problems, but now it makes sense why my limbs are so long. I try not to dwell on the thought of the differences between my sister and I. Grabbing several pairs of pants; I hold them up to see if any will look good on me. Some of them are on sale and that means I can scour the racks for more markdown items. Being an odd size pays off because I find a lot of pieces that mix and match well. The sale means what would normally cost eighty dollars will ring up for less than thirty. I'll have several outfits that I can wear to find a job and to work after I get one. Fi yells when she finds packs of undergarments unopened and I thank my lucky stars for that.

That's the one thing I refuse to buy second hand.

We head up to the register with our bounty and I know the elvish woman recognizes us. With a kind smile, she applies a generous discount and we end up barely spending fifty dollars put together. I make a mental note to remember her for later. If she ever needs help, I'd like the universe to remember her charity to people in need.

"We should get lunch. I know we weren't there long, but I've heard shifters need a lot of food to keep their fast metabolism running," Fi says as her face screws up in concentration.

Laughing, I reach into my bag and pull out two danishes. "We only need something to drink. I planned ahead because I remembered the same thing from school." She's right; this shifter metabolism makes me constantly hungry. That thought scares me—needing to eat all the time will drive up our food expenses.

Maybe once I figure out shifting, I can learn to hunt and help provide for the two of us.

I keep that thought to myself, though. Being a witch, Fi loves animals so much that she hates to see them harmed. My nature is the exact opposite of what would make her happy, and that pains me.

As we walk down the street munching on the pastry, Fi snaps pictures of the names of several vampire clubs we can go to, as well as a few Fae establishments that would likely pay well. She pauses when we pass a flier for a demon casino, but we share a look that says neither of us wants to get involved with that crowd. The clientele might get too handsy and, unlike at Philly's, we'd lose our jobs or end up in prison. I laugh when she describes what she'd do, knowing she's absolutely as serious as a judge and I'd have to bail her out.

Our conversation changes when we get to the witch district. It's hard not to feel the glares of the shop owners, who now look at us as if we have the plague. Yet again, something else I blame on myself as being the root cause of the problems for us. They've never really liked us, but they would have forgiven Fiadh for not having powers.

Why did I have to be a wolf?

My sister makes a quick stop at her favorite apothecary, but she makes the mistake of asking about getting a job with them. She's definitely qualified—she was in the top ten percent of our magic classes—but they took one look at me and shoved us out the door.

"If you want to work in this district, sis, you're gonna have to come back without me." I swallow hard, looking away as shame fills me. This is the lowest I've ever felt in my entire life, and I'm trying to keep all of that pain bottled up. Sadly, I know my tone is giving it away.

She grabs my hand as we come to what's left of the bar. "Fuck them and the centaurs they rode in on. If they don't accept you, I have no use for their money."

Fiadh is loyal to a fault and though I love her for it, I know we may have to make concessions in order to survive.

"I don't want you to suffer because of me. Once I learn more about my abilities, I can do more to help," I tell her as I grip her hand tightly. "I could hunt and it would cut down our food bill. And um… I could also… uh…"

Fi laughs softly. "Let's figure out how you shift safely before we figure out how to use that skill."

As always, Fiadh looks at this in a logical order. What she's saying makes sense, but I want to be part of the answer, not the question. Sighing, I dig around in my pocket to find the business card for the construction company. Once I get a hold of their secretary, she says we are in luck. One of their contractors had a cancellation and is in the diner down the road having lunch. She promises to call him and have him join us at the bar in about fifteen or twenty minutes.

"Finally, something's going our way." I stare at the phone. "Someone from the construction company is down the road from us. Their assistant said he should be done with lunch shortly and then he'll meet us."

"It's about freaking time! I've been wondering if some idiot hexed us when we weren't paying attention." Fi throws her hands up in the air for emphasis and I chuckle. My sister loves to exaggerate, and her dramatic responses to everything have always made me smile. She leads me over to a bench near the ruins of our home and plops down to dig in her purse. When she pulls out a handful of papers, I frown in confusion. "I woke up in the middle of the night and went downstairs to the guest computers to print this just in case we need it. Philly's copy went up in smoke with the rest of our stuff."

"Did you call them yet?" I ask. I didn't know she got up and did things while I was asleep.

She shakes her head. "No, I wanted to come here first, but I didn't expect someone to be available to meet today. I should probably do that now."

Just when I think everything is going well, we get a call back from the secretary. They have to move our meeting to tomorrow. Fi loses her shit, cursing the gods and kicking the stones. The only option we have is to head back to the hotel and wait for the next day.

It's not exactly how I would picture us spending our birthday, but sometimes fun has to take a back seat to things that need to get done.

Despite the urge to give up entirely, we return to the bar the next day. Standing out front with a thoughtful expression is a six foot, three hundred pound muscle man with his arms crossed over his chest. Dark brown hair and broad shoulders come with a scent that makes a whine escape my lips. He turns to look at me, tilting his head as he stares. I get lost in his hazel eyes before they suddenly turn amber—that must be his animal. I don't know how I know that, but it tastes true as I lick my lips.

His eyes dart between my sister and me for a moment before he notices Fi has the insurance documents in her hands. "You must be the ladies I'm here to meet."

I watch as he extends his hand to accept paperwork from Fi. His palms are huge, almost like paws, even in human form. Everything about this man is built sturdily—like the gods made him for this job.

He looks at the paperwork he has on his clipboard after scanning Fi's documents quickly. "I hope you don't mind, but I drew up a proposal for the repairs. I also included the apartment building above it because I figured that was in use by the rubble."

Fi accepts the paperwork from him, looking at it carefully while chewing her thumbnail. She does that when she's trying to make sure she doesn't miss any details and I know she's hoping the cost isn't more than Philly will be approved for by the policy. "How long do you think this is going to take?"

"If you hire us and the insurance approves the bid, we could start immediately. Once we dig in, it should only take a month, maybe two, depending on if we have to order some supplies." He looks at the building and then back towards us with a kind smile and my heart flutters.

What the hell is wrong *with me?!*

"That sounds reasonable," Fi replies distractedly as she continues to look at the estimate. "As far as I'm concerned, you're hired. You came highly recommended by the firefighter who helped put the blaze out."

A broad grin crosses his face and I notice he has dimples above his beard. He's got that big, burly lumberjack thing going on, and those dimples are the icing on the cake. "That's my cousin! He's always referring customers to us." He pauses, looking back and forth between the two of us. "May I be so bold as to ask if you two have somewhere to stay during all of this? I noticed what was left of your pictures on the walls upstairs and it made me thankful you both got out unharmed."

Can he get any more adorable?

"We're staying at a hotel right now," I squeak out before Fi slaps her hand over my mouth.

"But we can take care of ourselves. Thank you for your concern." Fi says and I can tell that her hackles are on the end.

Trust is hard earned with her.

I finally pry her hand off of my mouth. "What my sister means is that we appreciate your offer, and we would like to hear it, sir." I stare at Fi, letting the growl I've been suppressing bubble up. We haven't even heard his offer, and she's already rejected the help we sorely need. Perhaps it would be nice to hear his offer before we reject it.

"Please, you don't have to be so formal. My name is Torben—my friends call me Tor. I'm not just a contractor for this company—my family owns it." He shoves his clipboard under his arm and puts his hands into his pockets, trying to make himself not look as intimidating. "We have several cabins in the woods nearby that we rent out. It's getting close to winter, and I'd like to know the one empty cabin will be tended to. You could keep it nice through the winter in exchange for staying there."

I glare at my sister until she pantomimes zipping her mouth and pretends to throw away the key. Being bold for once, I turn and smile up at Tor. "We gratefully accept your offer."

He reaches into his pocket and pulls out a handful of keys with a rumbling chuckle. I don't know why, but I'm not afraid of this giant man—not even a little. Tor finds the key he's looking for and offers it to me. I grabbed the tip of the key and grip it in my hand. He grabs his clipboard and pulls out one of his business cards and then scrolls on the back of it the address.

"My personal cell phone number is on the front. If the cabin is to your liking, shoot me a text and then you're free to move in when you're ready. If it's something that you're not interested in, just leave the key on the table and lock the door when you leave, though I'd appreciate a text to let me know."

He bobs his head slightly at us and I nod back, thanking him again. He looks like he's going to say something else, but instead, he turns and walks to where his truck is parked.

I don't know why he's so interesting to me—usually guys that big scare me. *Maybe it's a wolf thing?* Being comfortable around another animal might be part of my DNA. Either way, I end up staring at the key and card in my hand. I'm thankful for once I stood up for what I believed in, even if it made Fiadh look at me like I'd grown a second head.

Today is my birthday and I'm starting it off on the right foot. I'm determined to go into the new year with a little more respect for myself.

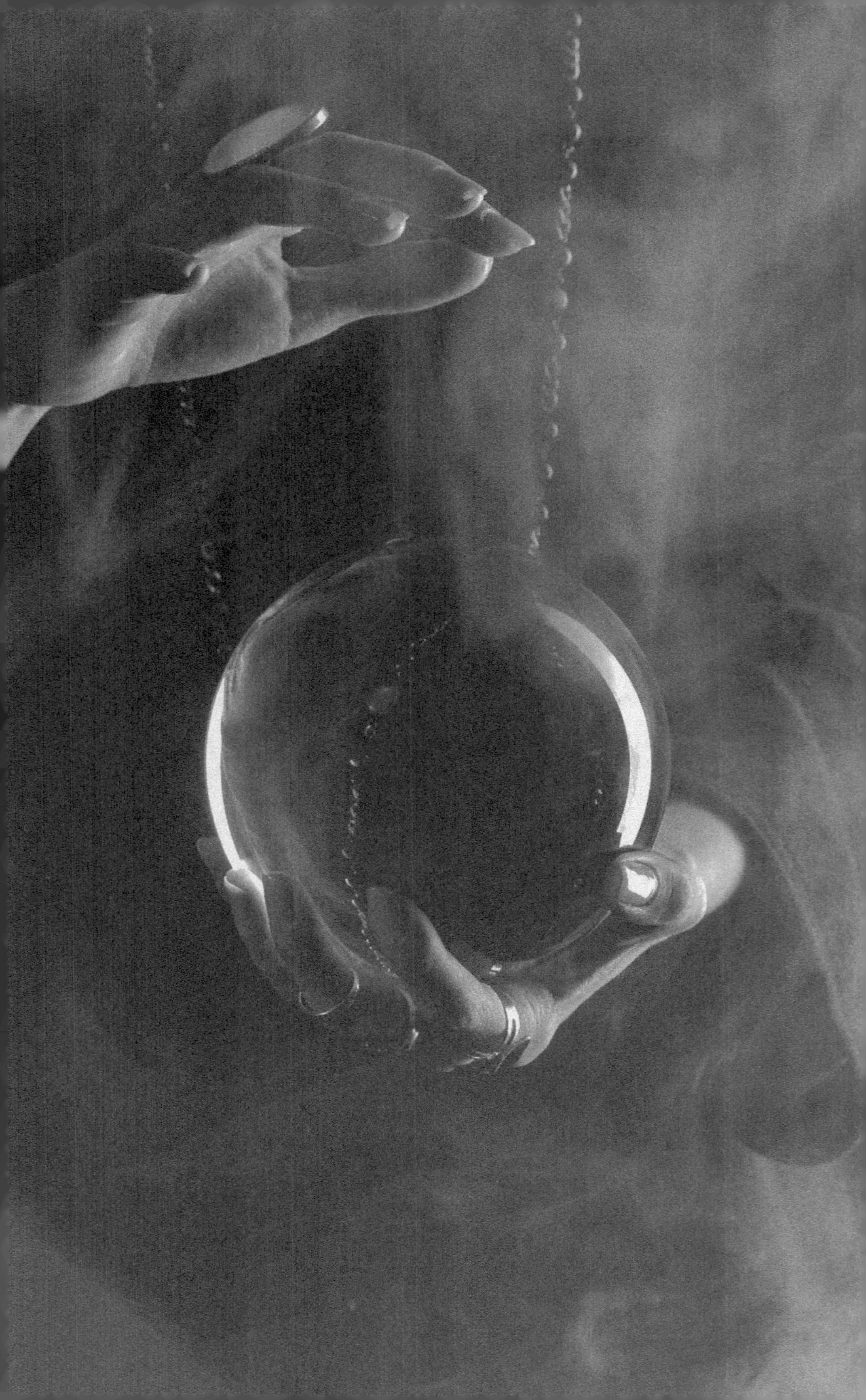

9

FIADH

I'm fairly certain Fer forgot we had plans for our birthday tonight.

When we got back to the hotel last night, she was so hyped up about moving into the cabin that she didn't even mention all the things we'd planned for today. Our birthday didn't fall directly on the Ascension this year nor on a good day for going out. We decided months ago to have a girls' day and go dancing at one of the exclusive Fae clubs in the entertainment district. It's been on our calendar since summer, but given that we no longer *have* a calendar because of the fire, I can see how it slipped her mind.

Of course, the shunning, loss of our home, unemployment, and the clown shoes that happened at the Ascension had something to do with it, too.

So I finish my breakfast, watching her pack her stuff as if she's not vibrating with excitement. I don't know why she's so willing to trust this guy we just met, but Feray is my sister and I have to back her play. It wouldn't be fair not to reciprocate the support she's always given me when I decide—even when they're wrong.

"It's small, Fi, but there's a kitchen and an office nook. We've never had an office! I don't know what we'll do with it, but I can't wait to get settled in. This place is nice, but we're so lucky not to have to live here for months." Fer holds up her phone, showing me pictures from the rental website she looked up.

Smiling to myself, I let her continue to babble as she finishes up her task and stares at me while I sip my coffee. Her brow arches as she turns to look at my things and I shrug. "It won't take me long. I'm just making sure I'm ready for our big day."

Her eyes widen, and I see it when the meaning behind my words hits her. "Shit! Our birthday outing is today. Will we be able to go now?"

"Definitely. I pre-paid all of our activities over the past few months and I had a little stash for incidentals. The spa stuff and club cover are taken care of. We'll be able to take our stuff and then walk back to the salon for our pampering."

The sound she makes is high-pitched enough that it makes *my* ears hurt and I laugh when she winces. I stand and walk over to her, hugging her tightly before I clean up the breakfast mess. Feray folds my clothes from the thrift store and loads up the bags, her excitement ramping up even higher than before. By the time I use the restroom and come back out, she's got everything squared away and is making the beds. I give her a fond, yet frustrated look and she shrugs.

"I'm faster at this stuff than you, Fi. You hate all the 'domestic' bullshit and I don't want to miss a single thing we have planned for today. With all the bad things that have happened in the past few days, we deserve a little fun," she says, planting her hands on her hips and giving me a stubborn look.

"Okay, okay! You win. Let's grab our shit and blow this popsicle stand, sis."

"That's more like it."

Feray tosses the surplus bag she put all our clothes in at me and I sling it over my shoulder. We grab our purses and the key cards, heading downstairs to pay the bill for our room.

As far as a start to our day goes, this one is the best we've had all week.

BY THE TIME we dropped our stuff at the cabin, we were winded. Lugging everything from the middle of town to the small cottage by the lake wasn't easy, but we managed. I'm not a fan of spending money we don't need to and I wanted to save the extra I'd put away for our special birthday pampering. Fer complained a little, but she seemed to handle it better than I think she would have before the Ascension. I think the release of her wolf might be slowly changing her physiology—and I'm glad for it. She's always been softer than me and the beast inside of her giving her more physical strength and stamina is perfect. Feray needs to be able to defend herself if I'm not around and that's never been the case in the past.

"What are you thinking about? Your face is all scrunched up," my sister asks as we hoof it back to the part of town where all the salons and spas are located.

That sector is mainly owned by a consortium of species who specialize in magic and artistry, so we're less likely to get completely shunned while we're primping for tonight. I let out a breath as I realize we should be relatively safe and turn to reply, "I'm excited to have someone take care of me for a while. You know, nails, hair, makeup... the full monte. We haven't done anything like this in a long time. With everything that's happened, it feels like we deserve to relax with cucumbers on our eyes."

Her eyes widen as she looks at her hands and then back at me. "Oh, Fi! What happens to my manicure if I shift? Or waxing? Am I gonna destroy it all if I lose control?"

I blink. *Shit, I didn't even think about that possibility and I have no fucking clue.* "Maybe we can ask the techs? You're not the only wolf in town, sis; hell, you're not the first new shifter, either. They have to know what to do or how to keep you looking nice for a bit."

"Okay," she breathes, looking a little less shaken. "You're right. There's probably a spell or salve or something they use on shifters to keep them looking nice."

Grinning, I sock her on the shoulder. "There's the spirit. No need to freak out until we know it's a real problem. This is *supposed* to be our relaxing time. Now that you got us a place to live, we can focus on other stuff tomorrow. Tonight, we're gonna let loose and have fun. Right?"

"Right!"

I just hope I'm not being naïve.

When we finish getting our hair, nails, and face done, Feray is giggling with me like we did as kids. The salon techs had no problem adjusting their services for a budding shifter and since they weren't witches, they had no problems with us based on our identity. In fact, it seemed like they had no idea who we were, which bodes well for our job search outside of our community later this week.

I always knew the assholes heading up the species' councils were elitist dipshits who were out of touch with their own people.

We're sipping on fancy coffee drinks and carrying the bags of products we deemed absolutely necessary as we exit the salon and I'm feeling better than I have since before the ceremony. That is, until I run smack into a hard chest and hear a hiss of anger aimed at me. Backing up, I glare at the offending moron with daggers in my eyes. After all, he almost made me spill my Faerie latte.

"Watch where the hell you're going, douchebag!"

The narrowed gaze and insolent smirk are familiar, as is the carbon copy standing next to him with an apologetic expression on his face. "Oh, look. It's Sassy and her sissy. Why am I not surprised that she's giving me lip for something that is clearly *her fault*."

Oh, hell, no.

Marching up to him, I poke him in the chest hard. "You! You and your criminal friends are the reason our home burned to the ground—your fight with those fucking fried chickens!"

His lips curve and he turns to his brother, muttering, "Fried chickens—I like it. Remember that, Khal." The nice one grins a little and pulls out his phone as if he's going to take notes and asshat turns back to me. "Listen, Sassypants. We had *nothing* to do with that fire. The only reason *he* mixed it up with those losers is because my bro doesn't like to see guys pick on chicks."

"He's right," the twin pipes up as he looks at us. "There were a lot of them and they don't fight fair. I didn't want you to get hurt."

I snort, putting a hand on my hip as I look at these two overly masculine dipshits. "I had it covered. I've worked in that bar since high school and managed to keep myself safe without two juiced up gangsters protecting me. Your egos are why our friend is in a coma and we have to find new jobs."

"I hardly think that's *fair*."

Feray steps forward, a low growl rumbling out of her chest. "What isn't fair? That we blame your rivalry with a bunch of other thugs for destroying our entire world? Newsflash: life is *definitely* not fair."

They both look at her in surprise, but the alpha twin speaks. "Good to know that fire runs in the family, Red, but we didn't antagonize them. Your lovely, yet ill-tempered sister knows that. I'll give you a break this time—but make no mistake, if you step up to the plate again…" His gaze cuts to me and a wicked grin spreads over his face. "Be prepared for what happens when you get your third strike, little witch."

"Gag me with a spoon," I mutter as I roll my eyes. "Come on, Fer. These idiots are wasting our girl time. Let's go have lunch somewhere less… toxic."

"And I didn't peg you for a… chicken. Sad, really."

That's it.

Whirling around, I drop my bags and haul my fist back, clocking him in the jaw hard. "Who's the chicken now, bitch?"

Khal's eyes widen as he watches his brother shake his head and rub his jaw. He looks at my sister, but she glares at him. "Wait, wait! Khol is an ass—it's his natural state of being. We're sorry. You must be overwhelmed with all the things going on in your life and his shitty attitude isn't helping."

"Duh," I reply in a voice so sarcastic that I'm surprised it isn't dripping on the ground. "Picking on homeless exiles seems perfectly in character for him, though."

"Exiles?" The jerk stops massaging his face dramatically and frowns at me. "What do you mean, exiles?"

"None of your business!" I pick up my bags angrily, noting one of my nails is messed up now. "Damn it, now I have to get this smudge fixed so I don't look stupid tonight."

Feray walks over and takes my hand, frowning at the fucked nail before she nods. "We can have Sasha put on a new one. Luckily, we have enough time before the next stop. Let's go back in, sis."

"Aw, how cute! She broke a *nail*!"

This time, Fer grabs me and holds me back with her freaky, enhanced strength and I notice Khal stepping in front of his mouthy twin. They exchange a look that doesn't sit well with me. *It's time to get away from these dudes before something even worse happens.* "I'll break your pretty face if you don't back off, jackass."

"Fi, let's go…"

"Khol, stop antagonizing her!"

The calmer siblings speak at the exact same time and I get this weird jolt when I look at the arrogant tool. I don't know why I can't just walk away, but I know I have to. I take in a deep breath, picking up my shit *yet again*, and take Fer's hand. She leads me back into the salon, but I feel the eyes watching us as we go like they're burning into my skin.

There is definitely something up with those guys and I'll be damned if I'm not going to find out what the hell it is.

10

FERAY

Thankfully, Sasha wasn't busy when we walked back in. She took Fi right away and fixed the smudge that was on her nail. I can't help thinking about the twins. The calmer one reminds me of myself, taking the back seat to our fiery tempered sibling.

Fi is rattling off the names of different clubs we can go to tonight and I can't help but feel excitement bubble up, then fear follows. "What if I lose control and shift?" I whisper in Fi's ear as we walk out of the salon.

Glancing both ways, she offers me a sympathetic smile. "We'll cross that bridge if it happens. You were in control of yourself the first time you shifted, so I'm positive we'll be okay." Fi smiles and leans into me, offering support.

The sudden urge to rub my cheek against hers sets me in motion before I can stop myself. A calming wave sweeps over me, and I can't help but smile.

"What was that?" Fi arches her brow as she looks at me.

"Not sure. Instinct, I guess." My gaze drops to the bags in my hand. Shrugging my shoulders, I look away. "Wolves are very tactile and social. I can only assume my wolf needed contact." Exhaling roughly, I go back to flipping through the club selections for tonight.

"There are three clubs that look interesting. *Red's Review and Nightclub* has dancing and dinner, then an all bear shifter male review. *Fangtasmagoria* is a dance club and rave—bar snacks are available at high top tables. Last, we have *Everglades*, a Fae owned establishment that promises a life altering experience." Laughing, I shake my head, trying to be serious. "The Fae club concerns me. It comes with portal warnings and offers drink covers at the door."

Fer stops in her tracks and steals the phone from me and looks over the listing. "Hard pass." She thumbs back up through the list, then passes the phone back to me.

"*Fangtasmagora* it is. The club opens at sundown in keeping with the vampire theme, so that's awesome. I hope wolf isn't on the menu." I laugh as I shove my phone in my pocket.

"If they think witch is on the menu, someone will eat a knuckle sandwich." Fi slams her fist into her hand, driving her point home.

Resting my hand on my sister's shoulder, I give it a squeeze before we move again. We head back to the cottage and I sigh as we walk through the city streets. The minute we step into the woods, my nerves settle and it's as if I can breathe again. Pausing, I breathe in deeply, taking in the scents of fresh earth, pine, and cedar. For the first time in a very long time, I feel at peace with everything. I get lost staring at the tiny gnats and dust particles floating in the air for a moment. The little things draw my attention before I notice my sister standing at the door of the little log cabin cottage.

I look over the construction of the structure as we approach. The cut marks of where the ax hit the wood tell the tale of the construction of the building. Long lines where the bark removal tool dragged along the length of the tree stand out. Reaching out, I run my fingers over the scrape marks, studying them before Fi clears her throat.

"Is it a wolf thing to be interested in sticks?" Her tone is mocking but in a fond, sibling teasing way.

A soft laugh escapes my lips as I pull my hand away from the log I was examining. "Maybe? I don't know; I've barely been a wolf for a week. Who knows what's normal for me?"

Tilting my head back, I search the trees as the sounds of the wind moving through the leaves catch my attention. "Everything is so much more intense, more beautiful. There's so many things I couldn't see or hear before. It's like I was born again, rediscovering the world for the first time."

Fi's face drops, and the joking expression melts to sadness. "I'm being a shit sister. I thought it would be easy for you since it's your real nature."

For once, my rock showed her genuine emotions. I know she's hurting and I can smell the change in her scent. Pulling Fi to me, I hug her tightly to me as I pull her into the house. "Where's my badass sister? You know, the one who is good at keeping us on schedule."

As soon as I mention the schedule, her eyes shoot to the grandfather clock Torben left in the house for us. "Fuck! Enough of this mushy shit. The sun will set in less than an hour. We need to get ready!"

Her panicked words make me laugh as I turned to head to my room to get ready. Keeping things organized is the one thing Fi can control, and it brings her comfort.

Pre-party jitters are kicking in and I groan to myself.

This is going to be the longest hour in history.

THE BASS THUMPS hard enough to feel like it's hitting my spine as we finally get to the door. The bouncer is a bear and he checks our IDs before letting us pass.

Squealing with excitement, Fi drags me to the bar. I get distracted looking at everyone around me as new scents assault me. I don't know if I need to cover my nose or my ears from the noise. *Damn these senses.* There's a faint scent that catches my attention —chamomile.

There are at least eight people in the direction of the scent. The dragon from our bank is talking to a strikingly handsome man. His chiseled features and unnaturally still, the way he's standing screams vampire. The banker has his tie loose and the top button of his dress shirt open. I stare at them a moment , wondering why they are taking care of business here.

Turning away, I watch my sister going over the drink menu. Tilly, the bartender, offers her condolences about Philly and the bar. I nod and look away, watching the other patrons who give the vamp and the dragon a wide berth. They are apex predators, so it's not a bad instinct, but my curiosity about them overrides my ability to reason.

"What are you two doing for work?" Tilly's musical voice draws my attention back.

"Not sure. Do you have any good leads?" Fi is always hustling, even when we're out to have fun.

"Several of the other vamp-owned bars are hiring. They are very selective about who they let in." Tilly's eyes land on me and I sigh. From what I read the other night, my bite is deadly to vampires, so it's not hard to read between the lines. More than likely, a vamp won't hire me; I'm too much of a liability.

Shaking my head, I lean my back against the bar on the other side of my sister. Several other shifters' eyes flash the color of their beast as they look in my direction. I'm not sure what they are, but I know they're there. Fi sounds like she's talking underwater again until a sultry male voice breaks through my people watching.

The vampire is next to my sister, and I feel the beast within me stir defensively as I look over her shoulder at him. The smoothness of his face and the strong angle of his jaw make him appealing. His voice is soothing as much as it's alluring. Narrowing my eyes, I focus on the lower octaves of his tenor; there's almost a reverb to it. As much as my sister is a badass, she's a woman, and he's laying the seduction on thick.

"Can I help you?" I break the spell he was trying to cast over my sister to stare openly at him. My gums ache, and I suppress the urge to bite him.

"Oh, I'm sorry. I didn't know you were together. My name is Dezi. I was offering your sister a job at my establishment." He casually flips his business card over his fingers back and forth like a magician would roll a playing card through his fingers.

Breathing in his scent, it reminds me of anise and lemon with a hint of leather. He wasn't the one who caught my attention before. "My sister and I are a package deal. She runs the floor and I run the bar." *Where this set of brass balls is coming from is beyond me. Perhaps it's my animal lending me her strength?* All I know is I don't like this male near my sister when he's got the vamp stuff turned on.

"Is that so?" He backs away, then extends his hand out to my sister, offering her the card. "Allow me to change my offer to include both of you. Whichever roles you are comfortable in will suffice. After all, it would benefit me to have a wolf on hand if some of my clientele get out of hand." He shows off his fangs, and I snort. A wolf in the house will keep the vampires in line better than a bouncer.

I watch Fi take the card and Dezi's eyes drop to look at where their hands are touching. My sister looks at her hand as she takes the card, shaking it, and then shoves it in her pocket. Dezi looks up slowly before he bids us *adieu*. I watch him head back to the banker before looking back at my dazed sister.

"You okay?"

Leaning in, I sniff her, but there's no acrid scent that I would associate with her being stressed.

Fi takes several moments before her face lights up and she lets a laugh escape. "Well, now we can really enjoy ourselves. We have a home and a job." She wraps me up in one of her bone crushing hugs and I can't help but laugh till the feel of the crowd shifts.

Turning to face the gathering behind us, we notice a gaggle of security surrounding a group of Fae as they enter the club.

"Ugh, just what we need is a haughty Fae Prince." Fi rolls her eyes and orders drinks for us and shakes her head in disgust.

"We shouldn't judge him. We don't like being judged." I offer half heartedly. Once Fi has decided, it's damn near impossible to change it.

"Why not? They judge us." She says as she motions with her drink to the entourage, following him in like he's the greatest person in the world.

Swallowing most of my drink in a single gulp, I try to gain some courage. "Because we are better than that. At least, that's what Mom would have wanted us to do." I mumble the last part. Of all people, I understand her anger and borderline hatred of others because of how they treated us.

Fi's hand comes to rest on my shoulder before she turns to face me. "It's hard to turn the other cheek when they always sought us out to hurt us." The way she's looking at me, I know she wants me to see things from her perspective. Sometimes it's hard because their actions are reactions to how we act around them.

"I get it, but maybe this year we can try to be a little kinder? Maybe it will change things for us?" Hopefully putting good vibes out will get the good vibes to come back to us.

"Always the optimistic one. You're definitely the better sister." Fi's lips land on my temple just as glass breaks behind us. We spin as one to see the mother of all fights break out.

Chairs and bodies are flying; fists and glasses are airborne. I smell the iron tinge of blood in the air and it makes my canines rip through my gums. The room changes—things are sharper than before and some of the vivid colors fade. The greens, yellows and blues are still as beautiful as they were before, but the other colors are now muted almost a gray brown in color. Things in motion slow down allowing me to move myself and Fi out of the way of the bottle headed in our direction.

"How the fuck did you do that?" Fi exclaims as I slide us out of the way of the next projectile.

"Not sure! Don't look a gift horse in the mouth; it's time to move. We need to leave or end this— your choice, sis." I catch a bottle inches from my sister's face as if to punctuate my point further, then shove a drunk patron back into the fray. A feral smile crosses my lips as I wait for Fi to make the decision.

Happy Birthday to us.

11

FIADH

A burst of adrenaline courses through my veins as I look around, trying to determine where the instigators are. Ending fights is one of my favorite things to do at *Dionysian Delights,* and with the bar on indefinite hiatus, I wasn't sure where I could get my fighting fix from—until now. Winking at Fer, I charge into the fray, new outfit be damned. As I duck and weave thrown fists and glasses, I slip through the mass of bodies to find out what assholes fucked up our birthday outing. When I see the culprits in the middle, I roll my eyes.

Minotaurs—goddess above, it's always *the monstrous fuckwits starting shit. They can't help themselves.*

I stomp up to the tall dickwad who seems in charge of the gang of douches that started the fight and flick my hair over my shoulder. "Hey, meathead! Your mother is a flank steak and your father smells like a slaughterhouse!"

His gaze drops to mine immediately and steam escapes his half-shifted features as he snorts. The gold ring in his bovine nose flutters and he scrapes a foot on the floor. It's covered in a steel-toed boot, but for all I know, it might be a hoof inside. These dudes have as much control as they do smarts—which is to say none. Lips hitch in a sneer as he peers down at me from eight feet of muscle and he huffs, "Be gone, witch. You are not part of this, and you smell like weakness."

As if this idiot can smell anything *well. It's not his species' gift.*

"You smell like you need A-1, but that's not the point, is it?" I shoot back as I drop into a fighting stance. Spikes of excitement zing along my skin, making me grin even wider. This might be painful tomorrow, but I guarantee I'll get some of my rage out, so I'll take it.

One of his friends steps up beside him, laughing in a piggish baritone. The bespectacled boar shifter looks down at me with a smirk. "Is this spice sucker bothering you, boss? I'll deal with her so your hooves stay clean."

I roll my eyes at them, not intimidated in the least. The combined brain power of these two morons wouldn't power a potato lamp and despite the size difference, outsmarting them will be child's play. "Yeah, boss. You look like a dude that isn't capable of fighting his own battles. After all, it's *coward*, not *pig*ward."

The minotaur narrows his eyes, reaching up to tug on the topknot his kind wear in agitation. Baiting him is accomplishing what is intended—it's drawn his attention away from egging his merry band of dipshits on. I can hear the fighting sounds dying down behind me, though I suppose that doesn't bode well for me. When his crew of jackwads aren't mixing it up with others, they'll all turn on me when he commands it. That's how herd animals work, even ones with minimally higher intelligence like these fuckers.

"I'll crush you like a grape, witch." He stands taller, looking down his snout at me with disgust as he leers. "Everyone knows who you are and you are beneath us. You have no power—you should take your pounding and thank me."

I think the fuck not, you egotistical knob.

Arching a brow, I smile and bat my lashes at the shifter as he tries to control me. Better manipulators than this chowderhead have tried and failed, so his feeble intimidation attempts are laughable. "Quit stalling, pot roast. Either square up and fight me or back your clan of fools off. I'm giving you a choice because even though I'd love to tenderize you, this isn't my bar and I don't want to ruin the atmosphere."

Muffled shouts echo behind me and I assume that either the bartender, the bouncer, or hell, any fucking security in the building has jumped into the fray. I know Fer dashed off to safety when I waded into the mess, so I'm not worried about her. However, I'd like to avoid collateral damage when this brawl starts, so I appreciated a little help with clearing the rest of the goons.

"As if I'd let an ill-equipped, monosyllabic twat get his miniature beef stick within a mile of me. Be fucking for real," I scoff. My hands drop for a moment as I slip them into pockets and come out with the spiked knuckles I keep on me at all times. "Now, are we doing this or are you going to talk me to death?"

"That's what she said."

Whirling to the amused voice to my right, I scowl. "It *is* what I said. Who asked you?"

The handsome guy with deep chocolate brown eyes and a bespoke suit looks at me with amusement. "No one, but you look like you could use a hand."

I snort, turning back to the minotaur and his Baconator buddy. "Answer my question, Bessie. Or are you less beef than poultry?"

"Merciful Bast, you won't quit," Hot Dude mutters under his breath.

While I'm waiting for the faux badass to respond, three more minions stalk up to form a semi-circle around us. Taking them in, I note a faun, a hippogriff, and a basan; the latter makes me groan low in frustration. *Why can't I get away from fucking fire-breathing chickens this week?* Scrubbing a hand down my face, I take in a deep breath as they all start chuckling as if they're big bads. The reality is they're oddballs—species who don't fit into the major populations in Briarvale and have formed their own gang. They have no more power or influence than I do, but they clearly enjoy starting trouble and bullying people.

I'm gearing myself up for a hell of a brawl when a hand lands on my shoulder and it's like an electric shock goes rocketing down my arm. My eyes meet the interfering muscle man and I squint at him. He's not a magic user and I don't have powers. *What the holy fuck was that?* I open my mouth to lambast him for daring to put his hand on me and when I hear a loud scraping on the floor.

Uh-oh.

What happens next feels like a blur. Large palms grasp my waist and yank me to the side as a fast moving pair of horns come charging through the spot I was in mere milliseconds before. My feet hit the ground and I spin around, letting a fist fly at the tusked asshole who follows the minotaur's lead. It hurts like a mother fucker to hit that bone, but I send him flying into the crowd like a sack of potatoes.

"Nice," Hot Dude says as he winks and half-shifts.

The beautiful white and gray spots of a snow leopard make me pause and I just watch him stomp over to the minotaur to yank the moron up by his horn. He grins with a mouthful of large feline fangs as he shakes the bovine like he weighs nothing and I swear to hell, the sight makes my thighs clench. Tiny tingles and shocks jump all over my skin, making me shiver, but I have to turn away when I hear the sound of another set of hooves.

I drop to a defensive stance again, but suddenly, my vision clouds. Wobbling a little, I have to put my hands out to the side instead to find balance. *What the shit is happening to me?* I shake my head, trying to clear it so I can prepare for the faun to advance, but it doesn't help. There are stars and sparkles all around me, glinting off lights and shiny sequins on clothing and piercings as the world spins off its axis.

"Help," I croak.

Shadows come bursting into the circle, grabbing at the fuckers lined up to come at me, but I can't make out who they are. Strong hands grab me again and I think I'm trying to fight them off, but that whiskey-tenor of the bemused leopard tells me to stop wiggling as I'm thrown over a shoulder. I flail anyway; I don't know this idiot from a shapeshifter on the street. *Who knows where the hell he's taking me while pretending to be a good guy?*

"Fi, stop! He's trying to help!"

Feray's voice cuts through the fog in my mind, so I pause my fight for a second to try and figure out what's going on. "Fer? Are you there?"

She chuckles and I can feel the amusement in the air like it's caressing my skin. "Yes, sis. This gentleman is carrying you to the bar. Please don't make it harder. He's doing us a favor before you keel over."

"Was I hit?" I ask in confusion. Fainting isn't my thing—I'm not someone who gets overwrought like that. I'm much more likely to do exactly what I was doing before this odd brain drain zapped me. "Did one of those shitheads have magic?"

"No," the shifter says, his hand squeezing my hip. "You were ready to rumble and started swaying like you were hypnotized. None of those morons have that kind of power, so I scooped you up while security dealt with them. Took them long enough to get there, too. I'm lodging a formal complaint with the owners."

"Complaint?" I echo blearily as the scenery blurs around me.

A sigh followed by a soft laugh is his answer at first, but then he speaks. "Yes. I'm private security for a VIP guest upstairs. When I saw the shit going down from the balcony and no response, I jumped down to contain it before it spread to my client's area. Of course, then I found a mouthy witch ready to take on a herd of live-stock with only brass knuckles on her side."

"Petty and Betty are all I need to take on assholes like that," I mumble as I focus on trying to lift my hands to show him. "I do it all the time at work—or I did."

"Not this time, Knuckles." His words make me frown as he lowers me off of his shoulder to bar stool—I think—and he places his palms on my thighs to steady me.

"Oooh!" Fer squeals and claps. "Knuckles. Fi, that's a great nickname for you."

I'm pretty certain I'm glaring at them, but since I can't tell whether I'm in my damn body or not, I don't know for sure. "It is *not*. People don't give me nicknames, Fer. Even Philly calls me by my name."

"I like it," she replies stubbornly. "And you should thank... what's your name, again?"

The fuzzy image of a beautiful, muscled bodyguard seems to smile when she asks. "Tiernan."

"You should thank Tiernan for helping me get you out of there before you passed out."

"Unlikely," I grumble. "I don't need some beefy bodyguard to bail me out of a fight."

His laugh crawls over my skin and I shiver again. "Keep telling yourself that, Knuckles. Luckily for you, I don't need the kudos; I'm just glad I was able to help."

"You're a peach," I say with an eye roll. "Can someone get me a fucking drink? I'm dry as a bone."

Feray turns to order and the leopard snags her sleeve. My vision is sharpening a little, but I still can't quite make everything out, especially far away. He smiles brightly. "She needs water with whatever you're ordering. Dehydration is no joke."

Hera save me, he's a fitness nut. Of course *he is—bodyguards have to be hella cut.*

"Got it. Can I get you something for being so kind?" Fer asks sweetly.

"No, ma'am. But tell Leroy to put it on the Court tab. I'd love to buy you both a drink. After all, your sister may have been foolish, but she was clearly trying to keep that brawl from spreading across the club. Even I could see that before I jumped in."

"Fer, quit batting your lashes and order the drinks. I want to make this shit go away so we can go home. Maybe I'm coming down with something." I know I sound petulant, but my sister is definitely flirting with this guy and for some reason, it bothers the hell out of me that he's flirting back.

Tonight is just the mustard on the shit sandwich of this week and I want to get far away from all these people.

Huh. Now I sound like Feray—who would have thought?

12

Feray

Chirping birds draw me out of my deep slumber. Rolling over, I snuggle deeper into the blankets and sigh. I slept better since we moved here than I have in years.

I wonder if someone furnished this house specifically for shifters. The calmness of the forest soothes me, setting my mind at ease. Stretching slowly, I test my muscles for soreness and for once, I wake up pain free. The battle royale last night was incredible. For once, I wasn't afraid and trusted my instincts, as well as the animal within me.

Turning to the side, I sit at the edge of the bed, looking outside at the stately conifer forest. I sense all the woodland creatures inhabiting the forest and it makes my wolf hungry. A voice inside me says *hunt* and I ponder its request. Fi would not be happy if I brought one of her little furry friends home for breakfast. Laughing, I picture my sister like Snow White gone bad—all the love for woodland creatures, but none of the love for idiot humans.

Part of me never wants to leave here. The apartment over the bar was nice, but I've changed. Being this close to the forest appeals to the animal in me in a way living in the city never could. Shaking my head, I push those thoughts aside for later. There's no way I would ever leave Fi—not until one of us is mated. Chuckling to myself, I banish that thought from my mind.

It suddenly occurs to me to look down at my knuckles, and I'm shocked to see there's not a single scratch left from the night before. *Go shifter healing!* Hell, if Fi had a clue how much I fought last night, she would look at me as if I'm possessed. When she wobbled, I jumped into the fray to protect her until the snow leopard could get to her.

For some odd reason, I didn't get defensive when he went to save her. I can only assume it's an animal thing; maybe my beast trusted him? I guess I'll never know—it's not like the odds are in our favor to see him again.

I tiptoe through the house. The ruffling of blankets tells me my sister is stirring in her bed. It's only a matter of time before she awakens and seeks her morning caffeine fix. The craftsmanship of the narrow hallway catches my attention and I study the wood-paneled walls. It makes me wonder how long it took for whoever built this place to do it. Everything is hand crafted and assembled with care.

My wolf nudges me, whispering that building shelters is an attribute of a suitable mate. I can only hope one day I will find a mate that is dedicated to me. Heading into the kitchen, I start the coffee for myself and I pull out an assortment of elven energy tonics for Fi. Thankfully, I remembered to purchase several flavors for her, knowing she gets bored with having one flavor every day. Goddess only knows how she hasn't exploded from one of these things yet.

Fiadh's grumbling and cursing echoes through the house and I know my sister has finally awakened. "Motherfucking son of a..."

Wincing, I can finish her sentence in my head. The slamming of her bedroom door sounds like it is right next to me instead of down the hall. Today is going to be an adventure. Fi never faints in a fight, nor does she ever lose, either. Besides her hand and possibly a few ribs being bruised, I know her ego definitely suffered some damage last night. Drawing in a deep breath, I brace myself for the force of nature that is my sister.

"Look at my fucking hand!" Fi's angry voice hits a pitch that makes me cringe.

Blinking in shock, I examine the swollen mass that is my sister's hand. "Well, no one said punching a boar in the head was a good idea. Just saying." Shrugging, I sip at my coffee as my sister glares at me. If she didn't break something, it would truly impress me.

"The jackass tried to bum rush me after his buddy charged at me." Fi slams her fists down on the counter then yelps in pain, shaking her hand and cursing under her breath.

"Need... Ice?" I bite my bottom lip, fighting the laughter that threatens to escape. Fi will murder me if I poke fun at her right now. I slap my hand over my mouth, trying to keep silent. Holding my breath to keep the laughter in, several puffs of air escape and hit my palm.

"Laugh it up, fur ball." She tries to point at me with her swollen hand and I fall off my damn stool laughing. "Ha! Enjoy the suck," Fi snarks as I lay on my back and cackle.

A new scent catches my attention and I roll over quickly. When my focus shifts, I head through the house in the smell's direction. My stomach growls as I get closer to the front door. *Fresh baked bread— why do I smell bread by the door?* Cautiously, I turn the knob to see a wicker basket on the porch. The delicious scent rises to me and I can't help but smile. Bread, possibly cured meat, and several other scents I can't discern without opening it.

"Don't touch it! It might hurt us," Fi cautions as I grab the basket and remove the hand towel covering it.

Under the towel, there are two round loaves of fresh bread, honey, and a jar of what appears to be butter. A curious square envelope sits in the middle of the basket. Under the envelope, I find a wedge of meat, several teas, and a soothing elixir in a blue bottle. Walking past a complaining Fi, I sit the basket on the tabletop and examine the contents.

"It might be poisoned," Fi says as she stares at the basket from the other side of the table.

"It's not poisoned." Rolling my eyes, I sniff the food again, then remove it and lay it out on the table.

"How can you be sure?" Fi pokes at the loaf closest to her with a knife.

Smiling, I point to my nose. "These new senses have some benefits. This smells homemade, as if they made it with love like Mom used to make for us." A pang of sorrow grips my heart as I think about our mother and how she would spend Saturdays baking for us. Memories of her putting me up on the stool next to her so I could help her mix ingredients make me a little melancholy.

Cutting open the first loaf of bread, I slide a slice over to Fi. "If you're so positive something is wrong with it, test it." I pop open the honey and the butter jars to offer those as well. I study the cured meat closely, looking it over before slicing some off and placing it in front of her.

Staring at the elixir in the bottle, I cautiously pop the top. The strong fragrance of lavender floats up to me. Smiling, I slip the bottle into my pocket.

"What was that, Fer?" My sister gives me a knowing smile.

"It's lavender essence; the smell is pretty and soothing." Blushing, I pat the bottle then reach for the note. The handwriting is blockish and very masculine. A faint scent of sandalwood lingers on the cardstock and I inhale it deeply.

LITTLE WOLF,
    I HOPE MY GIFT ADDS TO YOUR COMFORT AND SECURITY. IT IS MY HONOR TO PROVIDE FOR YOU. PLEASE ACCEPT THESE MEAGER ITEMS AS A TOKEN OF MY INTEREST.

The scrolled word at the bottom is far too elaborate for me to decipher who my secret admirer is. "Fi, does this mean what I think it means?"

She snatches the card out of my hand and smiles. "Oooh, you have a nickname *and* a gift. Wait, I remember reading about this in a textbook from fourth year shifter biology class." Fi runs to her room and I hear things falling as she hits her hand while searching. Triumphantly, she emerges holding the book in her good hand. She drops it on the table with a thud. "Boom!"

Quickly, I spin the book to face me and scan through the pages to the chapter on shifter etiquette. There's a huge section on visiting a shifter's home and what should be given to the host. The next paragraph is about what is offered in a mate basket. It describes examples of what each species offers in their gift. Bears leave honey and bread and other things amenable to the prospective partner. Gasping, I step back, prompting Fi to take the book from me.

"Oh, shit! That's a mate basket. What are you going to do?" Fi flips further through the pages as I have my mini meltdown.

A bear is interested in me? I feel like a redheaded version of Goldilocks.

"Wait, it's customary for the male to leave at least four to five in total before the female is expected to answer by leaving him something in response." Fi fixes me with a 'judgy sister stare.'

"Don't look at me like that; I don't know what to do! What if he eats me?" Panic sets in as I furrow my brows.

"Have you seen how long and dextrous their tongues are? That's definitely a win." Fi waggles her eyebrows at me suggestively.

Rolling my eyes, I shake my head at her. "I wasn't thinking with my hoo-ha, thanks sis. What do I leave him if I want to meet him?" Pacing seems like the best idea at the moment, especially after my sister explained what a bear's tongue can do. My damn hindbrain kicks in at the most inopportune times now.

"The internet says to leave a fresh honeycomb, a pastry, and two beers," Fi says, looking at me earnestly.

"Okay, I'll see what he leaves going forward." Reaching out, I take a hunk of bread and mix the butter and honey on it. Now I need to figure out where to find wild honey without getting stung. I also need to research how to harvest it without pissing off all the bees. Hopefully, this male is worth all this fucking effort. If I'm braving a hive for him, he better be a good man.

I stare down at my coffee mug for far too long as I picture having a mate. Someone to snuggle up with and be held by someone besides my sister would be nice. Reality comes crashing in when I remember we need to go job hunting to find a way to support ourselves.

Having a knight on a white horse rescue me would be epic, but I would rather rescue myself.

Tossing today's paper in front of Fi, I smirk. "Where to, Captain?"

The help wanted section flops open before her and she rolls her eyes. *Fi loves planning; why not let her have at it?* Leaning back, I eat my bread and meat. My sister is the project mastermind, so where she says we should go we will. I know one thing, the vamps won't mess with us with my wolf around.

For once, I am the one that should be feared.

13

FIADH

BEFORE WE VENTURED OUT TO POUND THE PAVEMENT, I WRAPPED MY hand in gauze. The friendly bear who allowed us to stay here had a well stocked first aid kit in the bathrooms and I knew if I didn't wrap this bruised mess up, it would invite questions I didn't want to answer.

Besides, it hurts like a bitch, and I don't have shifter healing.

That concession helped little, nor did my sister's plan of dressing a little more girly to make people see us as 'professional.' All that did was allow people to leer at us before sneering in disgust. Then they made absolutely sure we understood *why* they weren't interested in hiring us—the High Mage's decree at the Ascension finally filtered out into the other communities. We were already turned away in the witch quarter, but the Fae, shifter, and miscellaneous folks have heard now, too. That's what pushed me to pull the card out of my pocket and stare at it while my sister gnaws on the jerky sticks I bought her.

We have to check out the vamp and demon businesses.

I'd prefer not because the danger in those places is much higher than at Philly's and even if she has new powers, I don't want Fer around those kinds of guys. But we need money to survive and they all pay well—for a reason. The clientele and owners have extremely flexible morals and ideas about what's right and wrong. If we take a job there, we'll be in front row seats to some of the seediest deals and most kinky shit we've ever witnessed; I'm not sure my hopelessly romantic, idealistic sister is ready for that.

Me? I'm crooked like a question mark, so it won't even make me bat a lash. But I know deep down, Feray believes we'll find our Prince Charmings despite the mating fiasco. I will not take that hope away from her, especially since I believe the courtship basket we found is from our new landlord. He is handsome, has a good income, and seems kind enough to my sister. Even if he's not able to complete a fated mate bond with her, he'd make a good husband. If I destroy her romantic notions, she might reject Mr. Good Enough because he doesn't fit some silly daydream in her head that will never come.

Unfortunately, I'm enough of a realist to know our lack of mates at the ceremony spells the end of the fated mate fairytale we're all told about. If mates had rejected us, it would be one thing. But we weren't—they simply didn't exist. Knowing that helps me let go of the last of my childhood fantasies and move on; I'll be able to accept the reality once I've gone through all the steps of grief like I should.

But I can't let Fer know I'm mired in depression at the moment; she needs me too much.

Shaking my head, I look at Feray with a small smile. "I hate to say it, but we're going to visit the vamp and demon spots after dark. That fucker has blacklisted us everywhere that operates in daylight."

"Yeah, I know," she mumbles around the bite she's chewing.

I reach over and ruffle her hair fondly. "Cheer up. Those bars are bound to be more exciting and they definitely pay better. We can work less and make more; we'll just have to be very smart about watching our surroundings."

She rolls her eyes at my attempt to make our lack of options seem more positive. "Fine. But since we're stopping the search until dark, we need to go to the bank."

"Have I mentioned how much I *hate* that you won't let me do this shit online? I know you have dad's weird aversion to online money handling, but it's so inconvenient to have to go in every time we need to make a deposit or shift money around." I give her an irritable look and my hand throbs in the makeshift dressing.

Feray shrugs. "Dad always said it's not safe. There are hackers in the human and supernatural world. Money is the last thing you want to leave to chance."

"Dad also told us you were a witch. That wasn't true. Maybe some of the weird security shit he and mom preached at us growing up was more about hiding *that* secret rather than protecting ourselves," I grumble. "Since the Ascension, I've been questioning *a lot* about our life, Fer. You know, I've never believed that wreck was an accident."

"I know," she whispers as she looks at her hands. "I've never been able to look at it that closely because I feel so guilty. But now..."

Her sad face makes me feel terrible, so I use my good arm to haul her against me and squeeze. "That's a topic for another day, sis. You're right; we need to go to the bank and shuffle some funds until we work, but that can wait until later. The banks are open at night and I'd like to have a job before I look at our money. For now, let's get some coffee so we can chill out in a cafe until the sun sets. Sound good?"

"Sounds good, Fi. Maybe lunch will help me calm my nerves," she says as her eyes dance.

"You're going to eat us out of house and home before we even get one," I chuckle and turn us towards the darker part of town. We'll find somewhere to perch on the edge of the Night District until the businesses there open.

BY THE TIME the sun sets, we've eaten, consumed multiple pots of coffee, and dissected the mate basket thing to death.

I know Fer is interested, but her fear of the unknown is justified. We haven't been the recipients of much genuine kindness lately and I don't blame her for wondering if this is a humiliating set-up. It may not be high school anymore, but the way everyone acted at the Ascension and now after, it feels like there's some sort of conspiracy to fuck with us. I can't imagine what anyone gains from ostracizing us other than the perverse satisfaction they find in feeling 'above' someone.

My gut says this is real, though I can't explain why.

"Are you ready to enter the crypts?" Fer asks with a tiny grin.

Giving her an amused look, I nod. "As ready as I'll ever be. We should start with the club on this card. I feel the guy who gave me this is the owner. He seemed willing to hire us despite the rumors."

Feray stands and picks up our trash, walking over to stuff it in the cans before tapping her foot. "Let's go, then. If we get this job on the first try, we can go to the bank and get home early. That means we can have a movie night!"

"Okay, okay." I loop my arm through hers, and we head down the street.

The lamplight gets dimmer as we walk towards the Night District. When the vamps, demons, and various dark supernaturals formed a business district at the furthest end of town, I was only a kid. I remember visiting the dwarf district with my father, who complained the entire time that the council allowed the groups to build their own area. Vamps, demons, lower Unseelie Fae, incubi, succubi, and every morally gray species banded together to create a cross between Vegas and New York City on the outskirts of Briarvale.

I've been here once or twice, but never with Fer. We're very close, but she's 1989 Taylor and I'm more like Reputation Taylor. The succubus sex shops, incubus dance clubs, and dark Fae apothecaries have occasionally drawn me in on nights where she had to work and I didn't. Honestly, I hope no one recognizes me in front of her. I don't want her to get upset and think I left her out because I didn't trust her. This just isn't her scene.

The card in my hand says 'Cocktails & Screams'. I'm not familiar with it, but I assume it's not new. *Dezi Ruby* is the name printed in an embossed, flowing script dripping with tiny drops of blood that gather below the words 'proprietor of libation, exultation, and satiation.' I smirk at the design, finding it both irritatingly arrogant and charmingly old world. It makes me struggle with whether I want to work for someone with this much ego, but I suppose he saw who I was in the barfight. My attitude shouldn't be a big shocker.

I hope.

When we get to the bar, the front of it's completely blacked out, and they tucked the entrance in the alley on the side. There's a twenties-style ironwork sign with lights and an arrow that makes me think of the speakeasies we learned about in our human history class. *Cocktails & Screams* has ropes that lead from the door down to the end of the alley and around the back, so I assume it's a very popular fang hang. The big metal door looks like one from an ancient bank vault, so I roll my eyes and stride up to it. My fist bangs on the steel three times and a slot opens to show me deep brown eyes with red circles around the irises. It's a telltale trait of the vamps, so I know this isn't a thrall or some idiotic human offering themselves up as a blood bag.

"We're here about the job opening," I say as the vamp glares at me. I would have thought six p.m. was late enough, but the look in this guy's eyes says I was wrong.

"What opening?"

Fer growls behind me, and he hisses. Before the two of them can prove stereotypes right, I hold up the card I received at the club. "This one. I was told to come by to interview when it was given to me."

"*Merde! Combien de fois lui ai-je demandé de ne pas ramasser les chiens errants?*[1]" The vampire curses even more as I start hearing locks and tumblers click.

"What a dick," Fer mumbles, and a loud hiss comes from the doorway as the big door swings open.

A blond vamp in regency style clothing glares at her with eyes that have faded completely red. "No one asked you, fleabag."

My arm shoots out before Feray can respond, and I squeeze my fingers on the sides of the asshole's neck. I'm aware he doesn't have to breathe, so I'm not worried about hurting him as much as stopping the flow of his bullshit. "Don't insult my sister, you overgrown mosquito."

"Louie!" The deep voice booms in the background and the vamp in my grasp pales even more. "That is not how we treat our guests. Behave."

For the love of Hecate, I'm trying not to laugh at this shit, but a vamp in those clothes called Louie is just too on the nose.

The giggle slips from my lips before I can stop it and I let go of the weasel when I double over in laughter. Everything about this is so incredibly cheesy and I can't help myself. I look over my shoulder at Fer and murmur, "Is this fucking for real?"

Her eyes dance and she shrugs. "You're the one who said we had to come here."

"She was right to do so."

I whirl around, almost dropping into a fighting stance before I realize it's the vamp who gave me his card. He's dressed in a well tailored three-piece suit, but his collar is open and he doesn't have a tie on. I assume he was getting ready for opening when the mini-fight broke out at his door. His features are classically handsome—square jaw with a bit of stubble, roman nose, and full lips that likely draw women closer to his fangs by the bushel. Paired with that dominant vibe and his obvious wealth, I'm sure I'll be rolling my eyes at the line of drooling females nightly if I accept this position.

"Why is that?" Fer says as she steps closer. Her nose twitches as she frowns, scenting the air like the animal she is now. I shoot her a curious look, but she just gives me a mysterious smile.

What the hell, sis?

The vampire looks amused as he holds his hand out, gesturing towards the hallway leading further inside. "Shall we go inside to have a more in-depth conversation?"

I nod. "Fine. But if you attack us, I'll make sure there's nothing left for the cops to find, not even ashes."

"I *never* snack on the staff, much less the unwilling, witchling. But you are right to set boundaries early on. My clientele are well versed in boundaries and safe words—it's a requirement to belong." He turns and heads down the hallway, obviously expecting us to follow.

I hate following orders, but I have little choice at the moment.

We walk behind him, taking in the coat check and a bank of rooms that are marked 'Member Changing Area' with a number behind them. When we reach the heavy curtain at the end of the hall, he holds it aside, making room for us to enter the main area. My eyes nearly pop out of my head at the raised stage, dark black marble bar area, gilded stairs to an upstairs VIP area, and matching high top tables and soft seating areas around the room. There's room to dance between the seating and the stage, but I'd be willing to bet it's used less for that than watching whatever shows go on.

"The word is you both worked as bartenders for the fallen satyr. I need more alluring cocktail creators. I caught my former employees violating club rules, and I had to dismiss them. I take the safety of my staff and my clients seriously," Dezi says as he walks over to the bar and sits on a stool.

My eyes narrow. "How did you know where we used to work?"

He grins, and I see the hint of elongated canines. "I asked around, of course."

"Are you going to ask us questions or lecture us?" Fer trains her gaze on him, flecks of gold appearing in her eyes.

"Both, my dear. Don't let that new wolf part of you ride your temper. You need control to work here and I need to know you can learn it." He grins at me and points. "That goes for you as well. I would never tell you not to protect people in danger, but you must observe the situation before rushing in. This club is a BDSM haven, and there may be times when agreements are in place that you are unaware of."

I rub my hand over my face. *A bondage club? What in the hell are we going to wear to work somewhere like this? Is Fer going to watch this stuff without running around like a tomato?* More to the point, will the people here be super creepy and hit on us all the time? It's not like that didn't happen at Philly's, but since it wasn't a sex club, I could kick their ass and toss them out. Here, I'd have to... well, I don't know what I'd be allowed to do.

"You seem vexed. How about your sister goes behind the bar to show me some of her skills? I'd much prefer to audition you than ask pointless questions. It will give me a sense of whether or not you can handle the traffic here."

This fucking guy wouldn't get ruffled if a Cat 5 hurricane came ripping through this place, I bet.

Feray nods, walking behind the beautiful, well-stocked bar to look at the liquors on display. She picks up a few, humming to herself as she quickly pours, ices, mixes, and strains a drink. It only took her a minute, but she pushes the swirling purple concoction at Dezi with a satisfied smirk. I don't know what the fuck she made because Philly doesn't keep pretty shit like that at *Dionysian Delights*.

After he takes a sip, the vampire arches a brow and gives her a fangy grin. "That's delicious. What is it?"

My sister shrugs. "I don't know; I made it up. I've never had this much stuff to play with before."

"Could you do it again? Create signature drinks with names we can charge ridiculous prices for?" Dezi studies her as she thinks about it.

"Yep," she replies. "I'd have to experiment and come in before opening sometimes to work it all out."

"Done," he says. "You're both hired full time. I'll get you the address and an account card for Clementine's store—that's where you'll go to get suitable clothing for work. She knows what you'll need and how much to start. Anything else we'll negotiate later."

I walk over, taking a sip of the drink and blinking. *Damn. Now I get it.* "Wait a minute. What are full time hours? What are we even being paid? You can't just expect us to agree to—"

He takes the card I'm still holding and puts it on the bar. Pulling a pen out of his jacket pocket, he quickly scrawls a number on it and passes it back to me. My eyes damn near fall out of my head and I look at Fer.

When she nods, I take a deep breath. "We graciously accept. When do we start?"

"You have four days until the weekend to get yourself ready. Be here at sundown." His fangy grin makes my stomach flip a little as a weird electricity shoots up my arms into my chest.

Damn. Sir, yes, sir.

---

1. Shit! How many times have I asked him not to pick up strays?

FERAY

Venturing into the Night District yesterday was fascinating. I replay the events in my head and I'm concerned. *What if I can't control my base animal instincts?* I'm a late bloomer to begin with. Control? That's almost laughable. I feel as if I am coming out of my skin most times.

Every morning I'm awake earlier than my sister is—I guess some things haven't changed. A yawn escapes my lips as I head towards the kitchen to make coffee and breakfast. After yesterday's events, I've discovered I am more on edge when I'm hungry than when I have eaten. A brief laugh escapes my lips as I pull the eggs and bacon out of the fridge. Food is an instant fix for this grumpy wolf.

The crunching of leaves outside draws my attention away from the stove for a moment. I move the bacon off the fire to silence it so I can listen more carefully. Quickly, I move to the window and examine the woods around the house. Something or someone was outside just a moment ago. A slat in the wood floor creaking alerts me to Fi, trying to creep down the hallway. Turning to face her, I raise my index finger to my lips, then point to my ear before pointing towards the front door. Fi nods and grabs her bat out of the closet just in case it's needed.

With one hand on the doorknob, I focus on my right hand and my nails turn to claws. I arch a brow at my sister. Pride shines through in her gaze as she raises her hand and counts down from three to one. Soon as the last finger drops, I throw the door wide open. Nothing is there. Glancing around, I can see the white fluff of a buck's tail as he bounds off into the woods. "Well, that was rather anticlimactic." Smirking, I close and lock the door, heading back to the bacon in the cast iron pan.

"I smell bacon. What else are you making for breakfast?" Fi takes an energy tonic out of the fridge and takes her spot at the table.

"Bacon, eggs, and toast, at least for now. We need to hit the bank and move funds around." I shrug my shoulders slightly and return to the stove so that the bacon and eggs don't burn.

"Ugh, you know how much I hate the bank. I know we need to go. But it's still on my list of least liked things to do," Fi says as she plays with her fork at the table.

Using the tongs, I pick up several strips of bacon and some eggs, placing them on the plate. Purposely, I make a smiley face to make her smile. "Enjoy, sis."

I slide the plate in front of her before going back to the stove to finish making my breakfast. I'm the homebody between the two of us. Taking care of the house and my sister comes naturally to me, so I'm adapting to my new normal fairly well. Oddly, I am finding myself more territorial about my sister and the new house that we are living in.

The noises this morning couldn't have been from the buck I saw running deep into the woods. There would be no reason for it to get this close to the house, especially with me living here. I wonder if my mystery suitor tried to get close, then realized we were still in the house and didn't want to be seen. I reflect on the noise, the deer's distance, and it doesn't add up for me. Shoving the thought aside, I mentally prepare for the trip to the edge of the Night District.

"Hey, Fer," Fi says loudly.

Jumping slightly as her voice brings me out of my head, I feel my eyes shift and the colors around me change. I stare at the vase of flowers, noting how dull some colors are compared to others before I finally answer her. "What, Fi?"

"One, your eyes are golden. Two, we really need to get going soon," Fi replies as she dumps her plate in the sink. She steps into my personal space, looking into my eyes up close. "How different is your vision like that?"

Her curiosity isn't mean, yet it upsets my wolf just the same.

My vision returns to normal as I try to figure out how to explain how I see things. I climb up onto the bar stool at the end of the counter and turn to face her. "Honestly, my wolf wasn't happy you asked about our eyesight. But I understand your curiosity, so I'll answer. I can see blues and yellows very well. Black and gray are also very clear." I tilt my head, looking at my sister. "My night vision is phenomenal. It's almost the same as it is during the day for me."

"Noted." Fi smiles, satisfied with my answer. She grabs her bag off the back of the chair and heads to the door.

We cut through the forest and down into the valley, taking a shortcut to the Night District.

Fi points out the medicinal herbs on the way through and I can tell she's making a mental note on the way back where to stop. Crossing the valley was an adventure—we discovered three streams with no bridges. The dirt surrounding the streams has nests of fire ants and poison slugs. The worst part was crossing the sand and almost getting sucked into quicksand. I firmly cross this shortcut off the list, marking it as 'zero out of ten—do not recommend.'

The sand turns into a field again and we hear the sounds of commerce close by. Cresting the grass-covered hill, we emerge approximately two blocks from the Pendragon Savings and Loans. The Night District isn't busy during the day, but the bank will be. We make it to the main road and onto the sidewalk. Fi is cursing under her breath about her shortcut not being as easy as she thought.

"You never know until you try. Don't sweat it—it's not like we died or anything." I try to lighten the mood, but it does just the opposite. Fi seems madder that she put us in unnecessary danger to save us two hours of walking.

I grip Fi's shoulder and spin her to face me. "Stop beating yourself up. You didn't know how it would be till we tried it. We found a new place to gather herbs and possibly a field for me to practice shifting in." A sincere smile spreads across my lips and eventually Fi relents and smiles as well.

"You're right. When did you become the reasonable one?" Waggling her eyebrows, Fi hugs me briefly before heading down the sidewalk.

A half laugh escapes my lips as I jog to catch up. "I've always been the reasonable one. You're impulsive."

When I'm finally able to fall into step with her, we look into the windows of the shops as we pass. Most of the windows have a tint or a film over the glass to protect the shopkeepers from the sunlight. The higher end shops have wards and crystals that do the same thing, and several stores don't open till after sundown—I assume they are vampire owned. We stop several times to window shop along the way, learning who has what new items we may need.

The bank is Gothic in construction. Large pillars made of black marble adorn the front steps. They inlaid the steps—cobblestone recessed into granite—and from what the plaque out front says the cobblestone came from the village the bank owner was born in.

Fi tugs on my sleeve and drags me through the front door with her. She gets in line, giving me time to wander the interior for a bit. There are four cabinets lining the wall opposite of the tellers. As I get closer to the first cabinet, I notice the shelves are filled with coffee mugs. There's a different saying on each and some are funnier than others.

I walk around the perimeter of the bank, looking at the art on the walls. The painting of the wyrm skull dragon draws my attention. The artist that painted this image used thick paint strokes, layering the paint to give a raised appearance to the dragon itself.

Fi comes up alongside me and rests her hand on my lower back. "The banker seems to have a staring problem." She raises her hand up and points over her shoulder at the tall dark-haired man in the three-piece suit behind the large oak desk. Fi moves me to her left side and brings me back with her to the line for the teller.

My eyes keep drifting over towards the handsome man in the suit. Something about him draws me like a moth to a flame. *My beast is interested in him. She's awake and watching him.* Maybe he's a bigger predator than I am, and that calls her attention to him. Fi keeps moving to block me from his steady gaze. There's a flicker of something behind his eyes for a moment, and then it is gone.

"Fer, we need to go," Fi says as she tugs on my arm, snapping me out of the trance I was in.

"Sounds good. Can we get something to eat on the way home?" Smiling, I lightly tug on my sister's arm playfully.

"How can you always be hungry?" A soft laugh escapes my sister's lips as we push the double doors open and exit the bank.

Rolling my eyes, I allow them to change to that of my wolf. "I'm eating for two, sis." I wink at her, then shift my eyes back to normal.

"From what I can smell, there are several food carts down the road from here."

Motioning to our left, the street vendors can be seen rolling their carts towards the square that separates the Night District and the Elven District. I watch the carts roll by and it's almost like a poor joke. A satyr, a boar and a pixie roll past us towards the village square. We follow behind and wait for them to get set up for the afternoon. The moment the open signs flip, I head straight to the satyr. The scent of roasted beef on a stick makes me drool.

Fi is doing her best to hold back her laughter. The minute I make eye contact with my sister, she loses it and cracks up. "Fer, you're too funny." She pays the satyr and hands me three large pieces of beef on a stick.

"Sis, you're the best." I kiss Fi on the cheek before eating. Meat has never tasted so good as it has since the failed Ascension. I devour the three sticks and finally feel full. Gone are the days that the vegetables and bread sustained me. The animal within demands blood, and I don't know how my animal loving sister will deal with this change.

I spend most of the walk home listening to Fi talk about the new vampire bar we will work at and the benefits of it. The money is phenomenal, according to my sister, and I would agree with her. The money Dezi is offering us is far more than any other job we have ever worked before. Fi talks about the restoration of *Dionysian Delights* and getting Philly back at the bar where he belongs. It's not normal for my sister to be so hopeful and imaginative. Seeing this side of her warms my heart, and I can't help but smile at her, listening to the hope in her voice.

Coming over the hill, I can see on the porch a new basket has been left. Part of me is excited to see what's inside, but my rational side is frightened of the implications that the basket brings along with it.

As we get closer, I realize that my vision is enhanced and we arent as close as I thought we were.

"Fer! There's another basket on our porch." Fi seems more excited about the idea than I am.

Raising my brows I force myself to smile. "Yay!"

When we get to the porch I lift the towel off of the basket to see what's inside. This time he placed a roll of summer sausage, some spreadable cheese, more honey and another loaf of bread to round out the meal. Another card sits in the middle and I pluck it out before my sister grabs the basket saying something about testing it tomorrow. Shaking my head I wait till she goes inside before I read my note.

LITTLE WOLF,
I HOPE THIS DAY FINDS YOU WELL AND HAPPY. PLEASE ACCEPT MY TRIBUTE AND ALLOW ME TO FEED YOU TODAY. IF THERE'S ANYTHING YOU EVER NEED, LEAVE A NOTE ON THE PORCH FOR ME.

Again the eloquent scrolling signature at the bottom of the note. I can't help but hope a little that this male is a good man. That he is like all of the princes I've read about, a good heart and full of love. I know I'm overly romantic and have an ideal that is probably unattainable.

A girl can dream can't she?

15

FIADH

FERAY WASN'T HAPPY WHEN I REFUSED TO LET HER CONSUME THE second basket left on our porch until I tested it. I believe there's a bear out there leaving these for her, but I want to make sure he has the intentions we think he does. I know they're not *poisoned*—what I don't know is if he's setting us up for some nasty public humiliation. There weren't any of his kind's leaders at the Ascension and from what I've been able to gather from my secret internet searches, the bears stay away from all the politics. I'm hoping this is genuine interest, not something this guy has been talked into. It would crush my sister to find out she'd been led on.

I'd end up in prison for certain.

After our usual morning routine, Feray demanded we primp before we ventured out. Since we're going to the store, Dezi instructed us to visit for work clothes. She reasoned we needed to be prepared to try on *extremely* skimpy attire. I argued with her until she finally hissed that the uniform in a sex club might be ultra revealing and it wouldn't hurt to do some 'bodily clean-up.' Only my sister would say that instead of telling me we probably need to shave, so I laughed my way to the shower first, leaving her pouting in frustration.

Yanking her chain has always been one of my favorite pursuits, and this is no exception.

"Fi?"

Her tone pulls me out of my head, and I look over with a fond smile. "Yes, dear sister?"

"Do you think we'll have to wear really scandalous stuff? I mean, that would encourage people to misbehave, right?"

My lips curve up, and I shrug. "Maybe? Dezi seemed like he wouldn't allow his guests to harass or harm his staff, so I'm guessing sexy, but not a porn star. If he's buying, I will not worry about it. We can hold our own with most supes from working at Philly's, and his security should handle the rest. I saw one of them lurking in the background when we were there, and it *had* to be a rhino shifter or a fucking dragon. Dude was *massive*."

That mollifies her, and she squints at the card she's holding. "The name of this place is *Needful Thongs*." Fer pauses and tilts her head with a grin. "I suppose the owner is a Stephen King fan."

Hermes in a basket. I didn't even look *at the name.*

"What a painful pun," I wince as I shake my head. "And so on the damned nose."

She giggles and bumps my shoulder with hers. "Definitely. I'm kind of excited to meet the person who would think of that shit. Seems like a person I might like."

"A nerd who tells dad jokes? Yeah, I can see that."

As we cross into the Night District, I smile, glad to see all the nervousness has left my sister's posture. Besides the mess of this week, being thrown into a lifestyle she's not familiar with is going to be a change, and I want her to get comfortable before she's exposed to the *really* kinky shit at work. Browsing this shop may be the first step in loosening up her romantic, fairytales notions about sex. After all, I'm a hundred percent certain that, unlike me, Feray is as unspoiled as the communion wine in a human church.

I'm about to broach the subject when a bright blue sign blinks in a few doors down. It catches my attention because it's daytime and many of the places here aren't open, but clearly, *Needful Thongs* is the exception. I guess people need fetish gear twenty-four hours a day and the owner isn't a vamp. I'm not opposed to them, mind, but their mental powers give me pause. One of my biggest fears is having my free will taken away. Persuasion and getting into your mind are part and parcel with the bloodsuckers, so I usually avoid them.

And now I work for one, so that's going to be a change.

Shaking my head to clear the niggling doubts taking roost there, I grab the heavy handle of the ornate, dungeon-style wooden door to open it. I force a bright smile at my sister so she won't see the worry in my eyes. "Are you ready for this, sis? This won't be a bright, happy magic shop full of flowers and herbs."

Feray snorts. "I'm not stupid, Fi. I may be a little out of my comfort zone, but I have you to guide me. I've seen some of the shit you think you've hidden in your closet."

I blink. "Shit, really?"

"Duh." She waves her hand dismissively as she walks around me. "There's no shame in the game. If it revs your engine, go for it. At least I'll be able to ask you things so I don't look like a complete fool. If I had to bother any of the staff with a hundred stupid questions, that would make me look like a rube."

I'll be damned by a chaos demon.

"That doesn't mean I won't laugh," I warn her. "And for the love of Aphrodite's corsets, *do not* Google anything before you talk to me. I don't want to be flooded with a million dildo ads."

"Deal."

THE OUTFITS we selected weren't bad. The owner, Clementine, was the least objectionable succubus I've ever met, and she helped both Fer and I find things that would be tantalizing but not inviting. I'm sure she fed off every single pheromone we emitted as she explained various equipment and chatted us up about the atmosphere at the club, but surprisingly, I didn't mind. Her attitude was business-like, and she didn't let her lust fog out even once. That's unusual for her kind and it made me like her immediately.

We left with four stuffed bags full of clothes, shoes, and accessories, plus a promise to visit us behind the bar on nights she came in. Clem is a founding member at *Cocktails & Screams* and when she's not working, she assured us we'll see her often. I could tell by the way she handled Feray's quiet inquiries and shaky hands that she's a good person. It eased *my* fears about the guests Dezi allows to frequent his establishment, and I wonder if that's why he sent us here specifically.

Fucking mind readers are always suspicious, so I'm not sure.

"Clem said we should try the new fusion place on the way home. She said it blends all the cuisines of the Night District species and lots of famous people eat there. Plus, she told us to mention her name, so they'd give us a district employee discount."

I rub my hand over my face. My sister is a huge celebrity gossip lover and hearing that some of the royal families and stars who live in Briarvale might be there made this place like El Dorado to her. I have zero patience for rich dickheads and after our run-in with those two drug dealing thugs, I would prefer to avoid the one percent for as long as feasibly possible.

Besides, many of the species leaders who shamed us at the Ascension are part of that elite class. *What if they're in this place and start on us?* I don't know if I can hold my tongue when I'm not standing in the middle of a power circle. The need for vengeance on the assholes and bitches who treated us like garbage is still very fresh. Willingly entering one of the lion's dens seems like a bad idea.

"Fiiiii..." Fer looks at me with gigantic eyes and bats her lashes. "Pleeeeeease?"

Fuck.

Sighing deeply, I look at my sister and my iron will crumples like a beer can. "Fine. But if even *one* person starts something, you better hope we have enough for bail money."

Feray claps her hands and squeals in glee, nearly toppling me as she hugs me. When she gets herself together, she beams. "It's not far. A few blocks more and we enter the lobby right next to the blood bank."

"What kind of fancy restaurant is next to a goddamned blood bank?" I grumble under my breath.

"One that sources *all* of their food *ethically*," Fi replies as she swipes through something on her phone. "We *are* in the Night District, sis."

How is she completely okay with that and turns red as a tomato when someone shows her crotchless underwear? It must be the predator in her.

The building Feray points to is non-descript—it doesn't look like it houses some chi-chi restaurant frequented by royalty and celebs. *Maybe that's the draw?* It wouldn't surprise me to learn that the hoi-polloi in our town hide in secret venues when they don't want to be hounded by fans and crazies. I press the buzzer on the wall, waiting for the voice to answer. The tone of voice of the chick at the other end makes my hackles rise, but for Fer, I simply let her know Clem sent us. That earns me a bored huff and the door buzzes open soon after.

I'm definitely concerned about going in here now, but I can't let Feray down; she's practically vibrating.

We cross the plain marble hallway and head to elevators, stopping at the one marked *'Délices Coupables'* and pushing the fancy button for the elevator. I don't know what species run this joint, but someone was feeling full of themselves when they named it. It's not as bad as Garden of Eden would have been, but the sense of entitlement shines through just the same. I just hope I can make it through this meal without slapping someone upside the head—it may be a challenge.

When we step off the elevator, I'm suddenly *very* glad my sister insisted we dress up a little for our shopping trip. The chick from the speaker is standing at a sparkling crystal host stand, her eyes raking over us with disdain. Of course, she's a Seelie Fae clad in a wispy dress fashioned to look like a rosy pink tulip and her wings are glittering in the sunlight streaming through the wall-to-wall windows behind her.

How could we have known fucking Tinkerbell would seat diners at this place? What did she expect?

"Welcome to *Délices Coupables.* My name is Rhiannon Tanglewood of the Daybreak Court. Allow me to guide you to your personal oasis."

Feray looks at me with wide eyes as the Fae turns away. "Personal oasis? This. Is. So. Cool!"

"Calm down, Fi," I hiss softly. "She clearly thinks we don't belong here, even if she didn't say it. Don't give her a reason to toss us out before we even sit down."

I feel the excitement rolling off of her in waves as we walk up a gilded ramp to another level. They split the entire dining room between an outer ring of booths decorated to look like small fairy rings and four elevated platforms in the center where larger tables of people sit almost on display. On the top platform, a long, elegantly accented table full of Fae is talking and laughing loudly as they eat. After I study the room for a moment, I understand how it's laid out—each of the levels in the center are reserved for supes from different tiers of our society.

Son of an orc, it's a fucking stage for them to bask on while the lower folks watch in fascination.

"This is your table. Your server will be Griselda and she'll be along to take your drink order shortly."

The spring Fae stops short as she speaks and I damn near bowl my sister over as I whip my head back to look at them. We're in the outer ring, of course, and our table is facing the center head on. I don't know if that's on purpose and we're being set up, or if it's an unhappy coincidence.

The royals holding court on the highest level are a mix of all four courts and none of them look in the least bit friendly. In fact, they look so snooty that if it rained in here, they'd all drown. But I nod at the hostess, murmuring my thanks as I slide into the semi-circle booth and wait for Feray to join me. Of all the things I've endured over the years to make her happy, this isn't the worst; I can survive sitting in the sparkling glow of rich morons for lunch without ruining this for her.

Right?

"Fi, I'm pretty sure that's *Prince Revelin*. Oh my Hecate! He's next in line for the Daybreak Court throne!"

Squeezing her arm hard so she speaks more quietly, I follow her gaze to the lithe blond with spiked hair and a smug smirk on his face. I'm surprised to see him dressed in ripped black skinny jeans, an oversized sweater in midnight blue, and shining silver studded wrist cuffs that match the punk rock jewelry at his throat. There are streaks of color in his hair, but they're faint, like he might be growing it out before he switches. I've seen Fae royalty before and they never look like this. Usually, they're bedazzled like a jean jacket from the 80s.

"That guy is not the Prince, Feray. You've got him confused with someone. He looks like the leader of an emo band," I scoff. "Fae royals are always draped in designer shit and jewels, not dog collars."

My sister gives me a knowing grin. "You think he's hot, don't you? Bad boys have *always* been your thing. Like that irritating half of the twin sandwich who came into the bar. Leather and liquor, that's your preference, Fiadh. I see you."

I roll my eyes, but deep down, I know she's not wrong. And maybe if this dude wasn't lording over the dining room as if he could buy the lot of us, I might think he's hot. But snotty rich kids posing as bad boys are *not* my jam and I'm sure as hell not going to start with this dude. "I don't do fuckboys, Fer. Not worth my time."

"Well this one would be," she says as she holds up her phone. "Meet Prince Revelin, heir to the Daybreak Court, and lead singer of *Darkness Falls*."

My jaw drops when I see the haughty dude from the table on the cover of the number one album on the pop charts. *Holy shit!* I grab her cell and look closer at the broody looking Fae wearing a lot more makeup and sporting a huge pair of glittering bat wings. *Maybe he's not a poseur, after all...*

"So what?" I scoff as I hand it back. "I'm sure his popularity has *nothing* to do with his title and everything to do with talent."

Fer arches a brow at me, still grinning like a fool. "You're only saying that because you're mad that I'm right—he *is* a prince and you *do* think he's hot."

"Whatever."

Her response is cut off by our server's arrival and after we place a drink order, Feray scoots to the edge of the booth. "You can tragically lie to yourself while I find the restroom, sis. Hold down the fort until I'm back."

I look at the bags on either side of me and snort. "It's not an airport; you don't have to announce your departure."

She winks at me as she sashays off around the pathway in front of the commoner booths, completely unconcerned with the people watching her as she goes. Once I see her disappear down a hallway, I turn my attention back to the table of dipshits lording themselves over everyone else. It's odd to see the different courts mingling, but I suppose the draw of a rockstar is irresistible to the glitterati. I'm about to force myself to look away when my eyes clash with the Prince and something odd shivers over my skin.

His violet eyes stare into mine as if he's trying to read my mind, but I know my mental shields are stronger than that. I may not be able to keep a bloodsucker out, but a Fae—even a Royal—is a cakewalk. Smirking in return, I ignore the electricity dancing over my arms and wait until he looks away. Winning makes me grin at the menu despite the outrageous prices on it and I consider what I'm going to order as I congratulate myself.

"Who do you think you *are*?"

The shrill question damn near shreds my eardrums and my head whips up immediately. One of the Fae chicks from His Majesty's table is standing in front of me with her hands on hips glaring at me like I just pissed on the floor. "Excuse me?"

"You aren't fit to even glance in his direction, *witch*," she spits.

I rake my eyes over the Fae standing in front of me full of righteous indignation. Her dark curly hair is piled on her head in a messy bun that I'm sure she thinks is artful, but in reality looks like a bird's nest. Unlike most of the minions at her table, she's dressed in a weird BoHo sweater and leggings with knee-high boots and she's sporting small brown wings that look like a moth. Of all the women up there, I would never have expected *this* one to come down here and act like a fucking snot. "What's wrong with being a witch?"

That's when Feray walks up, her eyes fading light yellow as she scents the air. "Yeah. What's wrong with being a witch?"

The earth Fae turns and sneers at her. "About as much as being a mangy dog, I'd say. Who even let the two of you *in* here? You're not even fit to sit in the cheap seats."

Counting backwards from fifty in my head, I struggle not to ruin our lunch date by knocking this chick's teeth through the back of her bobble head. Mean girls are terrible—high school taught me that—but the girls who *want* to be part of the mean girl squad are even worse. They're so hungry for attention and acceptance that they'll sell out their mothers for one of the popular people's approval. This Fae's aura *reeks* of that kind of desperation and she'll do anything to get it.

That includes making an ass of herself in the middle of a nice place just to get brownie points with the big boys and girls.

"Listen up, lantern fly. I'm sitting here minding my own business and having lunch with my sister. I'd advise you to back off and go do the same with your friends. No harm, no foul. *Capiche?*" I give her a slightly unhinged grin, hoping that will scare her off before this becomes a real problem.

"Sister? How could—oh!" A look of absolute delight comes over her face and she claps her hands as she turns to the tiers behind her. "Ladies and gentleman, we are all in the presence of the truly famous. Behold the exiled witch and her mangy, halfbreed sister from the Ascension!"

Something deep inside of me sparks as I try not to stand up and punch the smirk off of her face. I open my mouth to respond, but before I can, a burst of fire shoots from my hand. It hits her hair, setting the mess on fire and my eyes widen in fear.

What in the name of Aries was that?!!

Feray squeaks in panic, reaching for the water glasses on our table and tosses the liquid at the Fae as she flails. Unfortunately, my sister misses the fire completely from her angle and only soaks the bitch's clothing, making her scream louder. My hands shake as I wiggle out of the booth, grabbing our bags so we can make a hasty exit before someone calls the cops. How would I even explain that I don't have any magic and I have no idea where that came from? It sounds ridiculous even to me and I know it's the truth.

The staff appear, some of them carrying extinguishers, and I jerk my head at Feray. She walks closer to me, following as we back away from the scene slowly so we don't draw anyone's attention from the wailing woman. My back hits something solid and I whirl around, expecting to see security ready to pounce on me.

Instead, another hard jolt of energy rockets through me and I meet the purple eyes of the Prince himself. His lip hitches in a sneer, but he doesn't even look at his flaming acolyte. He simply tilts his head to study me, then moves out of my way. I'm not sure if he's angry or puzzled until his eyes move to the earth Fae I accidentally crisped.

"Khorinea! You will cease your embarrassing wailing immediately. It is beneath you. Use your powers to—"

His command is cut short by the sound of fire extinguishers being unleashed. The thick white foam covers the crying bully from head to toe and that makes her screech like she's being murdered.

"Time to go," I mutter to Fer. She takes my hand and we make a break for it, heading for the front while everyone is watching the disaster.

I have a feeling we're going to pay for this someday, but right now, I honestly can't bring myself to care.

This might have been the best lunch I've had in my entire life.

16

FERAY

THE WALK TO THE CLUB IS MUCH SHORTER THAN I WISH IT WAS. Fi and I carry our uniforms tucked away in duffel bags. The dress code for the staff is insane; I feel like I should have a price tag hanging around my neck.

Fi raps on the door in a pattern Dezi taught her and the slider opens immediately. Glowing red eyes peer out before it slams shut.

The door opens quickly, and standing on the other side, Louie is smirking. "Now serving: a witch and a fleabag." He lets out a short laugh before motioning down the hall. "Come with me. I'll show you the changing room and break rooms for the staff."

He guides us past the coat check and the member changing areas, then beyond the heavy black curtain that shields the patrons from view. "We have about an hour before we open for business. My master has several things he needs completed before the night begins."

Louie calling Dezi 'Master' catches me off guard and I glance over at my sister. She motions for me to remain silent, then points to her ears. *Ah yes, the leeches have excellent hearing.* I nod so she knows I understand as Louie guides us to an area behind the gilded steps. There's a black door with a keypad and Louie gives us the code to get in.

Beyond the door is the staff break room and changing area. Snack machines and drink dispensers line the wall, but what shocks me most is the standing blood cooler. The blood is arranged by type and age—I had no clue those things mattered. All the blood is free except virgin blood.

Before I can ask, Louie comes over and points to it. "They gathered all the blood from willing donors. You'll meet most of them tonight. Part of the Thrall's membership is a donation—they do it hoping to gain a sponsor."

I tilt my head again, puzzled by what Louie is saying. For now, I decide it's best to keep my mouth shut; after all, I don't think he likes me very much.

Pushing through another curtain, we arrive in a locker room. "Open lockers have the locks hanging on them. Pick the one you want, cut your finger and place it on the stone on the lock. We had them enchanted to react to the owner's blood specifically." Louie's tone sounds beyond bored. I'm sure he doesn't want to be our tour guide for the evening.

"What happens when someone leaves? Do you throw out the lock or have them reset?" Fi voices the question I had been wanting to ask.

"There's a warlock in the founders' group; he cleanses the locks upon departure and wipes the memory of the clients that employee saw. Confidentiality is a cornerstone of our business, and secrets are worth their weight in blood." Louie's grin turns feral as he shows a fang.

I feel my wolf bristle at the sight of his fang, and I twist my head. There is no way I will let that leech get me fired for losing my temper. When I have calmed down, I turn and smile pleasantly.

"Thank you for showing us around. I'm sure this task was far below your station."

Shots fired.

I took aim for his pride button and scored a direct hit by the tight smile that graces his lips.

"Yes, this task was quite beneath me. But what Dezi wants, Dezi gets." His statement makes the owner sound more like a mobster than a vampire. Then again, anything is possible, I suppose. "Go back out through the door and out to the bar. Dezi will meet you there."

Before I respond, he was gone in a blur; the sound of the closing door is the only evidence we have that he had left.

"He's rather spicy tonight. I wonder who he ate that didn't sit well?" Fi's statement makes me look up from my duffel bag.

"Spicy? He's species biased! I've never done anything to him and he treats me like the scum on his shoe." Grumbling, a low growl escapes my lips as I return to fighting with my uniform for the evening.

Fer's hand lands on my forearm, stilling my movements. "I know. Trust me, if we didn't need this job, there would be a table leg where his heart used to be." The smile my sister gives me tells me she means every word she says.

Returning to the project at hand, this amount of cloth and leather they claim as an outfit amazes me. The booty shorts aren't as bad as the fishnets. The boots are okay, but this thing that they call a top is suffocating. The blood red silk and black leather corset presses my normally hidden breasts up so that they are almost bubbling out of the top. Every breath makes me concerned they will break free of their flimsy prison. It's not until Fi comes over and pulls the blood red spider web silk over the top does my concern lessen slightly.

Motioning to my figure, my sister waves her hand. "When did this happen?"

Fi motions for me to spin and I do. I'm far from perfect. I guess she's shocked that with the awakening of my wolf I'm toning up without trying. Thankfully, the girls have been spared for now. *Who knows what a wolf's body looks like?* Wrapping my arms around my waist, I have a bit of an insecure moment. "It didn't happen. You know I've never liked the way I looked. I don't have your confidence to expose how I look all the time."

"Oh, my Goddess, Fer! I didn't think about that with this job. If you want to leave, we will; no worries. We'll figure something out." Fi reaches for our bags and I stop her.

Forcing a smile, I shrug my shoulders. "I've got to get over the self loathing at some point, right?"

I step away from my sister and look at myself in the full-length mirror. The wolf in me has streamlined parts of me and left others alone. I can only hope I don't embarrass myself. My sister is a voluptuous vixen and looks completely at home in this kind of outfit.

"You have nothing to hate Fer, you're beautiful, intelligent, and are the best bartender I have ever met, and that's saying a lot." Fi's smile and her belief in me bolsters my own self image.

"Let's get it started, shall we? I have a bar to set to my liking and a night I'll probably never forget."

Looking over the lockers near us, I pick a top unit and toss my bag in and use my sharp canine to break the skin on my thumb and press the blood to the lock. Fi pulls a knife from between her breasts and cuts her finger marking the lock. When our belongings are safely stored away, I loop my arm with hers and we head back the way we came in.

Dezi is sitting at the end of the bar in his suit, hair perfectly coiffed and poised like the predator he is. He seems to sense us and turns, looking us over. From where I'm standing, it looks like his gaze lingers on my sister longer than I would like it to.

"Evening, ladies. There are several things we need to address before the night starts."

Dezi hands us two sets of laminated cards. One card gives the membership levels and where they may go, as well as what price code to use for food and drink. The second is a cheat sheet for the levels and what collar each group wears. My eyes linger on the collars and before I can ask, he drops two on the bar top.

"I will need your safe words for your tags." Dezi stares at me and I arch my brow, then remember the talk Fi and I had last night and again on the way here.

Hoping to look knowledgeable, I blurt out, "Pineapple." Fi and Dezi look like they want to crawl into a hole and I bristle. "What's wrong with pineapple? It's not something I'm going to scream out of nowhere."

Dezi reaches out and takes my hand gently; his icy grip is a stark contrast to mine. "You're so adorably naïve. Pineapple is a safeword that posers and idiots use. It's also how we sort the donors. People that choose pineapple are not educated enough to enter."

My eyebrows shoot up, shocked at my misstep. Dezi's free hand comes up and grips my chin. He turns my head from side to side, then smiles. He says something in a language I don't understand and passes the collar off to an associate. "Bubbles is perfect for you. You have a bubbly personality, like a fine champagne. It's fitting."

He smiles once more then releases me from his grip before turning to Fi. "What is your safeword pet?"

Fi's eyes narrow at the nickname and I know she's not pleased by it.

"Penguin." She says the word sharply, then crosses her arms under her chest in challenge.

"Done." Dezi smiles, pleased with Fi's answer, then hands off the other collar like he had done with mine.

The associate returns with the collars, and they appear to be different. The one that gets handed to Fi has a small sapphire teardrop hanging next to her dog tag. Mine has a crescent moon made of moon stone hanging next to my tag. I stare at it for several moments, then look at Dezi.

"For the safety and comfort of my patrons, they need to identify you from a distance. If a fight between rival houses happens, you may be called upon to end it permanently."

I put my collar on and nod. *I'm the last line of defense.*

Dezi helps Fi put hers on, then they walk off towards the servers' area. I hear them clearly as he explains the waitstaff's expectations and location of their items. Shaking my head, I focus on my task at hand. The bar is stocked with every liquor, flavoring, fruit, garnish, and shape glass imaginable. In the corner of the bar, I find the edible glitter, smoker, and other bar trick tools.

The start of the shift runs smoothly. I watch my sister from the bar. Fi snaps her fingers to get my attention and places her order from the rail upstairs. By the time she makes it to the bar, her order is set and ready to go. *I guess being a wolf has its bonus points.* Fi mentions how my hearing is a time saver and smiles before heading back upstairs.

My bar is hopping, but not to the point I can't monitor my sister. When one of the new 'masters' smacks Fi's ass, I get ready to hop over the bar. I'm ready to jump when I notice Tiernan stepping between my sister and the patron. I take that as my cue, handing the bar over to Mo so I can sprint to where my sister is. By the time I make it up there, Tiernan snaps the man's arm in two and bone is sticking out as his arm dangles freely.

I'll be damned.

Fi moves to go around Tiernan and he grabs her arm, stopping her. I watch their eyes flare and his voice rumbles as a purr escapes his lips. The hard mask that was over his face a few seconds ago is gone, replaced by a soft smile and eyes filled with wonder. "Mate."

I inhale sharply as the truth of the situation sinks in. Looking between the two of them in shock, I mutter, "Holy shit."

My words knock Fi out of the stupor she's in. Tiernan steps back and a blush creeps over his cheeks as he drops his gaze. The gears start turning at a million miles a minute in my brain—there's so many 'what if's' right now. I breathe heavily as the ramifications of the information shatters my former beliefs.

The simple act of touch alerted Tiernan to the fact that my sister is his mate. He couldn't resist the urge of verbalizing that my sister is his. Glancing down at my own hands, I attempt to parse this new information and apply it to what's happened since the Ascension. The revelation that we may actually have mates out there blows my mind. Looking up quickly, I watch how Tiernan watches my sister and the romantic in me is excited as all hell thinking that some-where out there my mate is waiting for me.

Anxiety morphs into excitement and for the first time in a long time, I can't wait to see what tomorrow brings.

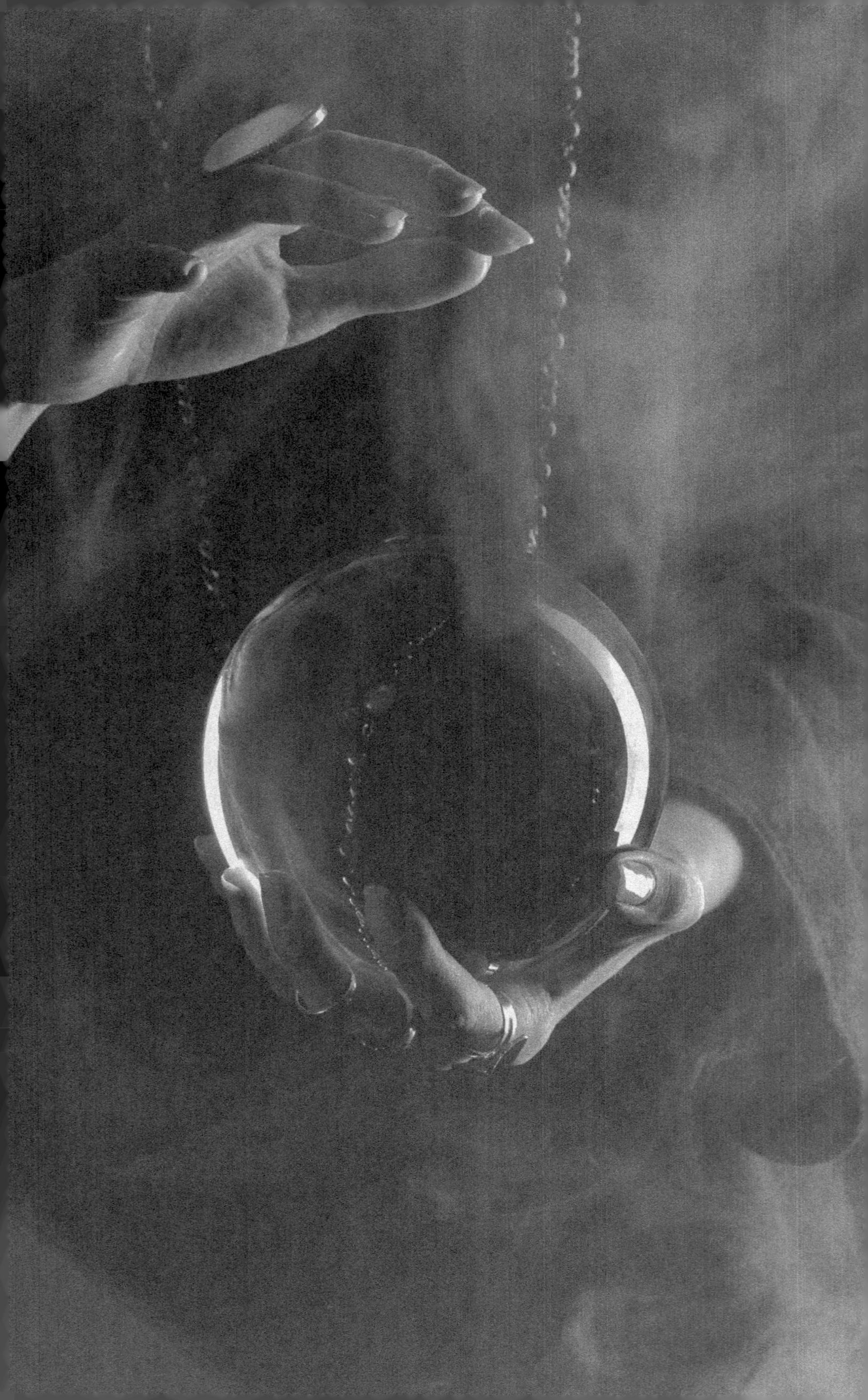

17

FIADH

This guy doesn't *seem* like he's full of shit, but I was in the middle of the circle at the Ascension. The High Mage said neither of us had mates and everyone laughed with him. No one corrected him or even quirked a brow. There definitely was a flash of... something... but it can't be that.

Now I realize why I've been so suspicious of Fer's baskets.

We were told this was not an option for us and suddenly two dudes are appearing out of nowhere to claim us. It feels super sketchy, although Tiernan helped get me out of harm's way the other night. The people in this town have been largely assholes to us, especially since Mom and Dad died, and I don't trust anyone but my sister and Philly.

But the large chocolate eyes of the leopard shifter in front of me are oozing sincerity and his expression is so giddy he might as well be a fangirl in the front row. Nothing in his aura is tripping my switches and Feray looks so excited that you'd think *she* was the one hearing she's got a mate. My lovey-dovey sister practically has cupids fluttering around her as she stares at us.

Embarrassing. People are going to notice soon.

"Both of you stop making those faces and get over to the bar," I hiss. Grabbing Fer's arm, I drag her off the floor as the snow leopard obeys my demand without question. When we're tucked at the far end, I look at him carefully as I ask, "How is this possible? The High Mage said we didn't have mates, and we didn't."

His eyes dance as shrugs. "I wasn't there. The Prince had another engagement that night; we sent other representatives from the Daybreak Court. Besides, why the hell would that old fool say such a thing? Not everyone in town, much less the world, attends that silly spectacle."

I blink, then look at Feray. It never occurred to me to question the premise of his words—it's the High Mage. And his entire band of cronies from the Council bobbed their heads like he'd handed down the wisdom of the ages, so why would I think he was full of shit? Except—I've met him and he's a complete d-bag. "Son of a bitch..."

Feray walks behind the bar, using a towel to clean it so she looks like she's working. "He's right, Fi. Everyone in the universe wasn't there. How could he know we don't have mates? Obviously, the baskets are being left by someone who wasn't there, either."

"Exactly," Tiernan says with a smile. "I noticed an odd tingling when I helped you the other night, but I figured it was adrenaline. I get amped when there's a fight—like all shifters. I didn't know for sure until I touched your bare skin tonight. Everything changed in that moment, even your scent."

I have the strongest urge to bash my head on the bar.

"We were told both by our parents and our school that everyone finds mates at Ascension if they have them. It's literally what they teach all the magic users. Why would they do that if we have potential matches out there who may not attend?" I frown, thinking about all the unhappy people who might be out there. It seems cruel.

Tiernan rubs his neck and makes an apologetic face. "Witches are known for being huge assholes about interspecies mating. They probably teach you guys that bullshit to 'keep the bloodlines pure' or some nonsense. It wouldn't surprise me at all."

"Those *motherfuckers!*" Fer says as she slaps the wood.

We both look at her with wide eyes. I reach over and put my hand over hers. "Fer, we need to keep a lower profile than that. Calm down. If that's true, it's reprehensible and they deserve a nasty case of the clap, but we have to focus."

"You do. 'Cause you might even have more than one mate floating around out here," the leopard says nonchalantly. "I mean, it's pretty common amongst shifters, and she's one of us. Who knows?"

More than one... has he lost his mind?!

"Whoa, whoa. Back that train up, buddy. What do you mean, more than one?" I back away a little, feeling my magic spark inside as I panic. The last time I felt like this, someone's hair caught on fire and we had to run, so I have put space in between us.

He snorts. "Don't worry. Your magic will know not to hurt me." His brow furrows, and he tilts his head. "Do you not have control of it? You said you ascended."

"I did!" I grind out. "But not only did we fail at having mates, I had no magic and she turned out to be a wolf. Where have you been hiding? This is the hot town gossip, as far as I know."

Fer walks over and grabs three rocks glasses, pouring a tequila, a scotch, and a whiskey. When she sits them in front of us, I'm surprised that she guessed exactly right. "We need a drink for this conversation."

"Look, I don't mean to sound shitty, but the rest of the species don't pay attention to you guys nearly as much as you think we do."

Tiernan shrugs and gives me a sheepish look. "I mean, some gossip hounds might, but in general? Not so much."

"That bitch at the restaurant definitely knew," I grumble under my breath as I sip the tequila.

His eyes widen. "That was *you*? I wasn't on the Prince's duty that day because the Queen requested me. But I heard about you setting that miserable little suck-up, Khorinea, on fire." A playful grin comes over his lips and he reaches out to squeeze my hand. "I wish to hell I'd seen it."

Ignoring the tingles from his skin touching mine, I let out a sigh. "I'm probably Public Enemy Number One for yet another species over it, but I didn't do it on purpose."

"You said you didn't have magic because it didn't appear at the Ascension." I nod and Feray joins in. "But you also said you didn't have mates because you didn't meet them there. I don't know shit about witches beyond what I've said tonight, but is it possible your magic wasn't… well, not 'not there' like me, but maybe not ready? Have you had other incidents like the one at the restaurant?"

"Yes, she has!" Feray claps her hands, bouncing in excitement. "Not as big, but some little things, especially when she gets emotional."

The way they both look at me makes my head hurt. I don't know if they're right and I don't want to let anyone down again. "I don't know, Tiernan. That's also totally different from what we've always been taught."

"Maybe the big wigs are teaching you guys bullshit to keep people from challenging them? That kind of shit definitely goes on in the courts. Rev would know more about it, but I've seen it, too. We should ask him. Not tonight, I mean, because I'll need to talk to him, but…"

Oh, I'm sure Prince Revelin has no *interest in ever seeing* me *again.*

"I wouldn't hold your breath, Tier," I mutter as I look up at the VIP area. A weird sensation crawls over my skin and I shake my head. I've stayed too close to this guy for too long; I don't even know I'm going to accept this whole theory. I need books and research and spells to help me feel truly comfortable.

He nods and tilts his head. "Don't count him out, firebrand. Rev puts on a lot of airs because of his title and the band, but deep down, he's a good guy. He just has a lot of walls up to keep people from abusing that."

"Does he come here a lot? I bet Fi would love to see you when he does," Feray chimes in with a mischievous expression.

That's it. I'm going to jail for sororicide.

Tiernan winks at me, then looks at Fer. "The Prince is a Master level member. He frequently comes here before or after we go to other clubs. Rev finds the atmosphere in the VIP area relaxing and he loves the shows. You'll likely see me."

Fer claps again, and I shoot her a dirty look. "You both realize I'm going to need a little time to… digest this, right? What you're saying makes sense and I believe the Council would do this kind of shit, but we've had many people being awful to us since the Ascension. It's hard to trust this is someone's idea of a cruel joke."

"Fi, don't be—"

"No, she's right, wolf. I don't have any proof that what I've said is true other than my instincts and our theories. I understand why your sister is suspicious." His expression is serious as he squeezes my hand and the tingles shoot up my arm. "Perhaps I can answer some questions about the basket you mentioned before? I'd like to show you I'm on your side."

My eyes narrow, but I nod, unable to keep my sister from the information she might need. "Okay."

"So, we moved into this cabin after the fire and now I keep finding these baskets of food, with brief notes about wanting to take care of me. We searched it and the stuff in it to see where it came from because the name is totally illegible. The honey and bread and stuff seem to be linked to bears?" Feray finally looks nervous instead of excited and tosses back a slog of her whiskey.

Tiernan's eyes widen and he grins wide. "It sure as hell does. Bears love to leave that secret shit. They're not very forward when it comes to mating and the baskets let them declare intent without direct rejection. It's *extremely* important to make up your basket and leave it if you are interested, otherwise they'll think you're rejecting them."

Her brows furrow and she pouts. "But I don't know who it is! I can't read the name and what if I don't feel this... tingle thing... you talked about? I'd be leading him on—or vice versa."

"That *is* a conundrum," he murmurs as he strokes his jaw. "Have you tried something magic to track the dude? I know you thought you didn't have any, but the fire on Khorinea's hair says differently."

For the second time tonight, I feel like a complete moron.

"No, we haven't. I can't believe we haven't even attempted it," I groan as I drop my face into my hands. "I am literally the worst witch in town, magic or no."

A low rumbling growl echoes out of him and the leopard flushes a delightful pink. "Sorry. My cat didn't like you saying bad things about yourself. You might have to start being kinder about mistakes, firebrand."

I blink. *His cat what?*

"Oh! My wolf gets mad when she does that, too! I thought it was just me," Feray says with a grin. "See, Fi? You have to stop blaming yourself for everything or you'll have your hands full of fur and fangs."

Hecate, help me—now there's two *of them.*

"Okay, that's enough picking on Fiadh for tonight." I give both of them a reproachful look as I finish my drink. Pointing at Tiernan then Fer, I tilt my head. "You, go do your bodyguard thing or whatever. You, go tend bar before we get in trouble. I need some fucking space to deal with this shit. Got it?"

They nod, both grinning like fools and it takes everything in me not to scream. I do *not* do well with surprises and I do even more poorly with shit I can't verify. Everything that's happened in the past two weeks has upended my entire world and I haven't had a second to come to terms with any of it. Now I've got a new home, a new boss, a new job, new enemies, and to top it off, a smoking hot dude who thinks I'm his fated lay.

The Fates truly have it out for me.

18

———

FERAY

Sleep eluded me last night as my head spun with new information. Our discussion turned my world upside down.

Everything we were raised to believe was a load of bullshit.

Tiernan questioned things we believed were gospel truths. The more I think about school and the curriculum, the more it seems like it was indoctrination for a cult. Staring at my hands, I raise them and will my nails to shift to claws. Huffing out a laugh of joy when it works, I allow the claws to recede.

Worst wolf ever might not be exactly right.

All I can shift are my claws, fangs, and shift my eyes; how in the world am I supposed to survive like this? *What if my mate rejects me because I can't shift?* My heart sinks at the thought. Tears well up at the edge of my eyes, threatening to bubble over. My poor heart feels like it's breaking. I rub the collar of my shirt against my eyes, hiding the tears I don't want my sister to see.

Thankfully, Fi sleeps later than I do, so sneaking into the kitchen to start the coffee is a simple task. I just want to be alone with my thoughts for a while. I'm happy for Fi—Goddess knows she deserves to be happy. She deserves a mate that will make her feel safe so she doesn't have to carry the weight of the world alone. I know she doesn't believe in the romantic ideals that I do, but I hope Tiernan will prove to her that some males are worth giving a chance.

Digging through the cabinets must have awakened her because by the time I find the pancake mix, she's sitting at the counter. I place a hand over my heart, feeling it pounding away. Before I realize it's happening, my claws and fangs extend and my eyes shift for defense. "Holy shit, Fi! You damn near gave me a heart attack."

Fi laughs so hard she almost falls off her stool. "Good morning to you, too, Fer. You should calm down before you hurt yourself." She smiles before taking a sip of her coffee. "Usually you know when I wake up. Why are you so distracted? It's not like you."

Sighing, I grab the bowl, dump the pancake mix in, add the milk, and whisk it all together. "Just thinking about what your mate said last night."

She winces when I say the word mate, and her reaction saddens me. "I'm still unpacking the 'M word,' Fer. Can we avoid it a bit longer?"

My wolf flares up when my sister says she wants to avoid her mate, and the bowl shatters in my hands. Pancake batter and glass goes everywhere. "Avoid it!? Do you realize how lucky you are?" A deep growl escapes my lips and, for once, I don't temper my rage—my wolf is pissed. I feel my canines gnash together barely able to keep the growl out of my voice. Turning away quickly, I use deep breathing exercises to get myself under control. "I would kill to know who my mate is."

"I'm sorry; I know how excited you are. I… I worry this is a spell to torture us more. You know how much the Council hates us." Fi sighs and I feel her hand rubbing my back like she used to when we were little. "I want this for us if it's real, but I'm trying to protect us."

She rests her forehead against my shoulder blade and I hear the honesty in her voice. She's not stomping on my dreams; she's honestly scared it's a trick.

Stepping away, I force a smile. "Then let's do today my way—no super secret conspiracy theories and no worrying about who is out to get us. I want to bask in the joy of you finding your mate and according to the mystery baskets, I have one, too."

Fi nods reluctantly then hugs me. I feel the weight lift off of my shoulders when she asks, "Have you looked on the porch this morning yet?"

"Not yet. I'm scared I took too long to leave him something in return. What if there's nothing left on the porch?" I rub my hands together anxiously, worry creasing my brow.

"Do you want me look for you?" Fi grins and walks to the front door.

"No, I've got it." Running past her, I fling it wide open to see a truly amazing basket waiting. This one is far larger than the last few.

Shit, I really need to create a response basket.

"What did you get— Holy shit, did he stuff half the store in there?" Fi stares at the basket in my arms as I walk past her.

"No clue, but the scent is quite strong this time. I may be able to track him."

Smiling devilishly, I dig into the basket, careful to sniff each piece of tissue paper I pull out. The heavy scent of sandalwood makes my wolf whine; she wants us to find him sooner than later. Inside the basket there are three beeswax candles with a lavender scent labeled as 'sleepy time candles.' Beeswax lip balm and several bath bombs round out the self-care items, but each one carries a familiar scent. The food he packed this time is venison jerky and more honey-apricot jam. I see two loaves of freshly baked bread wrapped in a checkered cloth as well.

I set the items in the basket and pull out the small note card. This time it has a beautifully scrolled heart in the center of the paper and nothing else—no written words, no signature. "Fuck, what does this mean?"

Shaking her head, she flips the card between her fingers. "I'm not sure. Maybe when we go to gather herbs to restock my stores, we can find you a beehive to raid?"

I decide I have to figure this out, so I turn back to the door. The beehives can wait; my wolf wants to know *now*.

"Where are you going, Fer?" My sister runs to catch up to me as I open the door..

"Back to Philly's bar. According to the email, you showed me the demolition and construction crews should be there today." She blinks and nods, clearly willing to indulge me. When we are both out of the house, I lock the door behind us before heading to the well-worn path that leads to town.

"What if he's not there?"

Drawing in a deep breath, I think about what I'll do if he's not there. "This is one of three large construction crews, so hopefully, I won't have to worry about that. If I do, it shouldn't be too difficult to find where the other crews are working so we can check them out."

We cross through the cedar part of the forest and I swear the roots are out to get Fi. Every twenty feet, I hear her complain about a root that jumped up out of nowhere. Since my wolf emerged, I seem to be less of a klutz than I used to be—yet another perk to being a shifter.

As we approach the edge of the woods, I stand behind one of the large, red cedars to observe the bears. There are two dozen men working on the bar and other tasks at the perimeter of the building. The wind is not helpful in the least bit; one minute, it's blowing from behind us, then directly in our faces. Shaking my head, I step out of the forest to take the metaphorical bull by the horns as I approach the building.

My mystery bear's scent is faint, but here, so I'm excited I'm on the right track. He's definitely not inside the building, but it smells like he walked through it earlier. Resigning myself to the fact he must be outside with all the other muscle bound bears, I head out the back door.

Fi talks to everyone on the way through; she must be doing her best Agatha Christie impersonation because she's in full-on detective mode. The bears she's questioned refused to answer because of 'bear code.' After two laps around the building's exterior, the wind finally cooperates with me. There are six males in the area where that breeze is coming from.

A frustrated whine escapes my lips as I stare at them. Four out of the six turn to look at me when I make the noise. Three I don't recognize, but one is the owner of our cabin. Glancing over at my sister, she smiles and motions back to the trail.

There are several things that I know are true: one of the four is my mate, he's a hard worker who is skilled with his hands, and he's very good at picking out gifts. Because of his species, I also know he has a robust sense of family and community. Those last two qualities trump everything else, but all of it makes my gut flutter. I smile to myself, content knowing that when the time is right, he will reveal himself and it will be amazing.

My sister is lagging and I turn abruptly and stomp my foot. "Stop gawking. I have to find a beehive and try not to get stung to death."

Laughing, Fi comes up and bumps my shoulder with hers. "I know something you don't know." Her tone is playful but slightly mocking, like she did when we were kids.

"That's a loaded statement, sis. There are plenty of things that you know I don't and vice versa." Tilting my head to the side, I shrug my shoulders.

"This is true." She moves ahead of me and stops me when we are out of view of the workers at the bar. She beams at me and whispers, "I am ninety percent sure I know who your mate is."

My wolf is dancing around in my head, but I decide to play it cool. Otherwise, Fiadh will torture me by holding the knowledge over my head. "I'm one hundred percent sure I will find out once I leave him the basket on the porch. I'm also sure I'm going to get stung while getting him a fresh honeycomb."

Fi giggles. "The things that we do for love, right?"

I move past my sister, smirking as I continue down the trail. "You're the resident expert now?"

"Not in the slightest, but I just found your honeycomb." Fi points to a rock formation thirty yards to our right off the trail. Close to the top of a jagged overhang, ribbons of honeycombs hang, the buzzing of the bees around them taunting me.

"Those are giant honey bees. Can't we find the average sized bees?" I glance over at Fi then back over at the inch long monsters.

She looks towards Philly's bar then back at me. "These are the first honeycombs I've seen in a long time. The comb itself is huge, so if you take that outer piece, they won't attack."

"That's too many 'ifs' for my taste, sis, but I don't have a choice at this point."

Moving away from her, I creep closer to the hive on the rocks. It's for the best that it's in the open like this—plenty of places to run for cover. Luckily for me, it's still cold, so according to my research, the bees should only be active when the sun is on the hive. I shift my nails to claws so I can climb the rocks and grin when I realize it's another shifter perk. Having extra grip makes the ascent much easier. Belly crawling across the flat part of the rock, I look over the edge. The comb my sister pointed out is barely attached. I look at both sides of the piece before attempting to rip it free. Once it's free, I notice a huge sluggish bee trying to crawl towards my fingers.

Thinking quickly, I scoot back from the edge and set the comb down. Panicked, I look for a stick to push the bee off, then run like all hell back to my sister.

"I didn't think you were going to pull that off." Fi looks shocked.

"Why?"

"Because you hate heights," she says matter of factly.

"I got lucky. The sun hadn't hit the hive yet and we had time to get out of here before they woke up." Gripping my sister's elbow with my free hand, I push her to get moving.

Instinct tells me that if they smell their honey, they will definitely give us a run for our money.

"Let's go home and I'll help you plan out your basket." Fi loops arms with me to head home.

Today has definitely turned around for the better.

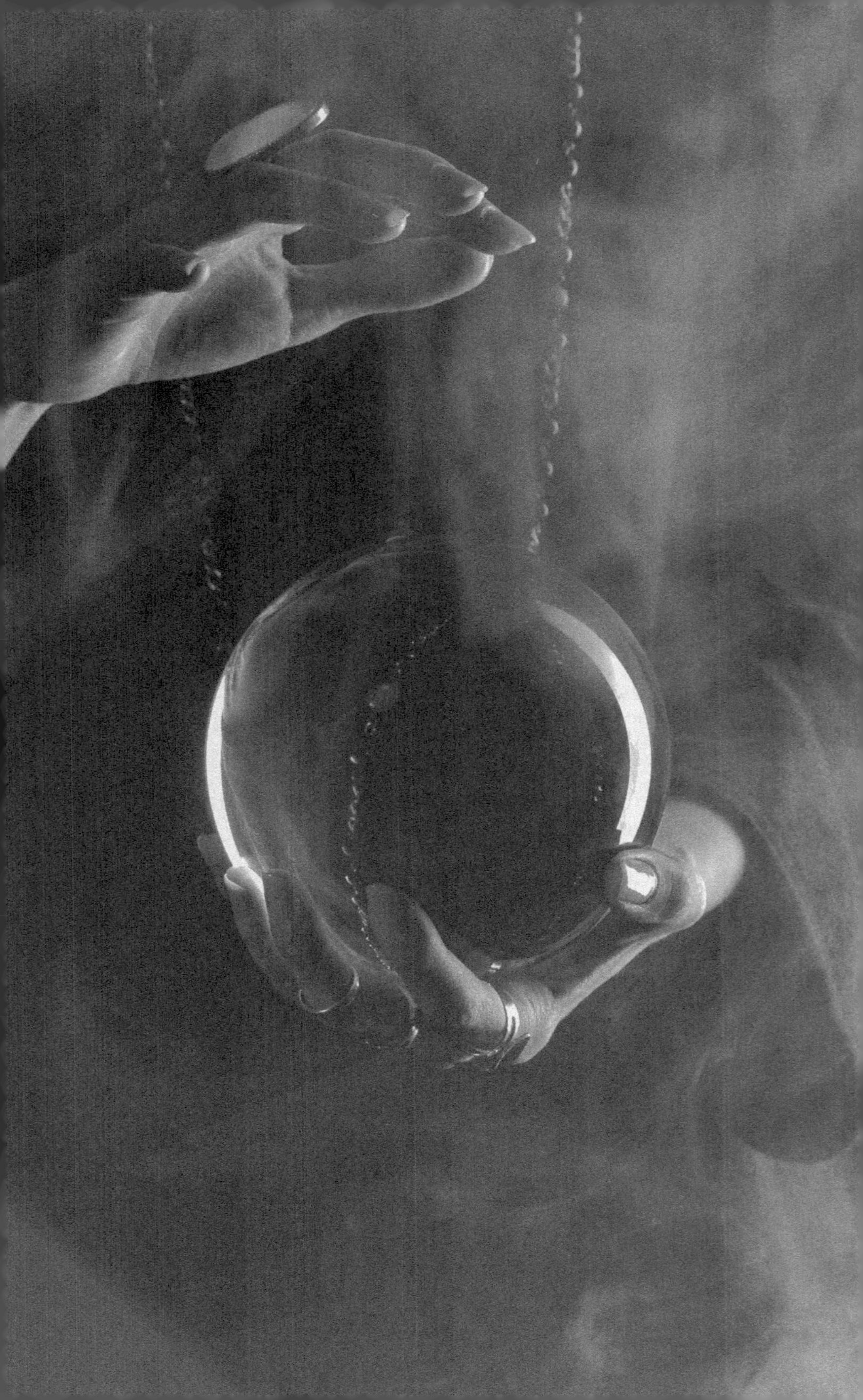

19

FIADH

I promised Feray I would be slightly less suspicious of the whole 'mate' thing and I'm trying. But we've been burnt so many times—not just at the Ascension, but when we were younger as well.

In elementary school, we were friends with a group of witches and elementals we adored. It didn't take long after we graduated to middle school for those same childhood best friends to dump us like trash when Fer didn't show any signs of having magic. The popular boys played their own games with us, pretending to ask one of us out and humiliating us later on. Dances were a nightmare; we quit going long before high school. It didn't bother me to only have Fer because I'm less forgiving of fools, but it cut my sister to the core. I almost got expelled in eighth grade for giving a handsy dickweed what he sorely deserved for leading her on. Our parents lectured us for weeks, but I'll never regret it.

That's when I focused my physical relief on older guys not connected to our community. It worked out for me, but not gentle Fer.

She didn't start dating seriously until after senior year and though she occasionally seemed happy, it never lasted long. As Ascension drew closer, expectations of their heirs to find suitable mates at the ceremony got stronger and casual dating petered out a bit. I know it made my sister lonely and I've always tried to be there for her anytime she needed to keep the rejection of our peers less painful.

All this bullshit is why I'm so damned skeptical of two random dudes suddenly sniffing around. I'm certain I know who her beau is and while I don't believe either of the men declaring interest is ill-intentioned, I don't know how to blindly trust what I'm told anymore. Too many people have betrayed me too many times.

I know what needs to be done.

Humming under my breath as Fer changes into loose clothes she can shed, I bookmark several spells in my phone. The coffee is hot and I have specific tasks I want to accomplish today, so I feel ready to put this topic to rest for good. It's not like we're going to have a line of dudes at our door waiting with flowers or candy, so I should only have to do this once and we'll know for sure. Wrinkling my nose, I look over the list of herbs and supplies I need to gather carefully.

- *Matches*
- *Three white candles*
- *One purple candle*
- *Mugwort*
- *Sage*
- *Lavender*
- *Calandula*
- *Bluebell*
- *Primrose*
- *Lapis Lazuli*

I put my phone down and grab the non-herbal items from my witchy stash. Tiernan's words about my magic needing time to develop echo in my head. If he wasn't lying about the mate bond, he might also be right about my magic. The fire and wind incidents seem to back him up and though I have no idea how to control either yet, the concept of having something I was told would never come excites me. I'm not allowing myself to be overcome, but I am nurturing a tiny spark of hope that I might receive my birthright as intended.

And I'll rub it in those motherfuckers' faces, too.

"Fer, get a move on! I want to do this shit before midday, so we have time to get ready for work tonight!"

Grumbling under her breath, my sister comes out of the bathroom in sweats, a tee, and a messy bun. I know she doesn't prefer going out all messy, but we're only going to woods next to the cabin. In theory, we should be alone as I gather and do spell work while she practices shifting. Taking a tour through the land surrounding us will help me get a feel for the access we have to common ingredients, too, because the solstice is in a week. I will have to do a solitary ceremony at home because that fuckknuckle exiled us and that means I'm doing it on my own. I'm sure Feray will watch, but I don't want to risk having her touch shit that might hurt her like the oils and incense at the Ascension.

I'll never say it out loud, but it would be nice to have someone to lean on every once in a while. I've been on overdrive since our parents died and I'm tired.

"Come on, sis. I want to see you get hairy before I do my shit." I throw an arm over her shoulder, stopping to pick up my bag and phone as I walk us to the door.

"That's assuming I *can*," she mutters.

"Either way, it'll be an adventure."

"ARRRRRGHHHH!"

The screech from the nearby clearing makes me chuckle, and I shake my head. It took me two hours to tour the closest part of the forest and pick up what I needed along the way. Fer has been in the clearing the entire time, torturing herself as she tries to control her shift.

Control might be a misleading term—she's still trying to make a full shift happen.

I have *zero* experience with that outside of the bedroom, so I can't even offer advice. She wasn't amused when I told her that and promptly banned me from recounting stories of how I got various shifters to go 'whole animal' for me. In fact, she plugged her ears and sang at the top of her lungs until I walked away like she did when we were kids. Her predictable shyness about naughty stuff made me snicker, and I finally headed to my little circle to clear and cleanse the space for future rituals.

After all, every witch needs a space for working her magic and since I'm not welcome in the community, I'll have to maintain it for celebrations as well. I might as well try to build the space I've always wanted—who knows how long we'll have to be here during the renovations?

None of the bears I talked to yesterday were clear on the topic and I got the sense perhaps they'd been ordered to be vague. That only backed up my suspicion that our giant, yet adorable landlord is the basket ninja. Torben doesn't want us making plans to leave soon, and though sickeningly cute, I still have to verify his intentions. He came out of nowhere, rescuing us like a white knight, and now he's declared my sister is his mate. I don't want to mistake kindness for trustworthiness and have everything crash around our feet again.

"Okay, Fi. You need to salt a large brush to sweep the negative energy out because your besom hasn't been replaced since the fire. Then you use that pile on the left to mark the circle and cleanse it again, and then set up the spell stuff in the middle. The rest will have to wait until you can afford to put some dough into materials," I mutter to myself.

A shout across the trees startles me. "I got one foot!"

Well, that's more than claws, I suppose.

"Way to go," I yell back. "We have to put a new caldron on the list once we get paid. It's non-negotiable, Fer!"

"Duh," is her reply, and I shake my head as I go about finding the right set of branches.

I could probably make my besom from the foliage out here until I can get a new one. There's plenty of twine and ribbon at the cabin and I'm low maintenance. It would make Feray crazy, but since we lost much of our mother's tools in the blaze, we don't have an option. Luckily, my sister is focused on trying to sprout hair from every limb, so she won't chastise me for not spending money on myself.

By the time I get the circle situated, Feray has gotten three paws and an ear. She seems excited, and I let her know I'll be starting the spell soon, so she takes a rest. I don't want to get distracted in the middle and screw up, nor do I want her to need help while I'm contained in the circle until the spell is finished. She offers to run back to the house for water, and I sigh in relief.

Closing my eyes as I step into the consecrated circle, I draw in a slow breath and let my magic flow through me. It spirals out into the air and into the ground, making me feel grounded. When I'm ready, I drop to the ground and light the purple candle. I take my athame and scratch the guys' names on individual candles. The last one bears both mine and my sister's name on it. Lighting those as well, I sprinkle the various herbs around the mini-altar, keeping the question I need answered in my mind. The last thing I do is place the lapis lazuli in the middle of the semi-circle they form.

> "May the truth I seek
> Be revealed to me
> May the hidden come to light
> In the quarter moons tonight
> May all intentions be known to me
> So mote it be."

A jolt of energy surges within me and I feel like a ribbon of light is swirling in the air around me. It grows and grows until it finally shoots into the small crystal, making it glow for a moment.

Holy. Shit. Balls.

"Fer!"

My sister comes running and I almost choke on my own spit. I have to cover my mouth with my hand because she looks *furious* when she sees the expression on my face. But...I can't help it. Poor Feray has one wolf ear sprouted, whiskers, a partial snout, and three furry paws. The rest of her is human and I have no idea how she expects me to take her seriously when she looks like she got rolled by a furry convention.

"Shut. Up. Fiadh. Amaranth. Morgenstern."

Her words are hissed, but I shake my head, hiding the tears of mirth behind my long hair. Her voice even sounds half-wolf, half-human and that isn't helping *at all.* "F-F-Ferrrrr..." That's all I manage to gasp out as I clutch my stomach and double over in silent laughter.

"Damnit, Fi! What did you yell for? I'm *obviously* in the middle of something *important!*"

No, shit Fur-lock.

I keep my witty rejoinder to myself as I wipe my eyes and jerk my head at the candles. "You... you missed it. I... uh. I made sparkles." Probably not the most eloquent answer but *goddamn,* she's funny looking.

Stomping her foot, Feray comes closer, squinting at the crystal and candles without breaking my circle. "Damn. I would have liked to see that. What does the crystal do?"

"I'll put it beneath my pillow tonight and I should be able to see the truth in my dreams," I reply. I've finally gotten myself under control, but that's precarious. I need her to quit doing the stompy tantrum stuff or I'm going to lose it again.

Her eyes narrow. "The truth about what?"

I use the athame to close the circle, then rise to my feet and walk over to her. "I asked the Goddess to help me see the truth of our suitors' intentions. I know you think I have to trust, but I *need* to feel more secure before I can wrap my head around this. If everything goes well tonight, you can put your basket out and find yourself a giant teddy bear. Okay?"

Feray looks mad for a moment and in her current state I have to look away as she gets that under wraps. I don't want to laugh again, but fuck. When I turn back, she's smiling fondly with fangs. "Okay. But I expect you to give the big kitty a belly rub to see if he'll purr. Deal?"

Snorting, I nod. "Deal. Although, do leopards purr? You know, I think they might. There are only certain kind of big cats that do because the others roar and—"

She starts laughing, shaking her head as she helps me pick up the extra items and wrap the crystal up to take home. "Only you would turn that sexy kitty into a Nat Geo special, Fi. Sheesh."

"What? I love that shit," I grumble as we finish gathering my stuff. "Now let's go try to get your mismatched body to comply so we can go home and get ready for work."

Her only answer is a long howl and I laugh.

20

FERAY

WHAT AN EPIC FAILURE I AM.

It's hysterical—I get a foot or two, but never a full shift. Frustrated, I flop on the ground and go back to my breathing techniques so I relax enough to shift back. I look like a little kid playing Frankenstein with their Barbie and a toy wolf. Luckily, Fi realizes her presence may irritate me more, so she's letting me be.

"I'll grab us some snacks, make a thermos of coffee, and be right back." Fi walks away and then stops looking over her shoulder at me. The look on her face speaks volumes; she's worried about me.

Smiling, I wave at her, hoping my false bravado is enough to get her to leave for a little. When she vanishes around the corner, I'm able to breathe easier. Concentrating on my body, I attempt to visualize myself as the wolf. I'm not even sure what color my wolf is—my paws were a creamy white color, so I guess I'm that color. I hoped my wolf was red like my hair; that would have been awesome.

After what feels like forever, I sprout a large, fluffy, white tail and let out a frustrated screech. I feel like a poor man's Kitsune. Pulling my tail in front of me, I try not to cry.

I'm the worst wolf in history.

"Are you okay?" A soft, deep voice startles me as it rumbles behind me.

Turning quickly, I use my sleeve to wipe my tears away. I realize it's Torben and I can't help blushing a brilliant shade of pink. "Maybe. Not really."

"What's the matter?" He moves closer, reaching out before he snatches his hand back.

Still holding my tail, I wave it at him. Several rogue tears escape and roll down my cheeks. "I don't know how to shift correctly."

Torben pulls a handkerchief from his pocket and offers it to me. Without hesitating, I accept it and blot my eyes. He sits on the ground in front of me, placing himself lower than me to ease my nerves. "When was the last time you fully shifted?"

"The only time was at the Ascension. Apparently, the amulet my mother gave me stopped me from shifting as a kid. I grew up thinking I was a powerless witch." Biting my lips, I stare at the handkerchief in my hand. *I don't know why I told him all of that.*

His large hand comes up to stroke his beard and he looks at me with the amber of his bear burning through the hazel of his human eyes. "That makes learning a little more difficult. But I'm sure you can do it if you learn the basics."

Moving closer, I can't help but stare into his eyes. The color fades from most of the world, and I know my wolf is looking out at him. "Your eyes are so pretty."

Now it's Torben's turn to blush. "My bear has never been called pretty before—thank you. Your wolf has a unique golden glow to her eyes that I've never seen before."

It's odd that Torben can study me and it doesn't bother me one bit.

Clearing his throat, he rises to stand, towering over me. A soft smile shows through his beard as he motions to the field. "How about I show you how to shift? Maybe if your wolf sees it being done, it might help."

"If both of you don't mind, that would be wonderful." My vision shifts back to normal in time to catch him pulling his shirt over his head. "What are you doing?"

He flushes pink again, looking at me sheepishly. "I forgot you were raised a witch. If you don't want to destroy your clothes, you need to take them off, especially with a shift as big as mine."

The confidence this man has is as impressive as it is scary. His megawatt smile does funny things to my stomach, yet still sets my nerves at ease. I note the light spattering of hair on his chest leading down past his stomach before disappearing into his pants. His muscles are huge, but not defined. He's built for strength and not show—something about that pleases my wolf.

Why would it please her?

He's our landlord and I'm about to see him in his naked glory, but it's to teach me. Torben kicks off his boots and pulls off his socks before his hands go to his belt. My heart is pounding in my chest—this feels huge, like it isn't just him being kind.

The fucker winks at me as he yanks his belt from his pants like the foxes did at the male revue Fi took me to a few years ago. Before I can get words out of my mouth to stop him, his hands unbutton his jeans. One by one, they pop open and I can't force myself to avert my gaze. My nostrils flare as I take in a familiar scent.

That smell... I know it...

But the idea of seeing him naked has short-circuited my brain, so I can't focus on where I recognize it from. The denim falls to the ground in a soundless lump and I unabashedly stare at his large semi-erect dick.

"Watch closely." His husky, lust-filled tone catches my attention and I lock eyes with him.

I forget how to breathe as I watch his body reshape itself. Each snap and pop makes my eyes jump to the parts of him as they change. Suddenly, I realize he's drawing it out for my benefit. Fur races over his flesh as his body seems to triple. Within moments, he goes from man to beast.

Having never seen a bear up close, I take this time to study him. "Can you understand me like this?"

His bear tilts its head for a moment, then nods and plops down on his ass.

"I've been terrified I wouldn't be me when I shift to my wolf." I circle his bear, knowing he won't hurt me. Leaning forward, I kiss the bear on the muzzle. His thick fur tickles my lips and nose, making me giggle. "I stand by my earlier statement that you have beautiful eyes, Mr. Bear."

Torben shifts back, looking at me in amazement. "You kissed my bear."

"He was so adorable, like a huge fluffy teddy bear." I shrug as I smile broadly.

Shaking his head, he pulls his pants back on then motions back to the field. "I've never been called a teddy bear before. That's a first." He holds his giant shirt out to me before saying, "Let's get back on track. Take off your clothes and use my shirt to shield you. Being new to shifting, you may still have an aversion to public nudity."

I take his shirt from him and can't help but sniff it before slipping it over my head. Covered by his shirt, I wiggle free from my t-shirt, bra, and sweats. Thankfully, Torben's shirt is as long as a dress on me, so I'm perfectly at ease following him dressed like this.

"For me, I feel my bear in my spine first." He runs his index finger down my spine and I close my eyes, listening to him. "Next, there's a warmth in my chest that radiates towards my limbs."

As he speaks the words, I focus on the feeling he's describing. Almost like magic, I feel the warmth build in the center of my chest then move towards my limbs. It feels like the earth is pulling me closer to it, so I chase the feeling, hoping it helps.

"Next, I feel my canines descend as the warmth wraps me up in a blanket." His voice seems closer now, louder than before. I feel him pull his shirt off me and embarrassment floods me; he's seeing me naked. "Open your eyes."

I open my eyes quickly and realize the world is how my wolf sees it. I tried this a million times and failed, but now I did it! I attempt to speak, but a bark comes out. Raising my head in shock, I look down to see fuzzy legs and paws. Whipping my head from side to side, I jump to my feet and spin in a circle. I can't look at all of me, but I know I'm fully shifted.

Best day ever!

Moving the field, I run to my heart's content. The freedom and speed she grants me is amazing. Torben is cheering me on as I race around the field happily. I don't stop until Fi returns, prancing over to her. She's holding my basket in her hand and she motions towards Torben. I shake my head 'no' for the moment. Walking back over to him, I nuzzle his shirt with my muzzle, and he slides it back over me before I shift again.

Shifting back wasn't as hard as it was to become a wolf.

"Thank you." My voice is still rough as I gaze up at him. I see love and affection shining back at me, so I offer him my hand. Shock replaces the soft smile he had moments before. Raising both of his hands, they engulf my little one. A jolt of recognition floods my system as I watch his eyes shift in time with mine.

Soft soothing peace spreads through me as if I have found a home within a person.

"I have waited so long for you." His voice is filled with wonder as he stares at me.

Looking over my shoulder, I motion for Fi to give me the basket and I hold it up to him. "I was going to leave this on the porch for you tomorrow. I made it myself; I even climbed the cliffs for the honey."

Scuffing my foot on the ground, I try to distract myself from the emotions because I want to cry and jump for joy all at once.

Torben removes one hand from mine to accept the basket then walks us over to the fallen tree on the edge of the field. He takes a seat then offers me his knee to sit on. Glancing over at my sister, I see her make the 'shoo' motion. I nod then turn back to Torben. Taking a seat on his knee, I offer to hold the basket for him.

He glances at it and grins. "It's a very sturdy basket. You did very well."

My inner wolf prances. *Fuck... do I have a praise kink?* "I hope you like what I put in there."

Torben lifts the towel to see the large chunk of the honeycomb and a deep rumble escapes his lips. "Is this from the giant honey bees? I've been dying to get a hold of some of this for ages."

Excitedly, he moves the tissue paper and finds the berries I harvested. He looks up before he pops several into his mouth. Sitting the basket down, he hugs me tightly.

Part of me wants to run, but my wolf tells me I'm safe.

He's ours and I don't need to worry. I hope my wolf is right because I would really like to keep him.

21

FIADH

WE SPENT MOST OF THIS WEEK EITHER WORKING OR DEALING WITH this new mate situation.

Fer and I took a lot of shifts at the bar during the holiday week because it was likely tips would be good. Many species celebrate this holiday—even if it's not under the name Imbolc—and being chintzy right before you make offerings to your higher power isn't good karma. Plus, as Fer so smugly pointed out, I desperately need more equipment for solitary practice. Losing most of it in the fire and being cut off from the community means I have to do *all* the witchy shit on my own or risk bad favor for the next quarter.

When we weren't hauling ass at Dezi's, we borrowed some of her bear's outdoor tools to clear up my sacred circle area. In between sisterly chats about the men who have declared their intent, Fer practiced shifting, and I started preparing my ritual space. Together, we even made room for several garden plots to grow various herbs, veggies, fruits, and flowers we'll want in the springtime. It was hard work, given the temperature, but we could sort out of some of the jumbled emotions we both have about learning the truth about how we were raised. It's not a simple transition to diverge from every-thing you've always known, but we're managing it.

That's why getting my spot ready is so important—if I'm going to have true magic, I need a place to hone my craft.

"I think we need to invite them to coffee," Fer says as she walks over from her clearing. She's doing much better at controlling the shift now, but every once in a while, she struggles. Today might be one of those times because she's got that cute tail wagging behind her like a hyper puppy.

I wipe my hand over my brow and ponder it. "Do you think they'll be able to come on short notice?"

"Yep."

My eyes narrow. "Is that because you already *asked* both of them?"

The mischievous look on her face tells me all I need to know. I glare, but it makes the tail wag even faster as she replies. "Possibly. And *maybe* we should go get dressed, so we're not late."

I knew it was a mistake to give her the passcode to my fucking phone.

Throwing my hands up, I growl. "Fine! But I won't be held respon-sible for what I do if you don't quit snooping in my text messages."

Her eyes dance, and she makes a small sound before the tail disap-pears. "You got it. But I'm helping you get ready."

"No!"

"Yes I am," she sing-songs as she tucks her arm in mine. "I promise you'll look hot *and* be comfortable. I just want us to make a good impression."

As if people wanting to be our mates aren't going to see us wake up with bedhead and drool on our faces someday.

"Ugh, alright. You win. No combat boots."

"Yay!"

Pinching the bridge of my nose with my free hand, I prepare myself for what is going to be a very excruciating experience.

AFTER A SHOWER and a torturous session with my sister's charred titanium makeup case, we finally finished dressing and headed out. Feray asked Torben and Tiernan to meet us at a small cafe in the shifter district that isn't far from Philly's bar. A sweet old bobcat shifter runs the place, and she makes some of the best pastries I've ever had. I assume that's why Fer picked it—she knows I have a weakness for the lemon-lavender cupcakes and violet tea.

"I like that we can take the shortcut through the woods and avoid all the creeps," she says as we emerge from the thick treeline. "It's convenient, but also feels kinda safe? I mean, I doubt anyone would accost us, but keeping you from landing your ass in jail is pretty high on my list."

I turn my head slowly, giving her a sharp look. It must not have the same effect as normal when I'm sporting fake lashes and 'bedroom eyes,' because she dissolves into giggles. "I can't help it if people are so criminally stupid that they decide to try me. It's not like I give off 'friendly and approachable' vibes."

"That's the truth if I've ever heard it," Fer mutters as she tugs me through the alley and up the street. "And I appreciate you wanting to protect me. But maybe what we're going to find out is that you don't have to do it all alone anymore."

Holy shit, did she read my mind? That's what I was thinking earlier in the week.

But I can't get her hopes up, so I grumble softly. "We'll see. Your bear accepted the basket, and you had a moment, but we have to see what happens next."

"Trust me, your kitty cat was *very* excited to get his invitation. He might have suspected it wasn't you texting, but he moved his schedule around just the same." Her expression is smug as I gape at her. I don't know what the hell unleashing her wolf has done for my sister's confidence, but the effect is startling.

"Fer, I love you, but I might actually *murder* you myself."

We approach the door to the quaint little coffeehouse and she winks at me before pulling the door open. "Save that fire for the furry one, sis. He seems like he'd be eager to please."

What. In. The. Actual. Fuck.

I follow her inside, my eyes immediately tracking the booth in the corner where the gigantic bear and the lithe leopard are waiting. Soft chocolate brown eyes meet mine and the energy pulling me towards him hits me hard. Torben greets us, but all I can do is murmur a response as I walk over to the chair next to Tiernan and sit down. I don't know if it's something that gets more intense over time or if maybe the simple act of acknowledging the bond out loud gives it power, but I feel like I'm magnetized to him.

"Is that a witch thing, Torben?" My sister's voice sounds far away, but I know she's sitting at our table.

His deep chuckle rumbles in the air. "It must be. For us shifters, scent is one thing that first draws us to a mate, but it's followed by sensations. Some people call it tingles, but to me it felt like my bear was pushing at me to shift every time I saw you."

Tiernan breaks his gaze from mine and looks over at them. "He's right. Scent first and then when I was close enough, this weird electricity shooting through me and an urge to shift."

That knocks me out of my trance, and I frown. "So I'm the only one who feels like I'm getting tugged in by the Death Star tractor beam? Awesome. Definitely seems fair."

Torben arches his brow. "You seem angry." He looks at Feray in confusion. "Is your sister angry at finding her mate?"

"Fi is naturally suspicious and after everything that's happened to us, it's amped up to a thousand," she replies.

I cross my arms over my chest. "Fi is right here and perfectly able to answer for herself." When Fer's face falls, I roll my eyes and sigh. "Okay, okay. She's right. People have treated us like garbage for whatever reason for most of our lives and the Ascension shit made it worse. It's hard to trust something I can't quantify. Feray is more of an instinct person and I bet the wolf has only enhanced that. But my magic isn't... working yet, so I have to run on proof."

Tiernan smiles gently, reaching over and placing his hand on mine. The effect on my frayed nerves is instantaneous—everything roiling inside of me settles and even my fingertips stop tapping on my leg. *Son of a bitch.* "That just seems like cheating," I mumble.

The three of them laugh and I make a face, but I don't pull my hand away. The barista comes up to the table, smiling brightly. Once she takes our orders, I try to relax. This meeting is to help us feel more comfortable and talk about what the hell happens next. I have to be more open or Fer is going to pout her way into convincing me of doing everything she wants.

"So... what happens... now?" I venture.

The leopard and the bear look at one another, doing that guy thing where they talk without words. Finally, Tiernan smiles at me. "For me, it's different from him. My kind are more solitary, so when I do anything in a group, it's usually with other big cat shifters who don't have full family groups in Briarvale."

"And I have an extensive family in town, as you know," Torben says with a grin. "I know you have a celebration coming up, but the next night is the sleuth celebration for the End of the Dark Times. It is like your Imbolc, I'd say, but ours is centered on waking from hibernation, of course."

I arch my brow. "But your people don't hibernate anymore."

"Fi!" my sister hisses as she leans towards Torben. "Don't be rude!"

"I'm not!" I shrug and give the bear a half-grin when Tiernan squeezes my hand. "I'm curious. Plus, I don't know what that has to do with mating.

Torben looks at my sister with a soft smile. "Do not worry. She didn't offend me; she's right. Most of us *don't* hibernate for the entire winter unless we live in really cold climates. Briarvale is temperate enough that we aren't driven to hide away for months, but we do celebrate the return of those who do. And it's a perfect time to introduce my future mate to my family because they will all be present."

My sister's face goes pale as a ghost and she's barely able to accept the plate of cookies and tea the server brings over. "Your...entire family?"

These guys don't know that we have some shitty history with other people's parents. For a second, I wonder what bullshit *didn't* happen to us as kids and only came up with physical abuse. I suppose that makes us lucky, but as I said earlier, it makes me suspicious as *hell*. I shift my gaze to the bear and watch him fumble a little as the fear radiates from Feray.

"Um, maybe I could come, too?" I say softly. "You know, to help her feel less surrounded by new people?"

It makes Fer's color come back and Torben notices immediately. He strokes his beard, nodding at me when he sees how my words affect my sister. "Of course you can, little witch. Bring the leopard as well.

Bear picnics are not closed affairs; we welcome outsiders to join our feast."

Blinking rapidly, I lift my hand to my mouth before the laughter gets out. They all look at me and I shake my head, feeling the tears gathering at the corners of my eyes as I hold back my mirth. Tiernan leans in, whispering in my ear, but I don't answer until Fer hisses my name. Reluctantly, I lift my hand and the chuckles start. When I finally get it under control, I look at Torben seriously, trying not to snicker.

"Did you just invite us to a... teddy bear picnic?"

Silence falls over the table and like magic, the laughter spreads from me to the big cat to my sister, and finally the amused looking bear shifter. He leans back in his chair, crossing his huge arms over his chest as his eyes twinkle.

"What if I did?"

I wipe my eyes and shrug, trying to gather myself. "I'd have to inform you that I'm *really* good at hide and seek and I can eat my weight in buffet items."

"Now that's a show I'd like to see," Tiernan says with a grin. "I'll have to schedule myself off, but I'm in."

Fer claps her hands, looking excited again. "Okay, I'm in, too."

Damnit. Every single time.

"Fine. I'm in, too. But the first person who tries to make me dance is getting stabbed."

The guys look at one another and shrug, then say, "Deal."

I guess we're going to a teddy bear picnic... with our mates.

What planet am I living on?

FERAY

Hunt... Need to hunt...

My wolf's voice wakes me from a dead sleep before the sun rises on the day of the party.

Creeping through the house, I grab my basket and knife before heading out the back door. I set up a changing tent on the back porch so I can shift in private. As soon as I'm naked, I fold up my clothes to take with me. After all, rocks hurt and I might need shoes. Shifting to my wolf has become as natural as breathing and sometimes I love walking around with my tail wagging. When my paws hit the ground, I shake out my fur and grab my basket with my mouth, taking off running.

There's a new found freedom having my wolf.

The world isn't as vivid as it used to be, but all the unfamiliar scents and experiences are worth it. I trace our steps back to Philly's bar until I find the rock formation with the honeycombs. Torben was so touched by my first gift of that honey; I want to bring his family some of it as well.

Circling behind the cliff, I shift back to get dressed. It's a shady morning, thank the Goddess, so the bees will be fast asleep. I lean over the edge and take a hold of the fatter combs. Pull some free from the rock without dragging it is damn near impossible. Carefully, I pick the bees off the comb and sit them on the grass. As I remove them, I thank them profusely and I laugh, knowing Fi would tell me to cut it out.

I carefully use my knife to cut the comb into squares that will fit in my basket. My eyes widen when I realize how much honey I have; there's no way I can carry the basket while shifted now. I didn't plan this out well and Fi will call me out on not thinking ahead. It's okay, though, because I don't care if I have to walk home.

I refuse to show up to Torben's party with his sleuth empty handed.

The walk home isn't horrible, and it gives me time to plan out the rest of my gift.

Fi is on the front porch with her coffee in hand, scowling at the world when I get back.

"Where did you go so early?" She tilts her head to the side, letting her long black braid fall over her shoulder.

"Back to the bees." I hold the basket up triumphantly.

"Did you rob them blind?" She takes the basket from me and grunts, not expecting the weight of it.

"I was careful not to take too much and I made sure to remove the bees on the comb and place them where the sun would warm them up." Smiling proudly, I take the basket back and head inside.

"Can I help with anything?" Fi sets her coffee cup down and looks around the kitchen with determination.

Shrugging my shoulders, I wince as memories of our mother flood my mind. "I want to make the sticky buns mom used to make. We can drizzle some of the fresh honey on top and it'll be a big hit." One by one, I pull the comb pieces out and set them on trays to catch the dripping honey.

Fi nods, gathering the ingredients with a soft smile. "I'll start the batter; you prep and wrap the combs." For Fi, taking control of the situation puts her at ease.

I watch my sister buzzing around the kitchen, mixing and singing random songs as she goes about her task. While she's busy, I clean and wrap the combs up in wax paper and decorative tissue paper with butcher's string. A brilliant thought crosses my mind and I dash outside to cut fresh wild flowers to tie them to the parcels. I'm glad I took the time the other day to make a bigger version of my previous basket. I place each comb into the basket with a few flowers lovingly tied on top and smile proudly.

"That looks beautiful." Fi wraps an arm around me and pulls me in for a side hug. "I'm sure his family will love it."

I get a little misty eyed at her words. It's been so long since we've been part of a family; I almost forget what it's like to have more than just the two of us. Fi's done her best to be the strong one for us by taking the brunt of the troubles on her shoulders.

"I love you, Fi. Thank you for everything." I kiss her cheek and pull her in for a full hug. My emotions choke me as I think about all the sacrifices she's made for us.

She kisses my temple back. "I love you, too, you big mush. Don't get all soft because you have a real life teddy bear."

I know when she deflects it's because she doesn't want to deal with her damage. Handling emotions is not her strong suit and she won't let anyone help her. Besides me, there's no one she lets in close. We pull apart and I sigh as I walk over to the counter.

Hopefully, Tiernan can break through and show her what unconditional love is.

Taking a small comb, I place it in a pot to melt down to separate the honey from the wax. About twenty minutes pass while Fi works on pulling hot pastries out of the oven to cool. I skim the last bit of wax off the top of the honey, laughing to myself as the frozen ladle trick mom taught me works yet again. "I'm ready when you are."

My sister motions for me to bring the honey over. We mix butter and cinnamon in with the honey before pouring it over the fresh baked buns.

Mom would be proud.

Fi takes the buns and stacks them on a serving tray. Once she seals it up, she turns to me and chuckles as she surveys our messy attire. "Let's get changed. We need to leave in less than an hour to be on time."

As we separate, I get a text from Torben. He tells me to relax—the sleuth is excited I'm joining them. His mom read the family the riot act so they won't make me nervous. I can't wipe the smile off my face thinking about how thoughtful my mate is. He reminds me that he tied scent ribbons through the forest so I can find my way to the gathering.

Butterflies run rampant in my belly as I think about getting to be around my mate and see how he is with his family and people.

My beauty routine is not as extensive as my sister's and I'm done long before her. I sit on the bar stool braiding my hair with flowers woven throughout the length. *We will be fine. He's our mate,* my wolf says to me. She's lending me her strength and stability which helps immensely.

Even when I'm alone, I am never by myself. The more I shift, the more in tune with her I am.

"You look like a fairytale princess, Feray."

Fi's voice draws me out of my thoughts and I turn to face her. She's dressed in a pair of tight, ripped skinny jeans and a slinky corset top with knee-high boots that look like she's going horseback riding. Her hair is piled on her head and she's got dark, smoky eyes and lipstick. I let out a sigh of relief when I realize she kept her promise about no grungy combat boots.

Standing up, I do a slight twirl so she can assess me. I chose an emerald green dress made of a moss colored crepe material I bought at *Feeling Thrifty*. "I made it myself."

Late at night, when I couldn't sleep, I embroidered the design of running wolves along the bottom hem of the dress. Around the neckline, flowers and butterflies are stitched into the material to make the sweetheart top pop.

"I cooked with mom; you sewed with her. Hell, I couldn't make a dress if I wanted to." Fi smiles as she gets closer, squinting at the detail. "This is amazing, Fer. If he doesn't appreciate your skill, I'll kick him in the nuts."

A soft growl escapes my lips and my vision changes briefly. Rubbing my sternum, I force a smile as I say, "I know you mean well, but we don't like you threatening harm to our mate." Grabbing my basket, I motion to the door.

Taking the hint, Fi picks up the tray with the pastries, and follows me out the door. When we get outside, Fi looks around the woods. "How do we know which way to go?"

I smile mischievously. Shifting my eyes to wolven, I allow my senses to heighten. Catching the bear's scent on the wind, I turn my head until my nose is in the wind. The scent of sandalwood fills my nostrils. Moving with purpose, my wolf drives me to want to run to get to our mate. "This way… Torben left me a scent trail."

"A scent trail? I don't smell anything." Fi picks up her pace as she tries to keep up.

Tapping my nose when I look at my sister, I giggle. "It's a shifter thing."

For once, I feel special. I wish I had known what species I was sooner; it would have made my life less painful. I wasn't bad at being a witch because I wasn't a witch at all.

The trail winds through the forest and along the way, we meet up with Tiernan. He followed the scent trail to us, and I smile when Fi and Tier end up deep in their own conversation. They don't notice the brief stops I make along the way. Torben scent marked flowers along the way for me so I stopped and picked every one.

It's not long after picking the bluebells that I hear the bears in the distance. My sudden stop and the noise puts Tiernan on high alert. Instinctively, he pushes ahead of me to look for danger.

"What is it? What made you stop like that?" His tone makes me tear my gaze away from the direction of the sounds.

"I hear Torben and his family," I whisper, looking into the distance nervously.

"Oh? That's all?" I nod and he smiles. "You stopped at a respectful distance, which is good. We need to let them know we are approaching." Tiernan tilts his head back and roars.

We listen for several moments before a responding bellow comes back from the bear camp. He smiles and tilts his head, looking at me. "Your turn. It's best to let a large gathering of shifters know when you approach if you're a different species."

His advice makes sense. Biting my bottom lip, I tilt my head back and howl. It's not a sad howl, but one of longing. My nerves are getting the better of me as we wait in silence.

The next thing I know, Torben comes barreling through the woods and picks me up off the ground, hugging me tightly. We don't need words as I bury my face in his neck and breathe in his scent, calming down almost instantly. Fi's hand touches my wrist and I release the basket to throw my arm around his neck. My giant teddy bear, as big as he is, is cradling me.

Tiernan clears his throat and I feel Torben stiffen. A growl escapes his lips as his head turns away from me towards the noise. "Not cool, man. You know I'm barely holding it together right now."

Instinct tells me to nuzzle Torben to get his focus back on me, and it works like a charm. He kisses my cheek, then moves me so he can carry me.

"I can walk," I say, softer than I had intended.

"I know you can. Allow me to hold you longer. Your howl made my bear angry because you sounded sad and lonely. He felt inadequate, so he drove to come get you." His explanation really knocks me for a loop. His drive to protect me and keep me safe blows my mind.

"I understand. I'd like to walk in on my own two feet, if you don't mind, when we get close to your family." I nuzzle his cheek, trying to reassure him.

"Of course, little wolf. Anything you desire." He buries his nose against my throat and breathes in deeply before leading us back to the gathering.

Looking over his shoulder over at my sister, she's making a hand motion about Torben being huge. Tiernan catches her and smacks her shoulder with a chuckle. I give him a nod in thanks and almost giggle when I see that Fi has him carrying my flower filled honey basket.

The trail narrows, and Torben sets me down gently. That hard, stoic mask he wore when we first met has been replaced by a gentle smile and dimples. "On the other side of the holly bushes is my sleuth."

Glancing around, I motion for Tiernan to hand me my basket. Once it's in my grasp, I thread the fingers of my other hand with Torben's and he leads us to his family.

"I'm back!" he bellows.

Everything from music to conversation stops immediately.

My eyes dart around, taking in all the faces. I am surrounded by larger apex animals and it makes my wolf a little jittery. Touching Torben's arm, I snuggle in against his side to use my connection to him to make my anxiety lower. I wave a little, waiting for someone to say something.

An older woman with golden brown hair and pale amber eyes approaches. "You must be my son's mate. I'm Mila, Torben's mother. The grumpy one in the corner with the stein of honey beer is Aleksei. The three men by the buffet are Elijah, Levi, and Logan—they are Torben's younger brothers. Last, but not least, is Torben's baby sister Evva, over by the refreshments." His mother's brilliant smile distracts me from my nerves for several moments.

Glancing up at Torben, he smiles and kisses my forehead. I draw in a fortifying breath and step forward. "I'm Feray Morgenstern and this is my sister, Fiadh, and her mate, Tiernan."

Fi's reaction when I announce them as a couple is priceless.

"Oh! I almost forgot. We brought gifts." I scoop out the flowers Torben marked for me out of the basket and give them to him to hold. Carefully, I pull out the largest section of honeycomb and offer it to his mother. Torben arches a brow in question, and I tilt my head in response. Our first silent conversation seems to go well —he understood I'm giving his mother the fresh honey as well.

The crinkling of the tissue paper redirects me to his mother. Her eyes widen when she sees what's inside the parchment paper. Shock is written all over her face."Is this what I think it is?"

"Freshly harvested this morning before sunrise. The giant honey bees were fast asleep. I was even careful enough to place them on a rock where the sun could warm them up."

His mom rushed forward and gave me a bone-crushing hug. "Are you sure you're not a bear?"

"I'm pretty sure. But it gets better. Fi, offer Torben and his mom the pastry you made this morning."

She steps forward and takes the lid off of the tray. The delicious scent of honey, cinnamon and butter draws a crowd. Torben and his mother moan over the taste of the pastries as they bite into them. My sister and I beam with pride. Aleksei and his sons finally approach and take a honeycomb and a pastry before walking to a picnic table to sit.

After his immediate family has taken their portion, Torben leads me to a table slightly apart from the others. Torben's voice is pitched low as he pulls the chair out for me. "Sorry if it's overwhelming. I asked them to tone down the intensity."

Sitting down, I watch his movements. He glances over to the buffet table before he walks over and starts making plates. I'm so intent that I don't notice when Fi comes up beside me.

"He's a gentleman. That's a welcome change."

I hum in agreement, watching my mate make plates of food for us. He's physically huge and I feel like a doll next to him. "It's nice for a change. How's Tiernan?"

Fi grumbles and sighs. "I'm used to dealing with grabby assholes. He's nice—maybe too nice." She narrows her eyes and I know she's being a Judgy McJudgerpants.

Doing my best Fiadh impersonation, I cross my arms over my chest dramatically and turn my head away. "Fine, don't be happy. Just because he's a good guy—not the bad boy asshole you're used to dating—doesn't mean he's not perfect for you."

Torben returns with our food, motioning to the other side of the table across from us. "Why don't the two of you join us? There's plenty of room."

Fi smiles and looks back at Tiernan. "I think we're going to go see Tiernan's people for their celebration. Besides sis, you need to get to know your mate without me here." Fi looks at Torben, extending a hand to him. "Thank you for allowing me to join my sister here tonight."

He gets up and hugs her instead. "If you ever need me, my clan and I will be there." Torben pulls back and shakes hands with Tiernan and I watch them walk off leaving me with my mate.

Watching his sleuth interact, I get a strong sense of family and my wolf is at ease. Dinner is divine and he won't let me skimp on eating.

I hope Fi's night goes as well as mine. Hopefully, she opens her heart and allows Tiernan to be the mate she needs.

But knowing my sister, she's going to fight this every step of the way.

23

FIADH

"I can't believe you agreed to come with me when your... cat group... was having a party, too," I say as I look over at the gorgeous man walking beside me. "I mean, I had to go to support Fer and make sure she was okay, but it's not your responsibility."

Tiernan gives me an amused look. "This is why I didn't mention it at first."

Frowning, I narrow my eyes in suspicion. "What do you mean?"

He stops for a moment, forcing me to as well, and takes my hands gently. His expression is earnest, and I'd love to trust it, but it's so damned hard. "Fiadh, this is what having a mate is like. Your happiness is bound to your sister because it's been the two of you against the world for years. The responsibility you feel for her would never have allowed you to decline the invitation and because I want to see my mate happy, I came with you. That's the compromise people who care about one another make. It wasn't even a question in my mind; you asked, and I came."

Blinking, I turn my face away. I can't look into his big brown eyes when he's saying shit like this. It's too kind and so very dangerous.

Having someone around who would change their entire life to see me smile is not what I'm used to. If I let him in and I get used to it, it will only hurt exponentially more when he inevitably leaves. Fer is the only constant in my life and I worry about her all the time.

How can I accept that this guy I just met wants to be part of my miniscule circle permanently?

"Hey. Don't get flustered. I'm not declaring undying love—yet." My head whips around and I guarantee my eyes are like dinner platters as I gape at him. He chuckles and squeezes my fingers. "Ah, there you are. So I have to shock the crap out of you to get your attention. Good to know."

"That's not funny," I grumble under my breath. "I've had a lot of really fucked up surprises lately. It makes me edgy around surprises."

Nodding, he catches my eyes again. "I'll try to help you work that with some positive reinforcement, but for now, would it help to talk about where we're going?"

My mouth goes dry when I think about meeting a bunch of people I don't know and trust. "Uh, yeah. That would help immensely."

"Okay." He drops one hand and tugs on the other until I walk with him. "There are a *lot* of cat shifters. Not all species have their own species specific group in every city, like wolves or bears. That's because while a bear's a bear, the cats vary in size and type. Obviously, Briarvale has a lion pride, a cheetah coalition, and a tiger ambush. But for the lesser populations like different leopards, panthers, jaguars, and the like... there aren't enough for a specific group. So those of us without a bigger collective do things as our own pack of misfits."

Son of a bitch, I had no idea. School taught us all shifters separated into their own groups. What the hell?

"I know you mentioned that our education might have... glossed over some things." I bite my lip and look at him nervously. Not knowing shit bothers the *fuck* out of me and I get the sense I'm about to find out a lot of what I thought I knew was wrong. "But they taught us that all shifters stayed within their own groups all the time."

His laugh is rich, and he gives me a delighted expression. "Oh, Fi. That's like... old folklore crap. Bigger collectives like I mentioned form their groups, but *lots* of species have melded groups. Again, it's just dependent on how big the population is in any city. And all the groups, even the mixed ones, get seats on local shifters councils. Obviously, the larger groups hold sway because of their populations, but we all get to take part. There are even smaller groups, like mythical shifters or bird shifters or aquatic shifters. Banding together gives us more votes."

"Holy fucking shirt balls," I mutter. "*Everything* I know about shifters is off. Is it that way about the other supes?" I look over at him with amazement, wondering if those old farts on the witch council truly screwed us up this badly.

"Possibly? I mean, the four Courts of the Fae are what you'd expect. Vamps and their ilk are probably how you learned. The general species haven't changed in centuries, so I doubt their info on them is off. But you might find that smaller sects have been misrepresented. I'm happy to help you learn, Fiadh. I can tell it's bothering you."

"How?"

A gentle smile is his answer as he holds our hands up. "You're going to break it if you don't ease off. I mean, I can heal it if I shift, but..."

Dropping his hand with a gasp, I back up and give him a stern look. He just grins and I shake my head. "Tiernan, tell me stuff. Don't be afraid to speak up. Look at how stupid I would have looked at this party if you hadn't offered to give me a run-down. I would have been so much more upset about looking dumb than I would be about you telling me not to break your freaking hand!"

"Okay, okay," he says as he holds his hands up in defeat. "Message received: tell you things even if they make you mad. Got it."

My voice is soft as I look up at him through my lashes. "I have an extremely hard time trusting people because of how we grew up. Feray and I try hard to be honest with each other, even if we have to cushion it a little to protect each other. That's probably more me than her, but we don't lie to each other. If you're going to be my mate..." I swallow hard and push the words out. "Do the same. Understand?"

Stepping closer, the snow leopard places a hand on my cheek, tilting my head back. His free hand brushes a few wisps off my forehead and he places a soft kiss there. When he looks at me again, he nods. "I understand. And in that vein, you should know that I swapped with another bodyguard to make sure I'm on the Prince's detail more often, which means I'll be at the club a lot. Hopefully, that doesn't make you too mad, but I felt like I couldn't focus on my charges if I was worried about you."

Again, I'm completely gobsmacked and I have no idea how to respond—this is becoming a habit.

Fighting against my inclination to scold him for assuming I can't take care of myself, I draw in a deep breath. If what we're learning about mates is true, the need to protect is *very* strong in shifters, especially predators. Tiernan is trying to be honest about how he felt and what he did to make it easier; he's not asking me to quit or live in a bubble. That alone means he took my feelings into consideration and I should do the same.

Learning to people is fucking bullshit.

I lean into his palm, enjoying the warmth before I reply. "I appreciate you telling me and that you didn't just try to force me to do something else so you didn't have to worry. Did asking for that change hurt you at work?"

He snorts. "Absolutely not. Most of the bodyguards *hate* being in the Prince's detail. He's surrounded by boot-licking groupies and fans, stays out all hours, gets wasted when he's bored, and frequently acts like a fucking brat. I practically got a promotion for asking."

"Oh." I grin a little and put a hand on his chest. "Well, good, then. That means I can see you more often in a place where I feel comfortable. That will help."

That earns me a suspicious look. "You feel comfortable in a vampire BDSM den? *That's* a safe place?"

Eyes dancing, I smirk at him. "Definitely. I'm bent like a paperclip, Tiernan. That world is based entirely on consent and trust, which though I struggle with, it helps me feel in control. Plus, anywhere I get to beat the shit out of drunken morons when they step out of line gets an immediate 'yes' vote from me. You should keep that in mind for later."

"I knew I should have brought a notepad," he mutters. I laugh and he yanks me closer, dropping a kiss on my lips. "Behave. We have to go see all these people from my work and I'd prefer *not* to arrive with a stiffy."

Laughter bubbles up again and I cover my mouth when the giggles break. *Goddess, I sound like Fer; what the fuck is happening to me?* It's his turn to look amused and I glare. "Don't even say it. And what do you mean, people from work?"

"The group of cats all work for the same company—we own it. So all the guys and chicks who are part of the security firm will be here. We're not celebrating the end of hibernating or a holiday as much as the change of season. I'm fine in the cold, but most of them aren't cold weather lovers. It's a big party when the weather starts to change."

I pause, digesting that for a moment when something occurs to me. "Fuck. You've shared a ton and I haven't done much besides admit I've been unwillingly sheltered. That's not right."

Moving away, he grabs my hand to start walking again and he shrugs. "I'm okay with you letting me in at whatever speed works for you, Fi. Don't put words in my mouth or I'll think of something better."

Damn. There went my concentration. Shit.

"Dirty pool, Tiernan," I growl as I shake my head to clear it. "But thanks. Maybe it'd be easier if you ask me something and I can tell you if I feel okay answering?"

"Hmm. I don't want to bring up anything hard, so I'll try to stick to easy stuff. What's your favorite movie?"

"*That's* easy?" I gape at him then turn back to the path through the woods. "I mean, I'm going to need more information. Which genre? What era? Can I list the top five? Do we mean entertainment or quality? I can't just spout off something like that!"

His hand squeezes mine and he chuckles. "I don't suppose books or music would be any different, right?"

"Uh, *no*," I reply quickly. "I mean, there's so much to love. And it's not all, like, award-worthy, but it's still fun, you know?"

"I think I opened a big can of worms." He squints over at me. "Just tell me Star Wars, not Star Trek."

I give him a look like he's lost his marbles. "*Duh.*"

"We're off to a good start, then." Tiernan is quiet for a minute and then he asks, "How about your favorite Christmas movie?"

"*Die Hard!*"

That earns me a broad smile and he pumps his fist in the air. "Perfect. If you'd said something sappy, I would have been very disappointed."

I roll my eyes and heave a giant sigh as I prepare to admit something only my sister knows. "If you tell anyone this, I'll skin you and wear your fur for a coat like a fucked up Disney movie. You understand?"

He arches a brow but nods. "Okay."

"I really love that fucking *Love, Actually* movie and it makes me watery even though it's full of garbage assumptions and stupid phobias." My nose wrinkles as I glare ahead in annoyance. "There. I said it."

That stops him again and he just looks at me with a shocked expression. "Really?"

"*Yes*," I grit out. "I actually believe in love and shit... I just can't believe it happens to people like me. Now shut up and start walking again."

I can tell he's smothering a chuckle when he replies, "Yes, ma'am."

Huh. I kinda like that.

That will be useful later.

24

Feray

The bears can definitely party.

Music, food, and drinks of all kinds flow like a raging river. Torben keeps pulling me to dance with him with every change to a slow song. Otherwise, I'm dancing with the females of the sleuth since it's improper for the males to dance with mated or spoken for females. A slow, sultry song comes on and my wolf takes over, moving my body in time with the sexy beat. Every thump, I arch my back and imagine my mate's hands guiding my movements. Closing my eyes, I keep swaying in time with the bass.

He's watching...

My wolf's tone is pitched low, and a whine escapes her lips. Soon, there's a heat at my back and the scent of sandalwood floods my senses and a real whine escapes me.

"Shhh, little wolf, I've got you." His cheek is pressed against mine from behind, and his arms are wrapped around me tightly.

"Why?" It comes out more breathy than I had intended. *Why does my body feel like it's on fire? Why do I crave him more than any male before him?* My hands cling to his forearms like a lifeline, afraid to let go.

His bear lets out a deep, pleased rumble, and he nuzzles my cheek. "It's the pull of the bond. It's why I said I was having a hard time holding it together. The pull is impossible to ignore, even harder to delay."

He nips my shoulder, and my core flutters in response. My breathing is becoming labored as his scent thickens around me. Boldly, I spin in his arms and press my nose under his jaw and inhale deeply. His scent is driving me insane. My wolf keeps repeating the word *mate* in my head.

"Get a room," his brother Logan yells.

Stifling a growl, I pull away and search the crowd. *I really need to talk to my sister about this insane pull.* Maybe she can help me stop thinking with my lady bits.

"Fi left with her mate shortly after you started dancing with the girls. Remember?" Torben supplies as he watches me look around.

"Oh, yeah, she did." Biting my bottom lip, I stare at him as my eyes shift and it's becoming more difficult to keep my wolf from taking over. She wants to complete the bond more than I do, and I didn't think that was possible.

"Let's take a walk so you can clear your head. All the pheromones must be driving you insane." Torben steps back and offers me his hand.

I smile at his thoughtfulness and allow him to lead me off into the woods. We walk for several hundred yards before I have control of my wolf. Breathing easier, my head slowly clears and I am no longer being driven by my primal urges. Tugging on his arm at the field edge, I make him stop and face me. "It's been almost two weeks. How have you kept it together all this time?"

His brilliant smile makes my heart leap in my chest and the butterflies flutter in my stomach. He rubs the back of his neck and he blushes. "Many cold showers and dips in the local river."

"I'm sorry." Looking down, I feel horrible for him having suffered this long waiting for me. A whine escapes my lips again when I think I've caused him pain.

Torben drops to his knees and pulls me to him so I can look into his glowing amber eyes. "I would go through those weeks a million times to be with you."

His sincerity makes my heart flip-flop and a rogue tear rolls down my cheek. Bending down, I kiss his lips softly, pushing the budding feelings of joy and maybe even the first tendrils of love to him. To have a mate is eternal, unconditional love; it's a blessing and a gift from the Goddess.

Torben kisses me back passionately before he stands up, taking me with him. Instinctively, I want to be closer, so I wrap my legs around him. One large hand cups my ass, holding me in place while the other splays across my back.

Breaking the kiss, I nip his bottom lip and smile. "Chase me."

A wicked grin crosses his lips as the glow of his bear intensifies. He double checks with me as I unbutton the top buttons on my dress collar. "You know what that means?"

Sliding down his body, I walk a few feet away. The dress hits the ground and my wolf rips free of my body. Dropping on my forelegs, I let a playful bark out and wag my tail, waiting to see what he will do. "I do. Catch me if you can."

Torben pulls his shirt over his head and drops his pants quickly. His massive cock juts out as I watch the beast take over. Gone is the man that had stood before me; he's replaced by a massive Kodiak bear. He rears up on his hind paws and bellows before landing and shaking the earth beneath my feet.

Turning quickly, I take off like I've been shot out of a cannon. My paws grip the earth beneath me, sending me flying over the land-scape faster than I ever could have imagined. The stream ahead gives me the perfect opportunity to lose Torben for a few moments. Leaping at the edge of the water, I sail over to the other side, landing on the soft bank. I run up the sandy beach and hide behind a juniper bush to see when my mate makes it here.

Remaining crouched close to the ground, I wait to see his huge bear lumber to the stream. He lifts his head several times, trying to catch my scent. Thankfully, the peat bog not far behind me smells strong enough to mask my scent. The minute he turns his back, I launch out of my hiding place and land on his back. Channeling my sister, I decide to step out of my comfort zone and shift back when I jump off. Standing here naked with a charging bear takes some massive balls of steel, but I know he won't hurt me.

Torben shifts back to his human form and scoops me up, carrying me. Not being able to resist anymore, I bite at his chest and nuzzle his neck. His bear makes a rumbling sound that gets louder the more attention I pay to him. Excited giggles bubble up as I hold on to my mate. The slap of his bare foot hitting wood jostles me. The cracking of wood and the impact of something heavy falling makes me finally turn my head away from his face. He kicked in the door to a log cabin and I'm assaulted with the thick scent of sandalwood as we enter.

He's taken me back to his den—a bear's most sacred space.

Carefully, Torben sets me down, letting me take in his den. My senses are on high alert as I walk around the room on the pads of my feet. I scan the area and poke my head into several doors, sniff-ing. There's a master bath off the bedroom with a large shower stall. Stepping into it, I flip on the light and turn on the water in the shower. After all the running and playing, I feel gross.

My bear follows behind me, grabbing towels and washcloths. For a man his size, he moves incredibly silently. I test the water several more times before deciding the temperature is perfect. I've never been a hot water person unless my muscles are insanely sore, or I need to relax before bed, so lukewarm it is.

Tilting my head back, I let the water fall down on me and soon I feel a soapy washcloth on me. Reverently, he washes every inch of my body, his hands firm but gentle. He massages the arch of my feet, eliciting a moan of relief from me. When I look down, a satisfied smirk plays upon his lips.

"Are you real? Am I dreaming? If I am, I never want to wake up." The words fall from my lips as I look down at him with my human eyes.

"I'm very real. Bears are raised to protect and serve their mates. A happy, well cared for mate is a point of pride for us." He kisses my calf, knee, then upper thigh. "Your pleasure, your joy, are my chief priority. Safety is the only thing that will trump the other two."

He says the words as his lips hover over my sex. His hand slides my leg over his shoulder, resting my calf against his back. His tongue slips free from his lips and elongates and reaches out, lapping at my folds.

Arching back against the tiles, my hand finds the rail to my right to help me balance. I watch him shift his tongue to his bears as he angles my hips and delves his tongue deep within me. "Cheater…"

Thrust after thrust, I feel my muscles tighten around his tongue. Just before my orgasm crashes over me, he pulls his tongue free and smiles at me. "Not yet, little wolf. You're still dirty."

A satisfied, playful grin plays on his lips as he picks the wash cloth back up, returning to clean every inch of me. His lips wrap around a nipple as he slides my leg down, letting me stand again. I take this opportunity to reach down and take his length in my hand and give him a firm stroke. His hand comes down and he gently removes my hand from him.

He kisses my cheek, then presses his lips close to my ear. "This is about you, little wolf. When I come, it will be buried deep within you with my teeth sunk into your shoulder."

I damn near come just hearing the words fall from his lips. A needy whine echoes in the shower and he pulls back to look at me.

"Patience, little wolf, all in good time." He licks my throat as his hand slides down and his fingers find my greedy core. His thick finger slides in and hooks up as he slides his finger deeper.

"I need you." I've never had a male make me whine or beg for sex. This is a first. My wolf is pushing me to climb him like a tree and ride him to exhaustion. My gums burn as my canines descend slowly, and I lean forward and grip his shoulder in my mouth.

That one motion snaps the last thread of his control and he withdraws his finger, leaving me hollow. Torben picks me up, placing my back against the wall. "I wanted to take my time, but I can't wait."

"Then don't." I bite his shoulder harder, almost breaking the skin. I need this as much as he does and I can feel him moving to line himself up.

The fat, hot head of his cock rubs over my wet silken folds before he pushes his way in. Every inch electrifies my core, and a warmth moves through me. So damn full it's almost painful. I give him a tentative wiggle, and he slams me down to the base. Crying out, I lean forward and sink my teeth deep into his chest, over his heart. Sparks shoot through me and my core clenches down around him.

Torben can't hold back any longer and starts moving. Long, slow, deep thrusts push me the rest of the way over the edge. In my heart, I can feel him and his bear. Love floods the bond and I feel whole for the first time in my life. I release his chest and throw my head back, howling through my release.

His thrusts become erratic before he buries himself deep within me, his canines grip my shoulder, then break the skin. Burning pain, then peace and warmth. The insane drive and need to complete the bond is gone, replaced with the urge to snuggle up and sleep with him. He finally releases my shoulder and reaches back to turn off the shower.

We catch our breath and, without skipping a beat; he carries me through the house and lays me down on his bed. His member slides free, and he bends forward and kisses my lips before vanishing for a few moments. He returns with a washcloth and a dry towel. Carefully, he cleans me and pats me dry before pulling the covers over me. Disappearing again for a few more moments, he returns with a bottle of water and offers it to me.

I motion to the bathroom, then look back at him as I take a long drink. "I've never been taken care of after."

Torben climbs into bed and slides next to me. I place the water on the nightstand and snuggle in close, resting my head on his chest. "That's because they didn't love you like I do." He kisses the top of my head and wraps his arms around me.

It's almost like an automatic off switch. The minute I feel safe, I fall asleep being held by my mate.

I RACE HOME as my wolf since she moves faster than my human form ever could.

Torben begged me to stay with him, and it physically hurt to leave him. I explained to him I had to go. It's my first week at my new job.

The conversation plays over again in my head and I feel a little better knowing he understood in the end. Just as my front paws hit the deck, I shift back and open the door, walking through the house naked.

I don't have time to be modest. I am so far behind, it's not even funny.

"Fer, is that you?" Fi calls from her room as I streak past the door.

"Yeah, I lost track of time." I yell as I decide to put my work outfit under an oversized zip up sweatshirt I bought at the thrift store. Digging through the closet, I find a long thin cotton skirt to cover the fishnets.

"It's not like you to stay out all night." Fi gives me that look that she knows what's up.

"Sorry." I tilt my head and adjust my skirt. If I'm honest with myself, maybe I should have skipped round three just before I left.

"Mmmm. Have a good night?" Fi gets closer as I grab my bag heading towards the door, trying to avoid the conversation.

"Yeah, Torben is a great guy. His family is very welcoming and affectionate." I get Fi out the door and head towards the trail.

Gripping my arm, Fi stops me. "Where's the fire?"

"We're late for work." I pull away now that I'm stronger than she is, and start back down the trail again.

"Okay. But you promise nothing is wrong, right? He didn't hurt you, did he?" The concern in her voice is genuine.

"He would never hurt me. He can't.. He's my mate. Ask Tiernan about mates. He'll tell you." A violent growl escapes my lips. *So angry...* Fi insinuating that Torben would harm me set my hackles on edge. I take a bit to get my anger under control. Slowly, I draw in several deep breaths before I force a smile. "Excited about seeing your mate at work tonight?"

Deflect and distract. Maybe she won't notice the bite mark. Hopefully, it fades enough before we get in the door.

A yawn escapes my lips as we pass Louie on the way in. For all of my false bravado, I am exhausted. I should have called out for tonight, but I won't leave Fi here alone. In the locker room, I grab my assigned necklace and tag from the hook it's hanging on. As promised, it says 'Bubbles' and has a crescent moon denoting me as a wolf shifter.

Without thinking about it, I take off my skirt and sweatshirt. The crash of something hitting the floor behind me makes me turn to face it. Fi has that *'I'm gonna bust your balls'* look on her face. "Good night last night? Something you need to tell me?" Her voice is too damn musical. I swear sometimes she's part Fae.

"Yes, and no. You obviously see the mating mark." Spinning on my heel, I head to the bar and start my shift.

Not even thirty minutes in, Dezi calls requesting a bloody martini extra dirty. Under the bar, there's a closed compartment with glasses that only the boss uses. Using the key he had given me, I take out his favorite martini glass that has rubies that line the rim of the glass.

He's just a little too fancy sometimes.

I take out the glass stirrer and slowly mix the blood into the martini just the way he likes it. After all, bruised platelets apparently taste bad. Passing Mo, I show him the glass and he understands where I'm going. Heading down the bar and to the office doors, I use my keycard to get into the private area that is forbidden.

Tonight's number of knocks is four according to the order. Knocking on the door, I wait till I hear the buzz then push it open. "Here's your drink, just how you like it. Stirred gently with more blood than booze."

His eyes go from human to brilliant crimson. In a matter of seconds, he's on me and I snap the stem of the glass in my hand. Dezi yanks my hand up and pulls the glass shard free as he breathes in deeply. His eyes lock with mine then drop to the bite mark before he shoves me away. Backing up to the door, I open it quickly. Something about the look in his eyes frightens me, so I run back towards the main part of the club.

Looking over my shoulder, I don't watch where I'm going and run into my sister. She sees the blood in my hand though, amazingly, the wound is almost healed already. "Fer, what happened?"

"I brought Dezi his drink. You know, the martini that's more blood than booze." Fi nods then motions for me to continue as she helps me to my feet. "I brought it in and his eyes ignited and blazed blood red. Next thing I knew, he had my wrist in his hand and I shattered the stem of his glass, sending blood and glass everywhere. He pulled the glass from my hand then shoved me towards the door."

Fi grits her teeth and I know it means my sister is going to war. "Stay here," she spits out

That said, she storms down the hallway.

I'm not sure if this is a good thing or an awful one.

25

FIADH

Rage ignites like fire in my veins as I stomp down the back hallway. I *knew* working at a vamp club might be dangerous, but they billed this place as a *safe haven* because of all the rules and regulations that come with BDSM. I felt comfortable after Dezi's orientation, and I allowed myself to believe his line of bullshit. And then what happens? The *minute* I'm not watching that platelet drinking asshole goes after my sister!

I yank the immense doors to his office open with energy vibrating over my limbs like someone electrocuted me. Reaching into my pocket as I burst inside, I slip my hands into my favorite brass knuckles and prepare to unleash all the anger inside of about the past few weeks on a *very* deserving target. "What in the *fuck* did you think you were *doing?*"

His eyes widen like huge glittering rubies as he looks at me. I'm surprised to see that despite the sharp fangs and altered countenance, he's as hot as ever. Tilting my head to crack my neck, I stride up to his desk as I push away those forbidden thoughts. It doesn't matter if he's a goddamn vampire Chippendale's dancer—he tried to hurt my sister and for that, he's going to pay. I don't care if he fires us, and I don't care if I end up in jail.

No one gets away with hurting Feray while I still breathe.

"I *said*, what in the merry fucking hell did you think you were doing, Dezi?!"

This time, the corner of his lips quirks as he watches me stand there with my fists raised and body tensed for battle. "I could ask you the same thing, witchling."

Tremors coast over me as I feel that new power unfurl within me and travel through my body. I have to be careful, but my fury is making it hard. Toasting one of the oldest vamps in town, even accidentally, would not be good. I won't be able to scramble out of here before someone gets a hold of me like in the restaurant. So I swallow hard and grit my teeth. "You tried to bite Feray! What happened to all of your *safe words?*"

The air in the room shifts and his eyes narrow as he tilts his head and sniffs, just like my sister does. Slowly, he stalks around the desk, still watching me as he bends to pick up one piece of glass still on the ground. Once he has it, he rises and scents the scarlet streaked stem. "She dropped a glass. I did not hurt her."

My patience with his quiet, predatory act is wearing thin. "She broke it because you were going to attack her!"

"Untrue. I was startled, and she is unused to her shifter strength, so she snapped the glass by mistake," he replies smoothly as his eyes coast over me.

The intensity of his gaze unnerves me, so I re-grip the knuckles and move closer. "But you're a vampire. You can hear shit in other towns. She wasn't quiet. How did she surprise you?"

"I knew she was approaching, but..." His voice trails off as he shakes his head, looking frustrated. "When she came in with my drink, I was—I simply had a moment. I did not mean to scare her, Fiadh."

He sounds sincere, but there's something about his words and his tone that says he's still hiding the truth.

"What do you mean 'you had a moment'? You promised us that working here was safe and that nothing would ever happen without our consent!" A tingling sensation runs up my spine and when I look at my hands, tiny sparks of energy are dancing over the ridges of my knuckle dusters.

Well, that's fucking new.

"Fiadh, you need to control your magic. It's leaking and it will only get worse as your anger increases," the vampire says as he eyes me seriously. "I did not lie to you about your safety. My behavior may have startled Bubbles because she's unfamiliar with my kind, but I have been alive for many years. I have not lost control and attacked someone since long before the Crusades."

Disbelief zings through me, and suddenly, I know what I need to do to learn the truth. I step closer carefully, watching his crimson eyes and fangs suspiciously. I don't know why he hasn't pushed his demon back, but since it's still present, I'm having trouble buying his words. Dezi doesn't move as I advance and he tilts his head as I come within inches of him. I reach out and take the glass, flinging it to the ground.

His brow arches when I grasp his hand. "What are you doing, witchling?"

I close my eyes as the skin to skin contact makes energy zing through me. My eyes pop open when I feel it: the truth. He really wasn't going to attack my sister. It was a miscommunication, and they both overreacted. There's something else flowing from him to me, but I can't figure it out. He hasn't vocalized it, so I can't analyze if he's lying.

"I think I'm testing you for truthfulness," I mutter when I finally look up at him.

The darkness of his demon eyes hypnotizes me, but not in the whole 'Renfield' way. Instead, I can feel a distinct pull to get closer to him. There's a magnetism trying to draw me in, and I know he can feel it, too. He licks a fang, and it makes me think of Fer when she's getting ready to devour her dinner since the wolf emerged.

Dezi is as much a predator as she is and he's eying me like a juicy filet.

"And what did you find out?"

My face turns red when his fingers caress over my palm. "You... you aren't lying about what happened."

"What else?" His lips curve up and he looks amused as his fingertips continue moving over my hand. The tiny motions are making me shiver, but I don't pull away. It's almost like I can't.

"Ummm. Just that. I mean, if this is... magic... I'm getting? I don't know how to control it yet." My face turns bright red and the urge to hide it makes me growl a little. It's not normal for me to admit weaknesses and definitely not to some fanged up bloodsucker who is my *boss*.

He narrows his eyes. "That. What were you thinking right then? Your energy changed."

Fucking seriously? Can he sense energy and scent shit?

I frown as I remember the fuckwits at school messed up all of our shifter knowledge, and it's very possible this vampire can do a host of shit I don't know about. Yanking my hand away, I look at him distrustfully as I wipe my palm on my tight leather pants. "I was thinking about how inappropriate it is to be holding my boss's hand in a private room in a sex club."

My words clearly fluster him and he spins away, turning towards one of the heavy inlaid bookcases on the wall. "Yes. You're correct. I apologize."

A zing of energy smacks into me, and I frown. He definitely did *not* mean that. *Holy fuck, how am I doing that without touching him?* I slip my brass knuckles off and put them in my pockets before I clasp my hands together. This whole encounter is so fucking weird and I have no idea what is going on with my magic.

Suddenly, Dezi turns around again and his eyes are wide. "What's wrong, witchling?"

"I don't know," I mutter. "I'll clean this up and go."

Dropping to the floor, I pick up the shards carefully, but my hands are shaking. I end up cutting myself on the biggest one and I hiss at the sting. "Fuck!"

Before I can stick my finger in my mouth to clean it off, the vampire is beside me. He grasps my finger and closes his lips over it as he looks at me. His eyes are so red they're almost black and the sound that escapes his mouth makes my lower stomach clench. That odd feeling comes back and my skin gets hot as his tongue cleans the droplets off of the digit.

The wet swipe over my skin makes my pussy clench and I suck in a ragged breath. It makes him snarl again and I feel the brush of a fang opening the cut more. My mind races as I get hotter, an intense desire for more rocketing through my body as he suckles. I swallow hard, knowing I have to put a stop to this. I have a mate, one I haven't even done more than kiss, and Dezi is my freaking boss. Everything about this is so very wrong, but it feels so right that I'm having trouble focusing.

You taste like fine wine... The voice that echoes in my head makes me gasp. I know it's his, but I have no idea how this is happening.

"Uh… th-thank you?" I stutter. The pull I feel intensifies as he scoots closer and I'm staring into those glittering red orbs so deeply you'd think I could see his soul. "I… I… don't do anything special…"

His countenance changes, the demon getting more prominent, and suddenly, he pulls away with a look of shock on his face. I'm still kneeling by the tiny pile of crystal on the floor, breathing hard as I watch him back away in horror. My hand shakes as I bring it to my chest, cradling it as I watch him struggle. He lifts his hand and points at me.

"You… you…"

My temper flares and I stand up, giving him an infuriated look. "Me, what? What did I do?" He doesn't answer, and it triggers all the feelings of rejection I've experienced lately. That makes the power flare under my skin again and I stalk towards him., "Me what? You were the one *sucking on my finger!*"

Shame flits over his expression and he growls softly. "You cut yourself!"

"Well, yeah, dickface! It's sort of my fucking job!"

"No, it's not!"

"Oh, really? Well, *enlighten me* as to what my job is and it better not be a quick bite between meals!" The two of us stare at one another, squaring off in yet another standoff. I highly doubt this one is going to end as well as the first because I'm practically vibrating with hurt and anger. I won't let him distract me from it this time.

Dezi stands up straighter, adjusting his collar with a deep breath before he speaks. "You are correct again, Fiadh. Your job is to do things such as that and I was inappropriate—yet again. I will leave you to it."

With a nod of his head, he backs away, grabbing a book on the shelf. The damn thing opens like we're in an Agatha Christie movie and my vampire boss disappears inside like he's fucking Batman before it closes. I'm left staring at the wall like an idiot, wondering what in the holy hell just happened.

My boss just sucked blood off of my finger and spoke in my head like he'd always been there.

I rub my face with the non-bloody hand, trying to process that plus the weird truth magic and the incident with Fer all at once. It's almost too much—everything that's happened, the mates thing, blood, mind speech? I'm going to lose my goddamn mind if the world doesn't quit throwing bricks at me over and over.

But what do I do now? I don't want to quit and Dezi swept off like a drama queen, so I have no idea what any of this shit means.

Maybe Tiernan's arrived. If I ask him, he might be able to tell me what that shit all meant. And he won't be a jerk when I ask him, so it won't make me feel stupider.

A smile comes over my face as I look at the pile of glass again and decide to ignore it. *You break it, you bought it, asshole.* Turning, I stride out of the office with my bloody hand tucked in my pocket so I don't accidentally tempt someone with even less control than my boss. If some idiot like Louie approached me right now, I wouldn't be able to do the responsible thing and not stake the living shit out of them.

All I need to do now is check on Fer and see if Tiernan is here so I can ask him all the shit swirling around in my head.

Next time I see that vamp, though... I'm going to knee him in the balls as hard as I can.

That should be a good enough revenge for the moment.

26

—

FERAY

I check the clock again as I wait for Fi to return. My pacing the mat for the millionth time between drink orders is driving my co-worker insane. Mo and I cleaned and restocked the bar, got ice, and he even let me in on a secret. There's something in shifter saliva, especially canine and felines, that heals wounds almost instantly. That explains why the bite I gave Torben healed moments after I licked it, versus his that took almost an hour to heal. Mo could be a good friend candidate if he weren't such a vain asshole. Then again, from what I've learned, foxes are narcissists and demand the spotlight in order to be happy.

I move to the end of the bar, switching places with Mo as I wait for Fi to return. His section is not as neat as mine, so I have to fix it before I can work. Every time I get stressed, I clean, so I don't give him shit about his half-assed job. Half way through resetting the bar, the hall door slams. My eyes catch Fi coming out of the office, looking visibly shaken. Jumping over the swinging door, I cross the room in seconds. Grabbing Fi, I look her over head to toe, making sure she's in one piece. "I smell blood. What happened?"

Several newer vamps' eyes shift and they stare in our direction at my words. Baring my teeth, I shift my eyes to wolven in warning. They back off immediately, returning to the entertainment for the night. My wolf is on edge, so I keep the younger vamps in my line of sight while I wait for my sister to speak.

Job be damned, I will bite every leech in here if I have to.

"I cut my finger on the glass in Dezi's office." Her terse answer and the mixed scents coming off her speak volumes. Magic, arousal, anger, and emotional pain make an acrid scent I will never forget.

A growl escapes my lips as I lead my sister to the storage room behind the bar. Mo is quick to pour Fi's favorite single malt scotch in a highball glass and follow me. He passes me the drink, then closes the door. *I guess he wants to live, after all.*

Fi downs it in one shot. She sits on the couch in the corner and pulls her legs up to her chest. Slowly, her aura settles and her scent changes. "Thanks. I needed that."

I still don't see the blood and it's making me more anxious by the minute. "Where's the blood, Fi?"

She holds her finger up and I see the cut that looks extended by a fang. Narrowing my eyes, I stare at it before I look up at her. "I'm getting Tiernan. I could heal this for you, but I think he'll want to do it."

Fi opens her mouth, but I snarl at her. "Keep your ass here; I'm getting your mate."

I motion at her hand and my canines descend. Her eyes widen, noting my teeth and wolven eyes. I'm so mad I can't control my animal, so she nods. *It's my fault she got hurt; I should have bit Dezi and been done with it.* But no, I ran like I always do. Seeing Fi injured now, I feel differently.

My wolf is an equal presence in my mind—her strength and resolve are mine to wield as mine are hers.

Turning on my heel, I leave before Fi can get a word in. I glare at Mo as I slam the door behind me. I jab my finger in the stockroom's direction and damn near bark an order. "No one goes in there. Do you understand me?"

He cringes, but finally lowers his eyes and submits. Tilting my head to the side, I hide my amazement when he's not able to make eye contact with me.

That's new.

I walk around the bar and through the lower level of the club, scenting for Tiernan. In theory, he should be upstairs, but if his client wanted a private show, he might be downstairs. By the time I finish searching, my wolf has subsided and I look completely human. Deciding he's not down here, I take the gilded stairs to the VIP room two at a time—it's packed with the Fae Prince and his legion of followers. Their combined scents send my senses into overdrive. Finally, the familiar spicy scent of my sister's mate catches my attention and I sigh in relief. Walking along the edge of the platform, the smell gets stronger, so I know I'm on the right track.

Voices flitter in and out of clarity as I hunt for my sister's mate. The words 'dog', 'mutt', and 'bitch' wash over me like water off my back. Brainless twits parroting each other's petty insults for clout crack me up; I don't have time for their childish bullshit. Something in me snapped when I saw my strong sister in the state she was at the bar. I'll have to unpack that revelation once I know she's safe with Tiernan.

A dipshit grabs my hair and yanks, but I'm not in the mood for games. Spinning on my heel, I'm face to face with the same Fae groupie who mouthed off at the restaurant. My wolf surges forward and she scrambles backward. Unlike Mo, she's not submitting, but she's also not carrying on like before. I want to bare my teeth and scare her more, but I see Prince Revelin and Tiernan just past her rat's nest of hair.

Instead of engaging, I shoulder check her. It knocks her down, and I grin to myself as I move through the crowd. Dipping my head in the Prince's direction, I lock eyes with Tiernan. I tilt my head to the side, indicating I need to speak with him privately. He leans in and speaks with the Prince. When the royal nods, Tiernan stands. Closing the distance between us, the leopard takes my arm gently to pull me away from everyone.

"What happened? Is Fiadh okay?" His tone is low as he glances around. Concern is putting his cat on edge and I scent it strongly now.

"That's a two-fold answer. Physically, yes—other than a cut on her finger. Emotionally is a different matter, and that's why I'm here."

For once, I'm the 'serious, take no shit' sibling and he notices the change immediately. My wolf is restless as I search the crowd then look down at the bar area. Mo doesn't have a sizable crowd, and I don't see Fi. Turning back, I watch emotions flitter over Tiernan's features. Rage is one of them and that cements my belief that he's good for my sister.

"Take me to her." He glances at another feline bodyguard and does some sort of hand signal before he looks at me again.

"Keep up." No sooner are the words out of my mouth, I'm sprinting down the stairs faster than I normally would. *Being one with my wolf may have cured me of my klutziness; I'll be damned.* I have to hand it to Tiernan, though, he's right on my heels.

Mo glances at me, moving out of the way quickly. "No one tried to go back there, and she didn't come out."

Arching a brow, Tiernan gives me a questioning look. He must know I don't like the fox.

"I lost my temper and put him on guard duty."

"She pulled an Alpha move," the other bartender hisses, still unable to look at me. His words draw another growl from my wolf and I slap my hand over my mouth.

Tiernan steps into my personal space, his expression curious. "Hold my gaze."

Shrugging my shoulders, I look deep into his eyes, watching the colors change until I'm faced with his cat's eyes. A wave of something moves over me and it pisses my wolf off. She surges forward and makes her presence known.

We break our gaze at the same time and he laughs. "Well, damn. I wasn't expecting that."

"Expecting what?" I ask as I pour my sister a second malt scotch. Handing it to Tiernan, I wait for his answer expectantly.

He shrugs. "You're not an alpha, but you have the sway of one. I'm not sure what that means, but I'll ask around discreetly tomorrow." He opens the door and ducks into the storage room.

Hopefully, he can help my stubborn ass sister.

Returning to my job, I mix orders with a practiced finesse. I've always loved the movie *Cocktail* where the guy did all the fancy tricks when he was pouring drinks. Several orders in, I feel eyes on me but it's not my mate. Turning to find out who's staring, I see the banker from *Pendragon Savings and Loans* sitting at the end of the bar.

When I approach, I note the founder's tag on his necklace and dip my head out of respect. I wipe the bar down in front of him and offer him my sweetest smile as I lay down a coaster and napkin. "Welcome to *Cocktails and Screams*. What can I get you?"

His eyes lock on my necklace before they find my face again. Eyes flicker to serpentine slits for a second as he stares silently. His gruff tone doesn't match his handsome face as he says, "A fresh Manhattan— don't make it boring."

"As you wish." I leave the quotable sentence hanging with a grin to myself.

Looking around until I find the fancy 'Founders' martini glasses, I select one that looks absolutely primal. The dark, gothic feel of the glass would be a good fit for the grumpy eye candy at the end of the bar. Oddly enough, my wolf doesn't like me calling him eye candy and I'm puzzled when I feel him watching me again.

Stifling a laugh at his arrogance, I decide to pull out all my tricks. I never got to do this stuff at Philly's because the clientele didn't care.

Finding the *Wild Turkey 180* and other higher proof fine liquors to make his drink is easy because Dezi's bar is so extra. The music downstairs changes and I draw inspiration from it. We have frozen cherries, so I drop them into the glass with a grin. Next, I use the smoker to burn some cherry wood to leave a rich cherry smoke floating over the top of a glass. Leaving the smoked glass on top of the drink glass, I carry it over to him. Before I remove the cover, I slide on my finger strikers to ignite the drink.

"You get an 'A' for originality," he says begrudgingly.

Before he can touch the stem, I remove the smoked glass and snap my fingers. It ignites the drink, and he jumps back slightly. Feeling bold, I wink at him before I turn away. He stares at the drink before blowing out the flames. After one sip, I hear a pleased moan— apparently my choice of flavors was correct. For some fucked up reason, his quiet praise me makes me extremely happy.

Maybe I have a praise kink after all.

My phone goes off in my apron, distracting me from the banker. Torben texted to ask how my first night at work is going. I give him a short recap of the night and he tells me he misses me. We chat back and forth about little things between my customers until it's time for him to go to sleep. I stare at my phone, wishing I was with him as he fell asleep.

Sighing, I glance at the closed door to the stockroom. My sister needs me, too. I'm torn, but she needs to let Tiernan in.

Then we can both have our happily ever after.

27

FIADH

HOLDING MY HAND TO MY MOUTH, I GLARE AT THE STOCKROOM shelves. I'm not used to my sister ordering me around, and I definitely don't think this stupid cut needs to be examined. Sure, an over-hyped bloodsucker made it worse, and I *let* him, but that's not a problem for Tiernan. That's *my* bullshit to deal with. Even if you asked me right now, I couldn't tell you why I allowed that shit to go on, except that I know I wasn't bespelled or whatever those platelet sucking assholes do.

Of course, I don't even know if they can *do that because our education at our supposed 'school' was so biased.*

The uncertainty is making me cranky, and waiting isn't helping. I'm not the 'sit around and ponder' shit kind of girl; I take action and if I need to, I ask for forgiveness later. It might not be the healthiest way to deal with my problems, but it's what I've got as far as coping skills. If people don't like it, they can fuck right off until they hit the ocean and take a deep dive to the bottom. I'm not here to make other people happy; they sure as *fuck* have never considered Fer and I.

I'm solidly in the middle of my mental rant when the door swings open and I see the usually calm Tiernan standing in the doorway, sniffing the air. His features flicker, giving me a glimpse of the long feline fangs of his cat, and he strides forward, slamming the oak door behind him as if it offended his ancestors. The gentle brown eyes of my supposed mate are gone—all I see are icy, glowing blue orbs glaring into the darkness. His steps are heavy as he stalks in and grabs my hand, examining it carefully. His features shift though the rest of him does not and a large, rough tongue laps over the cut slowly.

Holy shit, I felt that in my goddamn ovaries.

Sucking in a breath, I hold perfectly still as he looks at my finger and my pussy clenches. The air in here feels warmer, and I know my cheeks are flushed. It's taking every bit of my self-control not to touch him; in fact, I'm biting my lip to keep a whimper from escaping. I don't know what the fuck that simple lick did, but I've never felt the need to ride a dick so badly in my entire life. There's no way I'm not ruining these fucking pants, that's for damn sure.

I would choose today to wear a thong, wouldn't I?

My gut tightens as he stares and I can't stand the silence anymore. Flashes of snow leopard porn are running through my mind at light speed and if I don't get this train back on the rails, I won't be held responsible for what I do next. Gritting my teeth, I force words out, but my voice is raspy as hell. "It's not a big deal. I cut my finger on the glass Feray broke when she was startled."

The partially shifted cat's eyes whip up to mine, and he tilts his head, scenting the air. He makes an odd yowling sound, almost like a kitty moan, and his hold tightens on my hand. "It's torn?" he rumbles in a low, dark tone.

I didn't think they could talk when they shift like that and it's hot. I want him to do it again. Is that rude? I need it not to be.

"Uh, I… well, Dezi sort of licked it and his fang tore…" That gets another one of those weird leopard sounds and I hurry to distract him. The yowls are sexy, too, and I'd like to walk around the rest of the night without a sticky mess between my legs. "They told us shifters can't talk when they shift. And um, that you either, like, shift or don't? But you're… a little shifted?"

He snorts, which sounds *very* weird coming from the big cat's mouth. "Idiots. Not exactly true. Varies."

I assume he's short spoken because having the animal so close to the surface makes it a struggle to use the human part of his brain. That would make sense, biologically, so until he calms down and tells me I'm going with it. My eyes flick to my fingers and I'm surprised to see the cut completely healed and my skin unmarred. "What the hell, Tiernan?"

A slow, feral grin comes over his face as he steps closer and inhales. "Proof. Mate."

Annnnd cavecat is in the house, ladies and gentleman.

"Healing my cut is proof you were right?" He nods, advancing on me until my back is flush against the shelf behind me. His face is centimeters from mine when he licks his chops slowly. *Oh, triple Goddess, that's sexy as hell.* "So, uh, we're good then, right?"

His countenance shifts in a blink, and the handsome man is smirking at me. He has me pinned and doesn't seem eager to move soon. "More than good, Knuckles."

I frown for a minute, then I remember that the first time I met Tiernan, I was using my babies to take on that fucking walking BBQ slab. I've never been one for cutesy names, but this… it's badass, and I like it. I laugh softly, looking up at him through my lashes. "I'll allow that because it's not mushy. But you knew that, didn't you?"

"Maybe." He darts forward, pressing his lips to mine, and this time, I growl when his tongue brushes against mine. His hands land on my hips and, before I know it, I wrap my legs around his waist.

Shit, Fi, you can't do this now...

But smart Fi is not in control right now. Horny Fiadh hasn't gotten laid since before the Ascension and Tiernan is six feet of solid muscle that seems to be fucking *purring* against her chest. My nipples are ready to rocket off my chest as the vibration from his rumbles over them. I tilt my head back when our lips break, letting him run his nose along the column of my neck as I bury my fingers in his hair. There's no doubt in my mind that he wants me and I've definitely lost the plot, but he's being so careful.

Did I get lucky enough to find an alpha shifter mate that's a fucking submissive? No way the goddess is smiling at me that much.

I grab his hair and tug his head up, smirking a little as I look at him. "Tier, darling. We're going to fuck like sailors on leave and if you don't make me come at least three times, I'll be very disappointed."

Seconds tick by as I wait, and suddenly, his face lights up. "Yes, ma'am."

I am in so much trouble.

Before I can say anything else, he drops to his knees and peels my pants down my legs impatiently. I grin, lifting each one so he can toss them over his shoulder and he looks up at me with those eerie blue eyes. When I nod, he buries his face in the lacy thong with another bone melting rumble. Tiny bites with sharp teeth along the crease of my thigh make me shiver and I tighten my grip on his hair.

"More."

Tiernan slides a finger along the hem until it's inside, and I feel the brush of a claw seconds before he destroys my favorite fancy panties. *I'm going to make him pay for that,* I think to myself. His hands slide up my legs and he lifts my legs over his shoulders with a snarl, making that thought flitter away. Then he's feasting—there's no other word for it—and my eyes roll back into my head. Long, rough swipes of his tongue gather my fluids and I have to hang on when he dances it around my clit.

Every time I shudder or gasp, he seems to catalog it, repeating the motions until I'm trembling. The sensations bubble up within me so quickly that I don't even see the first orgasm until it slams into me. I bite my lip hard, hating the whimper of pleasure that escapes, but I'm not able to control it. He's so keyed into what I'm feeling that not a single move is wasted. I'm still pulling in deep breaths when two fingers slip into me, searching for the right spot to push me higher.

"Deeper. A little..." I barely get the words out before he does exactly what I was going to say and a throaty moan tumbles from me. My thighs press against his ears and I tug at his hair, liking how it makes him attack my clit with fervor. *The subbie leopard likes a smidge of pain with his pleasure.* I tuck that away for later as I ride the most talented head-giver I've met in my entire life. Anyone who let this kitty go was a fool; his feline lapping and swirling over me is making my fucking brain turn to slush.

And we haven't even fucked yet...

His hands tilt my hips back more and that's when I feel it—my magic lights up inside of me, coursing through my veins like a combination of fire, ice, and wind. The well in the center of my chest sparkles and tingles when he tugs on the steel bars above my clit gently, making me writhe even more. The pressure builds in me until I feel like I can't take it anymore, then in a burst of energy, another climax makes my entire body arch and shake.

All I can do is hold as the sensations flood my system, making me damn near incoherent. I'm pretty sure I'm babbling something, but hell if I know what. It could be ancient Sumerian for all I know—

I'm not present enough to give a solitary fuck what I'm saying. My hands tremble when the fire dims and I open my eyes, hoping I didn't just crisp the man giving me the ride of my life. When I see him smirking up at me with his face coated in my juices, I wing a thanks to the goddesses before I croak, "Get the hell up here and fuck me, Tiernan. You've earned it."

"My pleasure, Knuckles," he says before gripping my legs and lifting them off of his shoulders. I'm having trouble standing and by the preening look on his face, he knows it. He rises and lifts me again, positioning himself at my aching pussy. "Now?"

"Now!" I growl back, rocking my hips down as he slams his hips forward to bury his cock in me. It takes a moment for me to adjust to his girth, and I squeeze my muscles playfully. "Don't go shy on me now, kitty."

That earns me a fangy grin, and he pulls out, thrusting back in hard and fast. We find a rhythm and I wrap my arms around him, digging my nails into his back as I hold on. He's strong and the rocking makes the shelves teeter, but neither of us care. There's an urgency to our joining that's increasing as the power within me grows and spreads from my limbs to the air around us. Darting my head forward, I kiss him hungrily, loving the feel of his body stretching mine and his hard muscles pushing against my nipple rings. Every nerve in my body feel tuned to him as we fuck and it occurs to me that everything about this is different than I've ever felt before.

I tear my lips away and look at him as his dick sinks into me again. "This is…"

"New. Yes," he breathes as we stare at one another.

"Do you feel it?" I murmur.

His lips curl over the large feline canines and he nods. "Magic. Your magic is here."

"I don't know what it means." My head presses back against the wall when the head of cock feels like it's swelling to continually strike the same perfect place inside of me. "This is more... than it's ever..."

A hand slips between us and he tugs on the bar above my clit again, making me whine. His thumb brushes over my clit faster and faster until I tighten around him, squeezing hard as my body shoots towards another peak. "Come for me, mate. Take the barb and share my mate mark."

It should have knocked me right out of the bliss cloud but despite having no fucking clue what he means, I press my heels into his ass and nod. "Yesssss...."

Suddenly a sharp pinch inside makes my hips buck and I have the urge to bury my teeth in him. Nips along the column of my throat and his hand urge me to a spot at the crook of his neck where I bite hard. He lets out another one of those ear-splitting yowls before I feel the skin tearing in the opposing spot on me. Pain sears through me and my magic flares, sliding over my skin like a cool blast of water coating us. It helps send me over the edge and the orgasm that hits me this time damn near makes my eyes cross. Hot jets of come fill me, soothing the pinch inside, and I cling to Tiernan as if he's the only thing holding me to this plane.

When we finally come down, he smooths sweaty hairs off of my face then licks the wound on my neck with a soft purr. I give him a shy smile, not knowing what to say; I hadn't planned on this happening yet and we barely know each other. Yet he rocked my world so thoroughly I'd weep if he said this wasn't going to work out. Gently, he lets my legs down and settles me against the wall, making sure I won't fall before he walks over and grabs one of the clean bar towels. Very carefully, he uses it to clean me, his fingers nimble as he makes sure I'm not leaking.

That sort of attention makes me pleased, so I look down at him with dark eyes before I murmur, "Good boy."

The look on his face almost makes me say 'fuck this place' and head for home with him in tow, but I know I've tested the limits of how much Fer can cover for me. Tiernan takes the towel and the shredded panties, stuffing them in the inside pocket of his suit coat with a tiny grin. When I arch a brow at him, he shrugs.

"I don't want anyone else sniffing what's mine."

Well, that settles that. Fuck.

Clearing my throat, I bend to get dressed and he watches before he looks at me in a way that has my lady bits reconsidering my stay at work decision.

This guy is dangerous.

"I'll have them move you upstairs. I don't want you more than a few feet away for the rest of the night. And I'm taking you home."

Normally, I'd argue, but after that?

Sign me up, growly pants.

28

FERAY

The alarm sounds like an atom bomb going off in my head. Rolling over, I slap the alarm and smash it to pieces. *Damn shifter strength.* I still haven't gotten the hang of this part of my changes. Shaking my head, I look at what's left of the clock before getting up and cleaning the mess up.

I dig through my closet, trying to figure out what to wear for today when I remember the new outfit Torben bought me. The beautiful floral top is so soft against my skin and the loose-fitting pants have an elastic waist so I don't destroy it when I shift. Digging through the shoes at the bottom of my closet is a chore; I really need to get this organized. Several moments pass before I find the match to the sandal I have in my hand.

Stopping by the mirror, I run a brush through my long, wavy red hair. I decide to put it back in a braid to keep it out of my face. Once I feel ready, I grab my bag with my tip money in it and head for the kitchen.

Fi must have gotten up before me because her money is already in stacks, sorted by denomination. The only thing she didn't sort was the change because she hates it almost as much as people think coins are appropriate tips. My favorite hoodie hangs over the back of my chair and I slip it on before I add my money to hers.

Tiernan's scent is faint, but I know the leopard was here. Fi walks past me to the coffee pot right at the moment it finished brewing. She doesn't say anything about him climbing through her window in the middle of the night and out again before dawn.

Guess that means we're pretending today.

By the change in my sister's scent, I am eighty percent sure they are mated. She'll come to me once she's processed what happened so I'm not going to press her. There's a bounce to her step that wasn't there before and I like seeing it. With as high as my sister sets the bar for guys, he must be a hell of a bedmate.

"How did we make out?" Fi sits a cup of coffee in front of me before sitting across from me.

Shrugging my shoulders, I lift my cup to my lips, hiding how mentioning our old boss bothered me. Instead, I motion to the pile with a smile. "The club was very good to us. What we made last week is equal to what we made at Philly's place in a month."

"I have the list for the market. Whenever you're ready, I'm game."

My usually cranky sister is far too jovial this morning and I struggle to hide the grin trying to take over my face. I study her body language as she realizes how chipper she sounded and her expression closes down. Biting back a chuckle, I say, "Sure, I'll put whatever money you don't think we need away and we can get going."

Fi looks at her list, takes bills from several stacks, and shoves the money down in the front pocket of her jeans. I suddenly notice she's wearing a cutoff t-shirt for the Prince's band and I haven't seen her do that for a long time. That's yet another interesting snippet of information I'll save for later. Reaching out, I gather up the remaining money and run off to the secret hiding place Torben told me about. It will be safe there until we go to the bank.

Pushing the panel in my closet aside, I hang the bag on the nail in there before replacing it. When I come back to the dining room, I catch Fi texting like a fiend. Her thumbs are flying over the phone at the speed of light. "Ready?"

My sister damn near jumps out of her skin, tossing her phone in fright. Acting quickly, I catch it before it hits the wall.

"Fuck, Fer. You almost gave me a fucking heart attack!"

Ah, there's the Fi I know and love.

I try to hold back my laughter, but I fail miserably. "Sorry. I guess it's a shifter thing to tiptoe. Torben scares the shit out of me when he sneaks up on me, too." I rub the bite mark under my sweatshirt absently.

"How is that possible? He's huge!" Fi looks at me incredulously.

"Shifter?" Shrugging my shoulders, I steal the list from her.

"Hey! I was going to follow the list this time." Fi tilts her head and gives me a look only mom would fall for—the *'I'm serious, I will not grab things we don't need,'* look that's completely full of shit.

"Sure you are." Fi may take the brunt of the responsibilities but for food, she goes off the rails buying extra snacks and treats.

Shaking my head, I pour two coffees in disposable cups and herd my sister out the door.

The walk down the forest path was peaceful. We detoured to look at how the bar restoration is coming along. When we arrive, half the crew puts down their tools and come over to chat with us. Fi looks at me like I have twelve heads as I interact with them. Logan, Torben's youngest brother, tells me my mate is out getting supplies, but he'll let him know I stopped by. I give him a brief hug before waving so we can move on to the farmer's market.

"That was odd," Fi states.

"What was?" I stop walking just outside of the market and look at her.

"You were so chatty with them, which isn't like you. *And* only Logan stepped into your personal space."

"I'm spoken for, so that's out of respect for my mate. Logan is okay to get close to me because he's Torben's brother and family is different." I shrug it off. "It probably wouldn't be different if Tiernan has a sibling; I'm sure they would be allowed near you too."

Fi pales at the mention of Tiernan. "Yeah, I'm sure you're right."

Instead of pressing further, I wink and lead her into the market to start our shopping. Several stalls later, I groan when I notice the Fae trifecta of doom along with the rest of the Prince's entourage walking along the same aisle as us. Trying to steer Fi in the other direction doesn't work because she's fixated on something. I prepare for the worst when I realize we've been spotted.

"Aw, look at the 'almost' witch poseur in Revelin's band shirt! Isn't she absolutely pathetic? You're not even good enough to be a groupie, much less wear his merch." Khorinea's tone is snide and it gets the bitch squad to cackle.

As a growl rumbles in my chest, Fi whips her tee off and throws it in the approaching Prince's face. "I won't support a self righteous, pompous ass that allows his fucking followers to treat people like shit. That kind of person doesn't deserve fans *or* subjects—no wonder he's always hanging around this realm."

She's standing with her hands on her hips, eyes on fire, and seething in only her bra and jeans. I'm well aware Fiadh seriously does not give a fuck who sees her this way; it's not much less than our work clothes. But for modesty's sake in a public market, I take my sweatshirt off and offer it to her. After all, I have a shirt under it and she doesn't.

The Prince opens his mouth to refute her words, but I let my wolf surface just enough to partially shift. His eyes widen before he turns and barks at his people to get lost. His expression is unreliable as he looks at us until he finally turns on his heel to follow the crowd.

Shaking off my rage, I follow Fi as she curses up a storm as she storms away.

THANKFULLY, we'd mostly completed our shopping list before the Fae mishap. If we'd had to stay much longer, I would have gotten put down for being rabid. After we put away our haul, Fi excuses herself to accept a phone call. She keeps forgetting I can still hear her even if she leaves the room. I don't understand why she's still hiding that she's involved with Tiernan.

Several soft knocks sound at the door, and I know exactly who it is. Running to the door, I throw it wide open and leap at Torben. The big guy catches me with ease, laughing softly. He shuts the door silently and sets me down. His lips caress the shell of my ear as he speaks. "Someones excited."

"Always." I drag him over to the island in the kitchen and put on the kettle. Grabbing some of the honey I harvested and several tea bags, I work quickly. My lips curve as I take out the mugs that say 'somebody loves you beary much' that he gave me last week.

"Mom made some pastries. We thought you would enjoy them." He lifts the bag I didn't notice he was carrying and pulls out a tin with several honey based pastries.

A rogue tear threatens to break loose at how thoughtful his mother is. "Tell momma thank you for me, and give her a big hug."

Hearing me call his mother momma makes him beam and my heart flutters.

Fi comes back into the room, still staring at her phone. She heads for the fridge, not paying attention to us.

Torben's eyes widen as he looks at my bare shoulder then at my sister. I smile and mouth 'she knows.' He relaxes, laughing when the kettle whistles and Fi jumps.

"Sorry, sis. If it helps, Torben brought some pastries his mom made for us." Motioning to the tray, I draw her attention to the treats to soothe her.

"She made some of these for the celebration, right?" Fi asks.

Nodding, he pulls me to him and unconsciously kisses his mark. "Yes, except these are made with the honey Feray gave us. Mom thought she would enjoy the rich flavor the giant honey bees produce."

My sister gets a mischievous glint in her eyes. "Yeah, I'm sure she's not the only one that likes Feray's honey."

Torben chokes on the pastry he was eating.

"Fi!" I slap his back and go to the sink to get a glass of water for my red-faced mate. He clears his throat and kisses my cheek in thanks. "Behave."

"What? He obviously likes it!" She shrugs and bobs her brows at us, her shoulders shaking with laughter.

"I swear, sometimes I don't know what to do with you, sis." I finish making my mate his tea and bring the honey jar and mug over to him.

Just as Torben drips the honey into the tea, Fi starts up again. "So, Fer. I noticed you've been braiding your hair and keeping it off your shoulders lately."

Growling, I turn to face her. "We've established I have a mate bite. I have no problem admitting I have one, and I like that it's visible. Unlike some people, I'm not afraid people will see it."

Sometimes my grumpy sister needs to be poked to get her to deal with her own shit. It's easier if I admit to things myself to get her to look at her issues—like hiding her bond and the bite mark, I'm sure she has. Picking on me only tells me she's having issues working through it on her own.

But she gives me a wounded look and I fold. "Sorry I snapped."

She doesn't respond, only wraps her arms around herself and looks out the kitchen window.

Torben wraps an arm around me, holding me close. His bear rumbles softly, trying to soothe the frayed edges of my nerves. Soon I relax and sit on his lap, facing my sister. Being blunt and honest with my sister is the best policy—dancing around a subject won't be as effective with her.

"It seems like you're picking on us and my wolf is getting defensive. She doesn't like nitpicking."

"I'm sorry, too—to both of you." She motions to the room and then us. "I have a lot to get used to and I don't handle that well. The fire, the move, mates, *and* new jobs? It's a lot to take in." She waves her phone, smiling a little. "I need to run out for a bit. I'll see you both for dinner?"

That's her version of an olive branch, so I know to take it.

"Absolutely. Tor and I will cook and you should invite Tiernan." I smile innocently, hoping to catch her. Fi flinches and that seals my suspicion that she's meeting up with him when she leaves.

"I'll let him know about the invitation." Fi comes over and gives me a hug, then pats Torben on the shoulder before leaving.

"That was rough." Torben pretends to wipe sweat off his forehead.

Laughing, I climb onto his lap so I can face him. "That was easy. She's been mom and sister for so long sometimes she doesn't know when to let go."

Nuzzling my neck, he presses a kiss on my jaw. "Speaking of moms? Mine would like to have you come over for lunch sometime this week." He plants several kisses on my cheek as he pulls me closer.

Reaching into my pocket, I pull out my phone and look at the calendar. "I'm off Tuesday and Thursday this week, so either is fine. As long as it's a late lunch like around one so I can sleep in after shift."

I feel bad asking for the time concession because of my weird sex club job when it's lunch with his mother.

"Hey, none of that." He grips my chin, making me look into his eyes. "No feeling bad. You have work the night before and Mom will completely understand." He somehow makes everything better with barely any effort—I guess that's a side effect of the bond.

"If you're sure it's not a problem, then I'm good."

He holds his phone out where I can see what he's texting his mom. Almost immediately, she offers to have an early dinner instead so I can sleep more. Chuckling to himself, he hands me his phone so I can text his mom directly. I let her know it's me and give her my cell phone number as well. Not long after hitting send, my phone dings with a new text message.

I hold my phone where he can see what's happening. His mom and I go back and forth, setting up the early dinner at three. Nuzzling his throat I let his beard tickle my nose causing me to giggle. "You're the best mate a girl could ever hope for."

"I beg to differ; I'm the lucky one." He presses a kiss to my forehead before we start planning the dinner for tonight.

29

FIADH

Feray and I have settled into a pleasant rhythm in the past week. It's been over a month since the Ascension and the fire, but we've slowly made a new life for ourselves. On nights we work, we sleep late into the day, and since last week, I've taken Fer's place sneaking out to meet my mate. Unlike Torben—who shows up at dinner and then breakfast more and more—Tiernan and I aren't ready to be as public.

Okay, that's not fair.

I'm not ready for us to be that public. It's silly because he explained what we did and though I comprehend what it means intellectually, I'm still feeling very sensitive about allowing people to see such a huge weak point. Being my mate puts a target on his back with many people and the existence of mates for Fer and I also disprove the High Mage's declarations. I have no idea how that's going to go when it gets around. So, despite Fer proudly showing off her mark with every outfit and hairstyle, I'm holding back until I see what happens.

Plus, I haven't talked to Fer about it yet because I'm not there yet myself. I can't flaunt it if we haven't had sister gossip time.

The one thing I *have* shared with her was a random thought Tiernan had when we were snuggled up in his kitty nest at his place. We're sharing one secret or true thing about ourselves every day, whether through text or in person, and we ended up on my parents because I told him about the Ascension humiliation. Voicing that emotion to someone not my sister was hard for me, but he shared why he left his hometown. I had to tell him an equally traumatic story, so I picked the most recent one. I didn't expect to feel so comfortable and safe that I would delve into my parents' death. When he connected the dots between the Ascension events and the accident, Tiernan agreed with the questions Fer and I have been puzzling since she turned out to be a wolf.

Why did our parents lie? Why did we hide her true status for so long? Why is the official police report for their accident so barren of details? Why was the investigation non-existent and the ruling as accidental so fast? Most of all, why does the High Mage hate us so much?

Fer and I planned to look into this after our public shunning, but when we came home to find Philly's bar on fire, everything changed. We had to get our footing with our new status, find a place to live, find new jobs, and then the whole mate thing popped up. I felt bad admitting that I was so focused on those things that playing detective took a back seat. Our parents may not have told us the truth, but they *must* have had a good reason. Dollars to dick piercings, it's tied to my sister's hidden species and we need to honor them by not letting someone get away with murder.

I think.

Luckily, my easygoing leopard agreed with me. Tiernan said he'd poke around a little with people he knows in law enforcement who aren't on the Council's payroll, but he also thought we should do some research at the library. Paper is harder to track than internet searches and we might find things that got missed in a cover-up. His support made my heart feel funny, and I ended up staying at his place until dawn this time—which I never do.

Fiadh Morgenstern does not sleep at other people's home because I'm too fucking paranoid.

But I did, and the world didn't end.

I could tell Fer and Torben wanted to tease me when I got home in my usual grumpy morning state, but they held back. Now I'm so anxious to talk to my sister that I've showered and dressed, but I'm pacing my room as I wait for her mate to get lost. I don't want to growl at him, so I've tried hard to be patient. However, they are making breakfast last *far* longer than is socially acceptable. I'm not patient on a good day and right now, I'm so hyper, my magic is zinging between my fingers in little arcs.

It looks cool, but it doesn't do much still, by the way.

A low wail of frustration escapes me as I look at the clock and give in. I can't wait anymore; I need to go talk to Feray. We have shit to do and though she's being lazy out there because it's our day off; I know she's going to want to come with me. Stalking to the door, I stomp out of my bedroom and up to the table where Torben is poking raspberries in her mouth.

Aphrodite, smite me if I do that cutesy shit with Tiernan. I don't want to live being that vomit worthy.

"Fer!" I say, smacking my palm on the table. "When are you going to get ready for the day? It's eleven o'clock, for Hecate's sake!"

They both look at me in confusion and I just glare back. Finally, my sister quirks her lips, giving me a knowing expression. "Look who's all up and ready for the day like a go-getter because they're getting laid."

My eyes narrow as I lean forward. "Excuse me?"

Torben looks scared as hell because Feray is on his lap and he's effectively trapped between two sisters going to war. Fer leans back against him with a satisfied smile and shrugs. "I mean, usually you're barely conscious before eleven unless you've had almost a full pot of coffee. Have you *had* any coffee this morning, dear sister?"

"What? No." I frown at her, puzzled by the turn of the conversation. "We just have things to do and I want to get a move on."

Her laugh makes me grit my teeth and I see Torben hide behind her so I can't see his expression. My sister gestures at the perking pot on the counter. "Do have some and let's talk about what's got you raring to go out and deal with *people*—which you *hate*."

"*ARGH!*" I shout as I turn on my heel and head for the delicious smelling witch fuel she has going. She's not wrong that I'm a total addict and I haven't had my fix yet, but that's not why I'm frustrated. I need her bear toy to fuck off so we can talk privately and she's digging her heels in like she did when we were younger and had fights over TV time. "Why are you acting like such a pain in my nice, round ass?"

"Because you're acting strange, sneaking out, coming in after staying out all night, not sharing, and now stomping around like an under-caffeinated dictator!" My sister crosses her arms over her chest and I catch Torben peeking over her shoulder as it makes her cleavage deepen.

I guess that's one advantage of being so fucking tall; he can see over everything.

Sucking in a deep, calming breath, I pull out my jumbo mug and fill it with black coffee. After a sip, I turn to look at them as I prop my ass on the counter. "Okay, okay. That's true. I have been very secretive and I'm all worked up this morning."

"So tell me why."

Torben looks between us and clears his throat. "I can leave…?"

I wave my hand with a sigh and take another life affirming drink of my elixir that only the gods could have me. "No, no. I mean, I was worried before, but it occurs to me she's going to tell you, anyway."

That gets my sister moving, and I sigh in relief. She kisses Torben on the forehead before she replies to me. "Okay, I'll throw on clothes if you two will clean up. We can discuss what's got you going and then maybe Torben will drive us?"

I blink as she bats her lashes at the bear and he caves like a temple in an action movie.

"Of course. I would be happy to help."

Damn. Maybe there are benefits to this whole 'mate' thing I'm overlooking.

ONCE FERAY GOT READY, we had Torben take us across town to visit Philly first, so I had time to explain the conversation I had with Tiernan on the way. Of course, that meant I had to explain my sleepover at his house and a *lot* of ear-splitting squealing from my sister while her mate stared ahead at the road. Torben's ability to pretend he couldn't hear our girlish whispering was pretty goddamn impressive, and I told him so. Then I threatened to shave his entire body bald if he said one word about it ever.

That made Fer pout, and we all laughed. I wouldn't have pegged her for a beard gal, but it seems she's a little attached to his mountain man look. The entire ride made me wonder if it would have been even more fun if Tiernan had been with us, and by the time we pulled up to the hospital, I decided that it likely would have.

I have to bring my mate around and integrate him into what small bit of family I have; it's only fair.

Feray kissed Torben goodbye, and we thanked him for the ride in his big ass truck before heading inside. We've been visiting Philly a couple of times a week, either after shift or on off days, but it's hard. Most of the time he's on so much pain medication and so bundled up to prevent infection that we can't even squeeze his hands. It hurts my heart to see him looking so small and defeatable when he's normally a larger-than-life personality. Fer pushes the button on the elevator to get to the burn unit before turning to me with a sad look.

"Do you think he might be awake today?"

"I hope so. I'd like to ask him what he remembers about the fire and the wreck." My brow furrows as I wonder how long Philly's going to be here. The snooty phoenix is vague when we ask and the last time we visited, I had this weird sense he was hiding things. Since my magic has awakened, it seems to warn me when auras or words are off—almost like a mini-lie detector. But it's not reliable and sometimes, I don't get 'feelings' from everyone I'm talking to. I have no idea what that means, but I'm trying to hone it.

Maybe the library will have books on that, too.

The bell dings and the doors open as Feray murmurs, "I'm glad Tiernan talked you into going to the library to start this. But I'm even *more* happy that you're opening up to him. It's hard because of our damage, but so far, it feels like Torben is helping me heal some of that. You deserve to feel that way, too, sis."

Sighing, I give her a look. She knows my rules: no mush shit in public, especially when we don't know who's listening. As we walk down the hall to Philly's room, I weigh my words before I speak. "Thanks. I don't know how it will go yet, but I'm hopeful right now. And I will do what I promised and include him in stuff like you do with Sunshine Bear."

She snorts at my choice of nickname for the strapping guy, but reaches out to squeeze my hand. "Good."

When we walk in, I'm surprised to see they have Philly on his stomach and he looks even more bandaged than before. He's awake, and some nurse is feeding him jello, so it's an improvement. But something about the look on the doctor's face as he stands in the corner and clicks things on his tablet makes me suspicious. I don't know what's wrong here, but I'm going to find out.

"Hey, old man. It's good to see you awake," I say as I drag a chair over and angle it so he can see me while the chick spoons the goop for him. "Why are you lazing about on your stomach?"

"Humph!" he replies and cuts his eyes at the doctor. "Ask this asshat."

Fer pulls her chair over as we both look at the phoenix expectantly. He pauses and shakes his head at us. "That's a topic we'll discuss later."

I fucking hate *doctors.*

Rolling my eyes, I turn back to the prone satyr. "I guess we have to stew in anticipation. How are you feeling?"

"Like I pissed off a dragon," he grumbles. "I know you girls have to be handling all the shit with my place. You probably even have to deal with these hospital assholes. I owe you."

"Absolutely not!" My sister shakes her head and glares at him. "You took us in after the accident. Fi had to do all that insurance stuff and it left us with almost nothing. If it weren't for you, we would have been on the street. Of course we're taking care of you."

I doubt she did it on purpose, but that's a perfect segue to our questions.

"Speaking of that, Philly…" I pause, waiting for him to look at me. "What do *you* remember about that time? After the bullshit at the Ascension, I'm feeling a little nostalgic about mom and dad. A lot of our stuff went up in smoke with the building, so I want to take some notes."

Smooth, Feray mouths at me, and I shrug. They can't all be perfect, and I don't want him to clam up on us.

"Well, I remember you girls were just out of school. And there was a lot of… rumbling in the witch community. I don't remember what was going on, but it feels like Briarvale had a bunch of in-fighting going on. Like in the Councils because those idiots don't do anything but fight and spend money."

I nod, using my phone to type notes. "The insurance company fought like hell on payment because the police only kept the case open for a couple of days. It seems weird, don't you think?"

"The old chief was in charge back then, not the guy now. You could maybe talk to him. Or the detective who investigated. That accident was big news because of how… gruesome it was." He shakes his head, then winces. "I don't want to go into that because you girls never need to see that stuff again. But there were pictures all over the news of it and they kept droning on about this symbol on the car. But then suddenly, they declared it an accident and the detective said he'd found a report that said your family car was vandalized a week before it happened. I thought it was weird, but what the hell do I know?"

What. The. Fuck.

"I don't remember any of this, Philly," Fer finally says. "Not even the news stuff."

He sighs. "Docs had you girls heavily sedated during the first couple weeks, I bet. They seem to be doing the same shit to me and I don't have a clue why. They've already scrubbed all my *fucking skin off!*"

Before I can respond, the phoenix clears his throat and looks at us with an urgent expression. I nod and rise, looking at our friend with a grin. "P, I'm going to go grab a few coffees. We have a bit to stay and talk since you're awake. We're going to visit the library after and I want to keep picking your brain."

My sister takes the hint and starts telling him about the place we're staying in a bright voice. Once Philly is distracted, I walk out into the hallway with the doctor. He looks unsure for a moment and it surprises me, but I simply wait until he's ready. I'm dying of curiosity, but I don't want him to know. Seems like he'd lord it over me.

"I shouldn't be telling you this, but since your friend has allowed you in the room during medical conversations, I'm going to. Especially now," Dr. Bennu says in a low voice. "The reason he's on his stomach is that after finishing all the debriding, we did an ultraviolet scan to look at the underlying musculature. What we found this morning was… disturbing."

I frown as I study him. He really looks worried. "What did you find?"

The doc sucks in a breath and lets it out slowly. "Before he was burned in the fire, whoever did it *carved* a message into his back. The burns covered it until we were able to see what was below."

Holy mother of winged gods—that means the fire wasn't started by those flaming nuggets.

"What the hell did it say?" I hiss.

"It said '*We are coming for you, Children of the Moon,*' but that wasn't even the creepiest part."

I scoff at him. "No, of course not. Pray tell, what is creepier than some esoteric bullshit *carved* into my friend's back?"

"There was a really weird symbol below it and your friend just said your parent's car had a weird symbol on it before they had a mysterious crash. Seems a little… coincidental, isn't it?" Easton looks around as we talk, clearly concerned someone will hear him voice such baseless leaps of intuition and judge him.

Fuck this. I know what to do.

Using my phone, I google the search terms I think will bring up the best results until I find articles on my parents' accident. Sure enough, one of them has a picture of an odd looking symbol painted on the back panel of their car near the gas tank. I pinch the photo until it's bigger and turn the screen around to shove at the doctor. "Does it look like this?"

His face turns pale. "Yes. Yes, that's the *exact* thing carved under the words on his back."

Looks like our paranoia just became a lot less unbelievable.

Whoever was involved in our parents' deaths is also part of trying to kill our friend—and maybe even us.

FERAY

When Fi said she was going for coffee after Dr McHottie cleared his throat, I tried to get Philly to focus on me, but everything he told us is making my head spin.

There's so much I must have repressed, but I can't think about it right now.

"Philly, you need to see the house we're living in. It's an awesome little cottage in the middle of the woods." Beaming, I bounce in my seat, chattering about our new house while Fi herds the doctor out into the hallway by one arm.

A guttural growl escapes my lips and the hairs on the back of my neck stand on end—she's demanding to be set free. My vision shifts and the acrid scent of fear floods my nostrils. Whipping my head in that direction, Philly staring at me with his eyes wide .

"When did this happen?" He motions to my face, looking shocked.

Oh shit, he doesn't know yet.

Dropping my gaze, I rein my wolf in. "We didn't get mates or powers at the ceremony. Somehow, we went to Ascension and all I got was a lousy fur shirt." Shrugging my shoulders, I give him a slight grin as I joke. "It's honestly not bad; I'm adapting."

Philly closes his eyes for a few moments, then looks back at me. "I wonder how that happened? The wolf, I mean," he mumbles. There's hesitation in his voice and I know he's trying not to hurt my feelings.

I stare down at my hands for several moments before meeting his gaze. "People accused my mom of having an affair. Mom loved Dad too much to stray. Mates don't cheat," I say firmly, because deep in my soul, I know and feel it's true. "I think I'm probably adopted."

"It's possible, kiddo. Either way, they loved you both very much and that's all that matters." Philly forces a smile. "What else has happened post crispy satyr? Anything *not* depressing?"

Gotta love the old goat for changing the uncomfortable subject.

"I found my mate even though they said we didn't have any. His name is Torben; he's a bear shifter and the owner of the construction company working on your bar. He owns the house Fi and I are staying in." My thoughts drift to my mate and Philly chuckles so I know I must have a love sick look on my face.

"It's good to see you smile. It's been a rough go for you two." Philly yawns. "You have trust issues, especially that little firecracker of a sister of yours, and that won't make it easy going. Don't think I don't know you're not telling me everything." He smirks and I get a sinking feeling in my gut.

Shaking my head, I follow my instincts and let him into the circle. "We don't believe our parents' deaths were an accident. If it wasn't an accident, they were probably hunted." Swallowing hard, I clear my throat before looking back at Philly. "I'm scared to find out why they died."

My gut tells me it was because of me. Why else would a wolf be raised with witches?

I dare not speak of my dark thoughts for fear they will manifest. Instead, I reach out and rest my hand on Philly's.

"Everything will work out the way it is supposed to, Feray. It always does." Philly takes his 'dad tone' with me and I can't help but laugh. He waggles his eyebrows at me before he asks, "What's up with your sister? Any romance on the horizon for her?"

I focus my attention on the door, listening to where my sister is. "She has a mate and I know they sealed the bond, but you know Fi. She keeps her cards close to her chest." Philly nods along, listening intently. "Anyway, they've been sneaking around as if I don't know what's going on." Tapping my nose indicates I can smell the change of scent with my sister.

Philly nods again. "I bet that's an advantage. My sense of smell isn't as refined as yours, but I know her scent has changed."

Nodding along again, I sigh and listen to the muffled sounds outside the door. The jiggle of the door knob makes me raise a finger to my lips and point to my ear. Philly winks at me just as Fi and Dr. Bennu enter the room. My sister arches a brow and I grin like the cat that swallowed the canary.

"What are you smiling about, Furball?" Fi says with a playful smile.

I allow my canines to show. "Not much Sparky, just catching up with our friend here."

The sharp intake of breath from the doctor catches my attention, and I look at him. His eyes dart between Fi and I comically. Arching a brow, I tilt my head before turning my gaze to my sister. Fi rolls her eyes, then thanks the doctor for all of his help with Philly. He dips his head at us and finally departs like someone set his ass on fire.

My sister closes the door and comes over to Philly's bedside. The pain in Fi's eyes tells me she learned more from Dr. McHottie than she's letting on. "If what I believe happened, you can't say anything. You don't know us."

"I'll protect you. You're the closest thing to family I have at this point." Philly clears his throat as the first signs of emotion break. He winks at us and closes his eyes, dismissing us in his own way. "Now get out of here—you two have lives to live."

Fi grabs her bag and leads the way out of the room. Following her down the hall, I stop when I feel eyes on me. Dr. Bennu is standing there watching me with his back to the wall, sipping his drink. I dip my head in thanks before catching up with my sister at the elevator.

Once the doors shut, Fi gets a look that tells me the shit is about to hit the fan. "It's worse than we thought."

Scooting closer, I tilt my head. "What do you mean?"

"Philly had things carved on his back." Fi's voice drops.

Leaning back against the wall, I parse what she just told me. "It's definitely not a coincidence they hit his bar." I say more to myself than my sister and I see her nod her head.

Fiadh pulls out her phone, showing me the symbol on our parents' car again. "That's what's on his back."

The way she says it, I know she's not telling me everything. I take her phone, committing the image to memory. It's not a symbol we had to memorize for any of our magic tests. The elevator dings and I act like we were looking at something funny as we step out.

"Where to?" I'm pretty sure I know the destination, but I want confirmation. My sister doesn't answer, only nods as her eyes rake over the other people in the lobby.

Once outside, Fi turns north towards the center of town and finally speaks. "The repository will have all the old records and newspapers and other items that may hold information."

Thankfully, the repository is run by all the species and not just the mages. At least with all the species involved in its care, things are not being colored to favor a certain species over another. *Maybe I can find out why I am a wolf and not a witch while we are there?* Perhaps it's a dormant gene from generations back, like my red hair. Biting my bottom lip, I try to keep the flood of emotions from surfacing as we walk.

"You're quiet. Is something bothering you?" Fi knocks me out of my inner thoughts, and I force myself to smile.

I face her trying to find an answer as we pass the food trucks. That is, I'm thinking about it until my stomach growls. My sister laughs and we stop for chicken on a stick to quell my hunger. The repository is on the other side of the food court, so a quick snack doesn't impede our forward progress too much. "Nothing is bothering me but there are too many questions and not enough answers."

There's a faint glow on my sister's hand as she rests it on my arm and smiles. Her eyes drift around the food court, then back to me. "The lack of concrete answers is bothersome. I hope the archives have the answers we're looking for."

"Relax. Being a wolf has its advantages; I have a predator's sixth sense now. I can sense a shift in the group." Shrugging my shoulders, I laugh internally.

I really want to say my wolfie senses are tingling.

"Hopefully, your senses are enough to keep us safe." Fi still scans the area regardless.

A half shift would be helpful, but Torben told me it's frowned upon unless needed for defense. "I'm getting the hang of it. My mate has been helping me to hone my senses and reaction time."

Oh shit, I just left myself wide open to her picking on me.

"*That's* what the shifter kids are calling it: honing senses. Here I thought it was wild sex." Fi laughs as she takes a sip of her drink then almost chokes on the fluid.

"Fi, you have to swallow, *then* breathe." Hitting her with a one liner while she's down is one of her moves and I'm stealing it.

"I yield!" she cries out between hacking coughs and laughs.

"Blame yourself; once the student, now the teacher." I bow slightly before turning to head towards the Repository. The stone stairs are as wide as they are tall and there are thirty granite steps before the large, engraved wood and steel doors.

We push the door and it slides open with a creak.

"That's creepy," I whisper as we step inside the main hall.

At first glance, you'd think it was a museum. Period paintings and full sized marble statues line the walkway. Not far down on the right, a woman is sitting at a desk. Her hair is tucked in a neat bun and round glasses sit halfway down her nose. The style screams 'old fashioned school marm' but her smell is definitely some kind of reptilian shifter.

"Welcome to the Briarvale Repository. How can I assist you today?" Her tone is about as warm as a blizzard in the tundra.

"Can you direct us to the newspapers and news reports section?" Fi shoots back in a mockery of her detached, haughty tone.

Taken aback, the librarian clears her throat and pulls a map from a file behind her. Using a highlighter, she marks the path we need to take through the maze of a building. She slides the paper across her desk with the tips of her fingers till Fi takes it. "If you get lost, snap your fingers two times and a raven will assist you further."

"You've been most helpful." Sadly for the tight-assed woman, she took Fi's sarcasm as being polite.

I struggle to restrain the laughter until we are far enough away. Looking over Fi's shoulder, I stare at the map. There are several points of interest that we should look at before we leave. "Where did they dig her up?"

"Who knows? They ought to consider sending her back for a refund." She stops dead in the middle of the aisle then turns right, guiding us down the dimly lit stairs. "Didn't they pay their light bill? I can barely see two feet in front of my face."

Fi grips me as she tries to not get killed going down the stairs. I shift my eyes when she holds on for dear life. I place my sister's hands on my shoulders and so I can go down the stairs before her. "I can see clearly now."

"Lucky you. I can't see shit." Fi squeezes my shoulders as we make our way to what seems like a dungeon. According to the map, there are three levels below the one we need. After what feels like forever, we make it to the bottom of the winding stairs and I breathe a sigh of relief. "Stay here. I'll turn on the lights."

Sparks dance in the dark as Fi grumbles that her magic isn't helping her. I search the walls for the switch and when I find it, a low hum sounds before the lights blaze to life. The overpowering smell of musty old papers, ink, and mold messes with my ability to distinguish scents. Since we're alone, I partially shift, allowing my wolf's ears and eyes to remain to help me ensure we're safe.

"Any reason why you're all *Teen Wolf*?"

Flicking my ears, I turn them in every direction. "My sense of smell is fucked down here. So instead of taking the chance of being snuck up on…"

"Good thinking. We need to look for articles from three years ago referencing the Ferryman's Bridge accident." Fi motions to the racks of books and folders on the left side of the giant room.

I nod and walk off towards the shelves. Part of me wants the accident to be my priority, but my wolf thinks learning about what I truly am is more important. She obviously knows something I don't, but for now, I'll search for what Fi wants. I don't think it's the key to our problems—call it a gut feeling, but I believe there's more than meets the eye to this thing.

31

—————

FIADH

THIS PLACE IS KILLING MY ALLERGIES. I DON'T KNOW WHAT SPECIES they have working here, but obviously none are freaking cleaners. Every time I pull a book from the shelf, a cloud puffs up and I sneeze for two minutes straight. Hell, I didn't even *know* I had an issue with dust, but here we are.

Fer is sitting at a microfiche machine, flicking through films one by one for local and regional newspapers starting a couple months before the accident and a couple after, but I can tell she's having trouble focusing. This place has her on edge and I don't know what she's anxious about, but it's making her more a distraction than a help.

"Sis, why don't you go look in the records section and give me a break from this shit, making my eyes itch? I'll take over the microfiche."

Her eyes light up and she beams, pushing to her feet quickly. "Good idea! Trading will keep us fresh-eyed."

Uh-huh. I can feel the half-truth in that statement.

I don't comment on her white lie; instead, I get up and walk over to the ancient machine. The only reason I know how to work this thing is because of research papers for school. Witch and wizard professors abhor tech and they often require us to have sources from things other than the internet. I got super comfy with the microfiche viewer in our school library over the years. I probably should have remembered Feray never enjoyed using it; she always fobbed it off on me.

With a sigh of frustration, I move the slides slowly, straining to see if there are any mentions of accidental deaths, vandalism, or even plain odd occurrences. It seems likely that our parents weren't the only people targeted over the years and were even more certain that the people involved attempted their deed more than once. After all, our parents were excellent magic users, and we always had thorough wards and protections in our home. I thought it was because my dad was paranoid, but that's looking more like he knew they could have someone coming after them.

I know how much he did to protect us, so I truly believe whoever did this was actively stalking my parents, and maybe even us. I haven't gone through my memories to analyze every unpleasant incident from our childhood, but I plan on it once I get the new caldron. I'll cast a water-based memory spell and have the ripples show me anything suspicious. Maybe we'll even find shit we thought was nothing at the time but marks a pattern of unusual bad luck or events.

Calm down, Fi. You're heading towards tin foil hat territory.

Chuckling, I shake my head. I've always had an active imagination, and conspiracy theories are all about confirmation bias. I know better than that—simply because something fits what you expect to see doesn't make it true. Our minds love to free associate based on what we know or believe to be true. Truly intelligent people seek proof and demand evidence before they accept theories or claims. If you don't, you're no better than a petty schoolhouse gossip at a lunch table.

"Plenty of those to go around in this community already," I mumble to myself as I think about all the people nodding their heads at the vicious High Mage when he made false statements at the Ascension. They all treated us like trash afterward because of his self-serving bullshit and man, will they be eating crow when the truth comes out.

Am I a bad person for looking forward to it? I need it to be okay to marinate in satisfaction that everyone will find out what an awful bully that asshole is.

I squint as something passes by on the screen, stopping and flipping back to look at it. Fer walks over, arching a brow at me, and I give her a half-grin. "What?"

"Are you over here grumbling to yourself?"

Shrugging, I turn back to the microfiche. "Maybe. I was just musing about the politics of our community. Everyone was glad to follow the High Mage with no actual proof. They cast us aside and even actively worked to be hurtful, but he lied. When they find out, they're going to be ashamed—or they should be—and he'll be revealed as a nasty dictator, not a caring leader. I'm very much looking forward to his true face being unveiled. Is that wrong of me?"

She snorts and shakes her head. "Uh, no. I wouldn't shed a tear if he got hit by a stampede of minotaurs, Fi. He purposely set the dogs loose on us for not being perfect little automatons. Whatever punishment or consequences he faces, he earned. I'd called it justice, not revenge. And I'm not less forgiving of all the sycophants who followed him like lemmings. They should feel like fools and they should reap what they sowed."

Feray's words make me feel much better. I know I anger more easily than her and sometimes, I bite before I bark—which is a little ironic given her true species. My temper gets me in trouble all the time because I ignore every good instinct and act. But my sister agrees our tormentors deserve their fates, too. "Thanks. That helps, Fer. I was worried I was being a little *too* vengeful."

With a wink, she turns away and heads back to the books, leaving me to look at the screen I was focused on before she came over. The article I saw out of the corner of my eye mentions vandalism and several families being affected, but not ours. It's not from the time I was looking up and I frown at the screen. The date is over a decade before our parents' accident and it's about families in a small town about forty minutes from Briarvale. There were houses broken into and vandalized with weird symbols left behind. One of the families on that block declined to be interviewed, but the reporter notes they left town with their two five-year-old children not long after.

Could that have been us?

Fer and I weren't in school until we were six and honestly, I don't remember a lot about when I was that young. Favorite toys or normal kid memories, but I can recall what our house looked like or other kids our age being around for playdates. I know my mom stayed home until we were school aged and my dad worked, but it's like everything is super general and fuzzy.

I frown and send that to a printer, planning on adding it to our copies folder. Once we have enough primary material, I'll work on some internet searches, but I have to upgrade our software to make sure we don't get tracked by anything. That might require asking people if they know any kitsunes who don't cost an arm and a leg. Those multi-tailed little shits are obnoxious, but they're the best hackers around. Maybe Tiernan or Torben will know one? Wrinkling my nose, I realize Dezi might also know one of them, or maybe even a technomancer. Fer and I can't afford the latter, but maybe our boss has something on one?

That means you'll have to talk to him and that's a whole other ball of wax.

I groan and start skipping through slides again. Fer and I work again tomorrow and I feel I'll have to deal with the 'incident' from last week. I haven't seen the vampire since it happened last week, but there's no way he won't be in the house on a Friday night. Dropping my head to the desk, I bang my forehead lightly as I imagine how awkward *that* conversation is going to be.

"Hey, Fer? How's your search going? Did you print some stuff?" I call over my shoulder.

A sneeze followed by a growl is my answer and I laugh softly. "Yeah. I found some stuff. I'll go to the printer and grab it?"

"Sounds good. Should we keep looking for another hour and then head home for dinner?" There's a long pause and I grin to myself as I look at the moving screen. Feray has something to say, and she doesn't know how to say it.

"I invited Torben to dinner again," she finally says. "Do you think…"

I know where she's going with this and I've gotta hand it to my sister—mating and getting her wolf has really given her a brass set. Feray has been more confident and less accepting than ever; I love it, even when she's fucking with me. "*Yes*, I will text Tiernan and invite him. I know I need to include him more. Sheesh, *Mom*."

That gets a delighted laugh from her and I go back to research, feeling an oddly happy sensation in my chest.

Maybe things are finally going our way, after all.

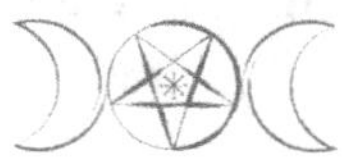

THE CABIN IS warm and cozy from the heat in the kitchen. Fer and I made a roast, so we stopped at the store on the way home from the repository and splurged. I made the marinade, and she cut the veggies while we chatted about what we found and our new life. It made me feel like we've finally settled in and even though the mystery of our parents' death weighs on me; I had a good time.

"Fi, did you get the table set?"

I chuckle under my breath. If we were rich, Fer would definitely have one of those fancy overly decorated tables for dinners with place cards and all the trimmings. She loves making things look pretty and I'm typically happy to eat in front of the TV while we sip drinks. We're a perfectly matched pair even if we aren't sisters or twins—no fuckery in our past can change that.

"I did, but you realize we don't have a lot of... finery to make this look fancy, right?" I glance at the plates, glasses, and silverware. Thank hell, they came with the cabin, but we're using paper napkins and plastic containers to serve. "It's as nice as I can make it look with what we have."

She bounds in from the bedroom where she was 'freshening up.' Feray's hair is tied back in a braid on the non-bite mark side and she's changed into a loose top and jeans. She looks natural, even with the light makeup she added. "I know. It's so basic, but we have so many other things we *need* before I start decorating this place."

I blink at her. "Decorating? I mean, once Philly's place is done, we're moving back... right?"

Humming under her breath as she heads to the oven to pull the roast out, my sister shrugs. "Maybe? I think Torben likes having me here and he won't ask us to move. Plus, I love Philly, but we have new jobs now. Living over his place and working somewhere else would be weird, not to mention how small it was. We have mates now, Fiadh."

Danger, Will Robinson. My sister is nesting here.

"Fer, we can't keep living here off of your mate's generosity. It's weird and feels wrong." I frown as I take the carrots and potatoes from her to place on the table. "That's not how we were raised, either."

Stomping her foot, Feray gives me an exasperated look. "We also can't live in a one room apartment anymore. Our lives have changed and Philly understands that. Plus, once we get on our feet, I'm sure we can work out rent with Torben."

Her mind is made up; I can tell. She used to get like this when we were kids and until her stubbornness gives way to logic, you can't reason with her. Paying her mate rent is a bit odd, too, and I have no idea how we will resolve this. But for now, I don't want to argue, so I nod. "We can revisit it when the bar is done, okay? I don't want to spoil the fun we've been having."

That makes her smile and she scurries back over to hug me tightly. "Thank you. I really want this dinner to be fun so our little family can spend time together."

"Me, too," I reply as I head for the fridge to grab ice for our drinks. "I'm glad you pushed me to invite Tiernan. I mean, I was thinking about it, but you asking made me go through with it."

There's a knock at the door and Feray claps her hands. "They're here!"

"How can you tell?" I ask drily.

"Smell, duh," she mutters as she rushes over to the door and flings it open. The way she throws herself into Torben's arms makes me grin and when Tiernan steps around him, he gives me a knowing look.

I'm not quite so outwardly affectionate—at least, not yet.

He walks over to me and takes my hand, kissing it lightly. "Thank you for inviting me."

My cheeks flush, both from the oddly adorable gesture and knowing the other two are watching us. "You're part of the family now, too. So… I wanted you to come."

Feeling eyes on me, I turn to see Fer giving me two thumbs up while Torben buries his face in her hair. If I had to guess, the big guy is laughing. The two of them think I'm dating deficient and they have to coach me not-so-subtly.

Oh, that's gonna piss me off all night.

Tiernan squeezes my hand and tilts his head at the table. "Tell us what you lovely ladies made for dinner. It smells delicious."

Yep. Tiernan is going to be the diplomat and Torben will let my sister do anything she wants.

I'm in trouble.

Feray

It's early Friday night at the club and it's already getting out of hand. Several fights have broken out, and we had to break them up. Being a shifter definitely has its perks; increased strength and being deadly to the vampire population makes my job a lot easier.

We've entered the Waxing Gibbous part of the moon cycle, and I can see its effects on most of the shifter population. Oddly, the moon phase doesn't seem to affect me except for increasing my strength, so I'll take that as a win. Torben has been working on the 'alpha' staring thing with me since that night with Mo and Tiernan. He and his mother believe I'm somewhere between an alpha and a beta with my ability to use dominance on lesser shifters. From what I've been able to dig up on my own, that would make a product of two powerful bloodlines—a natural born alpha, though females are usually referred to as lunas.

That tidbit gives me a lot to ponder and makes my adoption theory seem plausible.

Tiernan and Prince Revelin arrive at the bar an hour after opening, so I send the Prince drinks for his group. The leopard hangs out for a few moments, making sure I don't need anything. We devised an alert system together in case my beloved sister gets in over her head. He waves goodbye as he heads up to babysit the Prince for the night. From where I am, I can watch Revelin socializing and see how Tiernan keeps looking over the rail to clock where Fi is.

My sister is zipping around, taking orders and delivering drinks like it's a normal day. She's not even glancing up at her mate and I want to slap some sense into her, but I doubt it will help. Getting her to invite Tiernan over the first time was harder than herding cats with a garden hose. She's keeping her mate at arm's length when he obviously loves her and that doesn't sit well with me.

"Mutt, the Boom Boom Room is reserved tonight for the Bedia party. They ordered top shelf drinks and several bottles of champagne." Louie drops the list on the bar top with an eye roll, then disappears.

"Bedia party… I wonder who that is," I mutter to myself. They must be rich to demand a top shelf open bar in a private room. Growling, I pick up the sheet and look it over. Several of the high end items are in the basement or in the secondary storage room. I don't want to leave to get it, so I turn to the bane of my existence. "Mo, can you grab eight bottles of *EverFae* champagne and four bottles of *Viper* rum?"

I watch him roll his eyes before leaving the bar. I swear that fox has a death wish; the way he keeps pushing my buttons is going to snap the hold on my temper. He keeps pushing his limits with me and I swear to Fenrir, I will shift and make him a snack one day. Going back to my customers, I groan. Whoever closed last night was sloppy as hell. Everywhere I touch is sticky from an overuse of syrups that weren't mopped up immediately. "You might learn how to mix before playing at being a bartender," I grumble to myself as I scrub every inch of the bar between orders.

"Your wolf is showing, Fer." Fi saunters up with a couple tabs, leaning on the bar and looking concerned.

Reaching into the cooler, I pull out a fae energy shot for her and place it on the bar top. "The level of incompetence other people display astounds me." I motion to the filthy prep station before I mix the drinks she has on her list. "The lack of care and laziness speaks volumes. Also, it's easy to do this right; it's all proportions."

"Not everyone is as good with numbers or calculating volume like you. Maybe it's always been your wolf that made it possible. Predators need to calculate distance on the fly." She shrugs her shoulders.

Her words make sense. When in pursuit of prey, predators need to calculate the distance and speed to catch what they're after. "You're probably right. Is Tiernan good with numbers? I know Torben is. He has to be for his job."

"I would assume so." She glances over her shoulder and looks up at the VIP section. Her mate looks down at the same time and gives her a slight nod, then a wink. "I need to get my drinks up there. I'll be back soon."

Fi takes off like someone set her ass on fire and I laugh softly. Tiernan and I lock eyes for a moment and raise our water bottles in a silent understanding. I told him I would help him with my sister because it's so hard to get through that shell of hers. She's always so guarded and suspicious.

Scanning the room while I scrub, I know the exact moment my grumpy banker arrives. I work on his usual drink—a Manhattan with the cherry wood smoke is his new standing favorite. Switching it up slightly, I do a second drink—a whiskey based mule with cherries and a smoke layer. Both will ignite with a snap of my fingers once I get the strikers on. Three light raps on the bar top tell me he's ready for his drink and I head over with a broad smile.

"Welcome to Cocktails and Screams. I have your usual ready for you and a new drink I believe you may enjoy." Placing both drinks down before him, I motion to each. "On your left is your usual Manhattan with my little twist." Snapping my fingers, it ignites and he smiles slightly. I snap my fingers again and ignite the mule as well. "Here on your right is an aged whiskey cherry mule. Let me know what you think?"

The calming scent of chamomile fills my senses and all the tension I had melts away. *How odd.*

The banker blows out both drinks and takes a long sip of the mule first. "Hmmm. Smooth body, typical whiskey bite, good smoke and cherry undertones—overall I would call it a success, pet." He sips at the new creation and dips his head, dismissing me.

Pet? When did I earn a nickname from him?

As I walk away, Mo finally returns with the champagne and the rum. "I'm not your errand boy!" he snarks, drawing attention from the patrons at the bar.

"You are tonight."

Grabbing the boxes, I shove past him and head to the reserved room to set up. It takes almost an hour to make sure I properly cleanse the stage and seating, as well as stock up on ice and bring in sufficient glassware. There are several extra wide recliners and a bed in the corner, but only the rack in the corner mildly concerns me.

Thankfully I don't have to deal with that.

Before I leave the room, the Troublemint twins arrive and it occurs to me who the 'Bedia party' is. They are both scanning the room as if they are hunting for someone. Fi is coming down the stairs from the VIP lounge when she notices the twins standing there. She gets in the cranky one's face immediately, but by the look of it, they're enjoying pissing each other off. The nicer one is watching my sister with a perplexed stare like he's trying to understand whatever she's saying.

My sister throws her hands in the air and storms over to a stool at the bar. Throwing a hand back, she motions at Thing One and Two on the other side of the room. "Can you believe the nerve of him?"

"Khol Bedia reserved the Boom Boom room for tonight, according to Louie. They have a party of…" I dig inside the pocket of my apron until I find the note. "…nine. We're waiting for seven more people to show up." Wrinkling my nose in disgust, I shake my head and try to clear the thought of those two, their 'friends,' and the equipment in that room from my mind.

"Ugh. I hate being in there, but at least the tips are worth it." Fi takes the tray of drinks I made for her and heads across the room again. Each time she passes, the asshole brother has to say something to her and I watch her face contort with rage.

"Back off, lizard boy, before I turn you into luggage," Fi snorts on the next pass.

Inching closer, Khol's hand slides down and over his crotch. "Come on, Sassy, don't be like that. You may like what I offer."

"Ew, asshole! Inappropriate." Fi heads back to get her next round of drinks, and I'm amazed that she resisted the urge to punch him square in his dick hole.

The next time she heads out with drinks, I hit the rim of a glass with a fork, signaling Tiernan so he turns around. The minute he looks down, I point to where Fi is now toe to toe with the asshole brother again for the fifth time. *Secret request for help sent and received.* Tiernan nods, then heads for the staircase. Wiping my hands, I head to the end of the bar, ready to intercede if Tiernan doesn't make it in time.

"Join us, Sassy. I'm sure we can show you a good time." Khol's voice carries and I hear his lewd invitation clear as day. Their guests are almost all gathered, so I assume he feels the need to show off. Glancing up at the rail, I see Tiernan is gone, and noise is elevating in the bar. When I turn back to check on Fiadh, Tiernan is between Fi and the asshole twin.

"What do you think you're doing, Bedia?" Tiernan growls out.

"Back off, hairball. The lady and I are having a conversation." Khol says with a sly smile, knowing he's pissing the leopard off.

I see the fur rippling over Tiernan's arms from here; he's definitely going to lose it. "The conversation is over; she obviously doesn't want to talk."

"*She* is standing right here and *she* can fight her own battles." Fi glares at both men and I swear, it's like the temperature in the room drops by ten degrees.

Shit…

This will not end well. Feminist Fi is in full effect and no amount of reasoning will get through to her. Tiernan is doing what his instincts are driving him to do—protect his mate above all else. But she's too focused on proving she can take care of herself. *Immovable object, meet unstoppable force.*

I prepare to hop the bar, but suddenly, Tiernan throws Fiadh over his shoulder, smacks her on the ass, and walks away with her. My sister is kicking and screaming her head off until he leans in and says something too low for even me to hear. Right then, she stops fighting him, huffing as she let him cart her off.

The loudmouth twin rolls his eyes and beckons his crowd to follow him into the reserved room. His brother watches Tiernan take my sister away and then turns to me with a sheepish smile. There's something in his gaze that doesn't anger my wolf and I wonder why. His gaze is magnetic, distracting me until I hear a voice behind me.

"I'll take another cherry mule, pet," the banker calls me from the other end of the bar, breaking my trance.

I walk over, mixing his drink while still eyeing the gentle twin. He's a mystery wrapped in an enigma with a sprinkle of danger and I seem to want a taste. Clearing my head, I force myself to focus on the banker's drink. Every time I get myself back on task, the nice guy moves and draws my attention back to him again.

How does he keep doing that?

When I finally finish the drink, I place it before my regular client and ignite it for him. A smile tugs at the corners of his lips, and his eyes dance with merriment. He's as intrigued by the drink as I am watching him study it.

"What's the main propellant in the drink, pet?"

"Laphroaig, an Islay malt Scotch whiskey. I chose it for its rich smoky palette—it combines a high proof with a smooth, long finish. I figured being a Founder, you would appreciate the finer things in life." Slowly, I dip my head to him and move back down the bar to get to work.

As the drink orders pile up, I watch my barfly appreciate his drink. I never let him have an empty glass, knowing that will please him. My focus is divided between the banker and the silent twin. He keeps coming out of the private room, looking at the bar as if he's fascinated with me.

Morrigan knows why he would be interested in me, especially seeing my mates mark on my shoulder, but it seems I have a stalker.

33

FIADH

Tiernan isn't listening and my sister simply smirked at me, so I have absolutely *no* allies here. I'm kicking and yelling my head off, but my leopard isn't giving an inch. He strides back to the stockroom where we had our moment, kicks the door open, and then uses his foot to knock it closed behind him. Once we're locked in, he dumps me on a short pallet of glassware boxes with an amused look.

"Knuckles, learn to control your temper."

Is he fucking kidding me?

"I'm not the one who picked me up like a caveman and carried me off of the floor because some douche was getting fresh with me! Newsflash, kitty kat, that happens to women who work at bars *all the time*. Hell, it's how we make tips more often than not." I cross my arms over my chest, looking at him with barely repressed rage.

Sparks dance over my fingers and he still doesn't back away. In fact, he actually steps closer, grinning down at me like a lunatic. "Maybe so, but I'm not about to let some thug disrespect my mate in public.

Not only is it cowardly, but it would look very bad to the shifter community who are patrons."

I open my mouth, then consider what he's saying, and close it. Mates for shifters and magic users seem to operate differently—something I don't have the first clue about yet. Biting my lip, I try to filter out my outrage at being treated like his property and hear what he's saying. "You're telling me people would judge your… worthiness… if you didn't put him in his place?"

Big brown eyes light up when I respond and he nods. "Yes, they would. I don't have to be the dominant one in our relationship, but I can't allow another alpha male to challenge my status by ignoring my demands."

"I hate politics," I grumble as I kick my foot over the concrete. "This better not mean I can't fucking defend myself. I don't need rescuing and I don't want it."

"I don't have to rescue you, Knuckles. I enjoy watching you take care of business. But I do have to take a stand when a little shit like Bedia doesn't respect our bond." Stepping closer, he leans down and lifts my chin to look in my eyes. "Most mated pairs, even those with female alphas, appreciate when their bond asserts their claim. I would if you did. Leopards and other big cats are not as misogynistic as some species."

Sucking in a deep breath, I let it out in irritation as I turn his words over in my mind. Tiernan isn't saying I have to let him do the fighting, but there's some bullshit protocol about mating I have to accept. "Okay. I'll try. But you have to understand that I don't know all this shit like a shifter would. And I *hate* feeling stupid or out of control. So sometimes, I'm going to fuck up without meaning to."

His lips brush mine lightly and he murmurs against my mouth. "It would be my honor to teach you, even if you aren't always happy with how I handle it."

I wrinkle my nose. "The ass slap was a bit much."

"I didn't want you to kick me in the balls. We might need them later."

If you put it like that...

"Fair point." Grinning a little, I grab his face and kiss him hard before I let go and rise to my feet. "I don't have time for hanky panky right now, though. Louie fucking scheduled me in the Boom Boom Room and I have to deal with that asshat and his friends."

A low rumble echoes out of his chest and his eyes narrow. "They'd better behave or..."

"Calm down, Simba. I promise I'll get a message to you if they need a reminder. Okay?" I tilt my head, eyes dancing as I watch him struggle for a moment, then nod. "Besides, you have a dickhead prince to look after and I need you on the floor in case someone gets shitty with Fer."

He grabs my hand and kisses my knuckles before he tugs me towards the door. "I promise I'll keep an eye out as long as you promise to use your head before your fists."

"Fiiiiine. Deal."

ONCE WE PART, I walk over to the bar and check in with Fer, letting her know everything is okay. I let her know I'm headed to the private room and Tiernan will be watching from his perch upstairs. That makes Mo snort and for what feels like the umpteenth time, I consider skinning that vulpine shit for a blanket.

I know he's a lesser predator and definitely not one of the leader shifters like Torben or Tiernan, so his insolence is grating.

"At least T explained to me that different species call their leaders different shit so I don't fuck up and call every bigwig an alpha," I mutter to myself. "Though, I have no idea what these twin fuckers are beyond rich and sketchy."

Yanking open the door to the Boom Boom Room, I straighten my spine and stalk inside with all the confidence of a woman who didn't just get 'fireman carried' off by a dude. My eyes scan the room carefully, noting where everyone is and what's going on before I'm too far in. Several scantily clad women are lounging on the beds with inviting expressions on their faces. The men range in age and dress, looking like everything from dealers to businessmen. Most of them have drinks and a few are also indulging in question-able substances on tables and in armchairs. A thick, cloying scent tells me people are smoking unicorn glitter and maybe even catnip.

Great. I'll be working in fucking Wonderland this evening. I wonder where the goddamn caterpillar is?

A loud moan echoes through the room and I spin on my heel, locating the origin of the sound. It's a half-shifted naga female strapped to the rack in the corner and she's got a crowd of men and women around her. The pain doesn't sound like it's in the red zone, so I roll my eyes and head for the bar. I see Jazz, an incubus who works the bar on opposite nights from Fer, and let out a sigh of relief. He's the least objectionable person they could have called in to work the private room. His taste runs to men and non-binary types so he won't stare at my ass and he's not a shifter, so no idiotic rules to follow.

Perfect.

"Hey, Fi-Fi. I don't normally get to work with you." Jazz gives me a lazy smile that I'm sure his feeds and fucks find irresistable, but it makes me stick my tongue out at him. "Nice. I still think you should pierce it."

"I have quite enough steel, thanks. But if I change my mind, I'll visit you at *Scars and Bars*. How's that?" I lean on the bartop, watching for the mouthy asshole from earlier. The room isn't big enough for me to avoid him entirely, but if I can keep him from getting me alone, I'm more likely to hold my temper.

The incubus beams. "Aces, babe. You know I do shows here, too. I could make a show of it and we'd pack the house."

Turning back to him, I blink. "You do live tatts and piercings in the round? That's brave. The crowd has to be distracting."

Jazz shrugs. "I'm *just that good*. Besides, the vibe in the room amps up and I'm fed for *days* off that shit."

This is why I have trouble with lust lickers. Their idea of consent is... nebulous.

"You feed off me without permission and I'll pierce something you won't enjoy," I say as I take the tray he prepared while we were talking. "Guaranteed."

His laugh follows me as I walk away with the tray, looking at the handwritten ticket that tells me who I'm looking for. Frowning, I squint at his chicken scratch and when I finally make out 'blue bitch and horned god,' I groan. He might be the least troublesome bartender they could have brought in, but this kind of shit makes me want to strangle him.

I stroll through the crowd, finally seeing the blue haired siren sitting with a golden skinned demon with a body that did indeed look like it was carved by some deity to tempt people. Picking up my pace, I approach them with a smile, handing over the Blue Hawaiian and Fireball on the rocks. The demon hands me a wad of cash, not even pretending not to check out my rack, and waves me away.

At least he's a good tipper.

Folding the cash carefully, I tuck it in the tight corset top where it won't fall out. I refuse to keep that shit in my pockets because my brass babies have to be ready to go if someone dares to touch me. I know they'll look—the damn uniforms were made to encourage it—but no one gets away with using hands or magic. That's an automatic asskicking and I'll have the bouncers boot their asses.

"There you are, Sassy. I've been waiting for you."

The sound of his rich, low tone slithers over me and I whirl around, glaring at the guy who's pissed me off at two different jobs in the past month. "Look, moron. I don't know why you've made me your project, but I'm not interested. Buzz off."

"I'm wounded," he pretends to pout and bats his thick lashes. "I thought we were becoming friends."

I can't help it; I snort so hard I almost drop my tray. "You've got a warped understanding of reality."

His lips curve up in a slow, sexy grin. "Maybe so, but I know when a chick is fighting because she wants to leave and when she's fighting because she wants to stay."

"Again, you're deluded and I have drinks to serve. Get bent," I shoot back with an eye roll. Shaking my head as I stalk back to the bar, I mutter a string of curses that would make a kraken blush.

The whistle gets my attention and I see Jazz clucking his tongue at me. "He is *so* smitten, mama. If you don't want him, I'll happily escort him to Pound Town."

I grab the new tray, slamming the old one on the bar. I don't know why his flirting is pissing me off, but the second he talked about hooking up with the asshole, I felt something in my gut twist painfully. "Stop being a poster child for sexual harassment. We have shit to do."

"Fi-Fi, we work in a *sex club*," he chides as he wipes down the counter. "That's not a thing."

"Whatever."

Ignoring his ridiculous noises as I stomp away, I sigh to myself. Jazz isn't wrong and I know it. But something inside of me flashed red with rage at his words and I have no idea why. It's not as if I'm remotely attracted to that stupid gangster, even if he is hot as hell. I have a thing for bad boys, as Fer pointed out last time, but I'm not stupid enough to go for a guy that makes me want to kick him in the balls every time we meet. And I *have* a mate—that's more than I can deal with as it is.

So why am I ready to beat the shit out of Jazz for suggesting he'd like to take the greaser for a spin?

I growl in frustration and take the next round to a table full of shifty looking guys that are obviously gang members, noting the quieter twin sitting at it and watching me curiously. When I snatch the tip he offers and stalk away, I can feel his eyes on me the entire way back to the bar.

This is going to be a very long night.

34

FERAY

I FEEL THE CHANGE IN THE ROOM AFTER MIDNIGHT. THIS IS THE TIME of night when the seedier side of Briarvale comes out to play. The moon phase is wreaking havoc with the shifter population, especially those of the canine persuasion, and it makes shit worse.

Mo is more of an annoying ass than usual; I didn't think it was possible, but here we are.

Oddly enough, I don't feel the pull of the moon. I wish I had more free time because I'd like to look into that, but the amount of orders tonight is keeping me on my toes. Shelving those thoughts, I mix the drinks for servers as they rush over. The additional orders from Jazz's bar in the private room are driving me crazy. He should have checked his bar stock before starting his shift; I'll give him hell about it later.

Apparently, the Bedia party can drink their weight in liquor and they prefer more exotic cocktails. Jazz always defers more intricate cocktails to me, so he's got me hopping double time. Fi comes out with another huge list of replacement stock and hands it to Mo. The minute she turns her back, his eyes shift and I hear him grumbling.

Narrowing my eyes, I make a mental note to watch the fox closely. He's obviously affected by the moon phase and he could be dangerous to our clients. I'm not sure if a fox bite is as deadly as mine is for vampires, but I'm not about to find out. His shitty attitude makes me question why the first full moon phase since the Ascension is making everyone but me act like a fucking clown.

"How are you holding up?" Fi questions as she sips her pop.

"So far, so good. Mo's a cranky bastard today." I motion toward his end of the bar and Fi snorts.

"I couldn't tell from his pleasant disposition." My sister rolls her eyes, then goes back to people watching while I work.

"Louie said certain species aren't allowed in for the next week to prevent bar brawls. I wish he was one of them." Shrugging my shoulders, I mix the next four drinks without missing a beat. I've found my groove and I'm in the zone now.

That is, until Mo shoves a crate with Jazz's supplies in it at Fi's chest. "Take that with you, witch."

My wolf rises to the surface as I bear my canines at him. Moving Fi behind me, I advance on him until I'm standing between them. Tiernan, the banker, and Louie are suddenly focused on me—I can feel their eyes. My sister's mate moves to the rail, ready to spring into action if I need him. Looking up, I subtly shake my head 'no,' so he knows I have it under control. "Get out."

"You can't tell me what to do!" Mo yells as fur erupts on his arms.

Out of the corner of my eye, I catch movement. Louie steps away from his post to monitor the scene as I snarl at the dickwaffle. "I can and will. Unlike you, I am in full control of my beast. Leave *now*."

Louie comes forward, followed by the orc bouncer, and they immediately remove the borderline feral fox from behind the bar. Obviously, I read the situation correctly because Tiernan and the banker nod at me. Even the frilly vamp gives me a thumbs up as he comes back from the door. I'm still furious, of course, but I'm proud I handled that idiot without losing my cool.

Those narcissistic little vulpine bastards always believe they are in control, no matter how wrong they are.

Turning back to Fiadh, I look her over quickly to make sure the sneaky bastard didn't bruise her with the supplies. When I'm sure she's okay, she hugs me then returns to the private room to work. Exhaling roughly, I feel the pressure inside me abate. It was hard to restrain my wolf; she wanted to rip Mo into tiny pieces. I pause, settling my beast down before I go back to serving the patrons. From the corner, I hear the banker complaining about slow service and I note his glass is half full.

What is his deal? Maybe his species is also affected by the moon phase?

I make two of his drinks and place them before him, forcing myself to smile. He mumbles about poor staffing and I frown. *He thought I did okay removing my rude ass colleague, so what's his deal now?* Rolling my eyes, I return to the middle of the bar, finding a single white orchid. No branch—just the flower— sitting on the bar top in front of my station. The world stops briefly as I pick the flower up and fill a shot glass with water. Placing the stem in it, I rest the flower petals on the rim of the glass. A smile tugs at my lips as I stare at the flower, then go back to looking at orders I have to fill.

"You're exquisite when you smile."

The soft voice catches my attention and I look up to see the quieter of Bedia twins. "Thank you."

Thinking back to when I saw him pop out of the private room, I recall which drink he preferred. Mixing a Red Death, I push it towards him. The shimmer of the diamond on his safe word tag tells me he's a Master, so he gets charged a reduced rate. I ring it up and drop the bill print down in front of him. "Enjoy."

He sees the slip and drops a twenty on top of the receipt without looking at the price before he takes a sip. "How did you know?"

"I have excellent eyesight." My eyes flash to my wolf and back again as I get his change. I offer it to him and he closes my hand around it.

"Keep it," he says with a shy smile.

"This is not the 'Mating Games'! Leave the wolf alone so she can work, Bedia." The banker growls at him from the other end of the bar and I'm a bit surprised he knows who the twin is. *Maybe they bank with him, too?*

I go back to filling my orders after I give my new customer a sheepish smile. We need this job and the last thing I want to do is piss off a Founder. If I keep my head down, I can get through this night without more drama.

"Go back to your cave, old man. Leave the night to those of us that can still play." Clearly, the nicer twin has a bite when he wants.

Raising my gaze quickly, I reach over the bar and put my hand over his mouth. He doesn't care who the banker is, nor does he care what his rank is here, but I do. "Shhhh… He's a founder; please don't piss him off."

"Listen to the wolf, hatchling. Crawl back into the hole you came out of," the banker says as he slams back his drink. The muscles around his left eye tick as his agitation grows. Noting the empty glass, I mix his Manhattan, opting for the stronger drink this time. With a snap of my fingers, his drink ignites and he smiles briefly.

The Bedia twin removes my hand from his mouth and leans on the bar as he smirks at my grumpy regular. "I have met some pricks in my time, but you, sir, are a cactus!"

My mouth hangs open in shock as I look between the two males. Part of me wants to laugh hysterically, but the other part wants to run and hide. The banker stares at him then finishes his second drink in a single gulp. He moves to a booth on the other side of the bar with a dark glare. I stare in disbelief that he left his favorite seat.

"There you have it." The twin motions to him and raises his glass. Tilting his head to the side, he looks at me with a gentle expression. "I've been rude. My name is Khal."

Something is pulling me towards him now; this can't be natural.

Unconsciously, I reach up and rub the bite mark left by my mate. My fingers drift over the raised bumps, comforting myself. Khal watches my hand curiously. I know my mark is showing because I wore the uniform that has it on display. His brow furrows for a second, but that changes when I finally reply.

"I'm Feray; nice to meet you." Part of me is unnerved by the way he's studying me, but the other half is excited. *The excitement concerns me —we have a mate and one should be enough.*

"Your name matches your beauty. Would you do me the honor of going out with me sometime?"

Before I can gape at him in shock, he takes a pen off the bar, pulls a card from his pocket, and writes his number on the back. Sliding the card to me, he smiles shyly.

I pick it up and look at it curiously. It says 'Scaleon Pharmaceuticals' on the front. His handwriting is a beautiful scrawl and I wouldn't have expected that from someone who looks like a gangster. Anxiously, I flip the card around in my hand. I need to tell Torben about the invitation because I don't understand the feelings I'm having. "I really shouldn't; I don't think my mate would be pleased."

I have a mate; there's no way Khal could be a mate too, right?

"Hey bro! Watch out or she'll sick the kitty on you, too." The other Bedia appears next to Khal and I notice they're damn near identical, except the pissed off look the other one typically wears.

"No kitties for me, asshole. My mate is a bear." Smiling broadly, I allow my canines to descend and tilt my head to the side. I lock eyes with him and a tingle moves up my spine as if my hackles are standing on edge. "You can toddle your ass back to the far side of the bar. As far as I'm concerned, this is an AB conversation and you can C your way out of it."

"You're not worth my time." He pulls back and looks at his twin for a moment, then snaps his fingers before turning on his heel to walk away.

"That took a brass set, Feray. No one ever challenges my brother," Khal says.

Laughing, I look down at the card in my hand. I might as well see if it would be worth the conversation with Torben—I saw several members of his sleuth with more than one partner. "He can get bent. No one tells me what to do." My curiosity gets the better of me and I ask softly. "If I did agree to go out with you after speaking with my mate, where would we go?"

What am I saying?

A broad smile comes over Khal's lips as he looks at me. "That's easy. There's a beautiful botanical garden I would love to take you to see. It has some of the most rare and deadly flowers known in the world."

His eyes glow faintly for a moment then fade. I think his animal wanted to show itself and he stopped it. I'll have to ask him about it in a less public space because I recently learned it's rude to ask someone what they are. Khal has an interesting scent—it reminds me of the vetiver that grows in the meadows towards the north of our cabin. It's a clean scent, and I won't forget it, but I'd like to know what it is.

Turning my attention back to him, I make a note on a napkin to look up the botanical garden he mentioned. "I'll text you. You'd better get back to your party before your brother comes looking for you again," I say playfully.

He smiles at me then leaves, returning to the private room.

What the hell am I doing?

35

FIADH

I'VE NEVER BEEN SO GLAD TO SEE THE END OF A MOON PHASE AS I WAS this month.

Every shift from that disastrous one on April Fool's Day to the Full Moon on the sixth was a nightmare of epic proportions. Even the few since have been crazy—I guess Philly's bar being so small and not filled with partying rich assholes made the change in behavior less noticeable? Hell, I don't know, but I'm investing in serious weaponry and special padded clothing for the next one. It feels like the closer we get to Beltane, the more handsy people are getting, and that's just not how the witch community works.

Shifters going into the rut season will land me in jail; I just know it.

Shaking my head as I leave the cabin, I secure my bags on my shoulder. I have my usual messenger, but since we got paid overtime to help clean up some messes left by the rowdy moon-spelled patrons the past two weeks, I'm going shopping for new equipment for my sacred circle. The one we set up in February was as basic as possible since we'd lost most of our inherited or personal stuff in the fire. Unlike Imbolc, Beltane is going to require replacing the big stuff. It's a much more involved ritual, and I haven't figured out how to broach the subject of it with Tiernan yet.

Witches have affinities for certain holidays based on their power set, but I've never had enough to choose my favorite based on them. However, Beltane always drew me and I wonder if it's because it's about rebirth and rejuvenation. The Ascension certainly forced my sister and me to be reborn as completely different people in new circumstances.

Perhaps destiny had a hand in it and that's why I felt stronger during the May holiday than I do at the others?

It's not a far-fetched thought, but that doesn't make my task of teaching my new mate what goes on at this celebration in the witch community. The way we let loose for this coming together of the Goddess and the Horned God makes the Ascension matings look tame. I can only assume it will deepen our bond on my end and maybe even free some more of my magic. He needs to be prepared for it and a little spark of excitement dances in my chest when I think about being able to teach him something for a change.

Tiernan has been slowly helping me learn about various shifter types that live in Briarvale. I'm not an outstanding student when I feel dumb and his gentle corrections or additions make it easier to swallow. Feray wants to help, too, but I feel guilty taking her time when she has so much to learn about herself. I didn't turn out to be a totally different species than I spent my life training to be; they simply gave me bad or outdated info on others. The slow trickle of knowledge I'm gaining from T's help while we're at the bar is making me feel much more confident.

I stick my hand in my pocket, grasping the drawing I did of the symbol carved on Philly's back. While I know Tiernan has been quietly asking around the Fae community for me, I still believe the best information will come from magic users who stay on this plane. I brought the little sketch with me so I can pretend to be curious about it in the magic shops. Maybe one of the shopkeepers will recognize it or have a book that pertains to symbology that's older than the ones I've searched at the library.

"Don't know if you don't ask," I mutter to myself as I exit the forest near the main drag.

It's early, and that means the nocturnal shifters and magic users are still in bed.

Coming here without Fer means I'm more likely to hold my temper and the lack of crowds is even more helpful. I cross the street, passing the various groceries across from hotels and apartments as I make my way north to the witch district. It's closest to the elite areas because magic users are enormous snobs and hoard money like no one's business. Window shopping has never been my thing, but I see a few things I know Feray would love. Tucking their locations away for later, I smile as the sun shines through the clouds.

Having a stable situation and someone who cares for me is a lot better for my inner peace than I would have imagined.

Don't get me wrong—I loved working and living at Philly's, but it meant we weren't going any farther than exactly where we were. There's safety in that, but he couldn't pay us more than he did and we couldn't save anything to do any better. With Torben allowing us to live in the cabin in exchange for 'caretaking' and Dezi paying us as well as he does, we've finally climbed out of the gutter.

Okay, that's dramatic, but it's a more fiscally advantageous situation.

Being able to worry less about bills and shit has lifted a weight I didn't know was on my shoulders. We won't be rich anytime soon, but I truly believe we'll be able to do the things Feray and I have dreamed of, eventually. She wants to decorate and make the cabin homey; I want to replace the magical equipment with better, stronger tools that will encourage my magic to keep growing. If we continue like we are now, we might even take the first out-of-town trip we've taken since we were kids.

That makes me grin because I know Fer has Pinterest boards on her phone for the places we've always wanted to go. Being able to give her that would make my heart sing and I can't wait. The thought makes me so happy I whistle a merry tune as I walk through town until I enter the magical district. I feel the eyes on me the minute I cross the barrier, but I'm in a good mood, so I don't let their nosy bullshit bother me.

When I get to the herb store, I wait patiently for the exotic ones I can't grow myself and don't snark at the bitchy clerk. My stop at the candle and oils shop takes longer, but I don't get into a fight with the nasty old fucker who runs it. Even the snooty twin sisters at the bookstore don't bother me today. I show each of them the design and get puzzled looks, but I'm hoping to have more luck at the last stop.

Cards and Wares is the premier marketplace for magical equipment and I usually wouldn't even go in. Their prices can be steep and they sell nothing second hand. But I know I have the funds to be a bit more choosy this time, so I walk in with my head up. The staring is worse than on the street, but the gnarled old crone who runs this place is a mercenary mage. She won't refuse to sell me shit based on the Supreme Dickface's decree because she's too greedy to lose a customer.

That benefits me and it's about time shit did.

Ignoring the whispers, I walk to the caldron aisle, looking through the various floor models until I find one I like in a price range I'm comfortable with. Pulling the lot card for it, I make my way to the section with athames, besoms, and chalices. Those I'm able to select from the shelf, so I find a matching set made of durable materials that have pentacles and moons etched into them. The designs make me think of my sister and me: magic and moons. Fer would love being here to pick stuff like this out, but I came on my own despite her having plans with Torben.

She needs time alone with him as much as I do with Tiernan. We've been eating and living very much like a family, but finding time alone with no one around is a challenge. I don't think the guys mind that Fer and I are so close, but even I have to admit that being alone with Tiernan allows me to let go of the iron grip of responsibility in a way I haven't felt since our parents died. Knowing my sister is safe with Torben somewhere gives me an opportunity to simply be, and Tiernan is so very good at being a calming, quiet presence when we're by ourselves. The entire world quiets, and I feel like I can breathe more easily.

So I planned this brief trip while they were out and T has work to allow myself time to commune with my witchy self on my own, too. Feray loves being a wolf and I'm so happy for her, but I miss her being the other half of my spell work. I'd bet she misses doing it, too, but we won't risk exposing her to things that will hurt her like the shit at the Ascension did.

Damn, I've been fucking about in the Tarot aisle for like five minutes.

"Get it together, Fi." I chuckle to myself and pick two decks that feel like they're calling to me. My hands are getting full, but I'm almost done. I need a new set of runes, a few crystals, and a robe. Then I can head to the register to arrange the caldron delivery and pay.

I leave the Tarot section, hurrying towards the scrying and protection section to pick up the crystals and runes when I hear it. The voice isn't loud, but it carries across the store like it's caressing my ears.

"I have a standing order, Ophelia. How is it you never have it available when I arrive, even when I attempt to pick it up during *your* preferred hours?"

Oh, shit.

Dezi's voice is instantly recognizable, and I suddenly feel a weird pull in my veins. Ducking around the end of a row, I scramble into the section I need, tossing crystals and a set of affordable runes into my bag so I don't drop them. The need to get out of here before he sees me is strong, but an opposing ache in my chest is demanding I move closer. I'm torn and all I want to do is avoid him like I have been since our incident in the office.

"Why, oh why, did he have to come *here* on the one day I'm in the damn magic district? Is some god getting their rocks off watching me fumble like a fool?"

There's no one around to hear my frustrated question, but I head over to the clothing area carefully as I ponder a response. I don't think I've pissed any deities off, but I know I piss off others on the daily. Maybe I need to check for hexes or curses tonight. That *has* to be why my luck is so damn fickle. I might even have enough power now for that scrying to be more reliable.

He didn't seek me out, either, and I find myself a little miffed about it. An apology would have gone a long way and not only has my boss not given me that, but he's acted like I'm stuffed full of holy water and garlic for half a month. The nerve of it all makes my magic dance on my fingertips, sparking a little as I touch the lovely robes on the racks.

Fucking moody bloodsucker...

"Fiadh, are you over there muttering to yourself?"

Dezi's query makes my gut—among other things—clench and I bang my head against the cool metal of a rack in consternation. I should have known he was going to catch me. Now he has all the power because he spoke first. With an irritable growl, I step out from behind the rack of gorgeous and out of my price range ceremonial robes to look at him across the store.

"Yes, it's me. How are you today?" There. I was polite, but I'm sure as hell not giving him anything else.

His chuckle is low as he arches a brow. "Doing a little pre-holiday stocking?"

I nod, shifting my items around in my arms uncomfortably. "Yep. I'm almost done replacing the things we lost in the fire."

Walking away from the counter, the vampire prowls closer, and the bottom drops out of my stomach. He looks at the hand stitched silver and black robe I'm standing next in interest. It's really more of a dress with a hood and large robe-like sleeves that would allow me to work without being worried about catching anything on fire. This kind of tailored attire is what the wealthy witches and mages wear to big ceremonies in town—it's made by one of the premier designers and I'd have to sacrifice a fucking goat to pay for it.

"You should try this on."

Snorting in disbelief, I shake my head. "It would scare me to even take this thing off of the hanger. It costs more than I make in—my life."

"Ophelia, I need one of your staff to come relieve Fiadh of all her selections. She's going to the dressing room to try this piece on."

What? I certainly am not.

"It's okay. I was only browsing. I'm getting one of those over there," I protest as I gesture at the more affordable cloak rack nearby. "No need to put anyone out."

"Nonsense," Dezi says in a tone that brooks no argument. "Give your things to this chap and go try it on."

I blink as a small pixie zips up and holds out his hands for my things. There doesn't seem to be a way to get out of this without making a scene, so I reluctantly hand him my shopping bag and all the things I've gathered. Keeping my purse, I take the fancy ass robe the vampire hands me, frowning darkly. I don't like being cornered and I definitely don't like being forced to comply with demands he has no right to make.

Stupid, sexy, fang-faced dick weasel.

Stomping over to the dressing area, I slip off my bag and wiggle my way into the garment as best I can without stripping. I don't want to take my clothes off with him here, but I'll be damned if my skin isn't on fire. The fabric slides over what little exposed flesh I have with a sensation so amazing that I can't help but groan. This might be the nicest thing I've *ever* put on my body and though I don't have the small fortune to buy it, I'm glad I have something to dream about now.

"Perfect," Dezi murmurs, and surprisingly, I can hear him despite the distance between us.

I walk out and twirl around, deciding if he wanted to make a big deal of this, he'll have to handle me being a pain in the ass. "It makes my ass look bangin'."

That earns me an eye roll, and the vampire turns back to the old crone at the counter. "Find the materials for my wards, Ophelia, and put all of Fiadh's things on my tab—including this robe."

"No!" I shake my head in panic, struggling to get myself out of the damn thing and pick up my bag. "You've been kind enough to hire and train us. This, especially the robe, is *much* too… generous."

Dark red eyes glower at me from the counter as he takes the bag from the shopkeeper. "Don't argue with me, witchling. I will do this and you will let me. Think of it as… an apology."

I blink, putting my hand on my chest as the words hit me like a two-by-four. "An apology?"

"Consent is the cornerstone of my business and words are necessary. I should have asked." His lips curve up and he looks at me with a wicked glimmer in his eyes. "The rules will be set in advance in the future."

My brain is working overtime trying to come up with a smart ass retort, but before I can, he storms out of the shop like he's on a mission. I walk over to the register, still trying to understand what just happened. The irritated tone of the crone asking me when they can deliver the caldron brings me out of my trance and I have to shake my head back and forth for a moment.

"Uh. Tomorrow. We're off tomorrow."

She eyes me warily, scribbling information on a notepad. "You're close with one of the ancients, then?"

"Not really. He's my boss," I reply.

A loud snort surprises me and the woman starts packing my things in the bag I brought with me. "Is that what the kids are calling it these days?"

I frown. "I'm not fucking Dezi; I have a mate."

"Mmm. So you do," she says before she grabs my hand and flips it over, cackling in delight. "And so you will."

Eyes narrowed, I yank my palm back. "Reading without permission is *rude*."

"Seems to me you'd forgive me if I buy you a fancy dress—that's what the evidence says, anyway." The mage laughs again and slaps her palm on the counter. "I'm here all week, girly."

"Good to know." My wry quip is lost on her and I take my bags, hoping to get out of here before she tries a knock-knock joke. It suddenly occurs to me that I haven't shown her the drawing yet and I sigh.

Damn it.

I reach into my pocket and pull it out, smoothing it on the counter-top. "Have you seen this before? I saw it somewhere and was thinking about using it in a ritual."

"Ha!" she cries. "You should know better than to use something unknown in spellwork, girl. I don't know what it is, but I'd advise against funneling power into it."

Suddenly a flood of magic rushes through me and the sensations I've been feeling that help me suss out emotions start churning. The mage is lying and it's making her aura a sickly brownish-yellow. Rubbing my hands over my arms as a shiver runs through me, I watch her closely as she pushes the design back at me. I'm about to question her further when there's a whisper that travels through the air to my ears.

~She's lying. Don't push her.~

It's like time stops as I look around the store with wide eyes. I *saw* Dezi leave with my own two eyes, but that is his voice; I'd bet my sweet ass on it. Feeling unnerved, I take the paper and shove it in my pocket before I shrug at Ophelia.

"Thanks for looking! I'll see your delivery guys tomorrow then."

That said, I stride out of the store and start walking as far from the magic district as I can. I don't know what the hell just happened, but I am *not cool with it*.

I'll have to confront the King Batboy at work about using his powers on me.

I am *not* some simpering club bunny waiting for him to taste my blood for a cheap thrill.

He can take his Dracula cape and get superfucked.

36

FERAY

THE DIRT UNDER MY PAWS HAS A CALMING EFFECT OVER THE NERVES surfacing as I get closer to the gardens.

Over the last few weeks, Torben and I talked about the polyamory that happens in certain species. It seems over the last hundred years, more males than females have been born in a lot of shifter groups. He took me to meet other families in his sleuth where females have as many as six mates.

That's way too much testosterone for me to juggle and not lose my temper over, but it made me feel better.

During our discussion, I admitted I had asked because of Khal's offer of a date, and he froze in his tracks. He repeated the name, making sure he'd heard me right and it seemed like a very odd reaction. Torben is usually unflappable and his tiny flash of anger at Khal's name was unusual.

I go over the conversation in my head as I make my way through the underbrush. If I'm completely honest with myself, the pull I have around Khal tells me he's at least a potential mate. Torben confirmed my suspicions, but then his mood changed completely.

When he talked about what Khal could bring to the family, his biggest draw was security, but he stayed quiet when I asked about negatives.

Dropping the bag I carried my clothes in, I shift back to my human form and get dressed. Running a brush through my long hair, I watch the horizon, seeing if I can get eyes on Khal before he sees me. As Fi enjoys having the first word in a conversation, I prefer being the first to put eyes on my target to assess them while they are unaware.

I circle the Nightshade Botanical Garden several times before emerging from the wood line holding my bag. I didn't dress up in case I needed to shift and run. Ruining a pair of leggings and a sweater isn't a huge deal, but I'd be more upset about my fancy things. Anxiously, I braid my hair on the side opposite of my mate's mark and shift my sweater so it's visible. Even catching Torben's mark out of the corner of my eye soothes something in me.

When I finally walk closer, I see that the garden doesn't look like a garden from the outside. The twelve foot tall stone walls with a glass and wrought iron dome look more like a prison terrarium than a greenhouse. It's a very interesting structure and I wonder which species designed it.

"Amazing, isn't it?" The soft, almost hypnotic tone of Khal's voice brings me out of my fixation on architecture.

Turning enough to glance at him over my shoulder, a smile creeps over my lips. A giggle escapes and I realize it sounds more nervous than fun. "It looks like a terrarium prison for bad turtles."

"Bad turtles? Is there even such a thing?"

"Well, maybe snapping turtles. They seem mean," I say, shrugging my shoulders as I look over the structure again.

Khal steps forward and extends his hand towards me, then pulls it back and stuffs it in his pocket. "I got you something." He opens his jacket and pulls out a cream and gray-colored stuffed bunny, offering it to me.

Taking the cute animal from him, I can't help but smile at his thoughtfulness. "Thank you. I was looking at this the other day in one of the shops, but I thought it would be silly of me to purchase it." I hug the bunny to my chest, squeezing it tightly.

"I was worried you would be offended or think it was childish, but it sort of called to me." He places his hand at the small of my back and leads me towards the iron gates to the facility.

The witch at the gate appears scared when she sees Khal. She offers him the tickets and stamps the backs of our hands before opening the inner door for us. Just inside the door, there are pamphlets listing all the plants and herbs, including their poisonous agent and what species is targeted by it. The science nerd in me does a gleeful little dance and the part that wanted to be a powerful witch echoes the sentiment.

"Let's go into the greenhouse first. There's something I want you to be aware of for the future and they have some of it here." His tone says he's being honest, so I motion for him to lead the way.

As soon as we step inside, a beautiful yellow flower greets us, hanging upside in the air delicately.

"Be careful, dear. Don't let its beauty fool you," another witch inside says in a musical sing-song.

"Oh? What is it?" I flip through the pamphlet, trying to find it.

"It's called an 'Angels Trumpet.' The pollen it produces is a potent hallucinogen. In small quantities, it gives you an almost euphoric feeling, but too much will kill you. It depends on the person and the species as to how much is too much." The way she stares at the plant, I can surmise it's something she's worked with extensively.

Moving to the next area, Khal tells me about the hogweed and blue English that surround the laurel bush on the path. I didn't know the laurel bush close to the cabin was poisonous. I'll have to ask Torben to remove the bush so we don't accidentally get hurt. I'm sure he won't want a dangerous plant near our home.

The backs of Khal's knuckles brush along my jawline and the gentle pull I feel towards him intensifies. Staring up into his eyes, I see the faint glow of his shift, and then it's gone again. I finally give and ask. "For the life of me, I can't figure out what your animal is."

He tenses and backs away slightly. "My species doesn't have the best reputation." He drops his gaze for a moment, then motions to the next bunch of plants, changing the subject quickly. "What do you know about belladonna, nightshade, and nicandra?"

"We can find nightshade and belladonna locally. Nicandra isn't from around here so it has to be imported." I shrug my shoulders when he looks surprised that I knew. "Remember, I grew up thinking I was a witch. They hammered the different plants and their uses into us from an early age. Though some important plants were omitted from our education, obviously."

Sighing, he nods. "Witches are known for controlling the narrative." I can't disagree with what he's saying. It's the truth. "I'm a chemist by trade. It's important for me to know what I'm working with."

We find a bench in the middle of the garden as a vendor comes through offering snacks. I grab several sticks of jerky and he does the same. He's a carnivore, so that's a plus. "Well, at least I know our diets are similar. You must be a predator of some sort."

"I am a predator and I know you're a wolf." He leans in and draws my scent into his lungs. "Your scent reminds me of the geraniums outside of my lab."

Mimicking him, I lean into him and sniff. Unconsciously, my eyes shift and I feel my canines elongate. "Your scent reminds me of the vetiver field near to my home. Definitely not a wolf like me; I would feel it. You're not a bear like Torben or a cat like Tiernan." Tapping my chin, I keep studying him. "Scaring the witch like you did, I would say you're in the dragon family."

He bites off a chunk of the jerky as he shakes his head, smiling. "I'm neither as boring nor as lame as a dragon."

"No? What else is there then?" Apparently, not only have I been sheltered and lied to my entire life, I'm also the smartest dumb person ever.

"Promise me you won't freak out." He reaches out and takes both of my hands in his, clasping them. His scent changes and the slight acidic tinge of fear becomes apparent.

"Why would I freak out? You're an intelligent, kind man. I don't believe you would do anything to harm me." Giving his hand a squeeze, I try to reassure him.

Maybe he's a poison dart frog shifter, or a wild hog shifter? No, those aren't predators, Feray, be serious.

"Well…" He glances around, then leans in close to me, wincing as he says, "I'm a basilisk."

"See, that wasn't so bad. You're a giant armored snake; that's cool." I lean forward and give him a reassuring hug. Now that he told me, I stand up, wanting to get going again. Khal sits there wide eyed with his mouth hanging open and I reach over, using my fingertips to push up on his jaw to close his mouth. "I wouldn't leave your mouth open like that. Who knows what poisonous things may land in there?"

He stands up quickly and wraps an arm around my waistline, holding me firmly to his side. He presses his pillow soft lips to my temple. The warmth penetrates my soul and comforts me. "I was so scared to tell you what I am."

"Why? Because you don't have fur?" Bouncing up, I kiss his cheek. "You're a good man, Khal; never be ashamed of who or what you are."

Wrapping an arm around his waist in return, I realize I feel safe in his embrace. His admission of what his animal is has me wanting to see it, but I know it has caused him to be judged over the years. My acceptance of what he is comforts him, I can tell because relief had flooded his features almost immediately.

"I need to show you something very important." Khal holds me close like I am the most precious thing in the world to him as he guides me through the gardens. We make it to an area that has warning signs posted at the gates. 'No wolves beyond this point' is written in bold letters on a yellow background.

"Sir, your date can't come in here." The witch guarding the door looks at us, her hands trembling and eyes darting everywhere except Khal's eyes.

"She can and she will. I need to show her what's in here. Understand me?" The command in Khal's voice sends a thrill through me, making my wolf and I take notice.

Huffing as she walks out from behind the pedestal, the witch offers me a N95 medical grade mask, goggles, and gloves. "Please put these on, miss. Under no circumstances are you to take any of this off until you come out."

Her hands still tremble, and the acrid scent of her fear almost chokes me. *It's so strong.* My wolf is enjoying the fact that Khal's animal scares her this much.

I take the safety gear from her before she runs back to the pedestal. Khal adjusts the mask and goggles to fit me perfectly. After slipping my gloves on, he grabs the tape and tapes the gloves to my sweater.

It must be bad for him to take this level of precaution with me.

Once secured, he holds me tight to his side and leads me to the heart of the building. Beside a beautiful waterfall, there's a small field of flowers that look like large blue bells on stalks with leaves that have three main veins with feathery fingers shooting off. We stop about ten feet away and he pulls my mask away briefly so I catch the scent of the flowers. The faint whiff is *not* one I will forget —its dark, woodsy scent reminds me of the forest and leaves a bitter, acidic taste on my tongue.

"This is wolfsbane. It's also known as monkshood or aconite, and it's poisonous to everyone, but extremely fatal for wolves. A tiny microscopic amount can kill you, Feray." He looks back towards the door where the witch is. "The witches use it in their magic during the Ascension to root out wolves in hiding. It would burn your skin and make you feel ill. Ingestion can mean death."

My heart rate speeds up and my breathing becomes labored. I feel woozy when I realize the truth. Khal scoops me up and runs me out of the hazardous area. Once we're in the safe zone, the witch helps him rip the safety gear off and offers me water.

"I'm so sorry." Embarrassment floods me.

Khal pulls me into his lap and holds me tightly to him. It takes me several moments to calm down as the hedge witches retreat.

"The witches poison wolves on purpose? Why?" I don't mention that I've felt the exact sensation he described at the exact ceremony he mentioned.

"Not exactly poison—they want to drive them out of hiding. It helps them to sort out cross breeds since they are purists." A rattling rumble resonates deep in his chest and I notice the unique sound of his shift.

"That angers you." I reach up and caress his cheek, looking at the shifting of the bone plates under his skin.

He'd really freak out if he knew I'd already experienced this shit.

He closes his eyes and breathes in deeply. "Knowing what I know now? Yes, it does."

Leaning forward, he presses his lips to mine and the intense tingles of the beginning tethers of the mate bond wanting to forge. Pulling away quickly, I scoot backwards across the dirt.

"I have a mate…" My voice breaks as my wolf whines in my head. She's pushing me to go back to him. Mentally, I'm fighting for control over my body.

He crawls on all fours until he's sitting in front of me. "I know you do. Most bears and basilisks live in poly groups. We are experiencing the same problem as the bears are. For the last seventy years, more males than females have been born."

"You're okay knowing I'm already bonded? Because my wolf knows you're ours, but I don't want to hurt you or Torben. He knows about our date and he encouraged it, but…" Holding my head, I close my eyes. "I'm so confused."

The next thing I know, I feel Khal's arms around me and he rests his head on the opposite shoulder of Torben's mark. "You were raised by witches that usually only take one mate. You've spent your entire life believing you're a witch." There's a sadness in his tone that pulls at my heartstrings. He kisses my cheek and rests his head back on my shoulder again. "If you were raised a wolf, this would be so much easier for you."

"I need time, Khal." Raising my head, I turn and rest my cheek on his shoulder. "We need to talk to Torben if this…" I tap his ribs over his heart, "… is gonna happen. He needs to be part of the decision." Lifting my head up again, I smile, trying not to cry because it feels like it's tearing me apart inside. "I'm not saying 'no,' and I'm not rejecting you. I'm being respectful of my mate."

His lips curve up in a sexy smile. "This is why you're perfect. Your heart is as big as the moon and you don't hide how you feel. You don't judge people and you keep others' feelings in mind."

I hear truth and affection in his tone. "You can't have a successful family if everyone doesn't respect everyone's needs and desires."

Khal breaks away and stands up, offering me his hand. "Let me walk you home. It would be my honor to show I am worthy to your Torben."

Walking me home would show he cares and puts my safety before his wants and desires. Torben will be pleased that he's taking it seriously. Linking an arm with Khal, I point him towards the path to my house with my stuffed bunny in my bag. "I accept."

37

Fiadh

As we draw closer to Beltane, I feel my magic respond in a way I haven't ever felt before.

There's a hum in my veins and it seems to be intensified by certain phases of the moon or proximity to specific people. My sister was out on a date with the less objectionable Bedia twin on the New Moon and I could use the supplies Dezi insisted on purchasing for me without feeling guilty. But when she returned and vacillated between shy smiles and worried frowns, the power I'd gathered in my solitary ceremony didn't just spark at my fingertips playfully. Instead, a blast of water shot out, knocking several jars off the windowsill.

Once we cleaned it up, Fer admitted how she was feeling and the protective instincts flared up again. A small fireball charred the end of the house broom and I had to dump her water on it. That's when we figured out that my magic may not be listening to me—yet—but it definitely is listening to my heart. There are few people in this world I care about as much as Feray, and my frustration at not being able to help her with this made my magic go bonkers.

Not a brilliant discovery, given our jobs and the impending magical holiday occurring scant days before the full moon.

I sigh, trudging back to the bar with a resigned posture. My temper has long been my area of opportunity, and this little twist of Fate makes me even more dangerous than when I'm gripping my brass knuckles. When I reach Feray's, she's pouring another set of drinks for that aloof banker who seems determined to claim that one spot in the name of Spain. There's something about the way he refuses to sit anywhere else and the eagerness with which my sister works to impress and serve him that makes my witchy senses go off.

"You look troubled, Knuckles."

A low, rumbling voice whispers in my ear, and I smile to myself. Tiernan walked in with the Fae entourage an hour ago, and I was waiting for him to slip away for a visit. "My sister fawns over that uptight prick from the bank and the way he encourages it makes me... ponder."

"Feray is a big girl, love. You cannot keep her sheltered forever. If she wants to date one of the terrible twins or even that ancient asshole, it is between her, them, and her bear."

Gee, thanks for being logical instead of taking my side, T.

Frowning in irritation, I turn to face him with a look of consternation. "Are you sure mind reading isn't one of your gifts?"

His feline grin makes my body respond, and he shakes his head. "I'm sure. But I know a few supes who hold that power." He looks around, tilting his head as the very twins we spoke of earlier stumble out of the private room. "Speak of the Devil..."

Khol's inebriated smirk grows wicked as he sees me waiting for Feray to finish making drinks for his booze-swilling guests so she can take my orders from the floor. I'm not working that room tonight—thank Hecate—but Jasper and Mo don't seem to be handling their party's demand well. He and Khal trip over themselves as they approach Tiernan and me, making me groan.

What have I done to offend Dionysis this eve?

"Sassy, you look... delicioussssss." The asshole twin rolls his gaze over the outfit I'm wearing and arches a brow.

I frown, turning to look at Tiernan, who shrugs. The tiny black leather shorts, fishnets, knee-high steel toed combat boots, and leather bra halter allow my skin to breathe, but my feet to kick ass.

The closer we get to the full moon, the hotter shifter blood runs and there are a *lot* of reasons to be less covered. One, the amount of fights and weird drink requests lead to my clothes being covered in random blood or dyes. Last month, I lost several of my favorite pieces to stains we simply couldn't remove. Two, the frenzy of movement, sex, dancing, and drunkenness in the week prior to the moon change raises the temperature of the room significantly. I can't regulate myself the way many of them can and I'm sure not getting naked.

Hell, even Fer is wearing a tight crop top and matching shorts behind the bar.

"You realize it's a million degrees in here and I'm running through a crowd of people all night, right? I didn't dress like this to tempt little old you," I bite back.

Khal mutters something under his breath and takes off for the end of the bar where Feray is working. I share an amused look with my mate as we make the same silent assessment: chicken.

"Your sister has a mate. Why is she messing around with my brother? And who's the douche at the bar she's watching so closely?"

With a heavy sigh, I lean in to kiss Tiernan's jaw. "You can go back to your asshat and I'll deal with this one. See you later."

Tiernan nods, but hauls me against him hard, kissing me breathless before murmuring against my lips, "Fer isn't the only one who enjoys playing with fire, Knuckles. Make good choices."

I blink at him as he strides through the floor, slinking around shoving matches and drunken supes like a shadow. "What the hell does *that* mean?"

"Are you going to answer me, woman?" Khol is leaning against the bar like his bones are made of liquid, his expression taunting me.

Placing my tray on the wood, I put my hand on my hip and stare back. "My sister can date whoever the hell she wants. I'm not her keeper and you *definitely* aren't. Fuck off, Bedia."

He's fast—so fast, in fact, that I don't see him move until he's almost toe to toe with me. "That may be true, but you still haven't answered me. What is she doing and who is that man?"

For fuck's sake.

"Get out of my face." He steps back just a little when magic sparks on my fingers and I grin in satisfaction. "As to your questions, she seems to be dating Khal and enjoying herself. The man at the end of the bar is a Founder, and he works at the bank. He's here all the time. Why?"

His eyes narrow and he glares as he watches my sister and Khal talking near the man in question. "Interesting."

"Yes, it's truly fascinating. Now, move," I drawl as I shake my head. Feray is far too busy with moon-touched men to focus and I have to get these drinks before it sinks my tips. Louie had given the vamps at the table I'm holding up a wide berth and that made me suspicious.

"Why? I can't imagine you have more important clients to chat with." His smoldering look does what he intends it to, but it also activates the most stubborn parts of me.

Picking up my tray, I walk around him, whacking him in the ass with it as I go behind the bar and start pulling my own tabs. I take a few minutes to locate some ingredients since I'm not back here often, but once I get everything put together, I balance the full load on my hand easily. Khol watches me, clearly waiting for his response, and I roll my eyes at him. Such an entitled prick he believes he can't open his mouth without people being required to respond.

"I have customers over there and *you* have a private room you should be lording over. Get lost." I wave my free hand at him as I walk away, weaving my way through the crowd carefully. My brow furrows as I feel eyes on me and I reach out with my magic, trying to figure out who, beside the annoying twin, is ogling my ass.

The vamps are on a couch by the stage, watching the DJ spin and keep their red eyes on the undulating crowd. They're probably looking for thralls or donors; that selection isn't part of my job and I'm not offering any suggestions on it. I sit the drinks down on the table along with a check that wouldn't be necessary if their glimmering safe word necklaces had a tier higher than 'Master' on them.

"You're right, Grigori. She'd make a lovely shared treat," the blond woman says as I straighten.

Today is not the day, and I am not the one, Susan.

"I told you." The dark haired mate leers at me, licking a fang.

I'm about to let them both have it when suddenly, whispers start behind me. Turning on my heel, I ignore the inappropriate bloodsuckers to follow the direction of the buzz to the stairs to the VIP lounge. The Prince of the Daybreak Court and resident rockstar is coming down the stairs with some of his groupies following like ducklings. It's not unusual for him and his snooty followers to be here, but the full moon draws a different crowd than we normally have at *Cocktails & Screams*.

Tonight, the main room is packed with more lower tier clients than the rich regulars who aren't distracted by things like royalty. His descent from on high is causing excitement to stir within the gathered supes and that could either be good or bad, depending on how he behaves. More to the point, how his crew of designer clad dingleberries behave when they're among the masses.

"Just what I fucking need," I mutter as I watch Tiernan leap the rail to follow them. Speeding my steps, I cut around the corners, using my knowledge of the bar to make it there before the gorgeous Fae.

Feray comes scampering up to meet me, her voice full of girly excitement. "The *Prince* is coming!"

"Yes, I noticed the crowd parting like the clouds for Zeus," I retort. "Make whatever they want and send them packing. This is a nightmare waiting to happen."

My sister gives me a dirty look. "You know I want Dezi to let me work up there. This is a good time to impress them. Imagine the tips—we could get so much stuff!"

Now there's too much. Feray's enthusiasm, the threat of shopping for non-essentials, the two men watching her from her former spot, the impending rich assholes, my mate—all converging and to top it off, Khol is *still* here. *How is a girl supposed to keep from losing her temper and frying the whole damn place?* I stomp my foot and walk around the grinning bad boy, elbowing him hard as I join my sister. Four hands will be faster than two and if I can get these idiots back to their personal perch upstairs, the amped atmosphere in the bar will cool down.

"Well, well." The grating voice from *Delices Coupables* makes my whole body clench with anger and I slap my forehead in frustration. "Why am I not surprised to find these two serving deviants in a sex club?"

Fer lets out a dark growl and I hold my hand up to quiet her. I lean my forearms on the bar and look directly at Khorinea with a falsely sweet smile. "What can I get you this evening, deviant in a sex club?"

A choking laugh comes from my dickish twin and he covers it by taking a sip of his drink. He seems to have sobered a bit since he decided to haunt me and I wonder how much of his behavior was an act.

"Revvie, she can't be allowed to get away with such insolence!" The Harvest Court girl with her weird bird's nest hair and dark, glittering eyes lays her hand on the Prince's arm as she leans in.

The tension in the Fae is palpable as he turns to look at her, his blond hair slipping over one eye as the other glares at her. "Take your hands off me, Khorinea. You presume too much."

My lips curve and though I'd rather eat glass, I give the Prince a bright smile as I bow a tiny bit before turning my attention to him fully. "My sister will be happy to serve you, Prince Revelin, while your friend remembers her kindergarten manners."

That makes him laugh and he looks almost as surprised about it as I do. Up close, I realize his eyes aren't black, but deep sapphire blue and they focus on me with heat. "Again, you've amused me with your total lack of care for with whom you speak. I'd prefer you pour my martini, if possible."

"I'm not letting her fleabag sister make my drinks. She might have rabies!"

Giving the Prince an apologetic expression, I shove my hands in my pockets to grab the girls before I step on Fer's stool. She nods at me, yellow in her eyes as I look at the girl who has no reason to make trouble with me or my sister. We'd never seen her before the restaurant and it's only bad luck that she came downstairs on a night we worked. The only reason she's being rancid is because she can—something I've never been able to abide well.

"I'm sorry; I must have heard you wrong," I say softly as I prepare myself for her answer. The stool has me raised enough to measure the distance between us and I smirk when she doesn't answer immediately.

Khorinea senses the audience building around her and it feeds her ego far too much to allow her to back down. She looks back and forth at the people, including the Prince, and turns back to focus on me. "I *said* I won't let your *flea-bitten mutt* serve my drinks, nor will I let *trash* like you address me this way."

That does it.

Leaping over the bar with a feral grin, I funnel all my frustration at the bullshit I've dealt with tonight toward the bitchy mean girl intent on embarrassing me. I stalk towards her, a predatory look in my eye despite not being a shifter. My hands raise, the now familiar feeling of magic zinging through my veins and dancing over my skin as she backs away from me. I'm not surprised the rest of Revelin's entourage isn't backing her up; they may be rich and snooty, but they aren't stupid. The hunger inside of me to strike back at someone and drain the wells of my rage is too great to worry about the consequences.

"Fiadh…"

I shake my head at Tiernan when he speaks. He can't stop this; it's inevitable. At least in *Cocktails & Screams* there are too many people for me to really let loose. I'm only going to scare the pants off this chick so she leaves me alone going forward. "Where are you going, little fairy? You were talking tough just a moment ago."

"You're crazy!" The mass of unkempt hair on her hair bobs as she pretends to be frightened and I roll my shoulders. "Revvie, make her stop!"

My magic is swirling around me and I can feel the derision of the Prince behind me. I also feel Tiernan's resignation, Khol's intense focus, and my sister's resolve in the air. There are far more people watching me than I'm used to, but I can't worry about that. There's only one way to deal with a bully like this and given her desperation for the spotlight, I have to make it as public as possible. Otherwise, she's going to come at me anytime the royal contingent is here and with Tiernan assigned to the Prince now, that will likely be often.

I might piss off His Royal Rocksterness, but he's not exactly coming to her aid.

"I may be crazy, but I can back my mouth up. Can you say the same?" Closing my eyes, I reach inside of me and pray that what I'm about to do works rather than blowing the whole building to smithereens. I call the water to my palms, imagining compact balls of the element forming, then open my eyes. A feeling of pride and delight spreads across my features when I see I've done it. Bobbing my brows, I lob the two balls at her, snorting when one nails her in the face and the other catches her hair, making her look like a drowned rat.

"That was a bulls-eye, I'd say," the snarky twin remarks as he sidles up to me. "Do you feel better?"

Shrugging, I look at the sputtering Fae as she screeches in anger. "Not as good as punching her would have."

"Ah, but you accomplished humiliation, which for her, is almost worse." His lips curve up and he reaches out to tap my nose playfully. The spark that echoes through me at the tiny touch makes my eyes widen and panic floods my system. That only gets a smug look from him and he turns to the crowd. "I think we've all had our fun, yes? If not, Khal and I have plenty of friends in the private room who would be happy to join the fray."

"I don't think—"

Khol holds his hand up and shakes his head, his expression menacing as he steps a bit further into the crowd of Fae, lookie-loos, and other supes. "No takers? Go about your business, then. Shoo before I change my mind."

The last part is accompanied by a wave of his hand and like he has a magic of his own, the supes disperse slowly. I'm not sure how big this asshole's gang is, but clearly, people are terrified of them. He didn't even have to introduce himself; he just commanded and they followed. That is, except for the Fae, who are all looking at him like something a dog left on the carpet.

"You don't order my people around, Bedia," Revelin finally says as he looks at what's left of our audience. His eyes land on me for a moment and he smiles just a little. "Though it seems the brawler here could."

Why that makes my cheeks flush, I don't know.

Putting my hands on my hips, I let my magic recede as I give both of them an icy glare. "I didn't need to be rescued, nor do I need my ass kissed like you two egomaniacs. I have shit to do; go swing your dicks somewhere else."

I turn on my heel, intent on going behind the bar to help Fer get the long lines building up busted before I go back to serving when there's a shout at the entrance.

What in the name of Zeus' philandering dick is in the air tonight?

"I need to speak to Fiadh and Feray!"

Feray leaps over the bar this time, coming to my side without the aid of the stool. Her wolf is shimmering under the surface; I feel it in her aura. She let me handle the nasty woman and the trouble-makers, but whoever this is has called us both out.

There's a ruckus as the shouting person pushes their way through the crowds and finally appears in front of us. It's Dr. Bennu and his face is pale as he breathes hard. I'm surprised to see singed edges to his scrubs and lab coat, making me think perhaps his mode of travel was more fiery than his shout.

"Don't either of you answer your phones? There's been an incident at the hospital—your friend was attacked again and you need to come with me immediately."

I exchange a guilty look with my sister; we were too busy fending off the riff-raff to notice our phones going off.

"What are you waiting for? Let's go," the doctor says as he catches his breath.

If only it was that simple...

38

FERAY

MY WOLF IS TOO CLOSE TO THE SURFACE RIGHT NOW TO DEAL WITH this shit; I feel my fur rippling in waves under the surface. Between the war zone in the bar and the fiery, sexy doctor showing up, I'm about to explode into fur and fangs.

The minute Dr. Bennu mentions the attack, Khal is at my side running his fingers through my loose hair. His fingers soothe the savage beast within me. A crack from the large wooden door hitting the wall by the back offices draws my attention from the doctor and splinters fly past me.

"What in the name of La Magra is going on here!" Dezi looks like he's ready to go to war with how brightly his red eyes are glowing.

Stepping forward, I place myself in the vampire's line of fire, knowing one bite could kill him if he gets out of hand. "The fruit basket haired moron decided disrespecting your establishment and staff was a good idea." The tic in the corner of Dezi's eye worsens, telling me I hit my target. Sometimes being the smart, silent one pays off. "My sister and I handled it, so the House of Ruby's reputation didn't get tarnished." Raising my chin, I tilt my head to the side and wait to see if I pushed enough of his pride buttons to cover our asses.

"Get her out of here. She's on suspension until I conclude my investigation." Dezi watches as they escort Khorinea out of the building, then look at the doctor suspiciously. "Why aren't you at the hospital? This place isn't your cup of tea."

The doctor fidgets with what's left of his tie and clears his throat. "Your employees' close friend was attacked. Since they cannot answer their phones during work hours, I came to alert them."

His scent changes several times as he speaks—nervous to angry, then intrigued, then anxious. It finally occurs to me what his scent reminds me of: toasted bergamot. Dr. Bennu crosses his arms over his chest, his posture giving off an 'I'm better than you' vibe that's also familiar. Until his eyes drift to me and for a moment, I swear, I see them soften.

"Fine. One of you can go see your friend, but the other has to stay and clean up this disaster." Dezi fixes Fi with a glare, knowing she was the one responsible.

Fi walks over and gives me a hug, then whispers in my ear. "It's better if you go. If you need to shift and run, you can. I'll deal with these three stooges." Arching a brow, I look over at Tiernan, then back at my sister, who shrugs. "He'll help me wrangle them."

"I know he will." I kiss her cheek, then move closer to Khal. He returns to running his fingers through my hair as I think about what I need to do. Looking between the doctor and Dezi, I finally nod. "I'll go. Fi and the boys will stay and help put things back together. But I'll keep everyone posted."

Khal takes my hand, leading me towards the front door, smirking as he looks at the doctor. "We'll take my car—not everyone can fly." He laughs as he opens the door for me and I follow him out. Thankfully, his car has four doors, so the doctor climbs in the back.

I stare at the door of the club and a low whine escapes. *My wolf does not want to leave my sister behind.*

"Your sister is a tough witch. Trust me, she'll be okay. My brother won't let anything happen to her, and neither will the leopard." Khal reaches out and gives my shoulder a gentle squeeze.

Sighing, I turn back and lower my head. Wringing my hands, I fight to resist the urge to charge back to the club. "I feel bad leaving; I can't help it."

"I have to ask: how did this happen?" The doctor points his finger between Khal and I.

"Doc."

"Call me Easton," he says softly.

"Okay, Easton. Why do birds fly? There's a ton of mechanics and physics involved—including genetic modifications to bone structure and muscle development. That doesn't answer why they fly, it only answers how." His eyebrows raise and I assume I caught him off guard with facts and logic. "As for Khal and I, it simply is." A soft laugh escapes my lips. "A snake and wolf are an odd pair, but no worse than a wolf and a bear. We are all predators."

"Please don't add a rabbit, precious. That may be disastrous," Khal quips, putting the car in drive to head to the hospital.

I laugh as I ponder that. "Sure. We'll write whatever God or Goddess is in charge of selecting mates and ask if rabbits can be on the 'no go' list." Shaking my head, I realize what Khal is doing. He's trying to distract me from what I'm about to walk into.

Khal offers me his upturned hand. I stare at it for a moment before accepting the silent comfort he's providing. Mere contact with him sets my wolf at ease while my mind races, thinking about what I will find when we arrive at the hospital. He squeezes my hand and smiles, still focused on the road but able to knock me out of the dark spot.

Several things besides Philly being attacked twice are puzzling me, to be honest. Everyone knows Khal and his twin; they reacted with fear when Khol cleared the room. From what I recently read about basilisks, I see why others would react with suspicion, but it was bigger than that.

Easton directs Khal where to park just as Fi texts me to check in.

Her texts are full of irritation about the dick swinging still happening at the bar. Sadly, I expected it. My sister has always attracted bad boys and trouble makers. I tell her we just arrived and I'll be in touch. Looking up from my phone, I frown. This isn't the front of the hospital. "Where are we?"

"The staff entrance. I thought it might be best if you were not seen." Easton motions for us to follow and I stick close to Khal.

If my guesses about him and his brother are correct, they're pretty big deals in their world.

To the right of the steel door is another unmarked door Easton pushes open. The silence immediately sets my wolf on edge. My vision shifts.

Worst-case scenario, I'm prepared for anything as I look around.

"Shh, Precious. I've got you. The good doctor can torch whatever is in our path if there's a problem." Khal motions to Easton and he cringes slightly.

My eyebrows raise as I ponder the ramifications of having such power at his disposal. Maybe his elitist, untouchable attitude is because he's so powerful. He might even be more dangerous than Khal is. Hazarding a glance between them, I suddenly realize there's so much I don't know about in this world. I have to learn more or it's going to be a liability.

We make it to the upper landing, and Easton raises a finger to his lips before cracking the door. He pokes his head out and looks around before having us follow him. Moving as silently as possible has almost become second nature to me, so it's easy to creep through the corridor to Philly's room. Easton pulls us into the room and locks the door, drawing the window curtain shut.

A burnt scent that makes my eyes water assaults my nose.

Before I can say anything, Easton pulls his handkerchief out and presses it to my nose. He grabs the clipboard at the foot of the bed and looks over the records. "The smell that's making your nose burn results from a hex."

"Who did it?" My eyes drift from my prone friend to Khal, who shrugs. I look back at Easton as I wait for his answer.

Easton's eyes flare to life, burning embers replacing his eyes. He looks around the room once more before speaking. "We didn't catch anything on camera, nor can I see anything out of the ordinary." Blinking his eyes, I see them return to humanoid.

Stepping closer, I look at Philly. Allowing my eyes to shift, I use my wolf's eyes. They can see finer details than my human eyes. Looking closer to the area where the symbol was carved, I stare at it harder. "Do you think he saw or knows something he shouldn't? Maybe he doesn't know what he knows is important."

Or maybe he was attacked just because he was sheltering us.

Warmth radiates behind me and the doctor's hand moves to touch the spot I'm pointing at. The edge of his hand brushes along mine, and tingles erupt all the way up my arm. I know that tingle, but he doesn't seem to feel it.

Maybe it's because he's using a gift to analyze the change in the mark?

Clearing his throat, Easton pulls his hand back and adjusts his tie. "The change was the activation of the hex."

His clinical tone bothers me, but I'm not sure why. Shaking my head, I clear the negative thoughts and text Fi updates.

"Feray, I would strongly suggest you and your sister go somewhere safe. I don't know who has the power or reach to do this. It was definitely a focused attack and not an accident."

I let his words sink in, knowing I have two options. The first is to go home with Khal, but I'm not ready for that step. The second option is to call Torben to pick us up so we can discuss the best option together. I text Fi again, telling her to get home as soon as possible. We need to come up with a solid game plan.

Her mate runs a security company; if anyone knows how to keep us safe, it's him.

Moving to the window, I sigh as I stare out at the lights of the city. "I'll call my mate, Torben, and he will stay with us until we decide where to go."

Easton grumbles as he looks over the clipboard when I say the word 'mate'.

"I'll come with you. Two males are better than one. Besides, I'm mostly nocturnal, so being up all night is kinda my thing." Khal's genuine smile melts me. As soon as he opens his arms, I go to him, sinking into the warmth of his embrace. Easton complains under his breath, but now is not the time to engage him over his issues about having a mate that isn't a wolf.

I call Torben as I rest my head on Khal's chest, listening to his slow steady heart beat under my ear. When Torben picks up, I give him the short version of what's happened. He agrees to come pick us up and meet with everyone at our place.

"Maybe everyone can stay in our cabin? It's remote and hopefully, with all our mates and friends in one place, we should be safe," I say as I look up at Khal.

He smiles as he finishes his text message. "Sounds like a solid plan, Precious—even my brother is on board. Apparently, Hell froze over, because he didn't argue with me." Smirking, Khal bends down and kisses my forehead before snuggling me back against him.

I'm not sure what the look on Easton's face means, but it doesn't look happy. "Are you okay? I mean, you look like you have a terrible bellyache."

Shaking his head, he stares at me as if I'm supposed to understand what's bothering him. "It's not a belly ache. I'm fine; go wait for your ride. I'll keep you updated," he says before abruptly leaving the room.

"That was weird," Khal says as he maneuvers me out of the room and down the staircase.

My phone chimes several times, and I look down at it. The messages from Fi and one from Torben telling me where he's parked with a picture attached. I show Khal and he steers me toward where the picture was taken.

"Where's your car? It's not where we left it." Looking around, I don't see it anywhere.

"I had one of my guys pick it up." As soon as the words are out of his mouth, I see how uncomfortable he is admitting it.

Shrugging my shoulders, I lean into him. "Oh, okay. I was worried someone stole it." Beaming, I look up at him, hoping my answer sets his mind at ease. The tense lines around his eyes relax and a gentle smile crosses his lips before he opens the passenger side door to Torben's truck. Khal slides in beside me and helps Torben buckle me in place.

I thought I had one over protective teddy bear, but now I have an overprotective nope-rope as well.

"What's the plan?" Torben's voice has a deep, grumpy growl to it as he pulls out of the parking spot.

"Let's get everyone in one place and we can figure it out from there. My brother and I can keep watch tonight. You and her sister's mate can keep watch in the daytime."

Apparently, Khal is very strategic. I'm not sure how I feel about the guys taking control, but I'm not really in a mindset to deal with it.

Fi will definitely feel differently about it, so I'll let her handle that battle.

"Sounds like a solid plan." Torben says firmly, heading towards the cabin in the woods.

I stare at both males as they decide without me. This is not the hill to die on for me, but Fi may choose to not only die on this hill, but make everyone in her path wish for death. Either way, I get to sit between my mate and a male I feel safe with.

Hopefully, I can figure out my feelings for Khal soon—he's a perfectly complementary partner to be with Torben and I.

39

FIADH

It's hard to be worried about Philly when I'm stuck in a *fog* of fucking testosterone.

From the moment Feray left, I've done nothing but listen to Dezi bitch about losing staff, dirtying the club, having to rope off part of the bar while we clean, and whatever shit that's hitting social media because Louie keeps showing him. I glare at the blond vamp, pondering whether my boss would get rid of me if I set his stupid lacy cuffs on fire. He's purposely making this worse and needs a lesson.

Easy, Fi. This is the best place you and Fer have been in for a long time; he's not worth it.

"Louie, if you don't stop riling him up, I'll toast your ass," I mutter as I pass by him. Dezi walked away to get himself a drink, and I finally had the chance to put a stop to his meddling.

Khol overhears and smirks wickedly as he saunters up. "Don't get yourself in the shit, Sassy. I'd be *delighted* to cause this worm a little pain he won't soon forget."

Louie turns even more pale than his normal vampiric coloring and skitters off as if his ass is truly on fire. Whirling, I glare at the impudent twin in irritation. "I had that handled. How many times do I have to tell you assholes that?"

Tiernan comes up behind me and presses a kiss below my ear. "You don't have to tell me; I listen, Knuckles."

"Sometimes," I grunt. I can feel his pout, so I lean into him and rub my cheek on his. "Okay, mostly."

"More cleaning, less canoodling," Dezi says in a sharp voice as his eyes meet mine. The deep red in them tells me his demon is still riding high from the excitement—at least, I think that's why. He's been annoyed and brusque since Feray told him what happened and it's completely different from how he acted at the magic store.

Men are much more moody than women—we've been lied to. If I didn't know better, I'd think these fools were in their moon time, not either of us girls.

"Who the hell says 'canoodling' anymore? For that matter, who says that and owns a sex club?" I grumble as I pass by him with the mop. "You sound like a little old man."

Khol snorts, and even Tiernan has to hide a smile as the elegant vamp huffs and stomps around behind the bar. Puffs of smoke drift through the air and I look down to see the grumpy ass banker laughing as well. A smug look crosses my features and I stop, crossing my arms over my chest. That earns me an even darker look from Dezi as he lifts a brow.

"Perhaps it is unwise to cross someone with so many more years of experience with magic than you, witchling."

That finally gets the indolent Prince's attention, and he joins the fray with a casual retort. "Aye, blood bag, but your crusty millennia pale compared to my hundred years developing Faerie magic."

"As if the poison—"

If this doesn't stop, I may actually choke on the male bullshit and vomit on the floor I'm cleaning.

"Yes, yes. And the dragon down there could set us all on fire. You're all big and bad and *infinitely* more powerful than me. Don't think for a second I won't kick your asses up and down Main Street, regardless." Pausing, I take the mop, cracking the handle over my knee and spinning the pieces in my palms. "I'm a twenty-one-year-old *girl* who worked in a *dive bar* with no bouncers. You fools don't scare me."

All the men around me blink, watching the sticks twirl in my hands like I'm a majorette or a martial arts star. I wink at them, stopping the wood as I pretend to take aim to throw one. That makes Khol snort, then Tiernan joins in, and by the end, even the dragon seems to cover laughter with his drink. Dezi's eyes flash with fury, but he dips his chin and gives in.

"You may need anger management, lass," Prince Revelin says as his eyes twinkle. "I can recommend a few places. They've sent me many times."

"And here I thought you had the perfect, charmed, rich, royal life," I say as I walk over to the bar, standing in the middle of the four men who are oddly interested in annoying me. "I bet you've been to rehab, too."

Khol chokes on his drink, mumbling, "Like four times."

The Prince gives him a murderous look as he shrugs. "Rockstar life. At least I'm not the one who *peddles* the drugs."

That makes me rub my hand over my face. *I knew those guys were thugs the minute they walked into Philly's.* My sister is dating a drug dealer and I've been flirting with his twin for weeks. "Fuck my life," I grumble as I push away from the wood, needing to put space between me and them.

Sex club owner, drug dealer, rockstar royal, and bodyguard—what the hell? Am I living a smutty romance novel?

Tiernan walks up to me and pulls me against his chest, whispering in my ear low enough that I don't think even the vamp's ears can hear him. I raise my face, looking at him in confusion, and he winks at me. My brow furrows; he definitely *meant* what he said, but I don't know why he said it. Is this like what Feray told me Torben talked to her about? Does Tiernan think I have other mates out there and he felt the need to tell me it's okay *right now?*

The buzz of my phone saves me from the wild thoughts flittering around in my head and I look down to see Feray's message. "She says Philly is okay—mostly. He's stable and they're treating the injury."

"You don't look happy," Dezi says in his matter-of-fact manner. "Why is that?"

I shake my head. "There's more than I can share, but she says I have to meet her at home as soon as work is over. There's a concern about our safety because we lived in the last place they attacked and now they came back for our friend."

"I'm coming with you, it seems." Khol wiggles his phone in the air. "My brother says he's with your sister and her mate on the way there."

"Bubbles has more than one mate?" The vampire looks at us all, his eyes narrowing as if he's gauging something. "Of different species?"

"Ugh." I roll my eyes at Dezi and look over at Tiernan. "Why are all the old ones so damned fixated on that part? Feray told me the doc was giving her shit about it as well. It's like they're having a generational chasm issue with people doing what makes them happy."

Tiernan shrugs and comes over to kiss my temple. "Species, not age, Knuckles. Some of these assholes are *very* bound by staying within their kind to keep lines pure. Shifters are less concerned with that than survival. Things have changed over the years for those born with powers versus those who gain them through a gift or curse."

I look at Khol, who nods. "Agreed, cat. My kind are rare, anyway."

Revelin sighs before he adds, "Even in the Courts, there are issues with ensuring that not only the royals propagate their lines. Humans are destroying this side of the veil and some worry about overcrowding the Faerie—as if that could happen. However, mating and breeding with different species means different needs and... well, a lot of other boring Fae politics. The point is, we're born with gifts and are leaning towards intermingling now."

Dezi gives him a gobsmacked look. "The *Fae* are encouraging this?"

"I wouldn't say for *royals*," the prince says with a wince. "But for the populace, yes, it's been discussed ad nauseum in the Daybreak Court. I can't imagine Harvest, Midnight, or Reaping being any less forthright."

"It's a brand new day, Pops," Khol says as he slaps his hand on the bar. The moniker gets a snort out of the eavesdropping dragon at the other end. "You can join us if you're intent on listening in, Smokestack. We won't bite... Well, okay, the Prince won't bite. The rest of us do."

"*Au contraire*," Prince Revelin says as he flashes impressively pointed canines that look different from Tiernan's feline ones and the fang Dezi used on me. "We enjoy a nip or two."

This is going nowhere and despite enjoying them picking on each other and not me...

"Dezi, I need to go home to meet my sister. The crowd is dying down because of the fight and you have Louie, Mo, and Jaz. The private room will clear out if Khol leaves, too."

The vampire looks as if he's considering when our buddy at the end of the bar speaks up. "Oh, let her go, Ruby. You're only being stubborn. It's the right thing to do and you're not your sire."

I blink. *Hello, interesting information.* "Not your—"

"Go now, before I change my mind!" Dezi says before he storms away from the bar toward the office again.

"That bloodsucker has *got* to learn to control his damn temper," I murmur. "He's worse than a toddler."

The dragon snorts, and I give him a nod as I turn to the men still surrounding me. "Okay, so lizard man got me a reprieve, but T still has to work for this douchebag." I tilt my head at Revelin, who just rolls his eyes. "So, can I hitch a ride with you, asshole?"

"Coming from you, that almost sounds like a dirty term of endearment," Khol says with a grin. "In which case, I'd be happy to give you a ride."

"Hera in a basket, save me from all these fucking dudes smothering me in their absolute *dudeness*," I grumble.

Tiernan laughs and pulls me close, kissing me lightly. "Go home. I'll be there once I drop this douche—" he pauses to chuckle, earning him a glare from the Prince. "Er, this amazing example of Fae royalty back at his penthouse."

"You'll pay for that," Revelin says with a smirk. "Perhaps managing the groupies for a week?"

Tiernan pales and I pat his cheek. "Worth it, baby."

That makes him grin and I turn back to the twin. "Are you ready?"

"I'm always ready, Sassy."

Groaning, I ask him to wait while I go back to the lockers to get my things. I change quickly, stuffing the revealing clothes in my bag, but keeping my tag on. I've noticed having it on changes how people treat you when I go out during the day, and now I rarely take it off. Pulling a halter and tight skinny jeans on, I shove my feet in my worn combos before heading back to the bar.

All the guys are *still* there and as I approach, they seem to be having a conversation that stops when I come back. I arch a brow at them, looking suspicious, but no one says anything. That makes me roll my eyes and turn on my heel, heading for the door in purposeful strides.

Khol catches up with me, grabbing my hand. "How am I supposed to take you if you leave without me, Sassy?"

I give him a withering look. "Look. I'm game for getting to know one another, especially because your twin is dating my sister. But I refuse to let you wear that mask all the time. Be the real you, not this idiotic playboy jackass act that you put on in public. At least do me the courtesy of being genuine when we're not in a crowd. Okay?"

He blinks, looking shocked as hell. "I…Okay."

"Thank you. I can't tell you how much I wanted to punch all of you except Tiernan in the teeth tonight."

Tilting his head, Khol gives me a slow, dark grin. "You said be real, yeah?" I nod and he opens the car door for me, stepping in close before I get in. "Then you should know that if anyone else said that to me, I'd peel them like a grape and let the hyena pack take care of the evidence.

I asked for it, didn't I?

"Good thing I'm not anyone else," I reply primly. Throwing myself into the car, I wait for the door to shut, willing my heartbeat to slow.

Why the hell was that so fucking hot?

40

FERAY

MY ANXIETY OVER PHILLY'S ATTACK HAS ME BREAKING OUT IN PATCHES of cream-colored fur that randomly erupts all over my body. To top it off, my tail popped out and refuses to go away. I know my scent has shifted and I catch Torben watching me closely. His eyes flicker and flair to life periodically.

His bear knows I'm stressed, and he wants to protect me from the world.

Honestly, with everything that's going on, I couldn't blame him for wanting to hide me away. I watch his nostrils flair as his bear fills him in on what he's smelling. He leans over and I can hear him clue Khal in on my anxiety red flags. Not only is my tail out, but I'm baking.

Baking is my go to when I can't deal with what I'm feeling. Stress always equals me baking or cooking. Cooking is productive, and it's an easy achievement for me to complete so I feel in control. Sometimes that's all I need to feel better and be able to relax. So far, I've made three dozen cookies and several dozen pastries since we got home.

Khal, bless his heart, has tried getting close to me and Torben stopped him every time. He knows when I get like this I'm highly unstable and it's probably safer for him to leave me alone. It's nice to see that Khal will throw caution into the wind to take care of me. As leery as I am about taking a second mate, his actions are warming me up to the idea faster than I had expected.

Eventually, I switch from desserts to actual food.

Digging through the contents of the fridge, I find fresh trout Torben caught today before work. I descale the fish and stuff the cavity with breadcrumbs and apple slices. Humming to myself, I sprinkle herbs and spices over the top of the fish before placing it in the oven. Turning around, I find Torben and Khal slicing the fixings for a nice mixed salad. They work in harmony with each other and it makes me believe this could actually work.

Torben is a steady rock—the guy your mom wishes for you to marry. Khal is sweet, gentle, and thoughtful. His brother's reputation makes me question if he's part of the family business because he's simply a good guy. No matter how much of an ass his brother is, I know he's different.

I go back to the stove and make the butter wine sauce to drizzle over the fish. Stirring the sauce slowly, I realize that one of my love languages is food.

As a shifter, I feel like all I constantly do is eat most of the time.

Snapping out of my inner thoughts, I turn around and watch the guys for a few moments. Surprisingly, I find Khal making a raspberry vinaigrette from scratch. Turning to check the fish in the oven, I hear the front door knob click. Reactively, a deep growl escapes my lips and I turn quickly to face the door. As soon as I see Fi, I set my oven mitts down and race over to see how she's doing. I pull her into my arms and hug her tightly, as if she's my lifeline at the moment.

"What's with the half shift, little sis?" Khol snarks as he walks past me and heads over to his brother.

"I'm stressed." Part of me wants to pout and hide in Torben's arms, but the other part wants to put my claws to good use.

"Is that…?" The sentence dies on his tongue as I feel my wolf push harder at me, wanting to be turned loose.

Khol blinks and looks at Fi, who's shaking her head at him. "Leave her alone, Khol." Fi leads me back to the kitchen and sets me back to the task. "Do you need help with dinner? I see you picked the trout for tonight. How about I set the table?"

"Yeah, I figured everyone will eat it." I shrug my shoulders, trying to release some of the tension. Fi nods slightly and heads over to get the supplies for her task.

Tiernan arrives as I am pulling the trout out of the oven. I plate the portions for everyone and Khal helps pass out the drinks while Torben passes out the salad. Placing the butter wine sauce on the table, I flick my tail several times as I try to figure out how to start the conversation. We eat in relative silence as I ponder how I want to talk about what I have learned. The idea of someone possibly hunting us makes way too much sense and I'm scared for Fi. At the end of dinner, Khal collects the plates as Tiernan offers everyone desserts.

Time to rip off the bandaid, I guess. "We all know Philly was attacked again." Glancing at the others for confirmation, I cringe slightly as I pick at the pastry in front of me. "The doctor said they embedded the hex in the symbol carved in Philly's back. Easton also says it had to be someone powerful. There's no evidence of anyone getting in or out of the room."

"Easton? You're on a first name basis now?" Fi teases.

"I guess so. Anyway, back to important stuff." Huffing out a breath, I try to refocus. "Who attacked him? I don't think it's a coincidence."

I'm not sure how much I feel safe saying in front of Khal and Khol, so I say enough to get my sister's attention. Fi nods and I catch the minute movement. The look Fi gives the guys kills the conversation.

Torben moves from his side of the table and pulls me into his embrace. His fierce protectiveness settles over my frayed nerves. "Shhh, I've got you."

His gravelly voice makes my heart flutter for a moment, and I relax in his arms. He presses his lips to the crown of my head and I feel his hot breath wash over me. Dessert concludes and Torben still hasn't released me yet.

"Everyone can relax. Tor and I will get the kitchen cleaned up," I sigh as I lean against him. It seems like we need to discuss more, but my fear of being betrayed is preventing me from doing it.

Fi and Tiernan move into the living room, getting the sitting area ready. Khal and Khol linger for a moment, then wander around the house, taking everything in. Torben and I work in harmony—one washing the dishes, the other drying them. That is, until I hear the creak of the floorboard outside of the office with all our research in it.

The second creak of the loose floorboard tells me they've entered the room and I take off running, causing Torben to shout after me. Growling, I shove past Khol and face the twins. Using my body, I block the papers on the desk the best I can. "What in the name of Fenrir do you think you're doing?"

Unfortunately, the bulk of the research is pinned all over the walls with yarn drawing connections to things we've found.

"We were just looking around. We meant no harm." Khal looks remorseful for invading our privacy, but Khol is still snooping.

"What are these papers?" He keeps looking along the wall, ignoring my distress.

"None of your business," Fi pipes in. Her magic is sparking wildly over her body like she's a huge Tesla coil.

Khol plants his index finger in the middle of the symbol that was on our parents' car and on Philly's back. "I've seen this before."

Torben must have walked out and returned with a pitcher of his honey ale and glasses.

My eyes drift from my mate to my sister and I give her a firm nod. *If the twins are truly our mates, then they need to know everything.* After my bear's done passing out the drinks, he pulls me to the large armchair and pats his lap. *You don't have to ask me twice.*

As tense as I am, I need his silent comfort, especially since Fi is about to lay our world bare at everyone's feet.

Clearing her throat, Fi gets everyone to look at her and raises a hand before Khol says something that will get him smacked. "It all started three years ago when our parents died." She looks at me and I rest my head on Torben's shoulder, listening intently. "It was a sudden accident and there were no witnesses. Looking back at how we were raised after the Ascension made us question if there was more to it than a freak accident."

Deciding to speak up, I steel myself. Out of everyone here, only Torben and Fi know the entire story. "I was raised a witch. As far back as I can remember, Mom and Dad told me my magic would come at the Ascension." Smiling fondly at my sister, I get lost in the memories. "Fi always had magic—it may not have been dependable, but it was there. However, I couldn't so much as move a tissue; I was a failure as a witch."

Torben's firm hand forces me to turn and face him. "You are not a failure. You cannot fail at something you were not meant to be." He kisses me firmly, wiping away the pain for the moment.

I whisper my thanks to him before refocusing on the others. "It wasn't until the amulet around my neck broke and I shifted did I realize why I was having so much trouble. Wolves have their own magic. Why my wolf was locked away and hidden from me, I'll never know. They had to have had a very good reason to do it."

Sliding off Torben's lap, I stand on my own two feet. "That symbol you pointed at, Khol, wasn't only on my parents' car. It was also carved into Philly's back. Whoever hurt our boss and set his business on fire are the same people that killed our parents." I watch Khal and the other mates cringe and I can almost see their hackles raise.

The gold blazes to life in Torbens' eyes as he stares at me and the amount of dominance radiating from him is exciting. "I am not leaving you alone," he proclaims, staring at me.

"I'm not leaving you, either, Knuckles." Tiernan says and Fi rolls her eyes.

I swear her hatred of public displays of affection aggravates me sometimes.

Khal and Khol are off to the side discussing something as Khol stares at his dinging phone. He frowns and shakes his head, turning towards the door. "We're going to hit up some of our contacts and let everyone know what we find out."

"If you need me for any reason, don't be afraid to reach out. I'll answer day or night, Precious. Thank your for trusting us." He leans in and kisses my cheek then shakes hands with Torben before joining his brother.

"Khal isn't a bad guy." Torben says matter of factly as he leans back against the counter, holding me firmly to his chest.

"He seems sweet." A yawn escapes my lips and I turn in Torben's arms resting my head on his chest.

"You're tired; let's tuck you in. You've had enough excitement for today." He scoops me up as if I weigh nothing and carries me off towards my bedroom for the night.

Tomorrow's another day and a good night's sleep never hurt anyone.

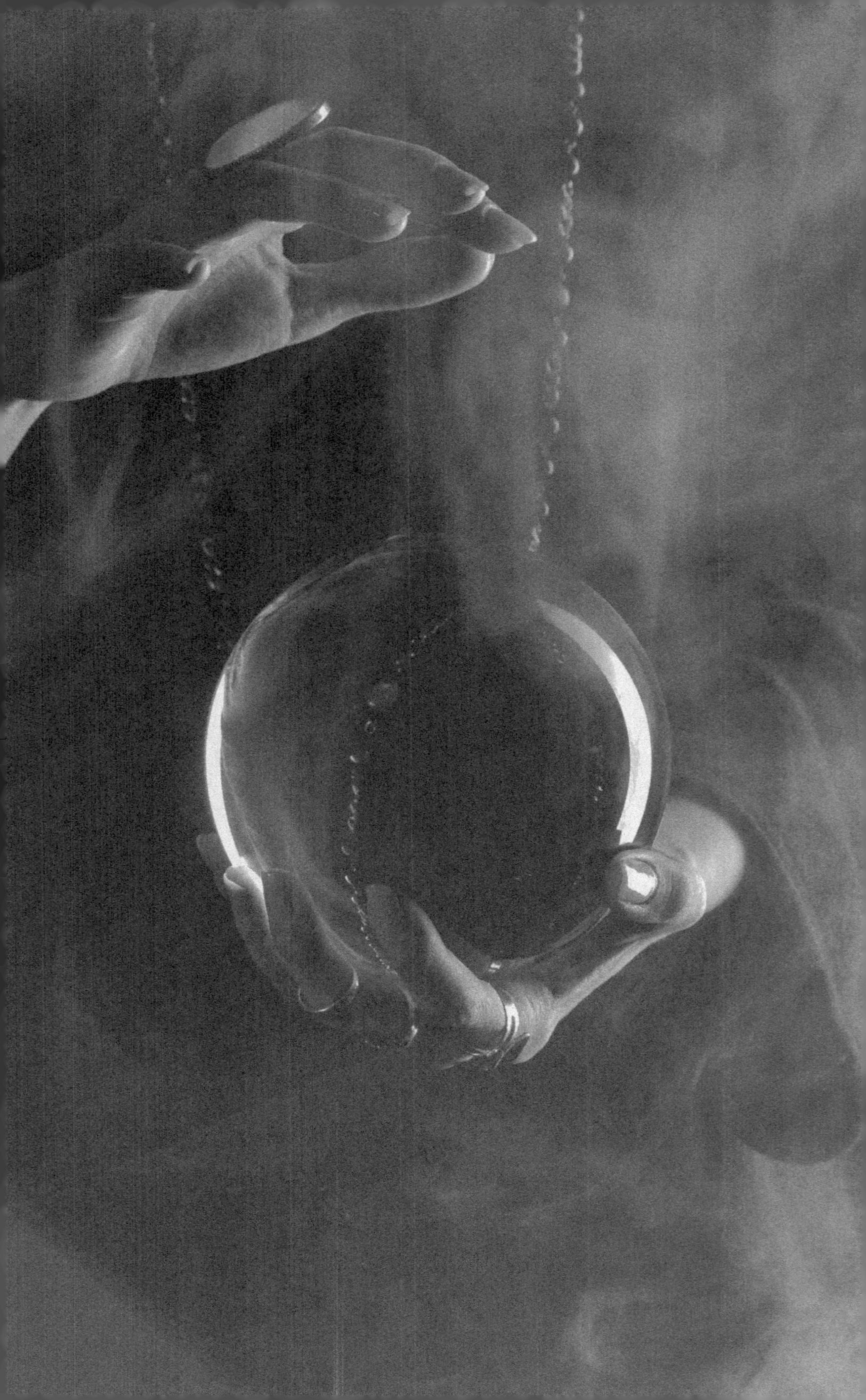

41

Fiadh

The sound of 'Midnight Prophecy' by *Darkness Falls* blaring from my phone jolts me out of an oddly dreamless sleep. Groping for my cell to shut it off before it wakes the entire house, I click the button on the side as I grumble under my breath. I've never been a morning person, but since Torben started sleeping over, his snoring echoes off the acoustics in this place. I've taken to sipping a little whiskey and melatonin laced tea before I go to bed to ensure I don't wake up every few hours.

It's a testament to his lungs, really, because I used to sleep over a fucking bar.

I swing my legs over the side of the bed, chuckling as I note Tiernan has escaped to get ready for his usual morning meetings. He often wakes before me and slips out; it would feel weird if I didn't know his job makes him run a split shift with late nights and early mornings. During the afternoon, he's cat-napping and catching 'Zs' before his evening protection detail with the Prince.

Padding to the bathroom, I clean up and toss on some comfy clothes so I can gather more herbs for the Beltane ritual in two days. Some things are only ripe and filled with power when picked at dawn, which is why my phone screamed one of the Fae Prince's songs to force me to awaken. Feray would give me a knowing look if she knew, but I figured if that jackass is going to show up everywhere, I can't pretend I hate his music forever.

I absolutely love it, but fuck if I'm letting anyone know I recognized him from the start—his ego is large enough as it is.

When I emerge from the small room, I'm freshened, dressed, and my hair is piled in a messy bun on top of my head. This is probably the softest I ever look willingly, but it's easier to connect with my magic and the earth when I let all of my shields down. Even when we're alone, I'm always worried about protecting us if we get ambushed or attacked—and that was *before* all this nonsense with Philly.

I used to think it was because my dad drilled many safety precautions into us I thought were normal; that is, until we started following this trail to find out who killed our parents and discovered we'd lived in other places neither of us remember. Now I know the edgy paranoia my father trained us to feel was a bid to protect us from whatever dangerous beast or magic is out there looking for us. He must have believed that one day, we'd be alone, and they'd be gone. That's why he pushed me much harder than Feray and why I always resist letting people in.

I was raised to be our protector without knowing it.

But now Fer is coming into her own power and as I walk into the sunlight with my basket, I have to admit she's learning quickly. It's possible my parents didn't think she'd ever gain her shifter powers because of the amulet, but I don't know. We have little to nothing of theirs that would have pointed to a secret life. I should know; I did most of the sorting and selling things off after their deaths. If Mom and Dad left us clues about whatever the hell was hunting us, they didn't keep them in that house.

Sighing, I walk into the area where I've set up my circle and adjoining gardens where I'm cultivating herbs, vegetables, spices, flowers, fruits, and plants I need for casting. Luckily, some of those things will also double as food sources when they fully bloom, and I know Fer will enjoy cooking with all of it. I can give her that, especially since she's enjoying playing hostess with Torben and now Khal. My sister is becoming more and more like our mother every day and while I wish I'd gotten some of her softer traits, I'm now realizing that perhaps we are a perfect balance.

The light and dark sides of the moon—reflections of one another, but complimentary in every way.

The poetry of that makes me shake my head and snort. I've got to get my gathering done so I can get back to the cabin and eat. I'm not sure what Feray has planned for the day, but given that we're being watched like hawks by roving growly men, I'm sure it will be interesting.

I'VE BARELY FINISHED GATHERING the morning harvest when my blasted phone vibrates in my pocket. Despite using the damn thing for almost every aspect of my life, I'm never more angry than when it serves its primary function: phone calls. Growling under my breath, I set my basket on a stump table and snatch it out of the pocket of my loose pants. I frown when I note it seems to have a blocked number calling that my spam app isn't kicking back into cyberspace.

"Stupid glitchy app," I mutter as I slide the bar and answer. "This is Fi. Who are you?"

There's no point in being polite when they're hiding from me, right?

"Ah, that lovely directness. I should have expected it."

Squinting as I walk around the circle looking for a few sprigs of dragon's blood for a perfume oil, I scoff into the phone's mic. "I'd say so when you hide your identity behind some sort of encryption or masking app. And you sound like you're calling from the bottom of a well. Who the hell is this?"

There's a pause and I can almost *feel* the smirk on the other end of the line. "That happens when you're calling a non-Fae from the Faerie."

"I'm sorry... what? You'll have to repeat that because I'm pretty sure some nut job told me they were calling from another fucking realm." Pressing the fingers of my free hand into my eyes, I briefly wonder if I ingested some sort of hallucinogen out here. There's a lot of natural growth and for all I know, some of it could make me trip balls.

This time I hear an annoyed sigh and someone whispering something muffled before the voice speaks again. "Fiadh. You cannot imagine how difficult it is to have *you* disbelieve me on one end and my *mother* squawking on the other. You know who I am and that I'm not lying about where I am, even if you don't understand *how* this is achieved. That is a topic for later, though, because I have a more important question for now."

"And what in Aries' bloody tunic could be more important than that information?" I cross my arms over my chest, feeling very concerned because an Unseelie *Prince* is calling me, possibly from his *throne room with the fucking Queen of the Daybreak Court* behind him. Nothing about that can be good, I guarantee it.

I mean, I serve drinks at a sex club and live in a borrowed house.

His laugh is almost musical. "That is an excellent point, but this question comes with... special weight. My mother would like... well, is sort of *insisting*... that I invite you to high tea this afternoon."

"No fucking way!" I blurt. Panic races through my body as I imagine so many terrifying things at once that I can't catch my breath. Parents, royalty, the *Faerie* full of tricksy Fae, a rockstar I barely know, and Aphrodite take me, I'll probably have to *dress up*. "I can't come and definitely not on this short notice. What in the Goddess' name would I even *wear* to tea with a *queen*?!"

That last part is almost a shriek and before the Prince can answer, a large wolf bursts through the trees. She's followed by an enormous lumbering Kodiak and I slap my palm against my forehead as this becomes a complete farce. Feray shifts immediately, striding over to me with fear in her eyes.

"Are you okay? Who hurt you? What's going on?" she fires rapidly and I just blink.

She's naked as a jaybird and hasn't even noticed—oh, how things have changed.

I hold up the phone, shaking it as an annoyed voice keeps talking. "This. This is... I don't even know *what* to do with this."

Torben shifts and frowns at me. "The phone hurt you?"

"No!" I grind out.

Fer grabs the phone, putting it to her ear as she listens. Her whole face lights up and a slow, happy grin crosses her features. "Your Highness, this is her sister. Yes, the wolf. Well, she's having a hard time... Exactly. What time? Mmm Hmm. Okay, I'll have her ready. That would be lovely. Yes, I'll pass on the message. Thank you. Okay, bye!"

My eyes widen like saucers as I watch her turn the phone off and whirl to me with a squeal. "Fiiiiii! You're going to tea with the *Queen of the Daybreak Court* and the *Prince!*"

"Absolutely not. What did you do?! I told him 'no,' Feray!" That tight feeling in my chest starts up again and I pace frenetically. I am not good with parents or families or royalty or… people in general.

"His mother was quite insistent, sis. Apparently, she heard about Tiernan and that you drenched the moron at *Cocktails* last night. The Queen has a very active grapevine and has decreed she needs to meet her son's new friend."

I don't know what crossroads demon I pissed off in another life, but this is getting ridiculous.

"Fer, I have *no idea* what the hell to do at high tea, much less high tea with the Fae version of the Queen Mum!"

The bear chuckles from where he's been watching and I glare at him, but he doesn't stop. "You have the internet, Fiadh. You and Little Wolf will figure it out while you get dressed. I'm sure you can do it if you can please my entire sleuth."

Dropping my face into my palms, I wail softly. "That does *not* make me feel better!"

"Don't worry, Fi. It will be fine; Torben's right. We have six hours to figure out what you need to do and how to fix you up. If it makes you feel better, Prince Revelin said he'd send something over in a couple of hours so you didn't feel self-conscious."

That would help if I knew whether he meant clothes or drugs, but I don't tell Feray that.

"Fine. But someone is feeding me when I get home, especially if I have to endure Fae protocol and fucking Feray makeover grooming shit," I grumble.

"Pancakes it is," Torben says with an easygoing smile.

I definitely get why Feray keeps him around.

"THERE'S no way I'm going anywhere in this thing. It's not me; hell, it's not even *him*. I look like a unicorn Barbie!" Throwing my hands up, I look in the mirror at the pastel, shimmery, fluttery dress thing Revelin had delivered as I mutter, "I wish it *had* been drugs."

Fer snorts and shakes her head. "Well, I'm glad it wasn't. The last thing I needed while Tor and I were trying to help you figure this out was you blitzed off your ass on fairy dust."

"Agreed," the bear says as he continues working on the meat for dinner. "You're a handful without chemical enhancement."

Thanks for the assist, Teddy Ruxpin.

"I can't go like this. It will set a precedent I can't live up to." Staring in the mirror for a moment, I watch a slow, evil smile come over me as I realize what I need to do.

I close my eyes and let my magic fill me, placing my fingertips on the frilly garment as I imagine something that will work for me. The satin shimmers with a warm glow before the dress wraps around my legs, morphing into tight skinny legged pants that connect to the strapless top. Humming, I wait as the soft pastels burst into warm jewel tones. The fluffy trim on the halter top turns to brilliant feathers circling the edge that flow in a long, intricate train down my back.

Now we're talking. Finally, my fucking power does something useful.

"Holy shit, Fi!" My sister walks around me, her eyes glued to the shiny purple and midnight blue fabric of the suit and the gorgeous emerald of the feathers. "This is so cool. It's fluffy like a Fae, but the pants scream 'get out of my way.' You need some tall 'I'll stab you with these' heels to complete the look."

My face falls. "Nooooo."

"Oh, yeah," she says as she goes running for the closet. The shoes she comes back with make me frown; what the hell kind of tips did she save up to afford those? Her flush tells me she held them back until she thought I wouldn't scold her for being frivolous and I roll my eyes.

"Fine, fine. I'll wear them." That's my concession and the relief on her face tells me she knows.

A loud knock interrupts us and I hop on one foot, then the other, as I put the strappy silver stilettos on while I'm walking to the door. When I open it, Revelin is standing on our porch wearing a messy white Oxford over a tight tee shirt, tight black pants, and his usual assortment of spikes, cuffs, rings, and jewelry that make him look the part of a rocker. He frowns when he sees the changed dress, huffing under his breath as he raises his hands. A swirl of magic lights the air, then swarms around him, changing the color of his tee and various pieces of the hardware he's sporting to match the new color scheme. Even the streak in his hair turns dark purple instead of lavender.

"Unable to accept anything at face value, I see?" he drawls as he arches a brow and holds his arm out.

I snort and shake my head, feeling the intricate braids and curls my sister wove into it move slightly but not fall. "Unable to pretend to be something I'm not, especially for someone who is both a queen *and* your parent."

"Oooh. Does your concern mean you've got your eye on me?" The smirk that accompanies that question makes me dig my elbow into his ribs as he leads me down the steps and into the front yard. His grunt makes me smile broadly, and he gives me a faux wounded look. "I'll take hate. It comes from the same place, you know."

"I agreed to this because you said your mother knew about Tiernan. I don't want him or his… group… to lose the contract with your family if I told you to get bent. Nothing more, nothing less." I sniff as I look around the lawn, feeling my stupid shoes sink in the grass. "Why are we standing out here like fools?"

"Because we have to enter the Faerie, lass. It's not just a drive down the block," he says, eyes twinkling with amusement.

"I know that, dick. But the Faerie portal is on the opposite end of town in the rich asshole district. We are in the forest in the shifter district." I heave a sigh, wondering if he's going to be this difficult the entire trip or if this is just an appetizer for him.

Winking at me, he raises his hand again, tracing a few runes in the air, then a big circle that immediately turns into a people-sized portal with a view into a lush, glistening land. My jaw drops and I stare at him in awe. There's only *one* way into the Faerie and it's a formal portal with a big fancy gateway that looks like it's out of a ridiculous movie. *Everyone* knows that—shifters, witches, demons, vamps… hell, for all I know the fucking human *Pope* knows it.

Revelin puts his fingers to his lips and makes a soft 'shhh,' sound. "You can't tell anyone, mind, but royals can enter our land any bloody time or where we want. It's a safety hatch for the four courts and its members."

Mother. Fucking. Bullshit.

"That violates… *all* the treaties—with everyone!" I hiss at him as I look around to make sure no one else is watching. "All the supernaturals and the humans. Your people…"

"Did not lie. You know we can't," he says as he takes my arm and leads me into the weird rip in the fabric of our realm. I open my mouth, but he shakes his head. "We built portals in cities and everyone *assumed* they were the only way to get in. It's not our fault no one asked the question."

He's not wrong, but this is the bullshit that makes everyone mistrust the Fae. Their cleverness and ability to work their minds around their own limitations while forcing others to fall for their traps will always make them suspect. And that would be amplified by a zillion if people knew the entire courts of the four kingdoms can rip reality whenever and wherever they like.

"Your Highness?"

My train of thought is interrupted by the very sunshiney, petite Fae with freckles standing in front of us. Revelin smiles down at her, his expression fond. "Thank you for meeting us, Cecelia. Where has mother set up her little tea party today?"

"The Royal Garden. Allow me to guide you," she says primly.

I arch a brow. Obviously, Revelin grew up here and doesn't need a tour guide, but he's indulging her by taking my arm and following. I wonder who this is? "Are we taking an actual tour or meeting your mother?"

"Meeting my mother. We're running a tad late because of some *difficulty*, so we'll forgo the tour for today, lass." His tone is full of mirth and I elbow him again for good measure.

Maybe if he has bruised ribs, he'll be less aggravating.

"Oh, your mother knew that would happen. She's been watching the leaves, sir." The bubbly Fae might be short, but she speed walks to the beat of her excited chatter. My feet are going to be a *mess* from these killer shoes when I get home.

"Of course she has," the prince mutters.

I lean over and whisper next to his pointed ear. "Why so glum, chum?"

He turns his face mere centimeters from mine as his eyes sparkle. "That means my mother is going to read you the moment they pour your tea. It's chased people away in the past, though that's never her intent. The future, even in nebulous terms, is hard for many to accept."

"No shit. I sort of get that," I reply as we approach a lush garden full of plants and flowers I've never seen before. "Whoa."

"Most of our foliage cannot grow in the other realm," Cecelia pipes up as she stops at an archway. "Be careful; some of it is poisonous to non-Fae, and some is carnivorous. Have a good afternoon!"

Blinking at Revelin, I mouth 'carnivorous?' and he just shrugs.

Gee, thanks for the warning, asshat.

We enter the garden through the arch and there's a beautiful silver-haired woman dressed in a flowing gossamer gown at a large table in the center. She turns to us, icy blue eyes and pale skin highlighted by a sparkling diadem that dips over her forehead. "Darling! I'm so glad you arrived safely."

The prince smiles, leading me over to her as his usual sneer fades to a smile. "Mother, this is Fiadh."

Marveling at the change, I step forward and do a small curtsey as I say, "It's an honor, Your Majesty."

"Oh, my, how lovely! You need not be so formal, dear. In this garden, you're a guest of my son and you may call me Niamh." Her pale eyes sparkle as she tilts her head. "It's not often I can pressure him into bringing any of his friends to visit; you must be special."

I blink, looking between the two Fae. Revelin rolls his eyes as he pulls the chair out for me to sit. "Don't be dramatic, Mother."

My feet demand I accept the seat, so I sink onto the cushioned chair with an appreciative smile. I'm not sure what to do with the Queen's statement, both in relation to calling her a casual name or her implication that the prince sees me as special. All the research I did with Fer and Torben was about formal protocol, so that's out the window. And I've barely met Revelin—how is it possible that he's elevating me above other people he's close to?

"I think you broke her, Mother. I've never seen Fiadh so quiet," the prince grins as he drops into his own chair. "It's almost a miracle."

"Revelin Ciaran Puck!" The tone the Queen takes with him makes my lips curve in and my eyes dance as he squirms in his seat. "You were not raised to be glad when women are afraid to speak their minds. Do you need a thrashing? I promise, you're never too old for your mother to box your ears."

Oh, this is delicious. I'll never let him live it down.

The Fae turns red from his neck to the tips of his pointed ears and I laugh softly, feeling much more comfortable now that he's been called out. "I'd pay to witness that, Niamh. Though, given his penchant for visiting my workplace, it's possible he pays for it, too."

Her eyes widen for a moment before she absolutely howls with laughter. Fluttering leaves and chittering sounds fill the garden as birds and animals come out of the foliage, looking around curiously at the sound. The Queen wipes her eyes, amusement written all over her face as we both watch Revelin go from red to almost purple as his embarrassment grows. "Oh, Fiadh! I have not seen *anyone* put my son in his place so firmly since he was a child and we had a dragon for a nanny. You are a delight."

I'm about to thank her when a tall, stern looking man appears out of thin air, frowning darkly as he stares at the three of us. The color immediately drains out of the prince's face and his head drops as he looks at the table. Winds shift and a cool breeze wafts over the table, ruffling the beautiful napkins and flowers decorating it. Stroking his beard, the man eyes me, then the Queen, and finally, the silent prince.

"I am less enchanted by your insolence, girl. You should not be so familiar with the Queen of the Daybreak Court."

His dark eyes drill into me, but I keep my chin up. After all, he hasn't taken the time to introduce himself, and though I assume this is the King, I don't need to show deference to someone who can't be polite. When his stare doesn't break me, he slams his palm on the table and leans over it, coming closer to my space threateningly.

Big deal. I've had a minotaur charge me, buddy, and you will not violate treaties by harming me when I've been formally invited.

Maybe those protocol lessons *were* useful; I'll have to thank Feray when I get home. Reviewing that info allows me to continue meeting the asshole's gaze until he formally announces his title. Otherwise, he cannot expect me to recognize a royal from a completely different species than me.

"Oliver, stop trying to scare the poor girl. You're doing a piss-poor job of it, for one, and beyond that, she's clearly aware you can't hurt her when she's been invited to our lands." Niamh arches her brow at the glaring royal as she picks up her tea pot and pours for all three of us. "Also, you're ruining my tea and you know how angry that makes me."

With a growl of frustration, the Fae stands up again and addresses me. "I am Oliver, King of the Daybreak Court, and ruler where the sun caresses the lands. You *may not* use my given name."

"Thank you for clarifying, Your Highness," I reply, dipping my head in faux deference. No wonder Revelin took off to our world to run around with a rock band; this guy had to be a fucking dictator as a parent. I can feel the waves of anger and discomfort coming off the prince as if they're my own.

The king scoffs and Niamh gives him a cool look. "Oliver, I warned you once about disturbing my tea. Do you not have soldiers to bark at rather than your son and the first visitor he's brought to see me in three hundred years?"

That makes *my* skin pale and I turn to look at Revelin in surprise. *The dude looks like he's twenty-five; I knew Fae didn't age, but holy goddamned frog balls!* His lips curve and he shrugs a little, looking at me instead of the tyrant who clearly dropped in to make him feel like shit. Feeling bad, I place my hand on his, squeezing gently. I had decent parents, but I'm fully aware that many people do not. Obviously, being a rich, privileged asshole came with a lot of drawbacks I wouldn't have known about had I not come with him today.

A tingle sweeps over me as our hands interlace and I tilt my head, letting it race over my skin.

"Oh, my," the Queen murmurs softly. I watch her shoo the King and after he disappears, she takes the cup she poured my tea in. Placing a strainer over it, she dumps the tea in the grass and places the gorgeous china in front of her. The hum of powerful magic fills the air and her eyes cloud as she looks into it. "Yes, that makes sense."

"What's going on?" I whisper to Revelin. "I've seen readers before, but not like this."

"Mother is…a different kind of Fae. Her powers are quite rare and this is one of them. It is unwise to interrupt and even less wise to ignore what she tells us when she is done."

Great. That's not gut churning information.

"Your power is not done manifesting, my dear. It will continue to grow until you are able to fulfill your destiny." The Queen hums a little as she studies the cup more. "The lies you were told were essential to your survival, as you and your sister are the Children of the Moon. When all is right and the eight are sealed, there will be a battle. Until then, you must learn everything you can, accept your fated, and grow strong. Do not allow those with ill-intent to prevent you from finding the truth or you will not be ready."

I groan under my breath, putting my free hand over my face as her words ring true in my soul.

Just what I needed: a fucking destiny.

42

———

Feray

So warm and comfortable wrapped up in my mate's arms...

For once, everything seems perfect, but something feels slightly off. A nagging feeling that wakes me fully from my slumber.

Get up.

My wolf insists, but I'm not used to hearing her voice occasionally echo in my ears. Nuzzling Torben, I get him to roll onto his back, so he releases me from his tight embrace. *Something doesn't feel right and I'm not sure what it is.* The air feels tingly, and the scent of ozone has filled the air.

It reminds me of that ionic air cleanser we had as kids because mom thought I had allergies. Now I realize my allergies were more than likely just my heightened sense of smell because of my wolf. The low hum from somewhere in the house isn't helping settle my nerves. Slipping on my fuzzy housecoat, I tie it tight around my waist and grab my phone before silently opening my bedroom door. Thankfully, Torben snores so loud he could probably drown out a concert so he doesn't hear me leave the room.

Creeping down the hall, there's a pulsing purple light flickering from under Fi's door. Pulling my phone out, I go to the calendar app and look to see if Tiernan is possibly here. This could be a weird sex thing or something less fun, but I'd like to know before I bust in.

Fi insisted on a house calendar app because of family dinners, mates sleeping over, and wacky work hours. No one wants to walk in on something they cannot unsee. According to the entry for tonight, he's on Prince duty, so it's not him.

Reaching out, I grip the handle and it's cold almost to the point of burning my hand. *What in Niflheim is going on?* The door is locked; Fi never locks her door. Tiernan left after dinner to go to work, so she wouldn't lock it for when he comes home. The glowing and the humming intensify the longer I stand here, and now panic is setting in. The ozone scent is the strongest here—it makes my chest tighten, afraid of what's happened to my sister.

"Fi? Fi, answer me! Are you ok?" I bang on the door as hard as I can, trying to get her attention. The silence makes my hair stand on end and I immediately believe the absolute worst has happened.

Wait. Are aliens real? Is this an abduction? Fi will be so *pissed if they probe her.*

Partially shifting is my go-to anymore, so I let my furry fly. It increases my size and my strength—making me feel less out of control. Gripping the doorknob, I ram my shoulder into it, breaking the frame. Wood fragments fall to the ground as I stumble into the room with the swinging door. I swear, the sight that greets me makes my heart stop: Fi is floating two feet off her bed, glowing like a neon sign at the bar.

Did she piss a demon off and now they took control of her body? Or worse, they took control of her body to incubate their little demon babies?

I stare at my sister helplessly before I shriek for help. "Torben!" Crossing the room, I use the phone I see on Fi's nightstand to text the guys. I'm only focused on getting help for Fi as I tap out distress texts on the blurry screen. When I'm done, I wait for answers as she hovers in the air.

Torben's heavy footsteps stop me from pacing as he races in, still buck naked. "What the hell happened?"

"I'm not sure." I glance from my mate to my sister.

"How do we fix it?" Torben asks.

"Pants would be good," I mutter. He blushes, walking down the hall to grab pants and when he returns, I shake my head. "I don't know what to do. Usually, Fi fixes the fucked up shit!"

The itch from resisting the shift is almost too much to bear. I'm damn near having a panic attack when my wolf finally takes over. I shift in the middle of my sister's room and howl in a wolven call for help.

Torben's bear is obviously on edge seeing how stressed I am. I leave the bedroom, needing to run some of the nervous energy in the living room. Furniture gets overturned, and I knock two vases off tables in my anxious state. My mate finally opens the front door, letting me out into the night so I can run laps around the front yard.

It feels like it's been forever since I texted everyone; where are they?

I circle back to the house to check on my sister over and over until the crunch of tires driving over the stone in the driveway stops me in my tracks. Seeing a set of headlights sends me sprinting back to the house. Torben turns on the porch lights, illuminating the front lawn and almost blinds me. When I get to the porch, I face the driveway with my hackles raised, ready to attack if need be. Waiting for the car to get closer, I tense—it's not a vehicle I recognize.

Torben leans in the door frame, blocking the entrance to the house, running his hand over my fur, trying to soothe me. "Little Wolf, it's the twins; it's okay."

"What the actual fuck is going on? This one is shifted, and it looks like you have a UFO in your house." Khol points at me, then over at the house, and Khal shakes his head at his twin.

"Not sure, man. Her sister is floating over her bed like a purple glow worm that fell into faerie dust." Torben's matter-of-fact explanation makes me growl and snap at the hand on me. The big guy jumps back and looks his hand over carefully.

"She doesn't like anyone talking bad about Fiadh," Khal says as he approaches carefully. He has his hands out to me, palms up. "It's okay, Precious. We're here to help if we can. At the very least, we can protect the two of you until we figure out what's wrong with your sister."

That earns him a tail wag, and I approach slowly.

The air shifts again, and the humming gets louder, sending me back into a panic. I race around, howling and barking at everything. A familiar sound gets closer, and I realize it's Tiernan's car. Sitting down, I throw my head back, letting loose the deepest, most mournful howl I can. It resonates so deeply in my bones that anguish nearly vibrates through me.

"Feray!" Tiernan calls for me and I run back to the house. He has the Prince in tow for some reason, making me sniff around suspiciously. His tone wavers slightly as he looks towards the light emanating from the house. "What happened?"

"We're not sure." Torben supplies as he inches closer to me. I know if he gets close, he's just going to snatch me up and carry me. I monitor my sneaky mate, but not the prince.

Revelin kneels down, looking at me at eye level. "I haven't seen a wolf your color in years." His tone holds a mysterious quality to it as he focuses on me.

"The darker coat she had when she first shifted is changing." Torben states as he ushers everyone inside. "That's not why everyone is here. Fiadh is floating and glowing like a snapped glow stick."

"I'll deal with the witch. You two deal with the anxious wolf." Revelin says as he moves towards the house.

Racing ahead of him, I run to my sister's room and place myself between her and the door. The instant Khol and Revelin step foot in Fi's room, I lunge at them, snapping my jaws and just barely missing Khol's crotch.

I'm not a match for the twins, but if I need to, I could hurt Revelin—I think.

"Holy fuck! She almost got the boys." He cups his hands over his dick, giving me a wide berth.

"Let her sister's bonded mate calm her down before you get eaten, you slithering idiot." Revelin sighs, remaining just inside the door with a sharp eye on my fangs.

"Feray."

Tiernan inches closer and I smell food. Tilting my head to the side, I flick my ears, listening to everything beyond the hum that is behind me. The leopard waves a cured meat stick in my direction and my wolf takes notice. "Take a deep breath. I need you to calm down so we can help Fiadh. I know it's tough when your animal wants to protect someone they love."

Whining, I look over my shoulder at my sister, then at Tiernan, and then Revelin.

"I agree." Tiernan looks over his shoulder at Revelin. "She thinks you can help Fiadh because you have magic and none of us do."

Furrowing his brows, the Fae Prince squints in puzzlement. "You understood her? How is that possible?"

"My cat sensed what her wolf was thinking and told me." Tiernan stands up and hands the meat stick to Revelin. "Give her the peace offering and she'll settle down enough that Torben and Khal can get her to shift back."

Wagging my tail, I wait for Revelin to get closer. Tiernan understanding me like this was awesome. Glancing over at Torben for confirmation, I yip happily when he signals that he can do it, too. I file that fun fact away for later.

"Fluffy, I just want to help your sister." Begrudgingly, Revelin takes the meat stick from Tiernan and moves to sit in front of me. He holds the stick out in front of him and I gently take it from him and offer him my paw. Gently, he takes my paw and shakes it before I move past him to Torben and Khal.

"What the fuck. She tries to take my dick off, but she shakes hands with you."

Khol is beside himself, but I'm not sure if it's anger or jealousy. Knowing Khol it's a mix of both—much like my sister, anger is his default setting.

"Get over it, Bedia. I'm prettier than you." Revelin snarks before walking over to examine Fiadh.

Khal and Torben nod at them, then lead me out of the bedroom to the living room. The guys set tables and chairs back to where they should have been while I watch. Torben directs Khal to the kitchen and he returns with snacks and smiles.

"You need to shift back, Precious. It's hard to have a dialogue like this." He waves a turkey leg at me just out of my range.

I grumble to myself mentally as I move over to Torben and stand up on my hind legs, looking at him with my front paws on his hip. When I tilt my head to the side, he finally gets the gist of what I want. "Can you see if she destroyed her housecoat when she shifted? It's in her sister's room on the floor."

"Okay." Khal sounds happy to help as he leaves the room.

"You and I both know he's yours, Little Wolf. But I respect your need to be covered up with everyone else here." Torben leans down and kisses me on my muzzle and his bear rumbles to me, setting my nerves at ease.

"Found it! Not a thread out of place." His excitement is almost contagious.

"Let's get it on her, but make sure to give her the food you brought out. She expels a lot of energy shifting between forms because it's still new," Torben informs Khal as he hands him my house coat. My bear gently lifts one paw at a time, getting me dressed before I land on all fours again.

"I'm not used to other shifters being shy." Khal says watching Torben taking care of my modesty.

My shift to human comes easily now. Rolling my shoulders, I adjust the fabric to cover me. My throat is rough and gravely from all of the carrying on I did earlier. Khal offers me a glass of water that I drink quickly. "There are unbonded males here and I'm not comfortable."

"That makes sense," he says before he looks back at my sister's room.

"I need to fill the others in on what the Fae Queen told Fiadh earlier. Revelin can help if I miss anything, but I think it probably has to do with this." I walk past Khal, grabbing the turkey leg and heading to my sister's room.

As I get closer to the room, I hear Khol and Revelin arguing again about what they need to do.

"Enough!" I bonk both of them with a turkey leg as I enter, moving closer to my floating sister.

"You did *not* just hit me with a turkey leg." Khol snarls, stepping forward, but Khal stops him.

"I did, and I'll bloody do it again." Brandishing the turkey leg like a sword, I wave it in his direction. Revelin is wiping the turkey juice off his arm as he frowns at me. "Prince, correct me if I'm wrong, but earlier, your mom told my sister we are called the Children of the Moon?"

"Aye, that's spot on. She also mentioned 'all eight being sealed,' but who the hell knows what that meant. We could assume she meant mate bonds, but we're missing some pieces if so." Revelin turns that bad boy rock star swagger up and he almost makes me weak in the knees.

"Cut that Fae magic shit out or Fiadh will cut your dick off and beat you to death with it." There's a growl to my voice that catches the Prince off guard.

"She can hold an Alpha's stare—intimidating her won't work," Tiernan chimes in from the other side of the bed.

"And she almost bit my boys off earlier, so she's crazy." Khol uses both hands to cover his crotch as he ducks behind his twin.

Growling, I stare at Khol as my wolf surfaces slowly.

Next thing I know, Khal is in my face, smiling. I see the faint shimmer of his shift in his eyes and the slit of his pupil. Hesitantly his hand comes up and caresses my cheek. Slowly his thumb runs along the edge of my jaw stroking it gently. His free hand grabs mine and rests it on his chest."Don't let my twin get to you. He's a dick. Breathe with me and calm down."

I feel his chest rise under my hand and breathe in with him. He holds his breath at the peak then slowly lets it out. We repeat the breathing exercise three more times before he stops.

"Feel better Precious?" He leans forward and presses his forehead against mine.

"Surprisingly, yes."

"Good," Khal tucks me into his side as we turn to face Revelin.

"My mother has theories about the girls from the tea leaves. Her reading seemed to indicate they were hidden for a reason. We just have to figure out what that reason is." He waves his hand in the air dismissively, as if getting that information will be no big deal.

"What are the Children of the Moon?" Torben asks as he looks from the Prince to my levitating sister.

"I don't know."

I turn to look at my sister. Perhaps Fi has the answer but we won't know until she wakes up.

43

FIADH

The moment Fer burst in here and had her puppy panic attack, I was aware of everything. Obviously, I have no idea what's going on with my magic, nor how to stop it, but I can hear and see all the chaos. I'd love to weigh in, because I'm nearly bursting with snarky commentary about the bear's bare ass, Fer almost biting the dick off one of the Ying Yang twins, and my big kitty baiting her with a doggy treat.

Alas, I'm stuck with all my brilliance trapped in my mind while they run in circles. This blows.

"I doubt she knows, either. Mother's ability to read is usually full of metaphor and rarely gives specific detail. We can add it to whatever research you two appear to be doing, but what's happening *right now* is more urgent. Fiadh's magic is increasing and this is a symptom," Revelin says as he watches me float.

"Anyone consider that taking her to the fucking Faerie was a bad plan?" Khol mutters. "That place practically dribbles magic on you from the second you step foot in it."

Tiernan and Revelin look at one another, then back at me, and I can *feel* their sheepishness. *Good. The Prince should have thought of this before he let his mommy push him around.* I like her, don't get me wrong, but my trip there may have caused this craziness. If only I could smack both of them with a bird leg like my sister did. *Sigh.*

"Shit," Tiernan mutters as he rakes his hand through his hair. "I never think of this shit, no matter how long I work for your people. It's become a little commonplace for me to feel the press of that wild power."

Revelin snorts. "Imagine how I feel. It's part of me so I definitely don't notice or think about how much mojo my lands give off. I just wanted to make my mother happy for once and… well, the next part isn't important, but I didn't think she'd get a prophecy and a power jump."

Khol rolls his eyes at them, walking over to me and I can feel his eyes roving over my barely covered form. "I think we should send the wolf out. She's a newly emerged shifter and still learning her powers and control. It's not helping. I can feel it and I'm not tied to her, so I'd wager it's helping to fuel this somehow."

"That's probably true," Revelin says. "Perhaps the less annoying snake and the bear can take the sister into another room and keep her calm while I consider what I need to do?"

Feray's glare has enough energy to crawl over my skin and I feel bad that she's being banished. She only wants to help, but I can't deny that her nervousness is palpable. She protests, but Torben rumbles something low and soothing to her that seems to work. She takes his and Khal's hands, pausing to look at the men in the room before they exit. "Hurt my sister and I'll rip your intestines out through your nostrils."

Go, Feray.

"Don't worry, Fer. I won't let anything happen to Knuckles." Tiernan's voice is soft, but the honesty in it rings through the air like a bell.

Am I hearing emotions now instead of simply sensing them? That's going to be very inconvenient.

Once my sister, the bear, and the quieter basilisk leave, I can focus my attention on what's going on with me and the men in the room. I know I'm glowing and floating, which is *not* normal, and I understand visiting the Faerie may have kick-started my developing powers. Beyond that, I don't know what to expect; the various bouts of elemental or empathic powers I've experienced in the past few aren't even close to this magnitude.

"Scaly, you and Big T back up a little while I see if I can get through to her," Revelin says as his eyes roam over me. "I don't want anything to bounce off if it doesn't work."

Khol snorts and I can feel the amusement rolling off of him in waves. "Big T, huh?"

That's when I'm surprised to hear the odd rumbling yowl of my easygoing mate followed by a muffled grunt. "The Prince is lean and willowy; I'm a big fucking dude with razor sharp claws and fangs. Picture clear now, you secret chamber reject?"

Goddess, I wish I could laugh.

"As amusing as that comparison is, old friend, I think we need to focus on the lady in the glowing cocoon."

When the two of them back down, I heave a sigh of relief internally. Revelin could definitely force them to dance a little with his magic, but I doubt that's the way for him to make friends and influence people. Something about this situation tells me I need them all to get along and if that's not worrisome, I don't know what is. Niamh's weird tea leaf reading left me vaguely uncomfortable and itchy when we returned. I haven't quite put my finger on why, but it's probably something to do with that phrase about the 'when the eight are sealed.'

I have three alpha dudes gnashing their teeth in this room and Feray has two more in the living room. Are they part of the eight and who in hell are the other three?

"Okay, Rev," Tiernan says as he walks over and clamps his hand on his shoulder. "Do your thing."

The rocker pushes his hair out of his eyes, drawing in a deep breath. The air in the room gets heavy, filling with the scent of grapefruit, jasmine, and ginger blossoms. Sparkles appear, raining down on me with another earthy, sweet one—patchouli, perhaps? The combination is heady and I breathe in it with pleasure, enjoying the feel of his gold and green magic twining with the deep purple and black of mine. My limbs tingle and I smile to myself as I feel my body lower towards the comfy warmth of my bed.

"Holy shit, he's actually doing it," Khol mutters. "I figured his magic was some bullshit trick with lights and sound at his shows."

"You ain't seen nothing yet." Tiernan's voice is full of laughter. "Rev keeps most of his true power under wraps. He's already a target for assassins and crazies as the Prince, not to mention stalker fans. The last thing he needs is his dickhead father sending professionals after him."

Again, important information I get to tuck away because no one thinks I'm listening.

When my body touches the comforter, the paralysis lifts and I groan as oxygen fills my lungs and makes my head spin. I don't know why I had to float around like Snow White at a rave, but my fingertips are *buzzing* with power. I'm actually afraid to see what it means, so I look over at the men with a sheepish smile.

"Hi," I say, wiggling my fingers at them. Flowers spring up on the floor, crawling up the ceiling and twining around the room when I do it. Gasping, I curl my digits into my palms and cut my gaze back to them with wide eyes. "What the *hell* is that?"

Revelin smirks, shrugging a little. "We think visiting my home brought more of your powers out. I can't decide what you are, to tell the truth. You've shown elemental powers, but on a scale far greater than those puny casters. We've also seen hallmarks of mindbenders, but again, to a degree that's not normal. I suppose this is earth finally showing up."

I let his words wash over me and all I hear in my mind is: truth.

Fuck. Me. Raw.

"Either of you guys want to comment on why she still looks like a Lite-Brite?" Khol says, arching a brow at me, then Rev and Tiernan. "Is that permanent or what?"

"He's got a point. If I'm going to glow like a lava lamp forever, I won't be able to go anywhere with my skin exposed." Chewing on my lip, I frown as I look at myself. It's a pretty glow, but it will kill stealth and make my life infinitely harder.

The Fae shakes his head. "I don't believe it's permanent. I think it's a short term issue, but I'm not sure what will make it go away. It's a shame, though, because you may have to cover yourself to get to sleep tonight."

"I worked that out on my own, asshole," I grumble under my breath. It occurs to me I'm so out of sorts that I probably missed a few normal person conventions and I sigh before I look at each of them. "Thank you for coming to help. I know Fer was freaking the fuck out and not all of you had to drop everything to run here in the middle of the night."

Tiernan beams, his face practically broadcasting 'good job' at my words. "I will always come, Knuckles. And oddly enough, my royal pain in the ass left the cadre of fawning Fae with little coercion."

Rev rolls his eyes and waves his hand dismissively. "I simply felt I may have had a part in your discomfort and it was my duty to help."

Lie, my brain tells me. My face screws up as I realize how goddamn annoying *that* quirk is going to get. I'll need to figure out how to shield my new mental lie detector so I don't lose my mind in crowds —like at the bar. Otherwise, it's going to get loud in there.

"I didn't have to be coerced," Khol says as he sidles up to the bed and drops down next to me. His arm lands on my shoulders and he gives me a wicked grin. "I couldn't resist seeing your bedtime sassy pants."

Pushing him until he topples over, I grunt. "Gross."

He just lands on his back and props himself on his elbows with a smirk. I adjust the tiny straps of my bralette, making sure that the unavoidable pitfall of wearing a tank top to bed hasn't happened to me. When I figure out that it hasn't, I mumble, "At least I don't have one tit hanging out or I'd be really embarrassed."

They look at me in confusion and I shrug. Finally, Tiernan gathers the courage to ask, "What?"

"There is no possible way to wear a tank top or loose bra-like top to bed without waking up in the morning with one of the girls escap-ing. It is known," I say with a shrug. "Now someone go get my sister so she knows I'm okay."

Khol doesn't move, so Tiernan looks at the Fae, who shakes his head. He gives up and strides out of the room, leaving the two least familiar supes watching me like a pack of hyenas. I scoot further down the bed and put my back against the wall as I look at the brightly glowing skin on my arms and legs. Since they're both ogling me, I figure I should get in on the fun as well.

"Sis!" Feray says as she rushes into the room. I hold my arms out for her to come hug me and another fresh burst of foliage springs up, decorating the other half of the room. "What the fuck?"

I flush bright red as I drop my arms and curl my fingers back into my palms again. "We don't know, Fer. I'm a rainbow Poison Ivy tonight."

Her eyes flick to Revelin and she puts her hands on her hips. "Don't stand there composing a song about your belly button! Do something to help her, you sparkly pretty boy."

My mouth drops open and so do the mouths of every single male now filling the room with rich, competing scents. None of us can believe she just scolded the prince like a naughty school boy and she's oblivious to our shock. Her posture is combative and she keeps glaring at him until he finally sighs.

"I'll try to bind her for tonight, but it's *not* a real solution. It'll wear off in the morning. She'll have to practice using and controlling her powers because when I leave, it will wear off. I don't have everything I'd need for a more permanent solution."

"Newsflash, pretty boy," I drawl. "I don't want it to be permanent. I'll learn; I just need to get some fucking sleep tonight. Hopefully, the glow isn't here in the morning and I can do exactly what you're suggesting: practice."

His lips curl up as he draws a few runes in the air, just like he did for the portal, and a bright flash nearly blinds me. When I open my eyes, I have to wait for a minute until the spots dancing in front of them fade. I look down to see there are two glittering runes on my forearms that look suspiciously like one of his tattoos.

"If he's staying to keep the magic fueled, I'm staying, too." Khol kicks his shoes off and gets comfy on the bed with a glare that dares anyone to challenge him.

"Obviously, I have to stay," Revelin replies.

Merciful Hecate, save me from this dick swinging—

"I'm not leaving." Tiernan gives me a grin and walks over as he glares at the other two. "And I call my usual spot. You two can tussle over the rest of the bed."

Feray giggles, her eyes dancing as she pushes the quiet basilisk and the bear out of the room. She looks over her shoulder as she goes, winking at me wickedly.

Great. She thinks I'm having an ultraviolet orgy tonight.

I'll never live this down.

44

───────

FERAY

Out of the three guys in my sister's room, I only trust Tiernan.

Who said cats and dogs can't get along?

I know as her bonded mate, he would never let anything happen to her. As much as I want to trust that things are okay, I know deep down they are not. My sister having multiple branches of magic can't be good. Then there's my fur changing color, which they say is odd.

What in the name of Fenrir is happening to me?

Torben leads us into the living room and I break away from the guys to pace the room. I'm trying to piece everything together, but the scent of the magic in the air has my wolf freaked out.

"Little Wolf?" Torben's soft tone catches my attention and I pause.

Turning to face him, I see a look of concern that is mirrored on Khal's face as they watch me fidget. My claws rise from my fingertips as fur covers my forearms and I stare down at my half shifted hands. *I feel more helpless than ever before.* I have the strength to keep

Fi safe, but I was kicked out of the room because I don't have magic. "I know I'm pacing, but I should be in there. We've always looked out for each other. Now I can finally protect her like she did me, but stupid magic has thwarted me again."

"Look at me." Torben's voice pleads with me, and I feel the pull of our bond.

Resisting the bond is almost as difficult as walking past a slice of cheesecake—you know you shouldn't, but it's impossible not to. I want to be wrapped in his arms, but if I go, he won't let go. Raising my eyes, I watch the amber of his bear rise and the pull increases.

"I know I'm new," Khal says softly. Boldly, he takes my hands in his. "But I also know she's safe. My brother can turn everyone in that room to stone if he desires. She's the safest she can be, all things considered."

Sniffing the air around Khal, I don't scent any dishonesty. While I'm distracted, Torben comes up behind me and wraps me in his arms. The deep rumble of his bear trying to soothe me vibrates through my body and echoes in my ears.

"Shhh… Little Wolf, everyone is safe. You don't need to be on edge."

The way the dominant words slip from his lips reminds me of when he denied my orgasm for what felt like forever. "No distracting me, you tease. I need to make sure those cock juggling ass clowns aren't hurting my sister."

I struggle in his arms, but he tightens his grip on me. "Naughty Little Wolf."

Torben ghosts his lips over my neck, moving to where my neck meets my shoulder. Gasping, I freeze, feeling his thickened length pressed against my ass. His hot breath whispers over my flesh and he uses his chin to push the fabric of my housecoat out of the way. Laving his tongue over my mate mark, he opens his mouth and applies a little pressure with his teeth.

My heart pounds and my core clenches in anticipation of a firmer bite. Khal's eyes illuminate behind his nictitating membrane. His mouth pops open and his fangs unfold to stretch out like a rattlesnake. Squirming, I attempt to break free; I'll never get to her if I give into them.

"My Precious." Khal's breathy tone sends my desire into overdrive. He glances at Torben and a silent understanding passes between them.

Before I know it, I am sandwiched between Khal and Torben. It's like I'm in one of my racy romance novels—two hot guys pressing me between them with their hard cocks. Khal leans forward and kisses my shoulder, then applies light pressure with his teeth. They both tease me with the bites and suckling, not stopping until I shatter in their arms.

Wave after pulsing wave of euphoria moves through me and I groan darkly. *We need to move this to a more private venue—like now.* Both males run their hands up and down my sides as I come down from my high. Perfectly synchronized, they release my shoulder from their mouths at the same time.

A deep chuckle escapes Torben's lips before he kisses my cheek. "Now you know why bears live in poly groups, Little Wolf. Sometimes two is better than one."

My bear leaves me in Khal's arms as the basilisk kisses where he pressed his teeth. Khal scoops me up like I weigh nothing, carrying me to the couch and sitting me on his lap. His voice is a whisper on the shell of my ear. "One day, I want to make my mark real."

I'm soaked, aching to be filled and perched on Khal's lap with a few thin layers of cotton separating me from what I desire. *So cruel.*

Torben comes back with three glasses of red wine and a charcuterie board loaded with meat and cheese. He pauses as he sets out the spread and hands off the wine glasses. "All things considered…We may need a bigger house."

"I love my house." Pouting, I turn to face him.

He smiles and takes my feet to place them in his lap. Torben's eyes flicker back and forth between human and bear. He rests his hand on my knee and gives it a gentle squeeze. "I know you do, Little Wolf. We can talk about it in the morning with the others."

"What others?" A non challenging growl escapes my lips and Khal runs his fingers through my hair, crooning.

"I believe boss bear is trying to say we need to include the three stooges and your sister," Khal says as he massages my scalp.

"Tiernan is her mate." I slap my hands over my mouth as I realize what they mean. "Crap on a cracker! The Prince and your prick brother are also her mates"

Khal nods and when I look over at Torben, he agrees with him.

Fuck my life.

"We," Torben motions between himself and Khal, "understand you and your sister don't want to live apart." I growl briefly when he mentions the living apart thing. "I can talk to my cousins about expanding the house you love so much."

"How can we afford to do that?" Sighing, I pinch the bridge of my nose. The exorbitant cost of such an undertaking would be astronomical.

Sitting up, Khal sets his glass down and wraps his arms around me tightly. "Let me worry about that, Precious."

"What do you mean, let you worry about it? Fi will kill you!" Jumping up, I move away from the guys and take a handful of meat and cheese off the board to take the edge off.

Torben moves closer and kisses my forehead. "Two of your sister's mates are self-absorbed assholes, but please be patient with the three of us who want what's best for the family unit."

I nuzzle him under his jaw affectionately and it earns me a happy grumble from his bear. He hugs me briefly and kisses my lips gently before turning me loose and pushing me toward Khal. He looks so unsure but relaxed at the same time. I snuggle in closer and press the bridge of my nose under his jaw. It's not a truly submissive thing to do; it's more that he trusts me enough to be this close to his exposed throat. A deep, relieved sigh escapes his lips, and he rests his head on top of mine.

I turn in his arms and press my lips to his throat, then my teeth. A soft growl escapes my lips. "You owe me for tolerating your brother, " I say before I back away and head down the hall.

"Where are you going?" Torben asks.

"Bed. Are you two coming?" I take off down the hall, listening to two sets of boots running down the hallway.

AFTER LAST NIGHT'S DEBACLE, I am exhausted.

The Fi laser light show and the guys giving me blue ovaries stressed me out enough to fall asleep fast. So many twisted dreams flooded my mind: I kept seeing two male figures, but I couldn't make out who they were.

The soft scent of vetiver fills my nose and I reach behind me where Torben should be. Noting the teddy bear is missing, I pop an eye open to see Khal laying flat on his back staring at the ceiling. I inch closer to him and rest my head on his shoulder, whispering, "Did you sleep?"

Smiling, he turns his head to face me. "I'm nocturnal, Precious. I watched over you like I said I would… but not in a creepy 'stalker' way," he rushes to add, looking sheepish.

I chuckle softly, rolling out of bed from Torben's side. "Let's head to the kitchen. I'm sure Torben already has breakfast ready. By the smell of it, I know there's bacon cooking."

Ducking into my closet, I switch out of Torben's t-shirt and slip into an oversized sweatshirt and leggings. When I'm ready, I step out and notice Khal is already gone.

I guess he was giving me privacy to get changed.

Heated voices travel up the hallway and when I enter the kitchen, the twins and Torben are arguing about what needs to be done first. Fi is in Revelin's face and Tiernan is sipping his coffee off to the side. He's the first to notice my arrival and wiggles my favorite coffee mug at me.

Thank Morrigan, someone has the forethought to provide me with coffee this early.

Taking the cup from Tiernan, we gently touch our cheeks together in greeting before I turn to watch the arguments happening around us.

"We have more pressing matters than housing!" Khol raises his voice, trying to be heard.

A low growl starts deep in my chest as I stare at him. He's yelling at mates and my sister. That is not a good way to start my morning. Handing my cup off to Tiernan, I stalk forward, knowing full well Khol can turn me to stone. "Hold my coffee." My voice is a mix of my wolven tones and human when I turn on the basilisk. "Who the fuck do you think you're yelling at, dickhead?"

"She shouldn't be able to do that." Revelin whispers to Fi.

I watch the scales moving under Khol's skin. His tone screams exasperation. "No one is listening to me."

Moving closer, I see the twitch in his nictitating membrane and narrow my eyes, allowing them to burn with the golden hue of my wolf. "You're overtired and irritated. I'm sorry we're keeping you up past your natural bedtime."

The tightness around Khol's eyes fades away and he nods. I turn to look at the others as they gape at me. "What? He's tired and having a tantrum. It's no biggie. Housing isn't a priority, but it is a necessity. There's no reason both issues can't be addressed at the same time."

Reaching out, I rest a hand on his shoulder and hope some of my calmness transfers to him. Khol's posture changes from tense to relaxed. He looks shocked at the change in himself. I walk back over to Tiernan and retrieve my mug. The silence in the room is eerie, so I turn and look around, only to find everyone looking at me. "Did someone draw a dick on my cheek again?"

Fi spits her coffee, and the guys crack up. *That was exactly the effect I was looking for.*

Revelin taps his spoon against the side of his mug to draw attention to himself. "Many new pieces of information have been added to the puzzle that is your lives, Lass and Fluffy. Follow me."

I watch Tiernan mouth 'Fluffy?' to Torben, and he shakes his head to dismiss it.

Revelin leads the way back to the office and gestures at everything on the walls. "From what they revealed to me, this mark," he walks over to the image of the car with the glyph on it, "has recently been discovered on their old boss, whose business burned to the ground. It also is where they once lived."

He paces around the room as we watch him in silence. My hackles are on edge because I feel like they have invaded my privacy. But on the flip side, he may help us. "From what I can gather, the accident more than likely wasn't an accident. Lass, you can't be left alone anymore. You and your sister are probable targets." The normally carefree Prince is deadly serious; that much is obvious from his expression.

Fi gets ready to protest, but Tiernan spins her to face him. He kisses her, holding her face in his hands.

Double blinking, I know for a fact my sister is going to kick his ass from here to the troll market and back again. She doesn't do public displays of affection.

When Tiernan pulls back, Fi is slightly dazed, then whispers something in his ear. I swear, I feel his cat cringe from here. She probably threatened his manhood over embarrassing her like that. Ball damage or stabbing are Fi's go-to when she's angry.

Thick arms wrap around me, holding me to the mountain of a bear behind me. Unlike my sister, my wolf craves contact with her mate and others. With wolves being more social than the witches I was raised by, it's a novel experience for me to want to be snuggled. My wolf opened an entirely new area of life for me.

I watch Khal and Khol move towards the walls, snapping pictures with their phones.

"We can watch the girls at night since it's our natural time to be awake." Khol offers and Khal pats him on the shoulder to reinforce his good behavior.

Out of the corner of my eye, I watch Revelin pull Fi off to the side. He leans in, discussing something with her that even *I* can't hear.

"He does that." Tiernan motions to the Prince and my sister.

"What do you mean?"

"He can keep his words from traveling beyond the person meant to hear them." Tiernan explains.

I swear, Revelin heard us gossiping because he turns and looks right at us with a smirk.

Clearing his throat, Revelin steps forward again. "There are several things we need to figure out to keep the girls safe."

He holds up his index finger. The way he looks at the guys, I think the sausage fest united without us and had a meeting about this. "Who or what are the eight that need to be sealed?"

The next finger comes up. The way he turns and looks at my sister, I think this was part of their private discussion. "Why does Fiadh have more than one branch of magic?"

I feel Torben tense up behind me when Revelin holds up his next finger. "Why has your fur changed color? The dominant coloration for wolf shifters is timber wolf or pitch black; you are neither."

The Fae examines every facet of me up close before turning those dark sapphire eyes away from me. "Finally, what that mark means and if it has something to do with why your shift and powers were sealed."

The ominous tone Revelin takes makes the hair on the back of my neck stand on end.

Tiernan moves forward, looking at us. "In short, ladies, one of us or the security detail will be with you from now on."

"What the actual fuck, T?" Fi growls and I watch the cat cringe. His cat wants to retreat, which is odd.

For now I'll file that bit of information away for later. We've got bigger fish to fry right now.

"During the day, it's either Torben or someone from Tiernan's team. At night, Khal will stay with me." Smirking, I lean against Torben then extend my hand out to Khal. I stare right into Khal's eyes and he smiles broadly at me happy I have accepted his presence in my life. "If all the bad things come out at night, I might as well fight fire with fire."

"Seriously, Fer? We have lives and work!" Fi shoves her way past the guys and flowers erupt in her wake.

"Um, Mother Nature? You need to focus on getting that under control." I point at the wildflowers now growing in the middle of our sitting room.

"Bloody hell, Revelin," she says as she spins on her heel to find him gone. "Where the fuck did he go?"

Tiernan chuckles. "He left a while ago to go work on answers. He does that a lot—you get used to it."

My sister throws her head up with a loud, frustrated growl and stalks out of the room.

"She's okay; it's a lot to process." Shrugging my shoulders, I smile at everyone apologetically.

I hope Revelin and our guys can figure this out; otherwise, my sister might explode.

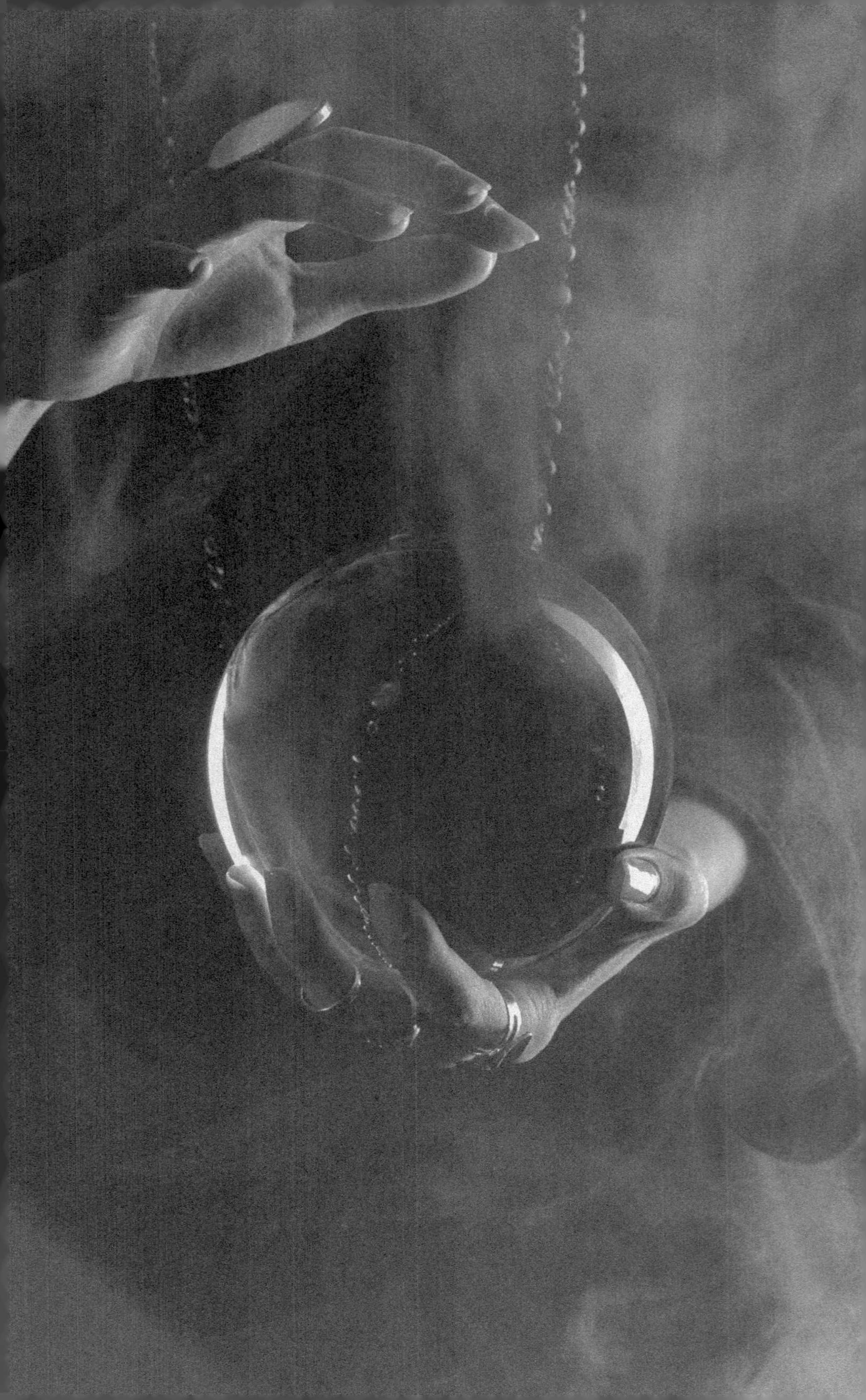

45

FIADH

"I HAVE MULTIPLE TYPES OF MAGIC," I MUTTER AS I WALK AROUND THE room. Luckily, they'd provided me with food and caffeine so I could get through this shit. One thing Torben is excellent at is making sure we actually eat and have energy resources—it's because of Fer's shifter side, I know, but I appreciate it just the same. I've spent most of my life subsisting off of caffeine and rage; it's nice to have someone prodding me to consume something substantial because I often forget.

Tiernan walks over and takes my hands, stopping me as he looks at me with his icy blue eyes. "Yes, you do, it seems. That's better than no magic by far, isn't it?"

Well, shit. He has a goddamn point.

"Way to logic her out of *that* snit, mate," Khol says with a smirk. He's leaning against my dresser, watching me like a predator, and I feel the snake shimmering under his skin.

Having a mate who shares my propensity for violence as a solution is going to drive everyone else *insane.* I blink as I realize what I said to myself: Khol is a mate. *What the hell did I do to deserve* this *horse-shit? We'll never stop fighting one another.*

Shaking my head as that irritating thought zings through my mind, I focus on the issues everyone brought up one by one. Obviously, the magic thing is outside of my control in terms of 'fixing' it. I simply need to practice my unique skills and since the only magic user is Prince Douchebag, it will have to be with him.

Great. That's going to go so *well.*

Revelin won't gently guide me through things like T has. He's going to push me until I break and then start again from the beginning until I get whatever he's teaching down. The Fae doesn't have to explain to me how he was likely taught; I've met his asshat father. I guarantee the method he uses will make us fight like wildcats and then drop to the ground when we're done. He's not a coddler.

"What are you thinking about?" Tiernan asks, as he looks at me in concern. "It's making your face do scrunchy things."

Snorting, I let go of his hands to flop on my bed. "I'm thinking that my magic crap is not a controllable problem—*which I hate*—and the only one who can teach me is Rev. That means we'll likely come close to killing each other until I learn."

Khol's lips quirk. "Spot on, Sassy. I agree with that assessment."

"He won't *hurt* you," the leopard cuts in quickly, his eyes wide.

"Yes, he will, but not permanently. At least, not something he can't help heal. He seems to think we're gearing up for some kind of battle or some shit, T. The Prince of the Daybreak Court was raised to prepare for war by a man who seems like a casual sadist. I'm pretty sure he'll do it even if he doesn't like it."

"Yep," Khol replies. "I'll do what I can to help develop your fight hand-to-hand, though, and so will Khal and Big T. For both of you, though, and the bear won't like it."

Nope. Torben's going to be pissed when Feray gets knocked on her ass a few million times because she isn't allowed to shift.

"Yeah," I sigh. "Okay. That's one bullshit issue down. The next is the house. I'm not deaf, nor profoundly stupid, and I've pieced together you idiots want us to have guards around all the time. By square footage alone, this place will not give any of us the privacy we need, if that's the case. I mean, look at this morning." I glare at them, putting my irritation at awakening to a bunch of shit before I've had my fucking coffee into the look.

"Don't worry about the house," Khol says, waving his hand. "Between the bear, us, and the Prince, it'll be fine. I'd bet that royal asswad is already making moves. He seems arrogant enough to be sliding chess pieces around and then demand forgiveness later."

I arch a brow, looking at Tiernan for confirmation. The sheepish expression on his face tells me he agrees with the basilisk, but doesn't want to say it out loud. "Motherfucker. I dislike accepting charity. I guarantee Feray told the others that."

"Pfft." Khol pushes off the dresser and prowls forward, looking into my eyes in a way that makes me suspicious. "It's not charity. This is *not* the standard of living Khal and I are accustomed to and the rockstar prince probably drapes himself in sparkling diamonds at night. Think of it as our arrogance demanding luxury and you two are along for the ride."

Tiernan coughs, trying to cover a laugh when I kick my leg out and almost catch Khol in the balls. "She's not fond of being called poor, even indirectly, nor does she like her choices being taken away."

I nod, leaping off the bed to meet the grinning bad boy until we're toe-to-toe. "He's right. Neither of those things makes me happy, nor do you try to use some sort of spinny-eyed compulsion, lizard dick."

"Oh, if only you knew…" Khol's face goes dreamy for a moment, then he shakes his head. "Stop distracting me with sex and threats. They're hand-in-hand for us, Sassy."

Again, helpful info. These boys have zero ability to keep their weaknesses to themselves and I love it.

"If beating your ass turns you on, I'd love to give you a big old happy right now," I reply as I grit my teeth. "But since I sense Tiernan will stop us from tearing up the bedroom, I'll save your reckoning for a more appropriate time and place, Bedia."

"Looking forward to it, Morgenstern. Bring it, baby." His expression is full of sin and violence, making my thighs clamp together involuntarily.

"Stop taunting her," Tiernan says with an eye roll. "We don't have time for that now."

I look over my shoulder at him, pouting. "You sure?"

"Unfortunately, I am."

The look of regret on his face is sincere and I huff my understanding. "Fine. So the Fairy Princess is going to do some rich guy shit and when I turn around, all of you will act *so surprised* that we suddenly have a fancy ass new house. Got it."

They shrug and nod, fine with that prediction. *Men.*

"The next problem is our research. Why are you all so pissy about the digging my sister and I are doing? It's not like I'm a blabbermouth. I've been *very* careful what trail we leave from the library to discreet inquiries about the sigil. No one's going to know." I cross my arms over my chest as I back away from Khol and this time, he pouts.

"Unless they're involved or know someone who might be," Tiernan points out. "Your notes show you did recordable searches in records at the Hall, which anyone could hack into. You asked questions about the sigil as a tattoo at quite a few stores in the magic district. Can you remember every single person you spoke to?"

Frowning, I think about it for a moment, letting the pictures in my brain whirl around as I flip through them. "I went to *Tarragon Alley* first and that nasty earth elemental, Cantato, helped me. She barely looked, though."

"Uh-huh," the leopard says as he types the lists into his phone. "Go on."

"Then I stopped at *Scandleous* for oils and candles, so I had to ask Grundy. He growled at me; that's all the old wizard does anymore, and not just to me."

Khol tilts his head. "Magic users have a lot of castes for people who all access power from the same fucking source. It's not surprising they're so damn snooty."

Giving him a look that drips sarcasm, I ask, "Would you like to be classified the same as a chicken since you're about the same bone structure, evolutionarily speaking?"

His eyes widen, and Tiernan laughs. "Atta girl, Knuckles. Put him in his place, but keep going on the list. I want to have some of Rev's spies and my people look into these names. Just to make sure your innocent questions didn't land you in hot water."

"I went to *Booked on A Feeling* and spoke to the witch twins—or I tried to. Willow and Figgy are rich bitches I went to high school with, so they sold me shit but barely addressed me. Last, I went to *Cards & Wares* to let Ophelia abuse me." I pause for a moment and snap my fingers. "Shit. Dezi was there. He *definitely* got all up in my business and I almost smacked him. We were fresh off his biting shit and he was being particularly controlling."

Khol puts his face in his hands, and I can hear him sucking a breath through his fingers. "Of fucking *course*."

I give Tiernan a weird look, but he shakes his head. "That's not important now. What is important is that I speak with the bloodsucker alone. I needed to anyway, and now I absolutely have to."

Khol nods at him, his eyes flashing yellow with his serpent. I throw my hands up in the air when neither of them speaks. "Keep your secrets, dickheads. But I promise I'll remind you of this when you get mad because I don't share."

"It's simply not time yet, Knuckles. But when it is, you'll know." Tiernan sends his text and comes over to put his arms around me. "I know you want to know and handle everything because you always have. People supporting you will take getting used to. But this will be a change for everyone and we have to communicate and trust each other for it to work."

Trust all these people because they say so? Has he even met me?

"I'll try; I promise. But you have to give me space to take care of shit myself, too." I look over at Khol with a firm expression. "I've been doing it for a long ass time and I'm not going to turn into a damsel to be saved because dudes are squatting in our house."

He raises his hands and grins at me. "I'm *never* going to stop you from giving someone who deserves it a beat down. Hell, I wouldn't, even if they didn't deserve it. The big kitty and the pointy-eared royal are more likely to pull you out than I am. I enjoy a nice bloody brawl, Sassy."

"Freya in a slingshot," Tiernan mutters. "Now there's *two* of them to worry about. I hope his fucking twin helps or I'm going to lose it."

I shrug and bat my lashes at him. "Would it help to say I like it when you get all feral and big cat fighter, too?"

"A little." He sighs and looks between us, running his hand through his hair. "Have we hashed it all out? I know we didn't mention the wolf's color thing, but that doesn't feel like something any of us can control, either. And Rev said he'd added it to the list of shit to poke around about."

Wrinkling my nose, I think about it. I don't enjoy giving the head-strong Fae such a long list of important shit to tackle, but I also know his network of contacts and asskissers might produce better results than my Nancy Drew act in town. He's far enough removed from the situation—at least, publicly—that people may not even ask why he's looking for the information. I'd never admit it out loud, but they may have been right about my attempts drawing unwanted attention.

After all, someone attacked Philly again.

"Shit," I whisper to myself. "Was that my fault, too?"

"Unless it was starting a fight at every bar you walk into, I doubt it, Sassy."

Smiling a bit at Khol, I nod, but I can't help feeling the weight of acting without looking at the whole board. I may have caused someone I love to be targeted and no kind words in the world will make that stain leave my hands.

Or so the lady said in the famous play—and she was probably right.

46

KHAL

Leaving the cabin is one of the hardest things I've ever done.

Last night, I shared a bed with my mate and she showed no fear of having me next to her. It makes me wonder if she truly understands what and who I am. Torben agreed to text me if he needs to leave her for any reason, plus he gave me a list of items she'd like for the house. He seems to be the key to the stability of the household. Tiernan, as badass as he is, bends to Fiadh—but maybe that's what being mated does to you.

Thunk!

"Ow! What the fuck, asshole." I rub my right pec where Khol's fist hammered against my chest to snap me back into reality. Whipping my head to the left, I face my grinning brother. Grumbling under my breath, I massage the sting away.

"I've been talking to you since we fucking left and you're in the clouds, man. What's more important than planning how we're going to protect the girls?" Khol hisses at the end of the sentence and I know his basilisk is near the surface. Scales ripple, moving along his cheekbone and just above his eyebrows before his pupils morph into the slits of his beast as he stares at me for a few moments.

Oh shit...

"Damn, I'm sorry. I was thinking about their safety and got lost in my thoughts." By the glow in Khol's eyes, I know that wasn't the answer he was looking for. "What do you think we should do?"

I watch for his usual tells, like the twitching of his left eye or his biting of his bottom lip. Neither happens; lately, he's become a much harder read than he used to be. I think it's because he's tired of me calling him out on his shit all the time.

Rolling his eyes, he refocuses on the road ahead of us. "I'll do whatever it takes to protect the girls. I'll check with our contacts to see what I can find out. Worst case, I beat the shit out of a few informants and boom! Answers will appear." The sinister smile that plays on his lips sends a chill up my spine. His idea of torture makes most human serial killers look like Sunday school teachers.

There are things you simply can't unsee and my brother's idea of coercion is one of them.

I shake my head at him, exasperated with the direction he's choosing. "You can't do shit that might blow back on the girls. Fuck, Khol —they're our mates, you asshole. If you fuck up, it could get them killed."

It feels odd to lose my temper with my twin. He's always been the dominant out of the two of us. My snake prowls under the surface, ready to go to war for our mate. Khol is always the first to say 'count me in, let's go' without thinking about the consequences of his actions. He's also been the one who's gotten us into some of the worst near-death experiences of my existence.

"Yeah, I suppose I have to rejigger things now that they are in the picture," Khol grumbles under his breath about 'sucking the fun out of things' and I laugh.

My phone pings several times as messages pop up. I'm almost afraid to see who's responding and what their answers are. Unfortunately, none of my sources know anything about a hit on the satyr or the girls. That's odd because our guys have a real in with the assassin crowd. I try several more that are in my inner circle, just in case they may have a better source of information. "Fuck."

"Did the guys find anything?" Khol asks before glancing down at his phone. It pings, so he hands it over to me.

Glancing through his messages, more cluelessness is all I see. Texts like 'no clue,' 'not us,' and 'haven't heard anything' are all he's getting. I mutter to myself as the idea of the conspiracy being tied to an elder or a demon makes my scales stand on end. "I get the feeling this goes much higher up the food chain."

"What makes you say that?" There's an edge of concern in Khol's voice I've only heard once before.

I turn off both phones and drop them into the cup holder. The crack of the phones falling into the plastic cup holders catches my brother's attention. That's our signal that what I want to talk about is too sensitive to take chances with being bugged. Khol's eyes glance down at the phones briefly, then he immediately pulls the car over along the side of the dirt road. We get out and walk into the woods far enough from the car that if it's bugged, we're too far to be monitored.

"What makes you think there's a bigger fish involved?" Khol looks around again, as if checking to make sure no one is around.

"First off, the way you're acting tells me you have a bad feeling, too. I know somewhere in that thick skull of yours, you believe it's a possibility."

He nods slowly, looks down at his feet, then back at me again. Khol shoves his hands in his pockets and then scans the woods, suspiciously watching the surrounding area. "What makes you so sure?"

I grip his shoulders and give them a squeeze. "My gut. It's never failed me before and something tells me we're not looking in the right direction. We're scraping the surface." I hope he sees how serious I am.

"It definitely goes much deeper—years of plotting have to be behind this sketchy ass shit." Khol paces, kicking a pinecone around. "I can't put my finger on it, but there's definitely something going on that we haven't considered yet."

The amount of truth that rings in his statement is almost scary.

"We have the security part down. The bear and leopard's guys watch the girls during the day, and us at night." I narrow my eyes, staring at the horizon when something bothers me, but eventually, I decide a herd of deer triggered my paranoia. "We need to consider sheltering the girls from the family business—at least until this is taken care of."

Khol turns to face me and shakes his head. "The witch will kick us in the balls so hard they will corner pocket our eyeballs. Being honest with her is the best policy. Besides, the wolf is highly intelligent and might assist you with your tasks."

My twin's assessment of the girls seems fairly accurate. I'm not sure they would want in on the illegal drug trade, but the fact he is making a joke about his mate kicking our ass concerns me. Either he is scared shitless of her reaction or he's not planning on saying anything until he has to. He's probably going to run on his tried and true philosophy of 'it's better to beg for forgiveness than ask permission.'

Fiadh is most certainly going to beat the living hell out of him and I'm going to sell tickets.

"I'm more concerned about the violence and killing that comes along with what we do. We have enemies all over. What if that bleeds over to the girls? Once we take them as mates, it paints a huge target on their backs."

I've dreamt of the day I would find my mate, build a nest and have a clutch of my own. My Precious is a soft skinned canine and my brother's mate is a witch with fickle magic. The witch has a propensity for violence, but I can't see Feray enjoying the work we do.

Khol directs me to head back towards the car. "Feray will shift and rip apart whatever comes after her. Did you see the fire in her eyes when she went toe-to-toe with me? She may be the soft-spoken one, but like you, she's got teeth, and she's not afraid to use them." He falls silent for a few moments as we approach the car. "Sassy has it on lockdown. She will pummel the fuck out of anyone that threatens her or her sister. Trust me, she will raze the world to defend what's hers."

That's two one hundred percent accurate statements out of my twin's mouth in less than an hour. I should buy a lottery ticket.

"That's a solid assessment. Do we call the next level informants now?" I stop walking about thirty yards from the car and stare at Khol's back when he pauses.

Smirking, he looks over his shoulder at me. "I'll call in a few favors with the Cadmean Vixen. If there are secrets no one wants spilled, Zia will know who to go to for answers." As soon as Khol stops speaking, he closes the distance between us and takes out his phone. He makes several short phone calls to some of our most trusted people, letting them know we're looking for the sneakiest information trader in Briarvale.

Khol doesn't mention our uncle Krystos, despite knowing he's the leader of our faction and knee-deep in Council bullshit. Waiting to question him is worse than waiting for the last of a shed to come loose. Even the thought there may be a slight chance of our uncle involved with everything going on has my scales standing on edge. "Khol?"

"Yeah?"

"Do you think…?"

"Don't even go there. It's like fucking summoning him. I'm way ahead of you, though, which is why I haven't called him." Khol stares at his phone for far too long. He runs his hand down his face and sighs deeply as he walks around to the driver side of the car. "Most things are a need to know basis when it comes to him. Right now, he doesn't need to know."

Sliding into the passenger seat, my mind jumps to several other topics that concern the hell out of me at the moment. The most important thing makes me grab my chest as the thought of it steals the breath from my lungs. "Khol, will our bites kill them?"

We don't get far before he slams on the brakes and turns to face me. The color drains from his face leaving him a sickly pallor. His brows knit together as he thumps his hand against the steering while he thinks about it for several moments. "I'm not sure, I'll have to look into it."

"I mean, in theory, if they bite first or drink our blood, they should be okay, right?" Thinking quickly, I take my phone and send several messages to others in our nest that have mates outside of our species. My eyes refuse to leave the screen as I wait.

"Staring at the phone isn't going to make the answer manifest," Khol says irritably.

It's amazing that we found our mates at the same time and they are sisters. He doesn't act like it, but he's excited, even though there are challenges. Suddenly, another issue occurs to me and I punch his arm for attention. I motion to my crotch, knowing that the boys may be an issue since they are unique to our species. "How are we gonna break it to the girls that we're built differently?"

Hysterically laughing, Khol shakes his head. "Sassy is gonna fucking love it! Are you kidding me? She's gonna be all over them like a kid on an ice pop! Ten bucks says she is going to say something along the lines of 'best day ever.' before she goes to town."

I can't believe how hard Khol is laughing. He's got tears in his eyes and he's wheezing from laughing so hard. Reaching down I cup my groin protecting the family jewels from an unseen potential attacker or should I say decapitator. "I'm worried about Feray biting the boys off."

Khol stops laughing and his mouth hangs open as he turns to face me at the red light. He looks down at his own crotch and the look of horror on his face is funny as hell. His right hand rests over his heart, then "Not the twins! Don't worry, guys; I'll keep you safe from the big, bad wolf."

"For fuck's sake. You named them?" I jab my hand in the direction of his jewels.

"You didn't? Damn, get with the program. No wonder you were born second." Shaking his head, he takes off when the light turns green.

I ponder how the actual fuck we're related sometimes. Clearly, he got the brawn; I got the brains when our embryo split. Thankfully, being identical he can't call me ugly because he's too vain for that.

I just need to figure out how to have sex with my mate without bodily harm to either of us.

47

TIERNAN

FIADH AND FERAY ARE IN THE HOUSE WATCHING *CHARMED*. Apparently, they like to make fun of paranormal shows and all the mistakes humans make. Torben is with them, listening to them yell at the screen like guys do when they watch sports. The bear is so laid back that he doesn't even mind when they throw popcorn, although he'll be the one vacuuming it up later on.

I have to say: I had no idea bears were such amiable mates.

I'm not volatile like Khol or Revelin, but I'm not *that* easygoing. It doesn't matter, though, because in mate groups like this, it works best when people are like spokes on a wheel—all supporting a distinct part of the group and rounding it out to make a perfect shape. Or, that's what I saw in cat groups when I was younger and the ones who were complimentary always seemed content and happy. It's interesting to watch *two* of those families form at the same time and know we're all going to support one another because the girls are so tightly woven together because of their past. The challenge will be getting the dick swinging alphas and my mate to find their groove.

Fiadh won't stand for any bullshit and that amuses me to no end.

Walking into the yard, I stroll further out towards the treeline and wait. I came outside to wait for my irreverent and perpetually late friend and employer to show up. Rev only bows to his father and his label, so everything else is a crapshoot. He promised to come back to give me an update after he visited home, though, and a few minutes ago, he sent a text claiming to be on his way. Since the girls are finally relaxing and having a good time, I thought I'd keep the atmosphere calm by filtering his shit before they have to hear it.

"Boo!"

I spin around, claws and fangs dropping as I face the intruder with a snarl. When I realize it's the prince, I let them slip back in, rolling my eyes at him. "Childish, Rev. We're on high alert and I could have gutted you first and asked questions later."

A smug look crosses his features as he shrugs. "The Wheel of Fate cannot be stopped by a simple prank, Tier. If you'd stabbed me, I would have known it was written that way."

The fucking Fae can be major pains in the ass with their whimsical bullshit.

"How are the sisters? Is the lass behaving?" His smirk says he doubts it, but he pretends to ask, anyway. I think he enjoys her outbursts as much as the snake does—a fact that means our lives will never be boring.

I point at him, irritation radiating off of me. "Stop being such a chaotic dick. Knuckles likes a good fight, but she will not put up with your royal asshat schtick. Both you and the basilisk need to figure out how to rein it in a little or it will make everything harder."

"Tiernan, are you telling me to stop bossing her around?" His amusement fills the air when I nod. "I hate to break it to you, but I think the fight turns her on. I assume when you mated her, it wasn't a gentle Hallmark love story? Fiadh prefers a bit of rough and tumble; I think she might even enjoy being bossed around if it's done correctly."

Rubbing my hand over my face, I groan. *This idiot is going to try to Dom her and she's going to kick his ass.* My lips quirk as I consider the Prince might need a woman who can put him in his place and I might enjoy seeing it. "She might, but neither of you two are the ones to do it. Trust me, I think there's a better candidate coming."

He frowns and tilts his head, looking thoughtful, then beams. "The broody vampire! Oh, this is beautiful. You think the ancient blood-sucker is one of her possible mates."

"I do," I reply seriously. "I think he knows it, too, but he's fighting it like a champ."

"Mmmmm." That's all Rev says as he leans against an enormous tree, his magic forming curling vines and little flowers around it as he ponders. "I could get behind that. I enjoy the fuck out of a dark, dominant male with an iron spine."

Having been in his detail at the club many times , I know that's true.

"Slow down, lover boy. Even if Dezi is one of hers, Knuckles doesn't even suspect it. The witches taught those girls an enormous pack of lies about other species and mating and fuck knows what else. I'm educating Fi on shifters slowly and everything normal supes know about us seems to be a revelation. It's not a leap to think she knows just as little about your people and even less about vamps."

He blinks. "Really?"

"Yep. The magic school seems to groom their young to be predis-posed to mate within their species by how they teach them. That Ascension ceremony is a giant sham, I think. Something about it tells me they've marked them with a spell or hex and the only non-magic users who get picked are vetted for political reasons. At least, that's the sense I get when I talk through things with our girl." I shake my head, not understanding why they would go to the effort to do all this in secret.

There are plenty of species who prefer not to interbreed with other supes, but that's a well known and advertised preference. Wolves are one of them, and so are some of the mythical creature supes like gorgons. There's no giant public ceremony where they pretend the Goddess has chosen all the mates and they're mostly magic users. The entire thing is weird, and I'd bet it has something to do with that asshole Mage who runs their shit.

Revelin arches a brow. "Interesting that our girls weren't marked for mates and then put on display. Fluffy not being a witch makes it even more suspicious. Is it possible they *were* marked in school, but whatever their clever parents did to them as kids prevented that from working?"

No, I didn't think that, but I do now.

"Maybe. They definitely had secrets. Knuckles says they had caution and suspicion drilled into them from a young age as if their father was preparing them for something. She didn't realize it wasn't normal to grow up that way because they didn't have many friends —hell, that could have been a spell, too. Keep other kids away so they could protect their secrets."

The Prince heaves a long sigh, looking up at the stars before he turns back to me. "This is such a fucking mess. I don't know how we can keep them safe with all this… unknown shit… floating around. Not to mention the impulsive snakes, the coddling bear, and an ancient fanger who's fighting a bond."

"Don't forget the giant lizard. I have a feeling about him, too." His eyes widen and he smacks his forehead.

"Merciful Mab, the dragon? How did these girls manage to attract a group of mates full of nothing but assholes, grumpy old supes, and two softies to balance it out?"

I snort. He included himself in the asshole category without hesitation. That kind of self-awareness is why I've always been fond of the Prince. He makes no bones about who and what he is—but now he has someone to worry about that isn't himself. "I don't know, Rev, but I guarantee Knuckles will torch all of our asses if anyone upsets her sister or tries to control her. We have to give her space."

"I'm not *opposed* to that," he murmurs with a grin. "But I play well with others, as do you. I worry about the snake and the vamp."

"They're a much smaller problem in the grand scheme." I look at him, my voice dropping as I ask the question I've avoided until now. "What about your family? I know you said your mother liked Fiadh, but she squared off with your dad. Is that going to be a problem?"

Pushing off the tree, he paces in front of me. "My mother will be fine. My siblings? Toss-up. The King will be an issue and so will the fans."

Son of a bitch. I completely forgot about his fucking fans and the goddamned tour in the Faerie.

"You have a tour of the realms coming up."

He nods and sighs heavily. "I do. You know part of how I keep Oliver out of my hair is bringing all that positive attention to our kingdom through the band. If I try to step back, he'll want me at the Court all the time, learning bullshit political crap."

I squint and tilt my head. "Do you think Fiadh has worked out that if she mates with you she'll be queen of the Daybreak Court someday?"

"Hell no and I'm saving *that* disaster for later, my friend. The last thing I need is our ass-kicking, brass knuckle fighting witch worried about people putting a crown on her head. She'll be more comfortable with whoever has a price on it instead." Revelin barks a laugh, slapping me on the back as he steps closer.

"Speaking of that, did you put out feelers while you were home?"

He nods, pushing his hair off his face. "I did. It will take time for my informants to ask around. I also made a few inquiries of the royal archivists, passing it off as research for the tour. Usually the ladies there are star-struck enough to keep their mouths closed."

"That's because they'd rather open their legs," I mutter.

"Tsk tsk. Don't be judgy, Tiernan. A healthy sexual appetite is encouraged in the Faerie. We don't have the hang-ups a lot of supes do."

I roll my eyes at him. He knows better. "Rev, you know I don't give a shit about who's fucking who. I care that our mate will probably gut anyone who looks at what's hers once she wraps her head around this. I saw her glare at that fruity Harvest Fae we kicked out and the blast she hit her with was harder than necessary. Fiadh didn't like how she was looking at you."

"That is an interesting observation and I plan to see what I can do with it the first chance I get." His eyes dance and a bad feeling settles under my skin. "I'm partial to a possessive woman who likes to claim what's hers; it makes my magic sing. I'd bet the other two assholes will enjoy it as well."

How am I going to keep the three of them from constantly riling her up? I can almost see *them pushing her to the brink all the time on purpose.*

"If you idiots piss her off on purpose, I'm not helping you fix it. You break it; you buy it, dumbass." I shake my head and look at the house. "You'd better come inside and tell them about your efforts. They'll ask if I come back alone."

Revelin pouts. "Can I at least magic the bed to allow us all to fit comfortably if I'm staying with you and the lass tonight? That's not going to cause a fight, right?"

I chuckle and shrug. "Hell if I know, man. Knuckles isn't predictable like that. But you might enjoy watching her and the wolf tear apart human TV shows. They've been watching one about witches and it's pretty funny. I've never seen two women angrier about the placement of candles in my life."

Grinning, the prince nods at me and follows me as I head back to the small cabin. I hope his travails included setting up the legal shit for expanding this place. I know the twins were going to work on furnishings and Torben called one of his best crews earlier to schedule the renovation. Both girls were suspiciously quiet when he said it was arranged, but I know they'll end up loving whatever he has planned. Even Fi has trouble telling the gentle giant 'no' when he insists on shit.

I'll have to have him teach me how he does it—I have the feeling we'll need it.

48

Feray

Sitting on my fluffy blue bean bag in the living room, I watch Torben and his extended family as they work on the expansion of the house. The buzzing of the chop saws and the pounding of hammers echoes through the house. Sheets of plasterboard and fancy wood panels are being carried through the house, past me, and into the two new wings.

Fi is going to have a fit.

Torben handed me a mini schematic of the plans, as well as a list of things that were being done each day at the start of construction. At least if I have the demolition and construction itinerary, I can talk Fiadh off the cliff when she loses control. He also was kind enough to introduce me to the entire sleuth working with him so I could pick who I was comfortable with having in the house. His sleuth understood it and complied, knowing that he mated a new shifter.

It's safer for everyone involved to let me have that tiny semblance of control.

Logan, his youngest brother, brings me pastries every morning when he shows up and sits with me before he starts. I think he has a female he's eying and feels comfortable enough to talk to me about what girls like. Being a good sister-in-law, I bought several perfumes I thought the girl might like based on his description.

Aleksei arrives and next thing I know, the entire sleuth is scrambling back to their appointed jobs. Laughing, I pull myself out of the beanbag and approach him. "Morning, Dad. Would you like a coffee or a honey lemon tea? I have honey butter biscuits if you would like."

We press our cheeks together and he offers me his arm to escort me to the kitchen. Laughing at my fluttering around the kitchen, he takes a seat at the end of the old countertop. "I see you've picked up the 'feeding everyone' thing from my son. Glad to know I raised him right. The tea and biscuits would be wonderful, dear."

Nodding my head, I turn on the kettle, cut the lemon, and grab a small chunk of fresh honey comb to drop it into his mug.

"Mind making me one, too?" Torben calls from where he's installing the new stove with a griddle top and six burners. I swear, some of the high-end restaurants would be jealous if they saw what my mate was building.

"Of course! I was already planning on doing it." I hold up his favorite mug and drop the honey chunks. Listening to his father laughing at us behind me makes me smile. *Who would've thought a bear and a wolf would be a good match?*

Before I know it, I have eight teas and biscuits prepared for the guys for their midmorning break.

"What do you think of the plans?" Torben asks as he wraps his arms around me from behind.

Reaching out to grab them, I look carefully. "It was a brilliant idea to use the old cabin as the heart of the new house." Flipping through my cards, I find the primary plan that gives Fi and I our own private wings that can be expanded. "Who's idea was it for the separate wings?"

Glancing over my shoulder, I see Torben blush. He glances up at his father and he shakes his head at him. "Well, you see…"

"Oh no, that talk is all yours, boy. Papa bear out!" His dad throws up a peace sign and walks away briskly.

"When mates… Um.. Well, the moon and…" Torben is stumbling over his words when his sister walks in and starts laughing.

"For Artaois' sake, move, big brother. You're confusing the poor girl." Evva shoves Torben out of the way and he heads back to work, looking panicked. She wiggles her eyebrows at me suggestively and I swear I stop breathing for a moment. "Now that the big softy is gone, the short version is for privacy for when your breeding cycle hits. I'm not sure if wolves go through it like bears do, but you will need the room and the privacy."

"Breeding cycle?" I look over her shoulder in the direction I last saw Torben, and he's gone.

How the hell did a six-foot-four, three-hundred-pound male disappear so fast?

"Oh shit, you have no idea. Um… Okay, so let's go sit somewhere more private and talk."

I lead Evva over to my bean bag and glare at the males nearby. They turn tail and run in the direction Torben escaped in. *Cowards…*

"I'm guessing it's like a human period?" I watched Fi go through them; Mom said I was a late bloomer when I only got them twice a year.

"Yes and no. It's when we can get pregnant. I'm not sure about other species, but bears need to be mated to conceive." I look around and this time, I see Torben peeking through the window in the kitchen, then he disappears again.

The big guy is afraid of this conversation.

Pursing my lips, I decide I need to research wolves more. I've been living as a witch with a wolf form, not a wolf with a human form. "Thank you for explaining that to me. I guess I have to find another she-wolf to ask the important questions."

We touch our cheeks together before she leaves to head back to painting the pool room. *I have no idea how I'm even going to approach this with…*

Fi comes storming in with a slight glow to her skin as if I'd summoned her. Every time something pisses her off, it's like instant 'lights on.' All the plants Evva brought to decorate suddenly bloom in Fi's wake. Shaking her head, she's bitching under her breath about the noise and dust and doesn't notice.

Moving quickly, I make it to the counter before she gets there. When she looks at me, I have her energy drink poured over ice to slide over to her. "It's not that bad, Fi."

"Not that bad? Have you looked around? I barely recognize the place."

Begrudgingly, she takes the drink from me. Fi is taking going nuclear to a whole new level with this magic glow stick stuff and I want to help her stay calm. Going over to the new fridge, I pull out her favorite pastry and hand it to her.

"What did you do?"

Her question sends a chill down my spine and I think about everything I've done in the last forty-eight hours. Smiling, I grab a second one and pour myself a honey-lemon tea like I would make for the guys. "Nothing Fi, the boys brought them with them this morning as a peace offering."

She uses her mug to point at me. "Now you're drinking like your mate. Where's my sister and what have you done with her?"

Baring my teeth at her, I remember the breathing exercises Torben and Tiernan have taught me to get my wolf under control. Once I feel my canines recede, I feel calm enough to address my sister. "Have you tried the tea? It's soothing and warm, the honey is good for our immune system and allergies. The lemon is a good cleanser and anti-infective for when you are feeling under the weather."

Shaking my head, I grab the tea bag and toss it on the counter in front of her. It's the brand she had blended for me once we found out I was a shifter. Pouting, I turn away from Fi. It hurts my feelings that she thinks I would change over a guy. "It has chamomile and lavender in it, combined with honey and lemon. I am taking excellent care of myself and everyone else here."

I hear Fi mutter 'fuck' under her breath and then her footsteps approaching. "I'm sorry, Fer. There's so many changes and I don't know how to handle them."

A soft laugh escapes my lips as I turn to face her. I shift my hand as I hold it in between us. "I have no clue what you're talking about. What changes? I spent my life thinking I was a dud of a witch." I force a smile as my hand shifts back to normal. "Problem is, I was never a witch. Growing up, I was jealous of what little you could do. Lucky for me, you and our parents never let me feel bad about it."

"I didn't know, Fer." Fi hugs me tightly and somehow it fixes everything like it always did when we were kids.

"I'm happy with who and what I am now." Laughing, I pull away slightly. "Tour time!"

Rolling her eyes, Fi reluctantly follows me. Thankfully, the subject of how I felt growing up is dropped the minute I show Fi everything that's being done in the kitchen. According to the plans, the kitchen will make a Michelin chef cry. Taking a cloth napkin, I tie it around Fi's eyes as a blindfold.

"Fer, you know I'm not a fan, right?"

Smirking, I roll my eyes. "If Revelin did it, you would be like 'yes, Sir, may I have another,' I guarantee it."

Lifting the blindfold on one side, Fi glares at me then lowers the blind fold and offers me her hand. "Doubtful. Lead on. Let's get this over with."

Carefully, I navigate my sister past the guys working and piles of debris throughout the house. I'm taking her to the oasis the twins insisted on building. Using my shoulder, I bump the button that opens the door to the atrium with the infinity pool lined with heated rocks. Around the pool, there is a massive garden with plants I have never seen before in my life. I can only assume Revelin had them imported from the Fae realm to add a bit of his home.

Of course, I have no idea how we're going to take care of them...

I take the blindfold off Fi and she looks around slowly. I don't pick up a change in her scent and she's not glowing yet, so I'm calling this a win so far. Pixies and other fair folk emerge from the foliage, and that's when I bow out. The Fae garden is a gift for Fi from Revelin and she should get to experience it alone.

The pool, however, is a gift from the twins to both of us. From what Khal told me, it will also help when he and his brother go through their shed. The garden will be a safe place for them to shed and be able to be close to us at the same time.

Heading back to the kitchen, I catch Torben handing a black credit card to the delivery guy. *Creeping through the house barefoot has its advantages.* I sneak up behind my mate and watch him sign for the marble that's being delivered outside. The credit card is lying on the countertop, and I lean over to read the name on it. It has *Scaleon Pharmaceuticals* printed on it with Khal's name underneath.

Gasping, I step back and my hands fly to my mouth as I look down the hall to see where Fi is.

"Shit, shit, shit. Little Wolf." Torben shoves the card in his pocket, then closes the distance between us with his hands up in a placating manner. The sharp tang of anxiety rolls off Torben. "I can explain."

Whining, my wolf urges me to go to my mate and soothe him immediately. *Fucking instincts.* I can't help but nuzzle him and rub my cheek against him affectionately. "Start talking, Tor."

"Okay, damn it. I told them you would figure it out. The twins and Revelin are funding the renovation. My crews are only costing us labor." Torben looks sheepish as he rocks from side to side.

Reaching up, I take both hands and hold his face, staring up into his eyes. "You guys are doing this for our family. You're providing shelter and a safe place for us to live together. Thank Fenrir you guys worked out so Fi and I don't have to separate. I don't know what we would have done if you made us move apart."

My bottom lip quivers as the crux of my fear surfaces. Leaning down, Torben kisses away my fears and makes me lightheaded as he ramps up the possessiveness of his kiss. He scoops me up, holding me to him..

"Get a room! Remember, Fer, we have work tonight and Dezi is expecting us early," Fi fires off as she smacks my ass as she passes by. When Torben raises a brow, she swats him, too, and runs away giggling like a madwoman,

Torben and I look at each other, trying not to laugh. Once the door is closed, we start laughing hysterically. Fi doesn't do well with public displays of affection, but actually spanked both of us. Miracles will never cease.

"You should get going Little Wolf. Don't be late for work."

"Good change of subject, Tor. Fi is going to lose her goddamn mind if she finds out who's paying for what." I cringe at the thought. My sister will see this as charity instead of our mates taking care of us and providing for the future.

"I'll talk to Tiernan and get a back up plan going in the event she loses her mind over it all." Torben kisses me once more before returning to work.

Grabbing my work bag, I head for the door. I hear the tail end of his crew picking on him for being a big softy. There's an extra bounce in my step as I head for my shift tonight. Other than the mysteries that surround my sister and I, life seems to be turning around finally. We are both in healthy relationships, we have a beautiful home and good paying jobs.

This is probably the happiest I have been in years.

Looking around, I realize I was so lost in my thoughts I didn't notice getting to work. I turn the corner and head to the door and knock.

Louie snickers. "Mutt…"

"Mosquito."

I hear him cackle through the door as he opens it and lets me in. "That was unique. Good shot wolf."

For once there's no edge of venom in his teasing. *I'm finally wearing the old blood sucker down.*

"Thanks. I can't wait to see what we come up with tomorrow." He nods at me before heading back to his post. I'll take that as a win for tonight.

Just when I think the night is going to be phenomenal, I see Fi toe-to-toe with Dezi. For whatever Goddess forsaken reason, she's decided to pick a fight with our ancient boss.

Drawing in a deep breath, I heave a sigh.

It's going to be a long night.

I glance at my watch—all hope is lost when I realize it's seven hours and fifty nine minutes until quitting time.

Morrigan save me.

49

FIADH

Gritting my teeth, I weave my way through the crowd on the main level. It's a Saturday night, so it's one of the busiest nights of the week and I started my shift arguing with Dezi over the suspicious lack of extra glassware Mo left for us in the reserve. I think the shitty little vulpine did it on purpose—as he often does—and he needs to be fired for slacking off. My tight-assed boss seems unconcerned with the poor serving staff etiquette of that douche, so he told me to make sure *I* refill it when we have a moment tonight.

I wasn't joking when I told Feray I feel very out of control with all the changes happening at once and this kind of shit is making me ready to rumble.

"Stupid self-centered, narcissistic *asshole* shifter," I mutter under my breath as I cut through the groups of vamps hanging out in the darkest corner of the room.

One of them salutes with his glass of blood, crowing, "You tell 'em witchy!"

At least someone agrees with me. My irritation with that runt is making me despise an entire species, for fuck's sake.

When I get back to the bar, my sister is slinging drinks for the other servers and patrons alike, chirping happily as she flips bottles like a pro. She never did this kind of stuff at Philly's and it makes my heart warm to see her so happy. Then I remember how much of our home is in a disarray that looks very expensive and completely out of our budget even if we worked for the rest of our lives. Frustration bubbles up inside me and I slap my palm on the wood to get her attention.

"Hey, sis! It's busy as hell tonight. We're going to rake it in." Fer does a little booty dance of joy and I almost lose my righteous anger.

Arching a brow, I look at her coolly. "Would that pay for even *one* appliance in the new kitchen, you think?"

Her eyes go wide and her face pales, guilt written all over her features. "I-I don't know. I mean, Torben is handling—"

"Fer, there's no way we could ever afford the extravagant shit being done at the cabin." She licks her lips and I glance at the banker nursing his favorite cocktails. "It's not like we took out a loan I don't know about, right?"

He huffs into his Manhattan, small wisps of smoke escaping his nose.

"I'll take that as a 'no,' and it confirms what I've suspected—the mates are funding this wildly over-the-top expansion," I say drily. "When was anyone going to tell me? Is everyone in on this?"

Feray fumbles for a moment before she puts her hand on mine. "I know it's hard to accept that our mates want to take care of us, but it's *normal*."

Another huff of derision comes from the end of the bar where the grumpy dragon is sitting and I give him an evil glare. "That's enough from the peanut gallery, Smoky."

Seeing my sister's dismayed look, I throw my hands up and head behind the bar to throw another rack of glassware in the big dishwasher while she's making the orders on the slip I left. Dezi's edict about handling the shortage myself is ringing in my ears, making me even more cranky, especially because I can feel his eyes on me. The cowardly bloodsucker is watching me from somewhere in the room while my sister is making that asswad dragon another drink because I growled at him.

My connection to the 'Force,' so to speak, is getting stronger every day and I can sense things going on around me.

That's another reason I'm so damned irritable because I haven't quite figured out how to control any of this new shit yet. I leave flowers and plants in my wake like a demented pixie, my magic is constantly touching everything, and I haven't been able to figure out how to fly like I did that night, so it hardly seems worth the trouble. I mean, what's the point of all this other shit when I can't fucking *fly*?

A zap of energy hits me when I'm checking the settings on the industrial dish cleaner and I turn, squinting to see what I'm being warned about. Feray is handing that grumpy lizard *another* fancy drink and their hands are touching. Her face turns a pretty shade of pink and it almost looks like he's smiling. *Shit.* Sighing, I run my hand over my face as I feel the headache coming.

Yes, Brunhilda, the dragon is one of your sister's mates.

"Well, that's fucking special," I mutter to myself as I walk back to the end of the bar to wait for Fer to stop flirting with him and get my drinks done. "Just what I needed tonight."

"I didn't believe it was possible, but you're in a worse mood than when you walked in, witchling."

The hits just keep on coming.

Whirling as my boss appears in front of me out of thin air, I growl low. I'm not a shifter like my sister, but I've got a pretty threatening snarl for a human, I think. Hopefully, it gets Dezi to fuck off so I don't get myself in trouble. He doesn't move and I wing a sarcastic remark to the Goddess again, making sure my displeasure with the events of this evening is known. "Yet here you are, looming like a gothic popsicle in my midst."

Dezi looks mildly affronted as he studies me. "The cold thing is a myth and you know it."

Now we're playing semantics? Okay, buddy. "Maybe so, but I'm not the weirdo stalking one of my employees, so…"

His laugh is warm and filled with a smugness I don't understand. "Witchling, you unnecessarily fight against so many things, even when it makes your life infinitely harder. Wouldn't it be nice to simply allow things to come to pass without struggling against the will of Fate?"

I give him a confused look, not sure where the conversation ran off to. "If you're asking why I don't just 'go with the flow,' it's because I don't *trust* the flow. Nothing in our lives has proven to be easy and when things *seem* simple, they go haywire. I can't just allow shit to happen."

The vampire arches a brow at me, looking at me with an unreadable expression. "I suppose I understand that sentiment. Very well."

Fer's giggle distracts me from his Mysterious Vampire Shit ™ and I watch as she comes bounding back to me with a broad smile. "Diaval is in a great mood tonight. I'm definitely getting good tips."

I snort, shaking my head. If she doesn't see what I do, it's not my place to rat the snarky dragon out before he's ready. "Are you done flirting so I can take those wolves at table five their shit?"

She sniffs at me, looking over at the vampire watching us. "Perhaps I am. And look..." Feray points over my shoulder. "...your favorite duo have arrived for the evening."

Both Dezi and I follow the gesture to see Revelin, his entourage, and Tiernan walking to the roped off stairs to the VIP area. The Prince's presence has the crowd stirring and people shuffling around in excitement. My boss shakes his head and mutters to himself, waving his hand at me and the upstairs lounge before striding away.

"Well, what the hell is his problem?" I murmur to myself.

Feray shakes her head. "You're all acting like you have crabs pinching your asses from the inside. Maybe some time upstairs with Revelin and Tiernan will help. Go forth and spread Fae dust, sis."

Gross. I'm never doing that—not ever.

How is this my life now?

Looking around the VIP lounge, I see Revelin sprawled on the big comfy chair with the long ottoman like the lazy royal he is. Tiernan is standing behind him, watching the gaggle of Fae women and men in his groupie pool carefully. At the other end of the lounge, Khol and Khal are parked with their various sketchy looking associates. The two groups are pretending to ignore one another, but I can tell that's not really the case.

I've been fetching drinks up and down the stairs all night because Dezi didn't put a bartender here—he obviously didn't know the Prince and the snake kingpins were going to take up residence this evening. His mood is foul enough and so is mine, so I haven't asked him to reassign Jaz or Feray to help. The club is hopping downstairs and the shibari demo on the stage has everyone in an awed frenzy.

He probably can't spare either of them, anyway.

My feet are killing me and I'm about to give in and plop down on one of the cushions to relieve the pressure when Tiernan catches my eyes. His flash yellow and he leans down to whisper something in Rev's ear. The Fae looks over at me, frowning as he watches me lean on the railing. He can't know I'm using it to take weight off of my tortured feet and calves, right? Definitely not. I'm being very subtle as I look out over the scene downstairs.

"Fiadh, come here."

Noooooo...

I draw in a slow breath and paste a smile on as I walk over to the Fae side of the room. The sound of Khorinea and her friends sniggering makes me want to blast something, but I ignore it to pull out my notepad. "What can I get you?"

Revelin rolls his eyes at me as if I'm the most annoying thing he's ever seen. "You can sit down and talk to me. I'm bored and I'd enjoy a conversation that doesn't revolve around my court or my albums."

A smirk dances over my lips. "I don't know if I believe *that*, Prince Douchecanoe."

He and Tiernan burst out laughing while the rest of the Fae gasp as if I've just told the Emperor he doesn't have any clothes on. "Good one, lass. I enjoy you taking a strip out of me every once in a while. Have a seat; there's much to discuss."

Thank Titania and her troupe of tittering pixies. My goddamned feet are about to fall off.

Tiernan ignores the hangers-on as they pretend not to be paying attention to the three of us, coming around to sit in a chair across from me. He smiles softly, holding his hand out until I prop one of my feet in his lap. When he takes my shoe off, I blink in surprise.

Maybe it doesn't matter if a bodyguard is giving a waitress a foot massage in front of the heir to the throne?

Hell if I know.

I bite my lip when the leopard's strong fingers work the arch of my foot. *Damn, that feels good.* Rev arches a brow, his eyes twinkling as he watches me for a moment before speaking.

"I spoke to some of the people we discussed, but I'm not having much luck—yet."

"Uh-huh," I say as I practically melt into the seat. "Why do you think it will be successful later when it's not now?"

His lips curve up. "Because I wasn't applying the same... pressure... I am now."

At that word, Tiernan uses his thumb to push on my heel and I grunt. These two assholes are doing this on purpose and I don't know why. Making me get aroused in front of the troupe of fools isn't exactly smart, especially if he doesn't want people to know about our connection yet.

Not that we've done anything about our connection yet.

Suddenly, the scent of lavender, cedar, and amber fills my nose and I know Khol is approaching. He pulls up a chair and straddles it, leaning on the back as he gives me a knowing look. My eyes narrow as I realize he was drawn here by *my* scent and any shifter in the area has to know what my mate is doing to me. That little power must be annoying as fuck in a place like this where everyone's a bit turned on, but the sneaky snake got to me in a flash when the massage made my lady parts tingle.

"Smelling tasty, Sassy," he says in a low voice near my ear. "I didn't know you had a foot fetish,"

"What? No!" I exclaim as I pull my aching foot back. "I absolutely do *not!*"

Revelin chuckles, waving his hand at Tiernan.

The leopard grabs my foot again and gives me a stern look. "Let me help you, Knuckles. I could sense your pain. The fanged fucker let you run those stairs enough to be part of a sports team. You're in pain."

He's not wrong. Our outfits don't lend to good, supportive footwear so I've been doing Bowser's castle in three-inch heels.

"What about the symbol?" Khol asks. "We're striking out on it on our end."

That makes T and Rev pause, looking around at all the people surrounding us. Khol rolls his eyes and mutters something about nobody paying attention while I'm moaning, but they shake their heads at him. The Prince sits up and looks over at the Fae near him and clears his throat. When they glance up obediently, he waves again. "Be gone. I want privacy."

I've honestly never seen that many people move so fast in my life. It's utterly astounding.

Once they've all fucked off, Khol looks over to his brother, who does the exact same thing with the exact same results.

Who the fuck are these dudes?

"Happy now?" Khol asks as his minions flee and Khal comes over to join us.

"Yes," Revelin says. "As to your question, no, I haven't been able to discern the meaning or who uses that symbol yet. My next inquiries will be within the Midnight Court because the less savory elements there have deep ties to those who run various enterprises in the Night District. I would assume that's some of where you've been digging."

Khal nods. "Yes. We started with shifter groups as they're looser lipped than some other species. Khol plans to have an… associate… speak with some of the mythicals next."

"Good," I murmur. "Who's brave enough to poke around the casinos?"

They all make faces and I roll my eyes. Tiernan lets go of the first foot and grabs the other, using the massage to pacify me. "Someone has to talk with the demons, guys. Let's face it—they know or are part of everything bad that goes down somehow."

"You're not wrong, but it's very tricky to pump them for information. They require finesse," Khal says softly. "One wrong word could leave you owing them a favor and no one wants that."

"Hence my sources talking to the Midnight Fae. If any beings can dance around words with the demons, it's the dark Unseelie," Revelin says with a grimace. "Though there may yet be a price. Much like the demons, Unseelie are not wont to give shit out for free."

"Is there a reason my entire VIP lounge was cleared out and my staff is being rubbed instead of working?"

I look up to see Dezi's dark countenance practically glowering with rage and let out another groan, though this one is in frustration. "Holy fuck, Count Chocula. Haven't you given me enough grief for today?"

His face screws up and I think this time I might have gone a little too far. But Revelin just gives him an oddly knowing look, batting his pretty lashes as he stares back and says, "You aren't part of this conversation, Ruby. I allowed you to stay last time, but if you want in, you need to *be in*. Otherwise, run along."

His face turns bright red, including his eyes, and he clenches his fists at his sides. None of the guys back down, though, and finally,

Dezi spins on his heel and stomps out through a panel in the wall I didn't know existed.

"His boxers are going to be in a knot for a while," Tiernan mutters. "Maybe you pushed too hard, Rev?"

I snort and shake my head. "I think he deserved to be taken down a peg."

Khol grins and winks at me. "That's my bloodthirsty girl. Give him hell until he folds."

"Folds what?" I frown, looking at each of them in confusion.

That just makes them all laugh and I wrinkle my nose. I *hate* when the menfolk all seem to know what's going on and I'm in the dark.

Assholes.

50

Feray

Waking up before the rest of the house is the new norm for me.

I get up early, shift, and get a run in before the others awaken. My wolf is more settled when I remember to let her out at the start of the day. Torben looked so peaceful sleeping this morning; I didn't have the heart to wake him up to run with me. He and his sleuth have been working so hard to finish the additions to the house. I know they are all very tired.

Yesterday, Tiernan and Khal helped me grill fish and steaks for the guys when they quit for the day. It was nice to have a large family-style meal. I know it's because wolves are pack animals that I'm enjoying everyone's company. Fi watches like a hawk, always expecting the worst to happen. I wish she would relax and enjoy the social aspect our mates are bringing to the table. Honestly, she's more like Tiernan than she realizes: his people live independently and only gather for holidays. If Fi had it her way, we would be isolated from the population in an area where she can control the environment. If what we found was correct, she was raised to be a protector, but why was she raised that way?

Am I what she was meant to protect? What makes me so special?

Shaking my head to clear the darkening thoughts, I look at what needs to be done today. I study my notes about what's left to be finished, pondering what I can help with. The main bedrooms need to be completed, but the mattresses are set to arrive later today. Both bedrooms have huge attached ensuite bathrooms with walk-in showers. We designed them with three shower heads and three benches so they would be room for entire families if they choose. The tiles are heated and everything is climate controlled with fancy touchscreens. The twins and Revelin insisted on luxurious vanities and sinks for everyone to get ready at, as well as giant detached whirlpool tubs. The last part made me giddy, but I know Fi will gape like a fish.

Who am I to argue with the people bankrolling the entire thing?

She is coming around to the changes, just slowly. I still feel like we are on the brink of a third World War half the time, but it's because Khol and the prince push her buttons on purpose. I don't know if it's actually a thing, but I think those two have a violence kink. Unfortunately, my sister seems likewise inclined.

The rich scent of sandalwood drifts to me, alerting me that Torben is headed this way. I get up quickly and pour him a cup of tea with honey.

Ding.

The timer on the fancy new oven goes off and I open it to find my breakfast pastries are ready just in time.

"Do I smell cheese danishes?" Torben's deep voice rumbles from behind me, sending a shiver down my spine.

"I decided to make one of Fi's favorites. Hopefully, she won't be such a wolverine if she has something she loves to eat waiting for her." Shrugging my shoulders, I slide a danish and a cup of tea to my mate.

A hearty chuckle escapes his lips. "For a little thing, she's terrifying." I watch as he takes the first bite and moans rolling his eyes back. He eats the danish like he was starving for days. "This is phenomenal. Remember, it's mine and Tiernan's turn to cook dinner. Khal and Khol said they are handling lunch."

Torben gives me the meal schedule and I'm honestly shocked the twins are pitching in together. Arching a brow, I look at my bear as I ask, "Khol is going to cook?"

Wincing, he looks away briefly. "Okay, he's going to shop for supplies and Khal is cooking lunch."

Resting my hand over my heart, I exaggerate my relief. "Thank the Goddess for little favors. What time are the guys starting today?" I flip through my itinerary and don't see any notes for today. I turn my day planner to face Torben. "Damn. It says Fi isn't going to be home most of the day, so we'll save her food from both meals."

Taking the planner out of my hand, he pulls my pen out and scribbles in my calendar. He hands it back to me and when I open it, his credit card is tucked inside. Under my note to go to the bank, he wrote shopping. I frown and hold up the card. "Shopping?"

Sipping his tea, he watches me wave his credit card. "I gave my guys the day off so we can do some cleaning around the house." I watch him text someone and shake his head before looking back up at me. "Apparently, Khol and Revelin have things they want to add to their wing so your sister being out with Revelin works means he can sneak it all in."

"You're avoiding the shopping question." I walk around the table to step between his legs and rest my palms on his chest. Pouting slightly, I tilt my head until the big guy's resolve breaks.

Leaning forward, he presses his lips to mine. "I want you to be happy," he says as his lips hover over mine. He places his index finger over my lips. "Do me a favor and go buy things that will bring you joy. I know you're going to argue and say you have everything you need, but it will make me happy to see you buy yourself nice things. Hell, buy your sister something, if that will make you feel better about it." He moves his finger, a cocky grin plastered on his face because he knows he's got me.

Damn perfect mate knows me better than I know myself some-times. "Okay, I'll go. But only because it will make you happy."

"Thank you, Little Wolf. You've made me very happy today." He kisses my cheek then smacks me on my ass playfully. The crisp crack of his hand on my butt echoes in the silent house.

Gasping, I look over my shoulder at the smug look on his face. *Do I like being spanked? I might.*

This is not the hill to die on today. He won this battle, but the war is far from over. Heading back to the bedroom, I sneak past a sleeping Khal and duck into my closet. I pick out a pretty forest green button down shirt, a pencil skirt, and the cute shoes Fi bought me for my last birthday.

Carefully, I move around the room so I don't awaken Khal. He and his brother have been working tirelessly to help unravel the mysteries that surround my sister and me. I leave a note on top of his keys and take the little location tag off his keyring. Clipping the tag to my bra strap, I hide it inside my cup before leaving the room. At least if he wakes up, he can find me quickly.

Walking out of the room, I grab my purse before heading back to the kitchen where Torben is putting the finishing touches on the cabinets he hung yesterday. "I'm heading out. I swiped Khal's key tag if you guys need to locate me in a hurry."

"Good thinking. I'll see you for lunch, but remember to enjoy your-self. Buy anything you want except a car." He arches his brows at me and smiles before he kisses me goodbye.

He knows I would never buy a car, I don't even know how to drive.

"Okay. Buy three cars and a truck, got it," I reply with a wink. He laughs because he knows I would never waste that kind of money.

Heading out the front door unescorted is interesting. I guess since the world hasn't ended and we're all in one piece, the guys have relaxed on the 'not being alone' thing. Walking along the woodland path is refreshing and soothing to my nerves until the wind direction changes and I catch the scent of a feline.

I've smelled the person in question before—she works for Tiernan. Pulling out my phone, I fire off a quick text to the leopard asking if he has a detail on me. It only takes a few moments before he replies in the affirmative. He's pleased my situational awareness has improved, so I send a smiley face to him and continue on my way.

At the edge of the forest, my senses go on high alert. Nothing seems out of the ordinary, so I step out onto the gravel and head towards the bank. I window shop on my way to the bank to make our weekly deposits. This area has a lot of... interesting shops, for sure.

Walking up the steps of the *Pendragon Savings and Loan*, I draw in a deep breath to prepare me for the perpetually grumpy dragon. Granted, last night he seemed to be in a particularly jovial mood, but I was pouring rather heavily for him. Pushing open the front doors, I finally look around the interior. I take in the artwork that's obviously been collected over the last few hundred years.

That's when I notice there's a piece of furniture that's out of place— a seven foot tall glass cabinet filled with glass coffee mugs in different shapes and sizes. Looking to my left, I see several similar cabinets also filled with mugs. I heard dragons always have a horde, and apparently, Diaval's treasure trove is funny coffee mugs.

The third cabinet is filled with mugs shaped like animals and one entire shelf is full of wolf shaped mugs. Staring at the mugs, I realize most of them bear a striking resemblance to my shift which is odd. As I move around the cabinet, I don't notice the nearby door open. I'm so focused on the wolf mugs that I almost miss the scent of chamomile. I freeze, then look around, jumping when I realize he's less than a foot from me.

"Geez, Diaval. You damn near gave me a heart attack!" Breathing deep, I try to slow my heart rate down. For whatever reason, I didn't partially shift like I usually do when I get frightened.

His hand goes to his tie and he fiddles with the knot several times, adjusting its placement inside his three piece suit. A soft wisp of smoke escapes his lips and the flicker of his dragon behind his eyes appears. "This isn't a museum, it's a bank."

"Watch out, D. Your dragon is showing." Arching a brow at him, I watch him step back.

His eyes widen as he processes what I said. He doesn't frighten me which takes him by surprise. Calling him something other than his given name seems to have surprised him as well.

Turning on my heel, I head over to the teller to conduct my business so I can leave. For once, I am thankful I am the one here and not Fi. She would be glowing like a snapped glow stick. The hairs on the back of my neck are standing on end from the feel of the room. There's a thick feeling of nervous energy and the scent of the teller has changed at least three times.

The woman in front of me is obviously a deer shifter. Stepping back, I give her a wide berth, knowing my wolf would set her nerves on edge. That's all I need right now is for her to become afraid and run—activating my new prey drive will not end well for either of us. There'd be dead deer and roasted wolf on the menu because I have no doubt Diaval would roast my ass in a heartbeat.

Sighing softly, I clear the vision of my possible demise from my mind. When it's finally my turn, I can't make up my mind what the teller is. Since it's rude to ask, I guess I'll never know but she's extremely pretty and delicate. I hand her Fi's deposit first, accept the receipt, and stuff it into my pocket. As I hand her mine, I hear

Diaval muttering about how my sugar daddies are making me a pampered pooch.

Deep down, I hear my wolf growling in my head. *Evil male,* she grinds out as she paces in my head.

I can't blame her for being angry; I'm angry too. As soon as I finish my deposits, I turn and face Diaval. He looks shocked that I stepped into his personal space, but doesn't say anything. My wolf surges to the surface as I stare up at the ridiculously handsome, grumpy jackass of a dragon. "You think I'm spoiled?"

Narrowing my eyes as the golden hue of my wolf blazes to life, I jab my index finger into his chest. "My sister and I have held two to three jobs a piece for the last three years to survive. Some nights we lived on bar food our old boss gave us because he felt bad."

I gnash my teeth at him showing how frustrated I am with him. Tears start to well up and I wipe them away roughly. "Maybe if you lived like regular shifters you would know what it's like to fight to live. Maybe if you came down from your self imposed pedestal you would see my mates are taking care of me. I think somewhere in this armored heart of yours, you are jealous."

Diaval flinches when I mention his armored heart and being jealous.

"Come see me when you pull your enormous head out of your ass."

Glaring at him, I wait until he finally steps back, raising his hands in a placating manner. Diaval's usually calming scent has changed and has the bitter edge of anxiety to it. His eyes are wide, shocked that I went on the attack though he could easily roast me.

I doubt anyone has ever stood up to him the way I just did. Channeling my inner Fi, I let go of everything I was holding in. We've been orphans, shunned and verbally abused most of our lives, especially me. Deep down, I know my wolf gave me the strength and confidence to stand up for myself.

Oddly, he doesn't attack back. Instead he shifts his weight from foot to foot as he messes with his tie again.

From what Tiernan and Torben said, my ability to maintain eye contact is rather unnerving since it's unusual for a female wolf to be able to hold an alpha's stare. Watching Diaval, I see the scales moving under his skin and his pupils occasionally shift to slits. He's fighting his dragon, but I don't know why.

"Why are you so nervous, Diaval? Wolf got your tongue?" My voice drops to a sultry tone—the same tone I use to get Torben to do what I want.

He leans forward before he catches himself and turns quickly, heading into his office.

Slowly, I calm down as I listen to him lock the door to his hidden office. Shaking my head I glance over once more at the mugs in the display cabinet and a soft laugh escapes my lips. "What is it with the ancients and escaping through hidden doors?"

I stand there for several beats too long before I turn to leave, noticing the rest of the patrons staring at me. *It's probably unusual for someone to stand up to Diaval and his egotistical nonsense.* Ignoring the rabble, I head off to shop like Torben told me to do.

The glass blowers shop is the first one I pass as I leave the bank; it must be where Diaval gets his mugs from. I end up picking out mugs for everyone, including one with a bear as the handle and the main part of the mug looks like a bee's nest. I also grabbed a snow leopard pattern with a leopard tail curved up as the handle. Since I wasn't sure what the twins' shifts look like, I go with a pair of black mugs with naughty sayings on them. For Fi, I grabbed a mug that says *'Kicking ass and forgetting names.'* Revelin's cracks me up because it simply says *'Magically Delicious.'*

I'll let Fi give him that one.

I can't help but stare at the all black mug with scales and a dragon's head and neck for the handle. Inscribed on the side, there's a phrase in a language I can't read. "What does this say?"

The shop owner comes over and smiles. "Until death. It is a phrase dragons use. Apparently, it holds a lot of meaning to them."

Nodding, I add it to the clutch of mugs I'm picking up. He places three wolf mugs on the counter when I ask about them. One is my color and the other two look like timber wolves. I grab the cream-colored wolf mug and look at it. "I wonder why we never see wolves this color? I'll take it."

"They were a rather powerful bloodline once upon a time." He sighs and wraps the mug in paper.

"What happened to them?" I couldn't help but ask—damn my curiosity.

"They were hunted to extinction and unlike my people, the council didn't protect them." He raises the hair off his forehead to reveal a faint lavender eight pointed star on his forehead that marks him as a unicorn. I nod in understanding.

Something tells me he knows what I am and he's warning me.

"Thank you for everything." I smile and lower my head to him out of respect.

He took a huge chance telling me. I'll have to tell Fi and the others after I process what it means. Taking my purchases, I leave the shop prepared to shock the hell out of Diaval when I see him the next time. I immediately run into Tiernan and lower my eyes to him.

That's become our public signal for 'I found out shit we can't talk about here.'

He double blinks at me and offers to take my bags.

This conversation will have to wait till Fi gets home.

51

Fiadh

"Are you sure we should be back here? Last time we visited, I came back with Lite-Brite syndrome," I grumble as Revelin leads me through the portal he created.

His lips curl as he reaches over and brushes a leaf off of my face. "I remember, lass. It was quite the after party."

Resisting the urge to duck my chin at the gentle touch, I turn my head and look around us. "This is a different part of the Faerie than we entered before. It's… not the castle."

Rev nods and holds his arms out, turning in a circle. "You're right. This is near the castle grounds, but it's on the way to a spot in the wild I'm fond of. I want you to see more of the Daybreak Court's lands and experience my home without a bunch of formality. That's why I said wear something comfortable rather than fancy, lass."

I follow his gesture, looking out over gorgeous grass in tones of sea green, blue, and midnight. There are copses of trees that look like they're straight out of a fantasy illustration and colorful flora every- where. The sky is shades of pale yellow, pink, red, and orange with two suns shining warmth down on us. It's beautiful and my magic is humming with anticipation.

"My magic *really* likes this meadow," I murmur shyly. "I feel it zipping around inside of me like a hyper puppy."

The Prince walks closer, his icy eyes coasting over me and turning a rich lilac. "You, Fiadh Morgenstern, are much more than you've been led to believe."

Frowning, I tilt my head and give him a puzzled look. "Why do you say that?"

He stops centimeters from me, our breaths mingling as he looks at me seriously. "Because very few magic users react to stepping into the wilds of the Faerie like you are right now. You can't see it, but your aura is radiating rainbows and sparkles like you're home. There may be some Fae deep in your line, though I don't believe it's my people."

I wrinkle my nose at him. "I don't think that's true at all. Don't be silly; my ears are normal."

"Oh, if *only* that was the only way to identify one of the kin." He boops my nose and takes my hand, turning to lead me across the fairytale-esque land. "But it's not, especially if your heritage is from one of the other three courts."

"Harvest, Midnight, and Reaping, right?" I ask as we tromp across the soft, pretty grass.

"Aye. They all have their own traits, though I suspect you've seen some of it in the group of royals and fans who follow me all over." Revelin looks at me with amusement in his eyes when I grumble something about the Harvest Court under my breath. "Easy now. Khorinea isn't representative of the entire court, love. She's a necessary evil, unfortunately, but not nearly as important as she makes herself out to be. Her fame is entirely in her head—I'd shake her loose, but she's got a mouth like a bloody foghorn. It keeps everyone from revealing what a rancid twat she is."

Snorting, I cover my mouth as giggles escape. I thought the Prince loved all the adoring Fae who trail him like teenage girls, but clearly, there's a strategy to whom he allows in the group. It makes me feel a *lot* less irritated at their consistent presence. "I haven't heard you talk like that before. Do you get… freer when you're not in public in our realm?"

No sooner than the question leaves my mouth than I realize how stupid it sounded. *Of course*, he's more comfortable in private and at home. Now he'll think I'm a fucking fool—

"Yes and no." Rev stops for a moment and gives me an earnest expression. "I feel more comfortable with *you*, and I don't know when that started. Your house, your family… all of it. Being in that environment makes me feel like I'm not on display—something I don't get to experience often. The stage and the throne sort of demand I'm 'on' all of the time, but with you guys? I relax."

That literally melts me inside and I give him a frustrated look. "Argh! You can't say things like that!"

"Why?" He frowns and crosses his arms over his chest. "It's true, Fiadh."

I stomp my foot and let out a low growl when flowers spring up in line, traveling across the ground from me to him. "It makes me… feel… things. That's why!"

Throwing his head back, he laughs. The sound is rich and trills over my skin like a feather stroking me. "Only you, lass. Not a single other soul—male or female—has *ever* complained when I offer my affections. You're allergic to emotions that aren't fury."

"That's ridiculous. I'll have you know I'm very fond of—" My mouth drops open and my speech stops when I see the creature approach behind him. The large snow white stag is glowing like it's made of moonlight and it has at least ten points on the enormous antlers it's sporting. Intelligence glimmers in its gaze and it paws the ground as it stops behind the Prince. "Holy Boy Who Lived, look at that thing!"

Revelin's eyes widen and he turns slowly until he can see what I'm looking at. When the Fae and the stag's eyes meet, the glow emanating from the animal gets brighter. He calls over his shoulder, "Come closer, Fiadh. This is an old friend."

Moving to stand beside Rev, I murmur, "What *is* it?"

"A feystag, lass. This gorgeous lady saved my ass from a hungry demon hybrid when I was accompanying my father as a boy. She scared the halfling away until an adult member of the Hunt could slay it and I lived to make trouble another day."

My brow furrows as I try to assimilate an asston of information in one go, but all I manage to ask is, "What the hell is she doing here now?"

Way to sound grateful, Fi.

"I'm not sure. This is the first time I've seen this creature since that Hunt and I'm not in danger—that I know of." He winks at me playfully and I shoot a small bolt of energy at him. "Aside from you, we're on protected lands so enemies aren't likely to be lurking in the bushes."

The stag paws at the ground again, looking at us as if we should know what we're supposed to do. I wish Feray was here or even Tiernan. Interpreting animals who can't speak isn't within my skill set and obviously Revelin isn't a Dr. Doolittle, either.

"I think she's trying to tell us something."

The Prince nods, scratching his jaw. "Feystag are known for hoarding magical items. Perhaps she knows we're searching for something specific?"

My eyes widen and I tug his sleeve. "The symbol! Should we show her the symbol? I can bring it up on my phone."

"That's a good plan. Bring it up and we'll approach her slowly."

Excitement pulses in my veins as I pull my phone out and scroll through the album until I reach the picture of the drawing I made. I zoom it in and hand the device to Rev so he can hold it out for the feystag. Its dark eyes study the screen, then look at us and when the words echo in my head, I almost lose my shit.

~I have seen this, but I have many objects and it may take time to sort through my treasures to find it. I will require a boon—a trade for my time and my treasure. Are you prepared to meet my terms?~

I look at Rev and he shrugs, looking amazed as well as he says, "She didn't talk last time; I swear it."

A boon won't be that hard; it's not like we'll be asked to locate fucking Excaliber, right?

"Okay, pretty deer lady. You have a deal. We will trade you for the item when you find it. How will we know when you're ready?" I look the magical animal in the eyes, acknowledging her willingness to be helpful, even if it is a bit self-serving.

~I will send a message to the Prince on the will-o-wisps. He will know what value you must replace.~

"Agreed," Revelin says, raising his hand and drawing a rune in the air with his sparkling magic. "You have my word."

The feystag dips her head, pawing the ground once more, then takes off across the meadow in a streak of moonlight sparkles. I watch them fade as she disappears, completely awestruck by the sight. I can't believe this is kind of shit the Fae see all the time; their world is so imbued with magic that it seems unreal in comparison to our world. I can see why they have to guard the entrance so carefully—the wrong people would ruin this lovely place.

"That was unexpected," Rev admits as he rubs his hand over the back of his neck. "I sort of intended to take you to my secret spot and have my way with you. It's a bit hard to top a mind-speaking magical animal visit, though."

Winking at him, I take his hand and tilt my head. "Does that mean you're not going to try?"

"Challenge accepted." Pulling me along, he heads to a set of flat stone stairs that lead to a far up hilltop. "Get the lead out, lass. I have seducing to do!"

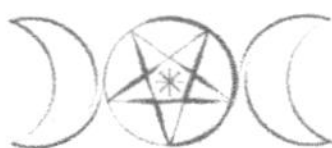

THE SOUND of the bubbling spring is soothing and I find myself relaxing into Revelin's arms as I look around his little haven. I wasn't a fan of all the damn steps, but once we got up here, I felt the pull of nature in a way I haven't ever experienced before. Trees, flowers, plants, and curious creatures surround us in the canopied alcove next to the water. I haven't seen one of the animals or creatures yet, but I can *feel* their presence.

The magic in this space is wild and strong—it calls to mine, tempting it to play.

Looking up at the prince, I smile a little. I wouldn't have expected him to bring me to this quaint, calm spot, but Fae are frequently full of surprises. His face is serene and his body relaxed as he leans on his hands with me settled between his legs. For all his talk about seduction, we've been sitting here soaking in the sounds and smells without a single wandering hand.

Revelin catches me studying him and arches a brow. "See anything you like, lass?"

Chuckling, I shrug. "You don't need me to tell you that you're good looking. You have plenty of fangirls to do that."

"You wound me." He pouts and bats his lashes. "How could their praise be as important as yours?"

I smack his chest playfully, turning my body a little so I can face him. "What did I say about that feelings stuff?"

"Hmmm. I think it was 'oh, Revelin, I *love* when you say all those mushy things that make me squishy like a girl.' Then you followed it up by making a kissy face." His eyes dance with mirth, but he does an admirable job of keeping a serious expression.

Elbowing him in the ribs, I roll my eyes. "No one would believe that tripe. You're lucky you can sing because acting is *not* your forte."

"Ugh. You can't help but stick a fork in me, can you?"

"Nope." I grin and dart forward, kissing the corner of his mouth on instinct.

The hunger that flashes in his eyes tells me I might have waved a flag at the bull. Before I know it, Revelin rolls us like a goddamn alligator in a death roll, pinning me to the fluffy colored grass with his body. I blink, adjusting to the change before I reach up and push the wispy hair out of his eyes. He flashes sharp canines at me and my eyes widen in surprise.

I had no idea Fae have fangs!

"The time for teasing has passed, lass." Revelin dips his head and kisses me, his tongue twining with mine roughly. His hips settle between my thighs and I wrap my legs around him automatically.

He's not as broad and muscular as Tiernan, but his lithe frame feels like it's coiled with power. Hardness pushes against me and I groan into his mouth as my pussy takes notice. Warmth floods over me and I arch into his erection, grinding against it. When the kiss breaks, I pant softly, licking my swollen lips. Desire and power are buzzing over my skin, making my thighs slick with need.

"I think these flowers have some sort of aphrodisiac in them," I murmur as I smirk up at him. "You're getting far more control than I'd allow otherwise."

"Keep telling yourself tragic lies, Fi. There's no one but us here to know you're hot for me—you don't have to pretend." His eyes slip to that lilac hue again and with a fangy smile, he lets some of his magic loose. "Now, hold still, lass."

Before I know it, vines slide along my arms and legs, twining around my limbs until they hold my wrists and ankles in place on the ground. When I pull against them, they tighten, but not painfully so. I arch a brow at the prince, waiting for him to speak before I decide whether I'll incinerate them or not.

"Tell me the word," he whispers against the shell of my ear. "We both know protocol from the club and I never break the rules of engagement."

Of course, the word is hanging from the necklace I'm wearing, but he's not wrong to set the rules.

"Penguin," I breathe. My pulse speeds up as he runs his nose along the column of my neck then follows it with his pointed canines. I rarely allow myself to switch to the submissive role and I don't know if he realizes how much restraint it's taking to allow him this moment. Control is my safety and I don't give it up—not ever.

But I am right now, despite what I snarked back at my sister, and I don't know why.

His chuckle rumbles over me, raising the hairs on my arms and making my sex throb. His magic dances over me again and this time, my clothes disappear. My skin is highly sensitive against the fabric of his clothing and I wriggle more, seeking the friction I need.

"Ah, ah. That's why the vines are there, love. Behave and you'll get everything you want."

"Tease," I grumble as I close my eyes. I'll never be able to stay completely; this is a test I'm going to fail like a pro.

Revelin nips and licks his way over my breasts, focusing on one at a time so thoroughly that a whine slips from me. The sound makes him happy because he tugs on my nipple rings firmly enough to make me moan. I keep my hips still, though, and he continues down my torso, rimming my belly button with his tongue. Every touch, every bite makes my nerves tingle; I have no idea how I'm going to do what he wants for much longer.

I shouldn't be so worked up by this small amount of attention, but with our magic feeding off the Faerie, everything is magnified.

Thoughts flitter out of my mind like petals on the wind when his mouth brushes over my mound. His tongue traces around the shape of me, circling my clit like he's trying to spell my fucking name with it. My legs tremble, but he pushes them further apart and his vines adjust without him uttering a word. When he sucks on me, I let out a strangled yell, my entire body tight as I fight the need to arch into him.

My struggle makes him smile against me and he turns his head, biting the inside of my soft thigh hard enough to leave a mark. "Good girl."

The orgasm that hits me is like a tidal wave and my eyes roll back into my head like I'm trying to see my goddamn skull. Limbs pull against the plant bonds as I ride the sensation, my harsh breaths the only sound beside the water still bubbling in the spring. After a few minutes, I manage to untangle my brain cells and remove my teeth from my lower lip before I bite through it.

That's it. I'm turning in my feminist card; I'm no longer worthy because I just came when a dude said 'good girl.'

"Stop thinking so hard, lass. If it makes you wet, who gives a shit if it's a little naughty?" Rev bobs his brows, ranging up my body with a hungry look in his eyes. "You can be a good girl and a bad ass. Everyone has layers."

"I'm never living this down," I rasp as he fits our bodies together. I suck in a sharp breath when he disappears his own clothes and I feel warm flesh and cool steel sliding against me. "Then again, who fucking cares?"

That earns me a bite just below my ear and I shiver. "I'm going to fuck you now, Fiadh. And when we're right at the edge, I'll bite and the magic will swirl around us. Are you ready for it?"

His pierced cock slides against my clit and I groan, nodding at his words. "Do it."

Revelin takes my lips again, kissing me deeply as his hips realign and his dick slams into me with one hard thrust. The feel of his cross and the stretch of his size almost overwhelm me with sensation and I buck up into him. He withdraws slowly, then crashes into me, repeating the pattern until my pussy is gripping him like a vise with every stroke inside. His fingers lace with mine as our bodies move and our mouths fight for control.

That's when I feel my magic swell inside of me, pulling from every corner of my body to rise up and twine around his power. I've never felt it so keenly before and combined with the mounting pleasure as he fills me, I worry that I'm going to explode in more ways than one. Pulling my lips from his, I look at my prince in awe.

"Is it… is this how it's supposed…"

"Better." He dips his head again and one of his fangs grazes my tongue. As the blood flows, his hips speed up and bang against mine as our sweaty skin slaps together.

I feel like I'm flying—my magic is unbound and swirling around us with his, filling the air with sparkles and sweet scents. His soft growls make my gut tighten and I know the pinnacle is coming. Panting against his lips, I whisper throatily. "Now, Rev. It's time."

His grin is feral and his eyes flash at me before he dives for my shoulder. I gasp when the points dig into my skin, piercing the flesh briefly. A burning sensation rockets over the spot he bit and I snap the vines on my wrists like they're made of cotton. Digging my nails into his back, I hold on tightly as the climax slams into me and my skin starts to glow.

"There's the lovely light show," he murmurs as he licks over the spot. His hips continue pumping into me as my walls shudder around him and within a few moments, he comes. Gripping him tightly inside, I arch my back and let the pleasure flow through me as the mate bond ties us together.

Tendrils of magic and falling glittery Fae dust fill the air around us as we come down slowly, wrapped together in the stillness of nature.

I open one eye and look up at Rev, glaring as best I can when I'm this sated. "I better not be covered in craft herpes forever because of you, asshole."

There. That'll teach him.

FERAY

The damn fox didn't stock the freaking bar after his shift again.

Wait until I see Dezi—this is the third time this week the lazy bastard left one of us with extra work.

Grumbling to myself, I clean the deck he left in a sticky mess and plot revenge on the asshole. The sound of the metallic slide on the front door's peephole catches my attention. It's still early in my shift and the first act is about to start. They're supposed to warm the crowd up for this exclusive tattoo and piercing demo Dezi booked for the end of the month. I glance at the entryway, waiting to see who is coming in. The bulk of the crowd doesn't show up till after the warm up act is over and it's still pretty calm here.

Shockingly enough, it's Diaval. He doesn't usually show up this early and he must be on edge because he's doing that thing where he adjusts his tie over and over. I can't for the life of me figure out why he does it, but everyone has their little anxiety things. Hoping to help ease his distress, I mix him a drink I'm calling a 'Nocturnal Tennessee Mule.' It's a mix of deep dragon bitters added to a normal

Tennessee Mule with a smoky topping. The deep dragon bitters look like black nebulas when added to alcohol and I hope he likes it. When he walks up to the bar, I place the new drink in front of him with a smile.

He opens his mouth to say something then shuts it and looks at the drink. Finally, he says, "I... was rude the other day." The dragon won't look at me while he talks so I know it must be hard for him to apologize.

"Forgiven," I say before reaching under the bar to place an ornately wrapped box in front of him. "I saw this the other day and thought of you."

"I don't understand; I was rude. You didn't have to get me a gift. " Diaval seems entirely puzzled by my gesture. It's as if no one has ever given him anything before.

"Think of it as my apology for losing my temper." As soon as the words leave my lips, he nods and starts to carefully untie the bow at the top.

"Girls!" Dezi yells as he comes down the hallway to the bar.

Arching a brow, I glance over at Fi and she rolls her eyes at his dramatics. "What do you want, Dezi? I'm in the middle of two large parties and the untouchable Mr. Fox is being a douche canoe."

Fi's anger is palatable; I watch tiny sparks dancing in her hair as she stares the vampire down. At least it doesn't look like the Rose Bowl parade, but I'm not sure how long that will last if Dezi pushes her.

"Laugh it up, witchling. Our volunteer for the exhibit called and said they can't make it. Apparently, they have a prior engagement." His eyes flair a brilliant crimson several times as he looks between Fi and me. "Any takers? Free mods if you accept."

Glancing over my shoulder, I see Khal and Torben arriving. They beeline for the bar and I know they heard what Dezi said. I wait for their reactions as I consider Dezi's offer. Torben pats the area over his heart, basically telling me to do what will make me happy. Khal gives me a thumbs up and I grin to myself.

"There is no way in hell am I giving up the tips on the floor for your sideshow, Bob." Fi says, noping her way out of the event.

I stare at her for several moments before looking back at the bar. I've never done anything like this before, so I check on my customers while I think about it. My eyes roam to where Diaval is carefully lifting the black dragon mug out of the box. The normal tension in his facial features slowly melts away as he stares at his gift. I can tell when he finds the inscription—he looks over at me before gently placing the mug to the side and returns to his drink.

Diaval's initial reaction pleased me, but his quick dismissal pisses me off to no end. Growling, I turn to face Dezi and he takes a step back as my wolf flares to the surface. "I'll do it." My voice carries and the silence around us is almost deafening.

"You'll do what?" Dezi asks, rubbing his ears as if checking to see if he heard correctly.

"I'll do the piercing and tattoo demo. It's time to take life by the balls... or is it the bull by the horns?" I look at Fi, furrowing my brow as I think about it.

"Either works," Fi says with a shrug. " You know there's a lot of pain involved with either option?" My sister strokes my cheek to soothe the wolf within me and I realize she thinks my animal is pushing me to do this.

"I understand that."

I look past Fi and see that Diaval is staring at me again. His mouth opens and closes several times, but he doesn't produce any sound. Torben looks shocked, but his expression says he accepts my decision. Khal has moved and when I turn to find him, the sneak is right next to me.

"Come with me." Khal excuses us from the group and pulls me over to a couch to sit down. He smiles at me softly. "That's a bold decision, Precious."

"I know what I'm doing, Khal. Please don't coddle me."

"No coddling; I promise." His soft tone and the gentle grip he has on my hands radiates concern and affection. "Have you ever been pierced or tattooed before?"

"Never. I've always been the good one—the one who never did anything bold. I've always wanted one of them, but I couldn't afford them." I drop my gaze, ashamed to admit how poor we were after my parents' deaths. My greatest fear is being rejected because of where I came from, especially since the Ascension.

He uses the side of his index finger gently to get me to look up at him. "Where you came from made you into the loving, giving woman that you are. Never be ashamed of that." Khal leans forward and presses his lips against the corner of my mouth making my skin hum.

"Thank you, Khal. I needed to hear that. I realize I just volunteered myself to be stabbed multiple ways, but can you tell me what I've gotten myself into?" We share a chuckle and I shrug.

A slow smile spreads over his lips as he caresses my cheek. "I believe it would help you to enter what we call 'subspace' while it's happening."

"What's that? Is it a place or a state of being?" Scooting closer as I ask, my leg brushes against his and the hum inside me spreads.

Khal strokes the area over my eyebrows. He starts at the space between them, then outward and down my brow line. It's a soothing movement that instantly gets me to relax and slow my breathing. "Subspace is a state of being." He continues the same soothing pattern while he talks. "It's different for everyone. Some say it's like floating, like an out of body experience. If done right, you don't feel pain and remain relaxed the entire time." The soft tone of his voice lulls me further into a deeper state of relaxation as I feel all the tension leave my body. A soft chuckle escapes his lips when he boops me on the nose.

I jolt suddenly, snapping out of whatever he did. "Was that it?"

"Yes." The end of the word is hissed, telling me his animal is close to the surface, but he kisses my lips tenderly. "I can help you get there when it's time—if you would like."

"I'll need it for the piercings. Will you stay with me for the tattoo?" I'm pretty sure Khal won't leave my side through any of it, but it doesn't hurt to ask.

"Anything your heart desires, Precious." He stands up, then offers me his hand. With a fond smile, he leads me over to the guest tattoo artist who is also the piercer tonight.

"You must be my canvas for tonight! I'm Salvador." He extends his hand and I shake it.

"I'm Feray and this is my mate, Khal. My other mate, Torben, is sitting at the bar." I motion to Torben and he raises his stein in our direction. Looking back at Khal, I see I caught him off guard by introducing him as my mate even though we haven't claimed each other yet.

"It's a pleasure to meet all of you. Let's start with what would you like to have tattooed and where?" Salvador helps me into the chair and I look at my left forearm.

"Can you do watercolor flames here?" I motion to the inside of my left forearm and then it occurs to me that I'm a shifter. A giggle escapes my lips when I think about my cream colored fur having oranges and reds on one leg. "Will it affect the color of my fur?"

Salvador shakes his head, but chuckles in amusement. "It doesn't change your fur color. That would be funny, wouldn't it?" The three of us share a chuckle as we picture our shifts with our ink showing.

Sobering, he takes a marker and draws freehand flames up my arm that stop at the bend of my elbow. He positions my arm carefully, then prepares the area for ink. Knowing I'm new at this, Sal explains in great detail about cleansing the area and shaving it so little hairs don't affect the needle. He asks me if I'm ready, and I nod.

I suck in a breath and look over at Khal when the needle touches my skin for the first time. Sal continues talking me through the process, explaining the importance of outlining. The buzz of the machine is almost soothing and the dragging of the needle leaves warm trails where it passes.

Khal is holding my right hand and watching Sal as he concentrates on the design. Leaning forward, he kisses my temple. "How are you doing, Precious?"

"I'm doing okay because I'm focused on matching your breaths. Thank you for being here with me." He has no idea how much this level of support means to me. My heart is ready to burst from feeling so very adored.

"From now until my last breath, Precious, and even beyond that." His voice has a dreamy quality to it as he responds.

He's so very thoughtful and sensitive; it's amazing.

When the artist takes a break to change to a different shading needle, I look around the room. Fi and Torben are laughing together. Diaval, on the other hand, looks like he's damn close to snapping the molding off the bartop. I can't figure out why he seems so stressed, but I have other things to worry about. Shrugging my shoulders, I adjust my body before Sal gets started again.

"Just a little bit more, Feray. You're doing phenomenal for a first timer." His smile radiates pride as he looks at me.

I guess most people don't sit as still as I am their first time.

He wasn't joking when he said it was only going to be a few moments. Before I know it, he's cleaning the tattoo and slathering the paste over it, then putting the protective covering on it. I gape as I look at it, amazed at his talent.

"No shifting for twenty-four hours. After twenty-four hours, remove the bandage and clean the area gently with antibacterial soap and pat it dry. You can apply this ointment if you need it." He hands me a tube of ointment and Khal promptly takes it from me.

"I will be tending to the tattoo. You just look beautiful as always." Khal kisses my cheek and I start laughing.

He is absolutely the sweetest man I have ever met.

"Okay, now for the piercing. What are we doing today? Perhaps your belly button?" Sal smiles as he cleans up the tattoo paraphernalia. From the look in his eyes, I bet most newbies opt for something like he suggested.

"Well..." My eyes dart around the room and Torben's eyes flare amber as I raise my brows. He cups his chest and I flush bright pink before I nod. "My nipples—definitely my nipples."

The corner of Torben's mouth quirks up and he nods subtly. Apparently, I've made him very happy with this decision and that usually works out phenomenally in the end.

Standing up, I untie the corset top I'm wearing and hand it to Khal. I reach behind my back and unclasp my strapless bra to set my breasts free. A soft gasp echoes from Khal as his eyes turn a yellow-green with slits in the center as he stares at my large, full breasts.

Salvador doesn't gawk—he's clearly a professional. Instead, he shows me different starter bars and explains the benefits of each. Khal steps in and pays for gold bars instead of the standard stainless steel. Arching a brow at him, I wait until he explains that he's concerned if there's any silver in the steel mixture I'll get sick.

He's such a thoughtful mate.

"Okay, I believe we are ready to start. Please climb up into the chair and we'll get started." Sal says confidently. He turns to talk to the crowd about what he's going to do and the services he offers at his shop.

In the meantime, Khal smiles down at me. "I'm going to help you relax before I return to my chair over there." He motions to where a chair has been placed for him and I nod. He kisses my forehead then moves to stand behind me. "Lean back and close your eyes. I will come and get you as soon as Sal is done, I promise."

Once in position, he starts with the tips of his fingers between my eyebrows, just above my nose. Then he follows the curve of my eyebrows out to my temples. His fingertips ghost over my skin in a slow, soothing pattern. I feel myself slipping into a deep state of relaxation like earlier. My breathing has considerably slowed down and I feel fabulous, almost like I'm floating on a marshmallow.

Khal and Sal are talking in low tones as Sal cleans my nipples in preparation for the piercing. Sal warns me before he places the clamp, but not when the sting of the needle pierces my flesh. Instead of pain, I feel my core clench as if trying to grip something that isn't there. The same thing happens again when he pierces the other nipple.

I'm curious as all hell about my response. That's something I'll have to ask Khal about later.

Next thing I know, I feel pillow soft lips pressed to mine and the scent of vetiver fills my nose. "There's my good girl. I'm going to take care of you now."Khal takes off his button down shirt and wraps it around me before he scoops me up and carries me away bridal style.

I look at the bar as he brings me off of the stage. My sister is shocked, chittering with Torben about what they just witnessed. Dezi raises his blood and vodka at me as if to say 'cheers.' I guess that's his way of saying thank you. Tiernan is waiting at the door to one of the private rooms and he holds the door open for us.

I didn't even see him come in.

"You did good, Fer. I'm proud of you." Tiernan says, lightly touching my hand before Khal brings me into the room.

There's a huge bed with red velvet sheets and soft lighting. A small bar is positioned off to the side next to what looks like a wash area. *Oh shit, this is one of the sex rooms.* I watch Khal, prepared to question him about what's happening. There's a knock at the door and when it opens, I see Khol with a basket. He doesn't say anything, just hands the basket off to his twin before leaving.

"I know you have a lot of questions swirling in your head right now. You're far too intelligent not to. This was the closest private room I could available to take care of your needs," he says softly as he kneels before me.

"This isn't what I expected from you," I blurt out. "I mean, your brother is a complete and total asshole. People are frightened of both of you for a reason." I feel like a blithering idiot when I fumble with words.

Nodding, he reaches into the basket and takes out a small assortment of candies. "Normally, I would offer chocolate, but all things considered, I don't know if that would hurt you." I accept the cherry candy from him and smile. The look on his face tells me there's more he wants to say. "I'm going to take care of everything from the smallest request to something unimaginable—whatever you need, I am here."

I think of what I really want to know before I speak. "I feel okay. I'm not too sore, but I am a little shocked I went to La La Land so easily.

Usually, I can't relax around so many strangers. Why was it like that?"

Leaning forward, he gently removes his shirt from my shoulders to look at the piercings. "There are a few reasons for that. Subspace removes the inhibitions you would normally have and shifts your consciousness so that pain becomes pleasure." He slips his tongue out between his lips and it shifts to his basilisk's. "I can taste your desire in the air and I'll handle it once I'm sure you're truly okay."

Blinking, I remember from basic biology that snakes use their tongues to taste things in the air. "You can't smell me like I can you?" He shakes his head as he uses antibacterial cleaner around the piercings. The soft stimulation makes my core pulse and I squirm on the bed.

"Oh, this is going to be fun. Someone's nipples are very sensitive now." Now there's a wicked gleam in his eye that makes me shiver.

"Always have been." I may as well be honest with the man that will be my mate.

Khal cleans both piercings and by the end, I'm soaked. He double checks the bandage on my forearm, then adds another layer of tape. "You'll feel the tattoo after the adrenaline wears off. Though, shifter healing being what it is, you may not."

There's an unmistakable hunger in his eyes as his forked tongue flicks out of his mouth again. He picks up two cotton swabs and teases the tips of my nipples, leaning so his body is between my legs. "Safe word Fer?"

It's plain as day on my tag, but I giggle as I look up at him. "Bubbles."

"That's a safe word as adorable as its owner. Lay back and relax, Precious, while I take care of you."

I trust Khal so I do as he says. He continues teasing one nipple with his hand while he slides my skirt up with the other. His hand slips between my legs until he reaches my apex to feel my soaked underwear. "Someone is rather turned on—I'm a very lucky man." He laughs as he leans down to kiss my thigh. "Torben will be thanking me later."

Before I can answer, he grips my hips and slides me down the bed till my feet hit the floor. In a blink, my thong is pulled down. Raising up on my elbows, I look down to see Khal smiling wickedly.

"You're so responsive." His breathy tone catches me off guard as he lowers his face to my sex.

The flicks from his forked tongue make me jump. Swirling his tongue around my sensitive nub makes my thighs quiver with every lick. Soft pulses start deep in my core making me crave him and want to tip over into oblivion.

"Khal please," I moan between panting breaths. He's driving me insane, edging me by slowing down and almost stopping before he licks again.

"Patience, Precious. Good things come to those that wait." He blows hot breath over my core, making it spasm as it anticipates being filled. His lips caress the skin around my engorged sex before the tip of his human tongue delves deep, teasing my entrance. He slides up between my lips to suck on my clit for several seconds before releasing it. "I can see why Torben is obsessed with how you taste. You're as sweet as honey."

"Khal, I'm so close." I reach down and thread my fingers through his hair to get a grip on it.

He hums as he presses his lips to my clit,and two fingers push into me. Between the sudden fullness and the way he curls his fingers, my orgasm hits me like a freight train. Bucking wildly, I ride his fingers while he pounds them into me. My core tries to grip him as he keeps up with my bucking. Tentatively, he bites my thigh—not breaking the skin, but sending me off the deep end again. This orgasm is different; with every pulse, I flood his hand with my juices. Tightening my grip on his hair, I pull on him, wanting him closer to me. He takes the hint and climbs up my body, slowing down his movements so I calm down.

Panting heavily, I release his hair and nuzzle him as soon as I am able to. The deep rumble of my wolf escapes my lips as I lay there, completely sated. He pulls his fingers out and kisses me before going to the sink to clean himself up. His undershirt and pants bear the evidence of my release and I flush. He chuckles, winking at me as he says, "Torben is going to take you home and finish what I started." Smiling, he rises and he glances over his shoulder. "You're welcome."

When he comes back, he cleans me up, explaining the full scope of after care. He wants me properly educated so I know how I should be taken care of. For a basilisk, he is surprisingly more tender than Torben—something I didn't think was possible. When we are cleaned up, he helps me to my feet and leads me to the door. We exit the room and I feel the shifters in the room take notice as their noses work overtime.

As predicted, Torben is on me like a bear on honey.

He fills us in on how shocked everyone was when I sat through the tattoo and piercings so quietly. His eyes flicker between bear and human eyes. Before I know it, he flings me over his shoulder and carries me out of the club.

I'll be damned. Khal was right—round two is all Torben.

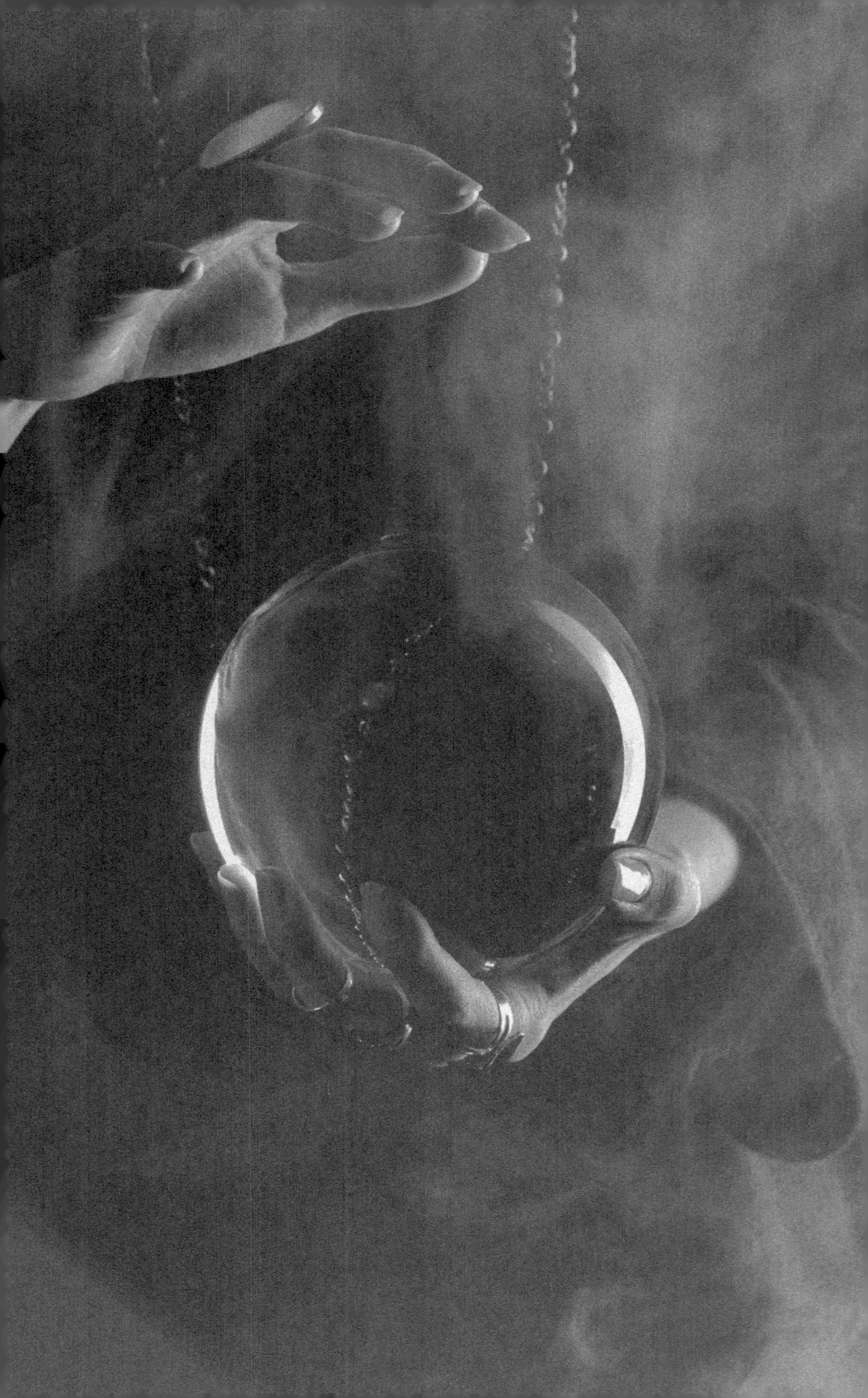

53

FIADH

I still can't believe Feray did that shit in front of the entire club.

Shaking my head as I smile to myself, I sneak a glance at my sister as she walks beside me on the street. We're headed to see Philly since it's our day off, and she'll be lucky if I don't spill the beans about her sudden badassery. Over the years I've scrimped and traded favors for the piercings I have, but never once did Feray tell me she was interested in trying it out. When she volunteered, you could have knocked me over with a feather. But here we are, striding down the main drag as the nipple twins and she's got her head held high.

"Are you sore?" I ask curiously. "I mean, I was sore for *weeks*. And the cleaning every day using shot glasses and salt water was no picnic, either. How's the care going?"

She snorts and I frown until her eyes flash with gold. "They're fully healed. I don't have to worry about any of it. Shifter for the win *again.*"

"You cheating bitch," I grumble. "I cannot tell you how much I didn't enjoy all the weeks of cleaning and care for all the shit I have. Being able to just poof it away because you're a wolf is bullshit."

Her laugh is light and I marvel again at how much our lives have changed since January. It's been almost six months since the Ascension and destruction of our home, but it feels like it's flown by. We have this insanely extravagant house being built around us, powers, a flock of assholes who track our every move, and jobs we don't hate. Every day, I wake up and wonder if today is the day the dream ends and we're back to scraping together money for Chinese food.

"Don't hate me 'cause you ain't me," Feray sings with a smirk. "At least you don't have to get re-waxed three times a month. There *are* drawbacks, sis. My chocolate fixation has me jonesing all the time, but I have no idea if it's a problem."

"We really should check into that," I mutter. "But you're right. I'm not a fan of having to do spa shit over and over. However, you also don't have flowers and sparkles shooting out of you when you get laid, so…"

Her eyes dance. "Your room is starting to look like a fucking botantical garden. Every time Tiernan trims it all back, those two bring it back with a vengeance. And Torben found glitter in his beard the other day—I thought he was going to have a heart attack."

My face turns bright red and I groan in embarrassment. "I'm a living embodiment of craft herpes and it's infecting everyone. Sweet baby Hercules on a winged horse, I'm never living this shit down."

Laughing as she pulls the door to the hospital open, Feray shrugs. "We've all gotten used to it. I check Tor before he goes to work or the guys would give him hell."

"I'm going to murder that silver spooned Fae, I swear on a stack of spell books." I rub my hands over my hair, wondering if I'm covered in the stuff now. "I did not sign on to look like a contestant for Miss Briarvale twenty-four hours a day."

"If it helps, I doubt he can control what your combined magics do when you're getting freaky. I know I don't have a lot of control of my wolf when she takes the wheel," my sister says as we step into the elevator.

The bell dings and I sigh as we head up to our friend's room. He's been progressing slowly, but this kind of injury takes a long time, even with all the magical intervention from our phoenix doctor. I've been poking around a little, researching if perhaps the symbol carved on his back after the attacks is connected to a hex. That would explain why his shifter biology isn't speeding the process up —something Dr. Bennu has been puzzled by for weeks.

"Do you think he'll let Philly out soon?" Fer looks at me with worried eyes. "Torben says the bar is almost finished, but the apartment we lived in is ready to be lived in. He can make it his own now since the back rooms aren't quarters anymore."

"I don't know. Philly needs a lot of care still and he's a stubborn old goat. He won't do it on his own and we don't live there to help. Who will we get to take care of him?"

Her eyes sparkle and I arch a brow as the glee takes over her face. "I know *exactly* who. Miss Florence from the bakery. That old bobcat has *always* had a thing for our Philly. If we ask her to check on him a couple times a day, maybe he'll finally give her a chance!"

I roll my eyes and sigh heavily. "Feray Morgenstern, you are *drunk* on love and trying to fix *everyone* up so they can be a couple. This 'mates' thing has you *out of control.*"

The doors open as she's clapping her hands and babbling about fixing Philly up with our favorite baker. I have no idea if she's right about Miss Flo eyeing the satyr, but I know he's just surly enough to scare off a gorgon when he wants to. She'll have a tough road to hoe if she's trying to get in his good graces—it took us *months* to get him to warm up to us when we first started working for him.

She ignores as we head for Philly's room, opening the door to see him sitting up and fussing with a nurse over the color of grass in his salad. I smile broadly when he bleats a bit and huffs when the swan shifter refuses to fluff his pillows again, especially near his ass. Some things *never* change, even when you almost die, I suppose.

"My two favorite girls are here!"

Feray looks so happy, I'm worried she'll burst when she rushes over to hug him carefully. "You look so good today!"

He does, but I'm always suspicious of too many good things happening at once. I squint at him carefully, watching as he and my sister chatter. Eventually, they turn their attention back to me and I blink. "What?"

"Wolf-girl here says you two have not one, but *two* mates each right now? Taking your revenge on that dickweed Mage a little far, aren't you?" The satyr grins, winking at me as Fer giggles.

Sucking in a deep breath, I let it out slowly on a long suffering sigh. "My sister is a blabbermouth. We've only been here for two minutes."

"Hey, I'm just sayin' your temperament isn't suited to having people around all the time and now you're living in a veritable frat house. I'd pay to be a fly on the wall there—laughs galore," Philly says with another guffaw. "And you're a peach in the morning."

"They've all learned to avoid her until she gets caffeine or energy drinks in her. You'd think *she* was the feral shifter," Fer says with a smug grin. "Then again, I suppose they could be avoiding her because of the glitter..."

My eyes widen and I rush over, clapping my hand over her mouth. "You hush, pincushion, or I'll share your new kink."

The sound of a throat clearing keeps her from answering and when we look over at the doorway, the very proper Dr. Bennu is standing there. He gives us an embarrassed look and I turn to glare at the two troublemakers. I let go of my sister and back up, holding my hands up in surrender. The doctor comes in and shuts the door, picking up the chart at the end of the bed.

"I see your friends are back," he says to Philly. "I'm glad to see they're here on a good day."

"Yeah, well, you're not skinning me alive anymore, doc, so that helps my sunny disposition."

"Be nice! He's helping you," Feray says as she swats the satyr. "Easton has been so nice to us. He came to get us when you were hurt again. Don't be a dick to him."

Philly arches a brow. "The wolf in you is making you bolder, kid. Your sister's right about that."

She shrugs and walks over to the doctor to see what he's doing. My eyes narrow when I detect the slightest wince as she gets closer. It's probably not the best time, but maybe I can use all these ridiculous powers I'm struggling with to see what's going on with him. I bite my lip, concentrating on letting my magic reach out to sense his aura. I don't want to violate him without permission, just get a sense of what's making him behave oddly.

"Why do you look like you're about to take a dump?" Philly says and my complete shock breaks my concentration entirely.

Both the doctor and my sister look at me in surprise and I whip my head around to glare at our friend. "If you weren't just getting your strength back, I'd kick your ass, goat-man."

"Gross," Feray says with an annoyed look. "Why are men gross all the time?"

Dr. Bennu huffs, tilting his head as he looks at her. "I wouldn't say all the time. You have several mates, yes? I assume they aren't objectionable constantly."

"Oh, they're all gross sometimes, but luckily, they leave us out of it." I grin as I shrug. "*That's* the benefit of my temperament, by the way. No one farts in our direction because I'll kick their asses."

That makes him stiffen even more and I can't help but chuckle. The kind Dr. Bennu is very proper and he's definitely hiding something based on what little I read before Philly distracted me. He seems to get uncomfortable when my sister approaches, so it has to do with her.

Oh, shit. Is he another fucking mate? No way.

I'm about to say something to Feray, but a knock at the door interrupts us. "What the hell? Is this Grand Central Station today?"

When it opens, two of Briarvale's finest are standing in the doorway.

Feray tilts her head, looking at them as she sniffs the air. I arch a brow at her and she pauses before saying, "Tigers."

At least we know it's not likely big cat shifters will show up and try to kill our friend. Tiernan assured me he'd made sure to spread our 'off-limits' status to the other cat groups, including the tiger ambush.

"Good afternoon, officers," I say with the sweetest tone of voice I've *ever* used in front of law enforcement. "How can we help you?"

The taller one has red hair and suspicious eyes, but I suppose that's not a bad thing. He looks at Feray and me for a minute, then nods. "We're here because the doctor finally consented to us interviewing the victim about his second attack."

My sister glares at him, stomping over and putting her hands on her hips. "What good would that do? You haven't figured out who caused the *first* attack as far as we know."

She's not wrong. Go, Fer.

"We're investigating and the crime scene unit has been—"

"Doing absolutely nothing, I'd guess," I interject wryly. *"Dionysian Delights* isn't exactly on the fancy end of town, so as long as the insurance paid, you're not worried about finding the perp. Right?"

"How would you know that for sure?" The second tiger is blond and looks like he's roided out to the max.

"Because that's how your department treated our parents' death and I highly doubt things have gotten better since then." I cross my arms over my chest, feeling the pain and anger from that time rise in me. "This victim, as you called, is who took us in when no one else could be bothered."

Philly leans back in his bed and I see Dr. Bennu watch him carefully. When his skin pales, he turns to the tigers and shakes his head. "Apparently, this isn't a good time still. My patient is still healing and since the girls seem to be right, I can't risk his recovery for a case you're not even actively pursuing."

Fer's eyes flash and she gives the shifters a smile filled with canines. "That means leave, if you missed his point."

Blinking, I mutter to myself, "What the *fuck* did getting your nipples pierced *do* to you?"

Dr. Bennu's eyes widen as his gaze whips to my sister, who is busy backing the cops out of the room despite her pink cheeks. "You did what? Where? Was it safe?"

I give the phoenix a suspicious look. "Uh, at our work. Yes. And duh. Don't be stupid."

"I highly doubt that the bar is clean and sterile. You could be infected!" he blusters as he puts Philly's chart down. "I should check the wounds to make certain they're okay."

"What?" Fer looks over at him and her face turns even redder. "Check them?"

"Oh, I am so out of this," Philly says with a huff. He reaches over and yanks the curtain around his bed until it slides a barrier between him and us, making me snicker.

I should point out to her that she just told me the damned things are fully healed, but I kind of want to see how this plays out.

"Well, yes. I should take a peek and just see that they look like they are okay. I don't trust anyone who does this stuff in a dirty sex club," Dr. Bennu says, looking as though he might turn green.

Glaring at him, I put my hands on my hips. "Hold up, Doogie. One, we clean that bar and I promise, you could eat off the floor in parts of it. Two, there is *nothing* wrong with sex clubs and exploring your limits, nor working at one. Three, you seem to be forgetting she's a shifter and her wounds are probably fully healed."

That earns me a dirty look from Feray, but his attitude got my hackles up. If she wants to play doctor with the doc, that's fine, but I'm not going to let him act like we're trash for living our lives. The doc puts his hands up, looking sheepish as he rubs the back of his neck.

"I'm sorry. That was rude and I shouldn't have said it." He turns to my sister, shrugging uncomfortably. "I only wanted to make sure you were okay."

Philly chooses to yell through the curtain at that moment. "Is anyone going to ask when I can go home and leave this hellhole?"

"Hellhole?" Dr. Bennu echoes.

I grin a little. "Anywhere not his place is a hellhole. But he's right, we should be asking that. I don't know how much longer you can hold the bill payers to keep him here."

He picks up the chart again and sighs. "Technically, he can leave in two weeks. But he'll need help with quite a lot of things when he first gets out and lots of check ups to make sure all the grafts and such are doing okay."

Fer chews on her nail as she looks at the closed curtain and back to the doctor. "We'll have to find a doctor who can come to our side of town. Bringing him here all the time will be difficult with our work and schedules."

"How about this? If you find someone to keep an eye on him for a while, I'll drop by once every three weeks until I'm satisfied he's on the right track."

Mmmhmm. I bet he's just doing this out of the goodness of his heart, not because he wants to see Feray.

"You would? That would be amazing!" Fer gushes at him, stars in her eyes and I have to cover my laugh with my hand.

Looks like Torben and the gang need to prepare for player three to enter the game.

54

DIAVAL

THE SILENCE IN THE HALLS OF THE BANK IS FAR LOUDER THAN I CAN stand at the moment. My concentration is shot and I am unable to recover. Multiple sheets are open on my monitors filled with thousands of numbers that I need to analyze. Yet, I can't bring myself to remain focused on the task at hand.

Tapping my pen on the desk, I try to convince myself I cannot waste anymore time because there's still work to be done. The newest addition to my horde sits on the corner of my desk within reach at all times. The simple but thoughtful black mug shook me to the core. Visions of my personal siren call to me, from the blue-gray of her eyes to the soft scent of geranium that vexes me. She just knows what kind of drink will soothe the frayed edges of my sanity. On the rare occasion that she touches me, flashes of what my dragon desires of her play like a movie in my mind.

Before I realize it, I've packed up my belongings and closed down my private office. *I never run on autopilot; what is happening to me?*

"Sir?" My teller Jada, a flighty peacock shifter, is dancing from foot to foot.

"What do you need?" I snap.

I'm crabbier than usual, but she's preventing me from going where I want to be.

Clearing her throat, her eyes dart around the room then back to me. "If you are done for the day, I can leave the remaining messages on your desk for you, or I can text them to you for review later." She smiles at me, her expression hopeful; I'm certain she wants me to choose the latter option.

Her anxiety kicks my predator drive into high gear and the thought of roast peacock sounds better by the minute. "Leave the messages in the usual bin. I do not wish to be disturbed for the rest of the day." Turning, I shut my office door and lock it before leaving the bank.

Much to my dismay, I'm breaking from my usual pattern to leave work three hours earlier than usual. I am of two minds that forced me to do so. The first *needs* to see the wolf and will not be sated until I do; the other thinks she is of short years unless I give her a scale or barter a feather from the phoenix. Walking down the marble steps, the crisp evening air greets me. The feel of it almost spurs me to shift and take off into the night sky. Clouds rolling over my scales is one of my favorite sensations I've experienced in my long life.

It's as if thousands of silken beads embrace every single scale on your body.

I become so lost in the memory of my last flight that I don't realize where my reminiscing has led me.

Frowning, I find myself standing before the door to the place I swore I would avoid today. This is the home of the siren herself: *Cocktails and Screams.* The owner of the bar is an ancient vampire and my oldest friend; Dezi is bound to torment the hell out of me if he figures out my weakness. Tiamat willing, he will still be sleeping in his secret lair, not ready to wake up for several hours.

I hesitate, staring at the metal door resisting the urge to knock and gain entry. Staring at the door for several beats I finally decide to bite the bullet and knock.

Thunk... Thunk... Thunk..

The deep metallic thump of my knuckles rapping on the door echoes in the alley. Beady eyes belonging to an annoying fox look at me when the slide opens. On principle, I want to roast him for the trouble he causes Feray. The little rat bastard half-asses his job and the sisters have to clean up after him. Without a word, he shuts the peep hole and flings the door open. I barely acknowledge the vulpine shifter as I head to the bar; he's of no consequence and I am not in the mood.

Reaching into my vest pocket, I pull out my silver watch, noting the time in disappointment. There are two more hours before she arrives. Huffing a puff of smoke, I sit in my usual spot and allow Mo to serve me. I don't trust this little bastard to mix my drink, so I accept a bourbon neat. He's very lucky Dezi has had a 'no eating the staff' rule in place for the last hundred years. Chuckling to myself, I reminisce about the good old days when Dezi would lose his temper and drain a fired employee before feeding the corpse to hellhounds.

"Diaval?" Dezi comes down the hallway straightening his vest as he steps behind the bar. He pulls a fresh blood bag out of his inner suit pocket and cuts the tube open to pour it into a pilsner glass. Once empty, he mixes top shelf vodka into it until it's what he deigns the 'perfect consistency.' Arching a brow, he leans back against the oak bartop thinking he has the upperhand. "You realize the girls aren't due for another two hours?"

"I wanted a bourbon; it's been a day." I feel my bone plates shifting, trying to realign under my skin. Fighting the urge to torch the smug, overgrown leech is growing harder by the second. My dragon slithers to the surface for a moment before subsiding. I slam back the last of my drink and glare at him. "You're up rather early. Waiting for a certain witch to arrive?"

"My bedroom routine is no business of yours, dragon." The vampire arches a single brow, centuries of restraint keeping his face unreadable. "I have more pressing issues to address than my erstwhile staff members."

Narrowing my eyes, I recognize that there is a chasm between what he is saying versus what is true. He's as in denial about awaiting the witch's arrival as I am about wanting to hear my siren's song. Catching the annoying fox's attention, he zips behind the bar and refills my bourbon on the rocks. "I'm sure you do. It must be quite pressing to be awake two hours before you normally rise."

I'm interested to see what else the stubborn vamp is willing to divulge.

"Dealing with those who do business during the day requires shifts in my schedule at times," he says with a shrug. "As much as I'd prefer to use only vendors from the Night District, I am forced to occasionally associate with diurnal creatures, especially since Feray demands unique ingredients for her special cocktails."

A deep rumble emanates from me as I resist the urge to echo my dragon's demand for an apology. It may be factual, but my dragon is defensive of his inamorata. Using her as an excuse for his true intentions is unacceptable. Smoke escapes my lips as my temper simmers beneath the surface. I stare at my old friend as my loyalty is tested. I've known Dezi for well over a millennium, but my dragon wants to defend my intended despite my insistence that I shouldn't claim her. "I highly doubt the wolf demands anything."

The vampire smirks, leaning against the backboard of the bar and crossing his arms over his chest. "Having a problem, Diaval? You seem… distressed."

"Deflection is as good as admitting I'm right, old friend. My problem is with you denying what's happening, though it's as plain as the nose on your face." Sipping the new drink, I attempt to quell my beast. Hopefully, once his siren arrives, her presence will settle him enough that I can move on with my evening. The slow curl of my lips always irritates him and this is no exception, so I know I hit the nail on the head. "You watch the witch as though she is a walking blood bag—ripe and ready for the taking."

The real question is, was it a direct hit or did I sink the battleship?

"Ah, but I am not the one who has smoke coming out of the nose that is most decidedly where it does not belong." Dezi's eyes glitter with amusement as he adds, "And you watch the wolf like a juicy lamb. You're not fooling anyone with your grumpy barfly act."

Staring at the bourbon as I tilt the glass in my hand, I watch the amber fluid coat the glass. "We are way too old for this." Shaking my head, I take a long sip of my drink before looking back at Dezi with a chuckle. "I have mugs older than the two of them."

"It is quite odd that these two would blow into our lives out of nowhere and turn very comfortable existences upside down. Even Louie has adjusted to their presence with more flexibility than he's had since the Renaissance. Their ability to worm their way into the hearts of so many men despite that old fool's decree is almost laughable." He taps his fingers on his forearm and cracks a rare smile. "I enjoy seeing the crooked leaders of our town dancing about like marionettes, though. My sources tell me the Council is up in arms."

When Dezi mentions the Council, the grip on my glass tightens to the point of stress fractures appearing near my fingertips. The tinkling of the glass starting to break makes me sit it down. Huffing, more smoke rolls out my nostrils as I think about it. "The Head Mage is a farce; they have controlled the bloodlines in this town for centuries. Selectively breeding and farming for the best possible magical or political matches. If I wasn't the only one of my flight here, I would have laid waste to them eons ago and enjoyed watching them melt in my acid breath."

Flaring my eyes open dramatically, my dragon's eyes blaze to life. He wants vengeance for what was done to his inamorata. One day, he might get it, but today is not that day and it frustrates him.

"There is change in the winds, friend. That, I am sure of. The whispers tell me I have a traitor in my midst and though I would prefer to root the coward out and place them on the rack until I have answers, I am being patient." He glances around, then continues. "The girls and their mates are looking into a dangerous subject so I do not wish to draw more attention our way. Perhaps you might get one of the library dragons to assist them with more... secret resources?"

Darting my eyes around the room, I glance at those I would suspect to be possible betrayers. "Given the hearing capabilities of those we share space with, that will make for an interesting situation." I ponder Dezi's request about some of the lesser dragons that work in the library. It would require more than a simple email or even a written missive to convince them to allow non-dragons into their most coveted documents.

Reaching into my inner jacket pocket, I pull out a single doubloon. Shifting my finger so my talon is extended, I drag it over the face of the coin. I place the coin on the bartop and slide it to Dezi. The weight this coin carries is more than what is obvious. "Give this to the wolf to present. My mark upon it will open doors locked to the lesser beings without question. Discretion is of utmost importance and this mark ensures their safety and privacy. Otherwise, they know they will have to answer to me." I pick up my bourbon and sip it without elaborating.

"I assume this offers more than simple access to ancient texts." Dezi gives me a knowing look as he takes the coin and slips it into the pocket of his vest. "If that is the case, I will have to likewise offer a shield to the witch to ensure those who might seek to harm them a similar warning."

Shit, we've both given a lot away. My mark on a coin is similar to a pre-mating present; it marks my intentions and extends my protection. I assume whatever 'shield' he will offer carries a similar weight and intention for vampires and other creatures of the night. "What else do you propose we do? They have all these 'mates' fluttering around, yet, none carry the firepower or wisdom we do."

His laugh is rife with mirth. "Youth is easily distracted. I'm more amused by what I can only imagine will be expressions of absolute terror on the faces of the Council leaders when the girls are seen with tokens from ancients. I might even deign to transform for the first time in centuries so I can witness it first hand. It's not often we get to see that sort of comic relief."

An answering chuckle escapes my lips as I shake my head. It's been three hundred years since I heard of Dezi transforming. I missed the event, but from what I heard, it was a sight to behold."It would be worth it for the laughs alone. If we could record it to watch it over and over again, I'd enjoy it greatly." Tapping my chin, I glance around the bar. "Don't you have cameras in this place?"

"Given that the leaders of the shifters, vampires, mythical creatures, demons, Fae and magic users seem to be terrified of two girls younger than my favorite scotch, I believe our involvement will have them all frothing at the mouth. That should give their baby mates enough time to help them develop their powers so they can continue on their little quest." He looks pleased with himself and I know it's because one of his gifts is visualizing the board as if he's playing in several dimensions. Dezi loves to tell anyone who listens that he played 'Go' with Mao himself and thrashed the despot.

Whatever he has planned is likely to unravel exactly as he expects.

The fox comes and takes it to refill, but it shatters in his hand before he can get to the sink. Dezi shakes his head, setting the bourbon bottle in front of me with a new glass. I pour a fresh glass and ponder what else we can do.

Swirling my drink I stare at the cube making its way around the glass. Lifting my gaze, I know he can see that I am itching to shift and blacken the sky with my wyrm dragon. "We should still keep close tabs on them and make sure unseen forces don't throw a wrench in their plans. As for their quest, we should carefully extract information about where in the planning stages they are. Perhaps our memories or contacts could make the trip safer or more productive."

"That is a salient point. I lived in many places before I settled on this continent and…" He stops short when the door behind us opens and the click of heels on the floor of the entryway echoes in the empty room. Lifting a finger to his lips, the vampire waits, watching as the sound of women chattering gets closer until they enter the main bar.

"What are you two weirdos doing sitting in the dark and drinking? You don't even have music on." The witch gives us a smug look as she crosses the floor in a trail of floral scent and sparkles that seem to float around her like toxic gas.

Feray stops dead in her tracks and her eyes lock on my glass. "Who was the genius that gave Diaval straight bourbon?"

Mo takes off like someone set his ass on fire.

My siren scoots behind the bar while Dezi tries to tell her he was responsible. She rolls her eyes and shoos Dezi from behind the bar. "Naughty elder. Scoot. This is my area." With that, she gets to work mixing my favorite smoked cherry wood bourbon manhattan. To soothe his rankled ego, she makes a twist on a Bloody Mary for the vampire.

"Thank you." My words are softer than I intended. Dezi makes a motion with his hand as if to say 'to be continued' and I get the feeling there will be more secret discussions in the future.

The witch rolls her eyes at us, then at her sister. "Ooh, look, I'm a broody vampire and dragon. I require special drinks and sit alone at the bar because I'm a grumpy old fart." She snorts and waves at Feray. "Come on, sis. We've got to stow our shit before it's time to work. If we stay here, we might grow emo bangs and have to listen to MCR."

I watch my friend's eyes flash crimson and for a moment, I think he's going to lose his shit. Instead, he simply smiles evilly. "Yes, run along, children. I'm sure you have many, many, many glasses to clean before the end of the night. You should get started before the crowd arrives."

"You get off on pissing the witch off," I mutter under my breath.

Shaking my head, I watch her clench her fists at his remark before the wolf drags her off towards the dressing rooms. My friend shrugs his shoulders at me before taking his Bloody Mary and heading back towards his office.

Let the games begin...

55

Feray

The warmth of the morning air caresses my skin as we walk towards the shops. Snuggling in close, I hug Khal to me."I'm shocked you're up so early."

"We needed to get house shopping done, so it makes sense for me to be here." He smiles before he kisses my temple. "It wasn't hard to flip my sleep schedule to be here with you. You know how much the control freaks hate when we do the shopping."

My sister cringes when I bring things home for the house. She doesn't realize the guys fight over who is giving me their credit card when I'm sent to get more decorations or housewares. Mind racing, I think about the aneurysm Fi is going to have at the amount of packages we have loaded in Khal's car. Fi will either spread an atom bomb sized craft herpes explosion or flowers everywhere when she loses her temper. "Clean up is going to be a bitch if my sister has the mother of all hissy fits about this stuff."

He freezes mid-step and looks at me. His smile falls and his brows knit together. He shivers slightly over the thought of the impending glitter bomb of doom. "Shit. We should give the others a heads up before we get home so one of the guys will distract her while we sneak the goods into the house."

"On it." Reaching into my sweatshirt pouch, I send a quick text to Tiernan. Several anxious seconds pass as we step into the next store.

The familiar *'meow meow'* of his text tone rings and Khal bursts out laughing. "He's gonna kill you for that one." He grabs the shopping cart and directs us down the dinnerware aisle as I pout.

"He picked it out! Tor picked out a roaring bear for his." Scrolling through my contacts, I pull up Torben's name and play the sound.

Shaking his head, he leans over and reaches for my phone. I barely elude him as he asks, "What's mine?"

"You're going to laugh—promise you won't laugh." I hold my phone close to my chest, prepared to guard it with my life to spare myself embarrassment.

He stops walking and slides his hands under my arms. Lifting me up, he sits me on a display to get me at eye level. "Show me, Precious. I promise I won't laugh."

Leaning forward, he presses his lips softly against mine. The touch sends a jolt through my system and makes my heart pound in my chest. My eyes close as the sensations pulse through my body. I want nothing more than to claim this man by sinking my teeth into his flesh. My wolf wants to taste his blood and make him ours forever. Unfortunately, for safety reasons, we need to find out if his bite will kill me first.

When I feel him pull away, I open my eyes with my wolf prowling near the surface. Interestingly enough, his basilisk is staring at me, yellow-green eyes dulled by his nictitating membrane. Drawing in a deep breath, I rein my wolf in and muster the courage to play his ringtone. It's not an animal sound like some of the others; his tone is a song called 'Believer' by Imagine Dragons.

"The words fit—every single one."

Khal doesn't care about the looks we are getting as he stares at me. Occasionally, he turns and sneers at the other shoppers and staff when they approach. When they realize who he is, they stay away from us. He cues the song up on his phone, watching the lyrics at the same time. When it gets to the section where the singer mentions blood, his eyes bore into me. He watches me for several beats as the song finishes then hugs me tightly. "We'll figure this out," he whispers, his lips brushing my the shell of my ear as he speaks.

I'm not as articulate as my sister, nor am I good at being forward when I want something. It was a huge step for me to share the song I pinned to my feelings for him. My struggles, my pain, and my belief that he will be as vital as blood to me wasn't easy to disclose.

Khal lifts up a box that holds a butcher block prep table I looked at before we started talking. When he puts it on the flatbed cart and then sits me on top of it, I look at him in puzzlement. All he does is smile. "Let me take care of you. I want to cherish you the way you deserve."

I can only nod wordlessly. *How can I object to that?*

Torben has his bossy over protective bear thing going on and now Khal has the soft handed, adore the hell out of me approach. I can't help but laugh to myself. Fi and I went from rejected orphans to coveted mates in a little over four months.

"You know I can walk, right?" He shakes his head and pushes the cart forward. I motion to the place setting aisle with a smile. The edge of the plate set I like is painted black with the phases of the moon circled around them.

"I do." He smiles as he grabs two boxes of the set I picked out. "I'm glad you're not looking at the tags anymore." Khal teases me, knowing full well this store has nothing marked anyway.

I looked.

Spinning on the box, I turn to face him. I feel like a little girl whose parents put them in the cart because they won't behave. Crossing my arms under my chest, I lift up slightly to make my breasts bubble up almost to the point of popping out of my top. "There *are* no tags, Khal. I concede defeat; you finally found a way to get me to shop without worrying about the budget."

Khal is fixated on my breasts and not my words and I grin

Now's the time to broach the subject of our siblings. I raise his chin—now that I have him boob-matized he should be easier to get answers out of. "Is your brother being a dick or is he into my sister?" He mutters some unintelligible things until I poke him in the ribs. "Eyes up."

He motions to my breasts and huffs, clearly frustrated. "You did the boob thing! You know I love them. Well, them and your butt." Running a hand down his face, he breathes in deeply before refocusing. "Khol is so obsessed with your sister that he blocked all his normal hook-ups from contacting him."

The family bad boy is behaving—interesting.

"As much as Fi complains about his ego, I think she actually loves that part of him, especially when they're fighting. She's so used to losing her shit and people bending to her will. I think that's when she loses interest—the minute they bend, they go."

I motion to the cutlery on the right side of the aisle. Khal directs the cart closer, picks up a rainbow set, and shows it to me. "They really aren't good at hiding that they are interested in each other, are they?"

Examining the colors, I add it to my pile. "They definitely aren't. Maybe we should set them up on a date. We can act like we want them along with us at one of the new clubs. If we push the safety in numbers thing, it'd be hard to say no to."

Tilting my head, I watch his brows knit as he ponders what I'm saying. The last aisle is loaded with table cloths, matching napkins, and napkin holders. We discuss our favorite colors and pick ones that everyone will like so no one feels left out. "Khol would be down to go to one of the new clubs. I'm pretty sure your sister would, too."

I scroll through a list of brand new clubs on my phone and show it to him.

"*The Devil's Kiss* looks like something that would distract Khol—the fact it's co-owned by one of our kind would make him feel more at ease and let his guard down." Khal supplies.

"Fi has been curious about your culture and so have I, to be honest. She'll go for it without a doubt." Smiling, I rest my hand on top of his. "According to the dress code, we need to be in semi-formal attire. I'll send you Fi's sizes so your brother can shop for her."

Arching a brow, he starts to laugh. "Are you sure that's safe?"

"Not in the least bit, which is why it will be fun." Opening my shopping app, I send Khal Fi's wishlist. Her profile has all her sizes, preferred colors, and cuts. "This should make his shopping easier. Score!" I fist pump, excited this plan may work out.

"You are cute as a button when you get excited." He kisses the tip of my nose and laughs. "The big bad wolf has an adorable side."

"There's nothing big or bad about me. My bite will kill a certain population, that's all." Shrugging my shoulders, I change the subject. "Can we get lunch? I'm hungry. We can devise our plan over some nice spicy food."

Chuckling, Khal turns our filled cart towards the registers. There's a man standing off to the side I haven't seen before. *I wonder who this is?*

"Zaze," he waves the dark skinned man over. "This is my future mate, Feray. Precious, this is Zaze. He's the head of... security for the family business." Khal's pause tells me he's uncomfortable discussing his real role, so I assume it's more violent than he's letting me on.

"Pleasure to meet you." I dip my head, not sure what's proper to do for his culture.

Zaze stares at Khal until he dips his head at him. "The pleasure is all mine, miss."

He lowers his head to me as Khal picks me up. Zaze takes our goods through checkout as Khal leads us away.

I wait till Khal has us out of the store before I dare question him. "He's not security, is he?"

Khal shakes his head no as he looks around. "Not normally. Today he is because we're outside of the Night District."

He steers us to a quaint cafe across from the park. We take a table outside and he opens the sunshade as the waitress arrives.

"Ah." I don't bother pressing him for more information. Khal is so afraid of what I might think because of his family. Khol let it slip several times what they do, so I'm not in the dark.

My new mate snuggles in beside me, putting the menu between us to pick. Once we make our selection, he waves for the waitress and gives her our order. Suddenly, I notice he's not as relaxed as he was earlier. Taking his hand in mine, I reassure him I'm there for whatever is bothering him. "Is something bothering you?"

"Honestly, I'm worried about two things. First, what happens when we exchange bites? I don't want to kill you accidently. I'm venomous; even the slightest nick of my fang can poison you. But Khol is looking into what we can do—for purely selfish reasons, I'm sure." He laughs and waggles his eyebrows, hinting it's because his brother wants to bite my sister.

"At least he's being cautious?" I grin and tilt my head. "I bet I know what the second reason thing is and it doesn't bother me. I work in a BDSM club and you don't judge me for that, so why would I judge you?." Resting my head on his shoulder, I pull up the club website again. "We need to figure out what we are going to use as a selling point."

"True." He squints and tilts his head. "It has a floor set up like *Cocktails & Screams*. Maybe we can say you want to check out what drinks they're serving?" he suggests as our meals are delivered. We each ordered different types of carnita subs. He cuts the subs in half and swaps them so we can try both of the sandwiches.

"Look at the uniforms! Definitely higher end. You know Fi would love to get on Dezi's ass over quality and presentation." I pick up the sub and take a big bite. The spicy flavor bursts on my tongue and I can't help the little happy sounds I'm making while I eat. "You definitely need to try the half I gave you; it's phenomenal."

Khal nods and waves his sub at me. "This one has a very good flavor. I wonder if your boss will ever open a kitchen with bar foods?"

He switches subs and I wait to see what he thinks of mine. His eyes practically roll back in his head and the moan that escapes makes my core clench. I swear, blue ovaries are no joke. Poor Torben is having the time of his life every time Khal takes me out for the day.

Hell, I'm already planning on hunting my bear later.

Shaking my head, I try to clear the thoughts running through my head. "*The Devil's Kiss* it is, then."

We clink our glasses with matching grins.

After the meal, Khal drives me home. It looks like Tiernan took Fi out for the afternoon, which leaves my bear all alone. Torben comes out, helping bring all the packages from our car into the house. I smile at them both, as they start unpacking.

Best. Mates. Ever.

LATER THAT EVENING, Fi and Tiernan finally arrive home. I burst out laughing when I see that poor Tiernan has tiny specks of glitter all over him. They are so small my sister's human eyes couldn't possibly see them.

"What's so funny, Fer?" Tiernan comes in for a hug.

Backing up, I hold my hands out in front of me. "Craft-herpes!"

Torben almost chokes on his water, but Khal is right there hitting him on the back trying to help him.

Fi zaps me until I yelp, so I run to hide behind the twins. "No! I don't want glitter pox!"

"Fer, I'm going to zap your wolf bald!" Fiadh growls.

The glitter and flowers have been my favorite joke since she got back from the Faerie and started spouting them.

Laughing, I come up behind Khol and hold a pepperoni stick from the counter to his temple like a gun. "Don't move or the wiseass gets pepperoni-ed!"

Khol is trying not to laugh; I can tell. Just when I think I'm safe, Fi manages to lob a wad of fuchsia glitter at me. Ducking quickly, I use her arrogant basilisk as a shield before I throw the pepperoni at her. She ducks and I grab a handful of cheese cubes to throw. "You'll never take me alive, sissy!!"

Torben picks me up and throws me over his shoulder, muttering something about being delirious from too much dick. He places his lips against my ear, softly threatening to withhold that dick until I learn to behave. With a quick smack on my ass, my cock hoarding mate sits me on the counter and gives me a pointed look.

"Ha!" Fi says triumphantly.

At least, until Tiernan whispers something in her ear and she stops her celebration.

When Torben lets me down off the counter, I assess the damage. Khol is standing in shock, his face half-covered with fuchsia glitter like Two-Face. Khal is trying not to laugh as he offers his brother a washcloth. There's pepperoni and cheese all over the floor.

Stepping away from the guys, I stick my tongue out at them and drag my sister to the living room. "We need to get 'double trouble' out there to go out with us."

I hope the direct approach works best.

"Where would we have Thing One and Two take us?" Fi takes a bite out of the pepperoni stick, pretending not to look interested.

Shrugging my shoulders, I take my phone out and start scrolling. "There are a couple new clubs opening, including one similar to where we work. We could spy on them and see if we can get Dezi to do some upgrades—you know he loves insider information."

My sister loves to have information someone else needs; she calls it 'banking favors.'

"That would be worth something to him, wouldn't it?" She takes my phone and flips through the website. I know I have her when she starts muttering to herself.

"This could work. Set it up with Khal; he's much easier to deal with than his brother. Tell them it's safer if they go with us."

It kills her to use that, but with the second attack on Philly, it makes more sense to be overprepared than caught unaware.

"I'm so excited! Thank you, Fi!" I squeal and hug my sister before I text Khal a thumbs up.

Operation: Secret Matchmaker is a go.

56

KHOL

THE SCREAMS ECHO OFF THE WALLS OF THE EMPTY POOL AND I SIGH IN irritation. Khal was supposed to be here over an hour ago and though I didn't *need* him to finish our latest assignment from dear old uncle Krystos, a text would have been nice. He probably took longer than expected on the shopping trip with his wolf and forgot all about me.

Oh, well. This is my favorite part anyway.

"Should we stop now, boss?"

I snort as Brick looks at me questioningly. Reptiles are very intelligent, but the lower level initiates in the clutch are not our best and brightest. It takes all of my considerable restraint to refrain from putting a bullet between their eyes sometimes.

Yes, yes. I could do all sorts of nasty things rather than shoot them, but I *prefer not to waste energy on losers.*

"Did I *say* to stop peeling him, Brick?" I tilt my head, my eyes fading yellow as I let the basilisk slip just a hair.

"Uh, no, boss, but you seem.. Uh…" The moron with a buzzcut and face tattoos fumbles for the right words and I roll my eyes.

Luckily, the one we call Spike saves him or we'd be here forever. "Distracted, boss. That's what he means."

Stalking around the captive bleeding out all over the tile of the former swimming pool, I look at my men with contempt. Finding good help is almost impossible when the leader of your gang lets them sample the merchandise as a reward. What little brain cells most of these fools were born with turn to gelatin once they've been working for us for a few months. That's when I have to deal with them because Krystos never gets his scales dirty.

Point of fact, this fucking cockwaffle in the chair.

"What do you think, Agnon? Are you ready to tell us where your people hid the shipment?" I stride up to the half-skinned demon, lips quirking as I take in all the black blood all over the ground. "I could make the pain in your veins go away with one swift slice."

The collector only gurgles a loud moan and my minions laugh like idiots. Obviously, the sound means he's still holding out and if we don't get the location or something to lead us to it, Krystos will be skinning them next. However, these dust suckers never think that far ahead and it makes everything we do that much harder.

I really wish Khal would get his ass here and raise the IQ in the room.

"Start again," I say as I wave dismissively at the five guys surrounding Agnon. "Perhaps bigger strips?"

"You got it, boss," Brick replies cheerfully.

Pulling my phone out, I barely register when the shrieks start again. I scroll through my texts, looking for the heads-up that isn't there with a dissatisfied snarl. It's not that I begrudge my twin time with his mate—I'm overjoyed that we've found them. But I need his calm, composed vibe to balance out my blood lust. I don't have the patience to manage the troops and when he's here, he deals with idiotic questions.

We really are the ying to each other's yang.

Suddenly, the door to the abandoned gym swings open with a loud creak and I see Khal striding in. He jumps into the pool, walking towards me with a sheepish expression. I glare in return, not wanting to show dissension in front of our guys. If they think they can get between us, the little tweakers will start trying to manipulate things. Khal and I learned *that* painful lesson as teens—junkies can *only* be trusted to look for their next fix, no matter how they get it.

Like almost getting both of us killed by our fuckwad uncle with rumors of a coup.

"Has he talked yet? Do we know where the nest is?" Khal arches a brow at me after he takes in the scene before him.

"Nothing but screams and bullshit," I reply as I push the hair off of my face. Khal nods, looking thoughtful.

Demons are a tough nut to crack. Their kind run the casinos, sportsbook, illegal lending, and whores in the Night District. Given there are so many kinds with such varied powers and appearances, it's damn near impossible to identify them unless they tell you or you find their sigil. Because that would betray them, the assholes are *very* good at hiding the sigils with magic and other techniques. They're also allied to specific families like the goddamn human mafia, so they get trained from a young age in academies for the skills they will provide when they graduate.

"He's a collector?" Khal walks around the edges of the blood spatter, studying the demon as Grizz and Brick pull off long pieces of skin.

I shrug and roll my eyes. "That's what uncle believes. No reason for a mid-level demon from the Drakon family to steal a baker's dozen of basilisk eggs from the nest up north. You can't eat or bespell them for displays—which means some royally rich scumbag wants a basilisk clutch for their collection."

My twin shivers and shakes his head. "Traffickers make my skin crawl."

"But you're fine with torture?"

Turning to look at the hulking demon on the chair, I smile in excitement. "Holy fuck, he speaks!"

Khal grins and a low hiss echoes from his chest. "I'm fine with torture. Selling any being for profit—whether it's sex or slavery or whatever—is the lowest you can go."

I dart in to look at the asshole who's been holding out for two hours, making crazy eyes at him before flicking my forked tongue out. "And you, my friend, are one of those scum sucking fuckwits who do it! Aren't we lucky we have you tied up and ready to receive your punishment?"

I can taste his fear on the air and I know it won't be too much longer before he gives in.

Backing up when he winces, I look over at my brother. "What held you up?"

"Shopping. But also..." he pauses and then shrugs as he continues, "...I was setting up a double date."

My eyes widen and I turn to the boys. "Try the barbed wire bats now. Maybe that will help loosen his tongue more. If not, I'll just pull it out with pliers." Going back to Khal, I nod. "Tell me more about this date."

He chuckles and shakes his head. "You and Fi are forbidden from watching *The Walking Dead* for a month."

"Shhh! Sassy likes bloody shit and the bats are fun. Why the hell not?" I shrug and bump his shoulder. "Quit holding out. What about this date thing?"

"Precious thought it would be fun for her and her sister to go out to one of the new clubs. When I questioned how safe that would be, she said maybe we should go with them so we could make sure they were safe." His smile is innocent, but something in his tone makes me wonder about the timing of this little trip.

However, I'll get to go out with Sassy without the others in an environment that demands little clothing and lots of touching.

Who fucking cares if its some kind of set-up?

I grin wickedly as I think about it and Khal clears his throat. "I like the idea. Have they decided where to go?"

My twin nods, his eyes dancing. "This new club called *The Devil's Kiss*. Fi thinks they can spy on it to get the vampire to make upgrades to *Cocktails*." He pauses and leans in to whisper, "Feray sent me her shopping app profile so you can pick something out and send it for Fiadh to wear. The info online said it was semi-formal."

"That place is owned by the Salazar Cubi."

I whirl around, turning to look at the hamburger face of Agnon at his pathetic croak. "The club is inside one of the demon family casinos?"

"I don't know if he can nod, boss. There's a spine showing back here."

As always, Brick is simple, but on point. "Fine. Groan if the club is inside the *Get Lucky*. Stay quiet if it's not."

The mass of blood and flesh groans.

"Shit. I didn't notice that when Feray showed me the website. Maybe she was only on the club's page?" Khal shakes his head and pinches the bridge of his nose. "We shouldn't go there. It's much more dangerous than I thought."

I scratch my chin and squint as I think. "It's also the perfect place to meet the Cadmean Vixen for that info we requested. A demon casino is the definition of a neutral ground for shifters."

"Don't trust…"

A low chuckle echoes out of my twin as he turns to the horned dipshit in the chair. "You really are trying, aren't you? Of course we don't trust her. If you'd tell my brother who has the eggs, this could end very quickly."

His tail flips up, the barbed end almost catching Spike in the gut. He hisses, partially shifting as he advances on the demon. I don't blame him; the barb could have left a very nasty wound he would have had for weeks. That doesn't mean he gets to kill this douche before he gives up more info, though.

"Spike!" My fangs descend as I rumble at him in warning. "Do not kill him. We don't have what is needed yet."

"All you seem to be getting is dating advice," Grizz mutters.

I'd chastise him, but Khal already has him pinned against the side of the pool, baring his fangs. My twin appears calm and collected most of the time—and he is—but when you make him angry, he reacts as violently as all of our kind when threatened. And everything about him is just as deadly, including his toxin.

"Anyone else want to comment?" I ask as I look between Brick, Onk, and Dre. "Feel like adding anything at all?"

They shake their heads, holding the bats in their hands as they stay perfectly still.

Good. Khal and I stay alive as long as we keep everyone lower than my uncle's main lieutenants terrified of us.

"Let him go, bro. We need to get this shit over with and get him what he wants so we can plan this little outing with the girls. I'd rather be doing that than dicking around with a demon."

Khal spins around and gapes at me, but he lets Spike go back to the group of minions. I shrug at him, eyes dancing as I walk over to the weapons cabinet and pick out another tool to use as persuasion.

"What? Booze, skin, sex, darkness, and possible fights? The only thing better would be getting her to help me do this shit. Now, *that* would be fucking *hot*," I say dreamily as I twirl the knife. "I just know she'd take to it like a duck to water."

"You are *not* conscripting Precious' sister into the family business, Khol!"

"I don't think I'd have to draft her at all." I walk over to the demon and hold the ballistic knife up, waving it at him as I look at my twin. "Something tells me she'd enjoy cutting off a finger or two."

To illustrate my point, I lean down and cut off two of Agnon's fingers, grinning as he wails.

"See? Super fun. You should give it a try. Or this idiot could tell me where to find the eggs and I'll shoot him. Then we can shop online and have Chinese."

Khal blinks. "Ooh. Chinese sounds really good."

"I've been craving Mongolian Beef for *days*," I sigh, then turn to Onk. "Make sure we don't forget to order as we leave so it's ready to be picked up on the way home."

"You got it, boss. I'll handle it."

Looking down at Agnon, I click my tongue. "See how well these guys obey? *That* is what you should do. Give me what I want so you can be put out of your misery and I can have fucking eggrolls!"

"You should visit the art exhibit… at *Get Lucky.*"

Frowning, I look over at Khal. *Is that a date suggestion or is he actually giving me a clue?* He shrugs and since we don't know why my uncle is looking for the eggs, I decide to hedge my bets. Walking over, I backhand the demon, not even wincing at the squishing sound the battered flesh on his face makes.

"Fine. You don't want to talk? I've got better things to do."

Before Agnon can reply, I use the knife to slit his throat, watching the black blood spurt all over. Turning to the guys, I point my knife at them. "Cut off his head, burn the body, and throw the ashes in the river. Then get the cleaners in here. We don't need his blood to infect anyone."

I drop the knife and jerk my head at Khal, who follows me.

Today has been an exceptionally good day so far.

57

Fiadh

I can't decide if I'm angry about the clothes that showed up this afternoon or not.

Fer, of course, was vibrating with excitement when the two sets of boxes and bags arrived. While I hate feeling like we're charity cases, the pack animal in her is basking in being taken care of. It makes her glow with happiness and that's why I've ignored all the expensive shit that keeps 'magically' appearing all over the house as the construction continues. This is the kind of home and life she's always dreamed of and I can't bring myself to ruin it for her by putting my foot down.

Even if it makes my skin itch with worry that something will go wrong, it will all disappear, and I'll have to pick up our pieces when it crashes down.

The difficulty I struggle with when it comes to trust isn't a state secret or anything, so I'm sure they're all waiting for me to explode in a cloud of flaming glitter or something. I catch the guys eyeing me with caution every once in a while and it makes me chuckle internally. My temper is pretty unpredictable and I know why they're all waiting for the other shoe to drop, but I care far more about Feray's happiness than I do lofty ideals.

So I unwrapped the shit Khol sent for me and let my sister treat me like a Barbie—*again*. At least this time, my outfit is short, tight, black, and made of leather. He even sent an asskicking pair of thigh-high combat boots in purple patent leather, so I won't feel like my fucking feet are going to fall off at the end of the night. Khol enjoys pissing me off, but not with clothing, unlike Revelin. Tucking that fact away, I stride into the living room to meet my sister.

"You look badass!" she says as she twirls around in the forest green mini-dress Khal sent. She has her hair braided and simple flats on, but she looks lovely. Her brow furrows for a moment. "It said semi-formal. You look good, but do you think we'll get in?"

I snort. "The note with it said he didn't give a fuck and he dared them to deny us entry. I'm going with no one will tell the psycho 'no' when he makes a scary face."

Feray blinks at me for a moment then shrugs. "Okay. Sounds reasonable."

Oh, how the tides have turned.

"Is Torben dropping us off? I hate to put him out, but I know the twins had some sort of thing earlier and they said they had to meet us there." I purposely didn't ask what they were busy doing that required them to go home and clean up before meeting us. Something tells me the old adage of 'never witness nothin,' you live longer' applies to a great deal of what they do.

"Yep! He's outside waiting. Let's go get our groove on, sis."

Grinning at her excitement, I tuck my phone in the pocket of my leather shorts and follow her out to the car.

This should be an interesting evening.

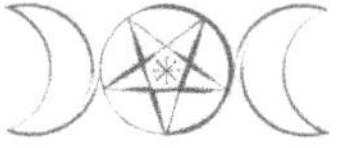

WHEN TORBEN PULLS UP to the sparkling lights of the *Get Lucky* casino, I shake my head at the opulence. It's designed to look like an oasis of sin— right down the huge water feature in front with palm trees, spurting fountains, and sand in a large playground for the guests in front. I can feel the magic in the air protecting the sphere in a superheated bubble that allows people to run around in every-thing from bathing suits to their birthday suits as they romp in the desert motif. I'm not surprised there's no dress code despite its public facing location; this place is owned by the Salazar Cubi family—incubi and succubi aren't known for giving a shit about conventions.

"Holy shit," Fer whispers and Torben lets out a deep chuckle.

Her comfort with nudity has gotten better since she found out she's a shifter, but my sister is still more conservative than me at heart.

I open the door, winking at her as I drop to the ground from the big ass truck. "The pickle parade is a bit much, I'll grant you that. Hope-fully, the club is a bit more circumspect with their rules."

She nods, ducking her head as her cheeks flush. Fer brushes against Torben's face with her own and follows me out of the vehicle, clearly keeping her eyes averted from the orgiastic scenery out front. "One can only hope."

Laughing, I grab her hand and tug her along until we reach the front door. The doormen nod quietly and I tilt my head as I try to identify their species while we wait for our IDs to be scanned before we enter the building.

"Hellhounds," my sister whispers in my ear. "The shifter version, so I guess they get enormous."

"Think they have three heads?" I ask as I watch the one with the scanner motion us forward.

She giggles and presents her ID first, then waits for me. "Maybe. We haven't seen them naked."

My eyes widen as we head inside and follow the signs to the club.. "Not *there*, Fer! Sheesh! That's... not normal."

Shrugging, she gives me a knowing look. "Lots of shifters have... extra accessories when they're mating. I bet you know *all* about that being mated to a big cat."

She's got me there; Tiernan's barb surprised the shit out of me the first time, but I'm used to it now.

"Hashtag truth," I mutter with a rueful grin. "And you haven't even asked what the snake boys are packing, I bet."

I think she would have smacked me if we hadn't run right into the men in question. Her gaze narrows as she shakes her head at me and I have to cough to cover a laugh. She's clearly done *something* with Khal—more than once, if my count is correct, but they haven't gone all the way. I'd give her hell about it since she jumped the bear pretty quickly, but it occurs to me that I haven't given Khol a chance to so much as smack my ass.

Do I want more? Is he really part of my... boyfriends?

"Precious, you look lovely," Khal says as he leans in to kiss Feray gently.

I arch a brow at his brother, who shrugs and says, "We both know you look fucking hot; I picked your outfit."

Gee, thanks, asshole.

That earns Khol a hard elbow from his brother, though I think I wasn't supposed to see it.

Shaking my head, I look at the motley group and sigh, realizing this is going to be a long night. "Come on, guys. Let's see what kind of debauchery the Cubi have for us here."

I HAVE *to hand it to the sex demons— they know how to run their club just on the edge of propriety.*

We've been here two hours and after Fer insisted we tour the whole place first, it became abundantly clear that this was geared towards people who want to play at BDSM, not be part of the community. As long as the half-naked dudes and chicks walking around like hall monitors keep them from doing unsafe shit, I don't mind it. I'd rather them come here than Dezi's because the people there are hardcore. Safe, but definitely not playing at the lifestyle.

The old grump will be pleased he can send people to a more appropriate place when they get booted for bad behavior. Score.

"Sadly, not our scene, Sassy," a low voice rumbles next to my ear.

I chuckle as I look down from the balcony, noting the people playfully cracking crops on their hands and tugging on leashes. "I noticed. Where are Fer and Khal?"

He shrugs, giving me a wicked smirk. "Probably hiding from the succubi who was following them around. She hasn't taken their very polite and totally not stringent enough brush-offs seriously."

"She'd better watch it; Feray is doing better but her control when it comes to what's hers isn't great yet. They'll get us all tossed out if she shifts." The thought worries me and I look around the lower floor anxiously, wondering if I need to track her down.

"Relax. Khal can handle it. You need to take the night off."

Frowning at him, I arch a brow. "From what?"

"Being the big sister." When I scoff, he shakes his head. "I know you're not older, but this is the same shit I had to learn with my twin. It's in my blood to be the scary protector, especially how we grew up, but I also had to learn to let him earn his own respect. You have to do the same."

Well, who asked you, wise ass?

"I think you're more fun when you look pretty and taunt me. Being all smart and shit is weird." I smirk at him as I turn away from the railing. That's when I notice how goddamn close he is to me in this dark corner of the VIP dance area and how loudly the bass is thrumming in the background—or at least, my *body* notices it.

His lips curve up and he presses closer, pushing me into the railing as his arms cage me in. "I contain multitudes, Sassy, just as you do. No one is only one thing or we'd be boring as fuck."

"Duh," I snark as I work to get my breathing under control. Being this close to Khol is making everything on me tingle and if he doesn't back up, we're going to be covered in fucking rave glitter or daisies. "I wasn't tying you down, just saying it's unusual."

"I could be down with the tying thing. If you make me believe it." He leans in and bites my lower lip, scraping his blunt teeth over the soft skin as he pulls back. "I have the feeling you'd enjoy both ends in the right circumstances."

Danger, danger, danger...

Before I can answer, a darkness swells inside of me and my magic roars to life. It's not flowers and sparkles, though—no, this is rough and hungry. My chest fills with the need to make him give chase and I don't know why. I look into his eyes as I prepare to duck and run, smirking playfully. "I enjoy lots of things under the right conditions, Khol. You'll have to catch me to find out."

That said, I bend and slip out of his grasp, tossing a wink over my shoulder before I take off into the writhing crowd on the dance floor. It's dark, hot, and there are supes everywhere moving to the loud industrial, but I use the magic humming inside of me to guide me through the bodies. It tells me he's hunting me, darting around as he sniffs out my trail.

I blink as something occurs to me: snakes smell with their long, forked tongues.

Woohoo!

I squeeze through a group of enormous aquatic shifters dancing with what look to be willowy equines, ignoring the grumbles and nickering as I continue to evade Khol. Fer told me that predatory shifters enjoy shit like this and I guess my magic decided I should give it a try. *Maybe Tiernan would like to chase me? He's a preda—*

The wind goes completely out of me as I slam into a wall in the back corner near the DJ stage. My cheek is pressed against the smooth marble and a *very* warm, *very* hard body is pinning me in place. I'm about to turn my head to figure out how to break the hold when I feel fangs slide down the skin at the nape of my neck, nicking it ever so slightly. Shivering, I close my eyes and let my frame go lax as the tingles of magic engulf me.

Teeth have always *been my weakness and my hussy magic isn't helping.*

"Be still, Sassy pants. We don't want anyone getting a free show." Khol's voice has a darker tone to it and the words with 's' in them are coming out as hisses.

I can't help myself, though. It's just who I am. "Sounds like someone is having a control issue. Did chasing me wear the widdle basilisk out? Maybe I need to find someone with more... stamina."

Note: when I die, it will likely be because of shit like this and someone should write 'shot her mouth off until it got her killed' on my tombstone.

"SSSSShhhhhhh…" He hisses before I feel a fang pierce the top of my earlobe then scratch behind my ear to the juncture of my neck. "Behave."

"Never," I pant softly as my ass pushes back against him. He can't play this game for too long or the scent of blood will draw unwanted attention.

I can't say I'd turn down a good fight when we're done.

One of Khol's hands lifts from the wall, plunging into the tight shorts without preamble. It doesn't matter, though, because I'm so fucking drenched that I'm lucky it's not running down my fishnet covered thighs. I don't know how he knew exactly what I'd enjoy without asking, but I buck against his fingers as he shoves them inside me. His thumb finds my clit and flicks lightly, making me squeeze until he adds another finger, fucking me roughly as his body smashes mine.

A tickling sensation near my jaw makes me gasp and I realize he's *tasting me on the air*—holy fuck, that's hot. I turn my head and look at Khol, taking in his serpentine features and the long, forked tongue as it darts out. I lick up his jaw as my hips rock on his fingers, feeling the pressure building in me as he works my pussy like he owns it. My teeth scrape over his jawbone and that gets me a louder hiss and harder thrusts.

When the orgasm hits me, I lean back against his shoulder, biting my lower lip until it bleeds so I don't scream. The sound of a zipper makes me wiggle against him, eager to be filled even if it is dangerous to be this distracted in public. Sweat sheens my face and I watch him lick his hand clean of my juices first then a bead of sweat from my neck. My hips grind against him, waiting him to free his cock and fuck me hard enough to rattle the drywall.

He's so arrogant that it has to be a monster, right?

My eyes pop open when I feel probing at my entrance and my jaw drops. Turning my head to look at Khol like I'm Linda Blair in the *Exorcist*, I watch the bright red color flood his skin despite the shifting scales and slitted eyes. "A little warning would have been nice, asshole!"

"Ssstop?" he asks, pausing as the pulsing of my sex and his rubbing together threaten to divert any ounce of blood from my brain box.

"N-no…" Drawing in a deep breath, I look at him with the dark magic flowing through me lighting up my gaze. "Don't stop. Fuck me—right here and now, Khol."

His fangs glisten as he leans in to whisper in my ear roughly, "What Ssssassssy wantssss, Sssssasssssy getsss."

And that's how I found out basilisks have two fucking cocks shaped like tiny goddamned snakes.

I barely contain the scream when his damn snakes move inside of me, twisting and writhing and slithering over every nerve and spot like they have homing beacons. His hips pull back and push in rhythmically, his hand dropping to rub over my clit as the wriggling appendages make my eyes cross inside. I don't know what the after-life looks like, but I'm pretty sure if I don't come soon, I'm going to die on the spot and find out.

"Faster. More. Make me come, Khol." My raspy plea is because my nipples are hard as jewels, my clit is throbbing, and I'm struggling not to moan so loud they give me a fucking job at this place. I've never understood people's fascination with hentai until Khol shoved these fuckers into me and they're playing my g-spot like a concert pianist handles a Steinway.

His fingers pinch and the shudders start as my orgasm crashes into me like Godzilla raging through Tokyo. Digging my nails into the wall, I hold on as my magic erupts from me, covering the both of us in a weird, black, sparkly dome of energy. I can't focus enough to marvel at it, though, because that's when I feel the piercing of two sets of fangs close to where Tiernan's barb usually hits.

OhmyfuckingGoddessthedamnthingsbitme!

That triggers another wave of pleasure and I whip my head to the side, glaring at the basilisk with aching eyes. "You'd better bite me and it sure as fuck better mean what I think it does, you motherfucker."

His smirk is wicked despite the snake face. "Asss you wissssh, dark Goddessss."

My eyes close and I smile in triumph when his fangs strike and sink deep. I grab his wrist, yanking it to my mouth and bites down hard as I hold on tightly.

Fucking perfect, is the last thing I think as my brain shuts off.

A loud screech brings me back to reality and I squint, seeing Feray and Khal staring at us like we just pissed on the carpet.

"Fiadh Amaranth Morgenstern!"

"Khol Liam Bedia!"

Uh-oh. Mom and Dad are mad.

Khol sighs against my neck, pulling all his snake-y parts away.

My body protests and I almost make a whining sound as he works to repair the clothing situation as I melt into the wall. I'm not sure I can move yet and man, do I feel fucking fantastic. When he finally spins me around and puts his arms around my waist to hold me up as we face them, I smile like a drunken leprechaun.

I can't see that, of course, but I can feel how goofy I look for sure.

"Did you…? Khol, you knew we didn't know…"

"In the middle of the club? Fi, have you lost your…"

Squinting at our siblings, I raise my hand. "I am too sated for incomplete sentences. I vote for the twins and their twins take us home!"

Feray gives me a puzzled look. "And their twins?"

Grinning like a Cheshire cat, I look up at Khol. "Tee hee. She didn't know, either. Fi, one; Fer zero."

"Yes, Sassy, you definitely win tonight." He smacks my butt and hauls me over his shoulder.

This time, I don't even complain—see? I can learn.

58

FERAY

My paws dig into the soft earth as I go for my morning run through the woods. Most of Torben's sleuth lives close to where we are and on occasion, I run into his family members out for a stroll. It took them a while to get used to seeing my wolf in their neck of the woods and some of the elders call me a 'forest ghost' since my fur is white and cream in places.

"Feray!"

I hear Torben bellow my name, so I stop and howl to answer him. As I hold the tone, birds break free from the canopy, taking flight in different directions. Between my howl and the birds fleeing, he knows exactly where I am now. Taking off at a run, I leap over the small stream and head back to the house as fast as my paws can carry me.

It doesn't take long to return to the house and squeeze between the shrubs in the backyard. Torben is waiting for me with a bathrobe and a tray of pastries sitting on the picnic table. Shifting back, I slip into his robe then dive into his arms, snuggling close.

"Mom sent some of her bacon-walnut pastries because she knows you love them so much." He nuzzles my cheek then kisses my lips, sipping from the bottom one.

"Your mom is the best. I have to get her to teach me how to make these."

Torben sits down then pulls me onto his lap and offers me a pastry, a huffed out laugh escaping his lips.

"She loves you so much. You've even made the sows in the sleuth step up their game. The guys go home and talk about what you do for the family and well... How you anticipate what the guys need is beyond what their mates do." He kisses my cheek and holds me tightly, nuzzling his mate mark and sending tingles straight to my core. "It took a she-wolf to show the bears what family is. I'm proud as all hell to call you mine."

"I'm sorry if I caused problems; I was just doing what felt right." I turn in his lap to look into his amber eyes.

"You've actually fixed a few den issues for the guys." He smiles and slides the box closer to me. "We've got a big day ahead of us. I got an appointment with the shifter elders. I want to help you find your people." Several emotions flicker over my mate's face, but the main one is his joy. He's happy he's able to do this for me.

"Today? This is the second greatest day ever!" I hug him tightly and he chuckles, kissing me on the cheek several times.

"Eat up, take your shower, and grab your water. We'll head out as soon as you're ready." He pushes another pastry to me and dips his head in the direction of it.

Taking my time, I eat two more of the pastries and then finish my coffee. Torben helps me off his lap then we head into the house. I pass Fi with her gaggle of men and wave at them. My mate stops following me to catch the rest of the family up on the plans for today. I hear Fi asking if it's safe, but Tiernan works to calm her down. I laugh to myself, knowing how impossible a task that is.

Once in my room, I grab my soaps and an outfit for our appointment. I select an off-the-shoulder, champagne colored dress and comfortable flats. I take my fastest shower to date, rushing through getting ready. Passing through the bedroom, I kiss Khal on the cheek and take his GPS tag from the dresser. Leaving him a quick note in its place, I duck out of the room to find Torben leaning against the counter.

He offers me his arm and walks us out to his truck. Opening the door for me, he places his hands on my ribcage and places me on my seat. Torben pops open the back door then closes it, and when he gets in, he offers me a water bottle. Raising his eyebrows, he pulls on the strap until I buckle the seatbelt. "Buckle up, Little Wolf."

Shaking my head, I open the water and take a good healthy drink. "It's not a long drive from here, so it won't take too long."

We drive deeper into the forest, going to a part I haven't visited before. You'd think we were in a horror movie with some of the old trees. The skeletal remains of something long dead on the side of the road accentuates my point."This looks spooky."

Torben glances at the skeleton and then refocuses on the road ahead. "Not all predators are civilized. Sometimes, the mateless choose to give themselves over to their animal so they don't feel the pain of loneliness."

There's a shift in his mood and I study the slight change in his expression. Reaching out I rest my hand on his forearm while he drives. The muscles twitch under my fingertips. "Did you think about giving yourself over to your bear?"

He makes a turn, heading down the left fork in the road. Forcing a smile, he glances over at me. "I'm still considered young for a shifter. Last summer, most of my friends miraculously found their mates. I felt like the odd man out, especially when two of my younger brothers found their mates before me."

AHEAD OF US, a mansion pulled out of a fairytale story stands alone on a hill surrounded by weeping willows. We fall into silence as I watch him school his features. For someone so expressive, the closed off expression reeks of sadness.

"That had to be tough. I watched Fi date all these handsome men and no one ever seemed interested in me. If you can't tell, I'm not as outgoing as my sister. I never felt like I fit in and I guess I know why now." Raising my water bottle, I take another sip as Torben pulls up and parks out front of the building.

"I'll tell you a secret." His soft tone tells me it's important. The amber of his bear blazes to life in his eyes. "The day I came to do the estimate, I swore after I took the insurance information I was going to give the information to my secretary then leave. My plan was to leave a note for my family dividing my assets between my siblings, shift to my bear, and never to return."

I grip his arm tighter, as I stare into his eyes. That day feels as if it was yesterday—what I know now as the 'mate tingle' was my wolf telling me he was mine. "Meeting me stopped you?"

"Best day of my life." He smiles and kisses the tip of my nose, breaking the heavy bubble we're in. Before I can say anything else, he gets out of the truck and comes over to get me. Leaning forward, I dive into his arms. He spins us for a moment, then kisses me passionately, before taking my hand to lead me up the stairs. "Let's go find your people."

Torben knocks twice and a man answers the door. By scent, I know he's an owl shifter, but I'm not sure which kind. The deep bass of his voice pushes a small amount of his alpha influence out as he says, "I have an appointment with the archivist that specializes in genealogy."

"Name?"

Interesting—the doorman doesn't even attempt to introduce himself. Can you say rude?

"Torben Barrett. This is my mate, Feray Morgenstern." I smile, loving when Torben calls me his mate. It never gets old.

The doorman hums to himself, finally allowing us to enter the building. Once inside, I feel like we've stepped back in time. The interior of the estate smells of old books, mold, and something I'm not fond of. Torben's boots echo against the wood floors as we follow the owl down the hallway. An ornate marble archway is on the right side where the doorman stops.

"Start here. If you're found worthy, you will be introduced to the head historian." He turns and hurries back down the hallway to his post by the front door.

"He was pleasant," I say as I roll my eyes. Every instinct in me wanted to stare him down and make him curl into a ball.

Torben pats me on my ass, shaking his head. "We need to tolerate the rudeness for now so we can find answers."

The way he says that has the hairs on the back of my neck standing on end. Eventually, I look away and we walk into the room. The leonine historian behind the table gawks at me. "Did you just stare down a Kodiak?"

"I stared down my mate." Stepping closer, I see stacks of family trees on the table.

"A she-wolf shouldn't be able to do that. Who are your parents?" He looks from me to Torben then back to me again.

"I was raised by the Morgensterns—a witch couple from Briarvale." Biting my bottom lip, I remember only finding a record of Fiadh's birth in their archives when we searched. I assume that means one of two things: I was adopted or my mother had an affair with a wolf.

Torben pulls me back against him, murmuring next to my ear despite knowing the archivist can hear him. "Are you sure they aren't your parents?"

"There was no record of my birth in Briarvale. Either Mom had an affair or I'm adopted." I sigh, looking down at the piles as sadness fills me.

The archivist appears before, his voice soft now. "I've been rude. Forgive me. I'm Josiah." A soft, understanding look crosses the man's features and I feel a little more defeated. "For the record, unless the wolf who sired you was your mother's mate, she would have birthed a witch. It's part of shifter magic to protect the young. A human or a witch wouldn't understand what to do with a shifter child, especially when they first start shifting."

"So more than likely, I'm adopted," I say softly. My heart breaks all over again. A low whine escapes my lips, making Torben crush me to his chest.

"Adopted or not, you are loved. Fiadh loves you and that hasn't changed since your first shift, has it?" Torben raises my chin so I look at him while he talks.

"You're right. Fi will never leave me and I'll never leave her—blood or not, she's my sister." Somehow, the big guy got my sadness to switch to anger. I turn to face Josiah, determined to figure out what my history is. "Can you help me find my birth pack?"

He taps his chin several times before smiling. "Not my area of expertise, but I'll take you to Roman. He's the Alpha for the Blackmore pack and he's in charge of the records for the wolf packs."

With a renewed sense of hope, we follow behind him down a flight of stairs to a different room.His voice has the slight grit of his beast's roar as he speaks. "Roman, I have a packless she-wolf who needs help locating her people."

"I hear you. I might be old, but I'm not bloody deaf!" Roman yells as he emerges from the back room.

You know those Jedi movies with the old guy that guides the next generation?

"Come forward pup." That's what I feel like we stepped into. Roman looks like Father Time—thick beard down to his stomach, missing an eye, and just as surly as Fi is without caffeine. I have to admit I'm kind of concerned. He leans against the table and I glance up at Torben. He motions for me to go forward. There's a growl in the wolf's voice and a wave of something that washes over me that makes my wolf angry. "Don't look at the bear; I told you to come forward."

Tearing my eyes away from Torben, I growl and bare my canines at the man. I know I shouldn't, but my wolf refuses to be told what to do by this male. "No."

As soon as the word leaves my lips, I watch Roman's knees buckle for a moment. He steps forward cautiously. "Impossible. I don't sense her being dominant. What color is your wolf?"

"White with cream colored markings." I glance at Torben to confirm and he nods stiffly. His bear isn't thrilled with me being tested. Looking at the Alpha, he nods.

"It's been a very long time since a wolf was born with that coloring. You need to see the resident expert. He can trace blood lines all the way back to the first beings of your family tree."

Roman moves to the back of his room and presses his hand upon a seal. The sliding of stone on stone catches my attention. We watch as part of the wall moves away and reveals a winding staircase. "At the bottom of the staircase is where you should find the answers you're seeking." Roman extends his hand out to Torben and they shake hands. "If my gut is correct, your mate is more than she seems. Guard her with your life."

The Alpha motions for us to pass and I can't help staring at him. *It's unnerving to have men talk around me as if I'm not here.*

Heading down the winding stone stairs, I feel the temperature drop steadily. The sound of dripping and the musty smell of stagnant water float up to us. Our steps echo louder as we go deeper into the bowels of the building.

"It's rumored this place was built over catacombs. The crypts of the first shifters in the area are down here. It's a seat of power and the archivists use it to keep all of us safe." Torben's voice carries, but it doesn't echo like our footsteps.

Reaching the bottom of the stairs, the glow from the torches guide us to a room set back from the open crypts. The scent of myrrh and frankincense dominate the air; thankfully, it covers the musty odor from the stairwell.

"Hello?" I call out.

"Step into the light child, so I can see you." There's a soft purr to the male voice—yet another feline working here. Cats love their secrets so it makes total sense.

Looking around the room, I find the brightest area and step into the light. "I wish to find my people. I am among the packless, orphaned as far as I know."

It takes a lot to keep the emotions out of my voice. I have no clue if the Morgensterns are related to me at all. The historians are my only shot at finding out where I truly come from. Knowing what Roman told us, unless my father was mated to my mom, I would have been a witch.

A cloaked figure steps out from the shadows. He pushes up his sleeves and lowers his hood. We are in the presence of a real live Sphinx. "I may be able to grant that request. First, you must open my puzzle box and solve my riddle."

"We will do our best," I say confidently. Reaching back, I take Torben's hand, giving it a squeeze.

"Take as much time as you need, but know, nothing is as it seems." His mysterious words echo in the room as he walks out the way he came.

The box in question sits on a pedestal in the center of the room. It's as large as a medium sized tool box. Torben circles the box, looking at it from all angles, nodding to himself. "I don't see any hinges so however it opens it either slides apart or something slides out," he says confidently.

"Nothing is how it seems." I look at the patterns on the outside—each side is different. With Torben being in construction and my penchant for puzzles, we shouldn't have too much difficulty."Each face is a puzzle. Let's start with the side closest to us and go from there." I instruct.

Torben

Feeling the maelstrom of emotions ripping through my mate is infuriating my bear.

He wants to break free of my body and destroy whatever is causing her pain. The relaxed mask she wears hides so much from the outside world; it's almost insane. Her ability to school her features so well angers me because it means there's far more abuse that she hides. It makes sense why Fiadh is quick to anger while Feray is cold and calculating. They are opposites in how they handle things, but out of the two, I'm more frightened of my mate.

We search the puzzle box for a hint on how to decipher its secrets. The low frustrated growl that escapes Feray's lips makes the hairs on the back of my neck stand on end. When her wolf rises to the forefront, her face takes on more wolven qualities. Suddenly, I see recognition flash in her eyes.

"Tor, use your bear's eyes. It has pictures like a jigsaw puzzle."

Feray's excited tone settles my bear and he rises to do her bidding. "I'll be damned! There it is. Good job, Little Wolf."

She preens at my praise and the brightest smile I've seen in a while graces her lips as she tries to make the puzzle work. Tilting her head as she walks around it, I notice she let her tail out and it's swishing side to side as she ponders what to do. "The pieces aren't moving."

On a hunch, I half-shift and use my bear's claw to touch the puzzle. The piece I am trying to move slides with ease. "Use your wolf's claws. This puzzle isn't for man to solve—only a beast."

The minute the words are out of my mouth, I watch her hands shift to white fur with cream accents. An excited giggle escapes her lips as she focuses on the puzzle before her. By the time I finish the side I am working on, she is halfway through her side. She stops her movements before she moves to the final side, looking around.

Something caught her attention.

"Tor, please watch the area. My wolf is uneasy." The glow in her eyes intensifies and a wave of her energy washes over me, so my bear complies immediately.

I've felt Alphas do something similar, but her energy wasn't demanding like an Alpha's command. It was like a nudge, almost like a mom would do with her cub.

Once Fer is sure I'm on guard duty, she returns to the puzzle. When the last piece slides into place, the wooden cover falls away in pieces. There's a second puzzle within—it's an orb with symbols and lines on it. She immediately starts twisting and turning the layers, spinning the orb in her hands.

I knew my mate was intelligent, but this is beyond average intellect. She's solving puzzles I can't even comprehend. My skills are nothing to shake your head at—I can estimate a distance by looking at something and be accurate to within a quarter of an inch. What my mate is doing is next level calculations and spatial reasoning far beyond what I can do.

"How's it going, Little Wolf?" I move to allow her to lean back against me while she works.

"Good. I think I'm almost there. I can hear the pins lining up." She flicks her wolven ears to illustrate her point. A wolf's hearing and eyesight far exceeds my bear's abilities, so what she lacks in strength, she makes up for in cunning and speed.

The spinning of the orb pieces draws the Sphinx out to watch what she's doing. He moves to get a better look at what my mate is accomplishing. "No one has made it this far in a very long time."

With the last twist of the orb, the metal pieces fall away in her hand, leaving a small parchment scroll. Unrolling, Feray finds a riddle inside.

> *To some a source of trust and love,*
> *To others, ball and chain,*
> *For me some go beyond, above,*
> *While others but complain.*
>
> *For I'm a thing you cannot choose,*
> *You're stuck with what you've got,*
> *But I'm a thing that one can lose,*
> *For granted, take me not.*
>
> *The leaves, the branch, the roots, the seed,*
> *The living crimson flow,*
> *As each of them their lives they lead,*
> *Forever shall I grow.*

She reads the riddle as she paces around the pillar. Talking seems to be her way of working through puzzles and problems. She pauses to stare at me for a few moments as her tail thrashes behind her. The more she stares at the parchment, the more I begin to worry about it going up in flames.

"Ball and Chain...," she mutters out loud, continuing to circle the pillar then stopping suddenly. "For humans, a ball and chain is a wife; for us, its mates."

Her brows furrow as she stares at me. I watch a myriad of emotions flicker over her features and her eyes glow from her wolf. Apparently, circling the pillar isn't working anymore, so staring at me is the new thing. "I'm a thing you cannot choose."

Biting her bottom lip until she draws blood, it trickles down her chin and she reaches up to wipe it away. Feray stares at her blood covered fingers, then spins in the direction of Thoth. She holds up her bloody fingers as if they're the answer to the universe. "The answer is family."

Clapping echoes as we turn to face the Sphinx. He moves to stand before us, smiling broadly. "Congratulations! You are the first in several generations to complete that puzzle—in record time, too. Therefore, as head archivist, I offer you one boon. Make your request of me and I shall grant it."

Feray looks up at me and all I can do is nod. She shifts back, leaving her tail out and swishing behind her. *This is the moment she has been waiting for.* I know how much she loves my parents and tries to spend time with them. But the loss of the parents who raised her caused more damage than she lets on. The opportunity to find her birth parents or pack is at her fingertips and she needs to grab it with both hands.

Bowing her head slightly to Thoth, she finally speaks. "I would like to know my true bloodline. Who are my people? Where is my pack?"

Her tone wavers and Thoth nods and dips his head to her. He heads back to his table in the corner. Curled up parchments lie on one side while dozens of jars of herbs like the other side. "Come with me child; we have some work to do. I will need a sample of your blood."

Feray offers her left hand to him. He places a bowl next to it, dropping several herbs in while speaking an incantation. When he's ready, he cuts her palm, allowing her blood to drip into the bowl. Once there's enough, he places a paste on a cloth then wraps it around her hand.

My mate comes over, snuggling into my side. She only does this when she's anxious, so I hold her tightly.

Thoth pours her blood onto the herbs and they ignite immediately. His eyebrows shoot up as he jumps back. His eyes dart to Feray, then back at the herbs. While the fire burns, he unrolls one of the parchments and uses stones to make it lay flat. "That's never happened before."

The fire slowly dies then extinguishes. Taking out a stone rod, he gives the inky black mass a stir before pouring it in the center of the parchment. The fluid pulses several times before spreading out to show three generations back. Slowly, names come into view. The majority of the females are labeled as 'Lunas' or 'pack mothers.'

It's shocking, but at the same time, not really.

The blackened mass stops after the bloodline before the fourth generation that would be her parents is revealed. It puts the name 'Feray,' but a piece of the mass undulates where her surname should be.

Looking at the rest of the family, we see the other parts of the fourth and fifth generation and what town they reside in.

Thoth reaches forward and rests a hand on her shoulder. "It appears you have some relatives living in Blackmore. I would look there for information on who your parents are. I'm sorry I couldn't be of more help. Someone is using very powerful magic to hide your parents." The sphinx's tone is sad and I can tell he's sad for her.

"Thank you for trying." My mate sounds like a lost little girl, her voice choked by emotion as she struggles to keep the tears at bay. As much as she tries, she can't stop the tears in her eyes or the redding of her cheeks. She's making a valiant effort to hide what she's feeling, but her emotional pain throbs through our bond.

The archivist hands her the scroll, looking at me with a grave expression. ~*Protect her at all costs.*~

His voice echoes in my head as his eyes glow and I frown. *That ancient bastard just invaded my mind.*

Feray is so withdrawn I can barely sense her. She's hugging the scroll like we had discovered the *Arc of the Covenant.*

I steer her to the staircase, leading her back to the main floor. Not a single word falls from her lips the entire time. We pass Roman on the way to the front. With a tilt of his head, he motions to the scroll in her hands. I shake my head 'no.'

No answers—only more clues and a deeper mystery, and I know it's killing her that Fiadh's name didn't appear next to hers.

We make it to the truck and I open the door, waiting to see her reaction. She's barely blinking. I pick her up gently, sitting her in the passenger seat, then close the door. As soon as I'm behind the wheel, she places her head on my thigh facing the dashboard. Any other time, I would tell her she's facing the wrong way, but now is not the time to joke. I put the truck in drive and turn on instrumental music for her.

Sending a short text to the group chat, I alert everyone to what happened. As soon as the message is sent, I thread my fingers through her hair, trying to soothe her the best I can. There's no way I can fathom what is going through her head. Her sister isn't her blood sister and her parents names are hidden by magic even the Sphinx can't get through.

We have more questions than answers and I don't like it.

At least we have the name of a town she has distant relatives in… it's a start.

Fiadh

Time has passed so quickly since Beltane. It was like I blinked while all the chaos was going on and suddenly it was summer. Given that we spent most of June dealing with men, a home renovation, and working our butts off at the club, I'm not surprised the days flew by.

Briarvale always has a big festival for the Thunder Moon and since it's so close to a human holiday, the rowdy festivities don't draw the attention of humans. Businesses set up booths and stalls in the large park in the chi-chi part of town where they also hold the Ascension ceremony.

Despite its location, this is a universal shindig, so every district is represented by vendors and demonstrations. The schools even have booths to sign children up for the fall semester and a few universities set up, too. Feray and I used to avoid it like the plague—our lack of standing and money made it hard to enjoy ourselves. Besides, Philly never paid for a stall; he much preferred to accept the overflow of ne'er-do-wells stumbling home from the big party in his hole in the wall.

I can't say I blame him; I'm not fond of being in this open space with all these people, either.

Unfortunately, our enigmatic boss finds participating amusing. He's had Torben's crew building this weird Gothic looking biergarten all week and now we have to work it. Louie is wrangling the stage and performers at the far end, so he's no help at all and to no one's surprise, that fucker Mo called in. That left me and Fer to run this monstrosity alone for the duration of the day and long into the evening because Jaz was already booked for piercing demos with Sal.

"Just my fucking luck," I mutter to myself as I stack our new, unbreakable glassware Dezi commissioned for the event. He swears if it survives this, he'll get more to use during the full moon weeks, and *that* I can get behind.

Feray bounces over in her all black and blood red sexy *kellner* outfit, her eyes dancing with excitement. She does a quick twirl, watching the fluffy short *dirndl* and petticoats as she moves. "This is so much more fun than our normal outfits. Clementine outdid herself."

Letting out a slow, aggravated sigh, I look down at myself. I'm wearing a similar one in black and amethyst, right down to the knee high socks with matching bows. At least he let me wear the kick ass boots Khol bought me in case I have to bust some drunken heads. The likelihood is high given the amount of alcohol, drugs, magical food, and moon shenanigans that will go on today—which is how I won *that* argument. "I *hate* them. I would have preferred barely there leather or vinyl to this shit. I haven't worn this many ruffles and ribbons since I was a little kid."

Her lips purse as she looks at the fat raven braids full of ribbons she helped me achieve. "You still look hot. Like... a Gothic Barbie. Use it."

"I am *not* worried about looking hot. Besides the fact that we're going to be busier than one-armed weavers, I also have plenty of dick hanging around crowding me at this point."

"Speak of the devils..." My sister beams and rushes around the bar to jump into Torben's arms like a goddamn koala bear gripping a tree.

Which... is a fair comparison, I suppose.

Tiernan ambles up with his charge in tow, but I'm surprised to note they don't have an entourage along. He winks at me, his lips curved when he sees me frown in confusion. "Something wrong, Knuckles?"

I look over at Feray dusting kisses all over the bear's face before he finally lets her down and shake my head. "More than being dressed like this and forced to make nice with the rest of the population because my boss is a *sadist*? No."

Dezi appears like I fucking *summoned* him, arching his brow as he casts his gaze between Feray and I. "Excellent. I will have to send Clem a bonus for her speedy and skilled work. You, too, Barrett. I have been complimented many times as I walked the grounds on the design and quality of your work."

Torben smiles easily, dipping his chin in response, and he looks down at my sister. "You look lovely, Little Wolf."

A grumpy knock sounds from the end of the bar nearer to the stock area and I roll my eyes. "Jesus, what are *you* doing here? Are you magnetically attracted to bars belonging to Dezi or what?"

Fer whirls around and smiles brightly despite my cranky question. "Diaval! I didn't expect you'd be here, so I don't have *all* the fancy stuff, but I can make do. Give me a minute."

Throwing up my hands as she babies the cantankerous ancient, I walk out from behind our prison to see Tiernan. He tugs me into his arms, rubbing his face on mine quickly, then spins me over towards the Prince. The royal is wearing matching accessories again, and he rests his forehead on mine for a second, using that weird whisper power to say something wholly inappropriate in my ear. My face turns red and I smack his chest, yanking myself out of his grip to stomp on his toe.

When I look at the others, I find a wolf, a bear, a vampire, and dragon all staring at me with their mouths hanging open. Narrowing my eyes, I let sparks dance across my fingers as I glare at them. "*What? Are we pretending to be landed trout or something?*"

"You…you… they…" Feray sputters as she points at me, then looks at Torben when words fail to exit her mouth in any comprehensible format.

The big guy grins like he just won the lottery as he looks at me.

Hell, he almost looks… proud?

"*What* is everyone's *problem?*" I grind out as I put my hands on my hips. If people don't start talking soon, I'm going to knock some heads.

A pair of arms slide around me as a low hiss travels to my ears. I turn my head and give Khol an angry look until he finally speaks. "You let them touch you in public. It's unusual, Sassy."

That's why they all look so shocked?

Irritation and embarrassment flood me, making flowers pop up around my feet and throw an elbow back at the basilisk. He grunts and I turn, socking him in the gut for being so damned amused. "Stop making a big deal of it. We have shit to do and you jackasses are distracting us."

I stalk away, heading for the bar again as I fume. *Of course, it's likely I look like a pissed off pixie with this ridiculous outfit bouncing around me.*

That thought makes me even madder and I let out a shriek of frustration as I storm behind the curtain to the stock area.

Their laughter follows me, making my temper flame hotter. *Why is everyone so damn focused on my... relationships?* I kick one of the kegs, feeling mollified when the steel toes of my boots make a dent in the side. *I mean, I did mate with those three assholes; of course I let them touch me. How else would they give me orgasms?* Shaking my head, I flop down on a stack of crates and cross my arms over my chest as I think about it.

I suppose it is odd that my dreamy, romantic, marshmallow hearted sister has only mated with *one* of her two intendeds and she's been on board with the whole thing from the start. In contrast, I've been suspicious and resistant from the start, but each time one of my three mates came to me, my magic *insisted* I complete the bond. Between my hussy magic and greedy pussy, I begged all of them to not only fuck me into oblivion, but finish the deed.

Okay, maybe I have been giving mixed signals, but it's not like anyone gave me a fucking handbook.

"Is there a handbook?" I mutter to myself. "There better not be, because I wasn't issued one and I'm going to beat someone's ass if they purposely excluded me from distribution."

No one's here to answer me and I groan as I bury my face in my hands. I was such an organized, controlled person in every aspect of my life—even the bedroom—until this Ascension bullshit happened. Now everything is completely off the rails. Our past is a lie, we don't have to scrimp, there are people everywhere, and I have officially lost my everloving mind by mating with three dudes I've known for a couple of months.

I lift my face from my hands, shaking my head as I chide myself. "Fiadh Morgenstern, you are a hot fucking mess."

Rising from the boxes, I pause when I see a faint glow through the crack in the curtain at the very back of the stall. I squint as I walk closer, stepping quietly and carefully so I don't spook whatever the hell is stalking us. When I whip it open, I'm pretty sure I see a trail of white light that reminds me of Rev's feystag friend. But that can't be—she can't leave the Faerie, right?

It's probably a symptom of my mounting insanity, I think as I turn back. Grabbing a rack of glasses, I stomp towards the front curtain, pushing through it to emerge from my hiding place. I feel eight sets of eyes on me as I stride down to the glassware stacks, dropping my load on it without a word. I know they're all scared to say anything since I was probably glowing like a nuclear reactor when I tore into the back, but I'm not going to make it easier for people to tease me by talking first.

The sound of a throat clearing gets everyone's attention; it ends the standoff as we see the good doctor approaching. He looks at Feray, then me, and then the crowd of silent men with a curious expression. "Is something going on?"

Torben smiles and shakes his head, ever the peacemaker. "Not at all. It's nice to see you again."

I roll my eyes to myself, mumbling about yet another stalker following my sister, but I doubt he hears me. Dezi, however, definitely does and he gives me an amused look before cutting his eyes to Tiernan, Rev, and Khol. Flipping him off as Easton makes conversation about the festival with the others, I head down to where the banker is sitting with *three* fancy drinks in special glasses.

"We should have asked if you were coming so Torben could work you into the bar, considering you're always holding it up wherever we go," I say as I slap a bowl of jerky on the bar next to him. "You're like our own personal gargoyle."

He huffs at the comparison, smoke rings floating around him as he gives me a death stare. "Your employer is one of my oldest friends. I cannot help that you are but a child in comparison to almost everything around you."

"Huh-huh-huh. I'm a crusty rich old dragon who haunts bars and taunts the young waitresses. Look at me, aren't I so cool because I'm old and young people are dumb? Huh-huh-huh," I mock him in a derpy voice as I set up a few more snack bowls to place along the bar top. "Okay, *Renaissance man*. Hope that bourbon is preserving you well enough."

"Fiadh." Dezi's voice distracts me from taunting the dragon as he clearly struggles not to set me on fire.

Sue me; I'm self-destructive when I get pissy.

Turning on my heel, I walk over to my boss, looking up at him with a faux sweet smile. "Sir, yes, sir!"

His eyes widen, turning that bright red at my words, and he clenches his fists at his side. It takes a moment before he speaks and he grits his jaw so hard that I think he's going to crack a fang. "Stop taunting the customers; Diaval will roast you like a chicken."

I arch a brow and shrug. "If you can't take the heat..."

"You absolutely *cannot* take that heat, you stubborn... little... minx!" I blink at him and he growls darkly, fangs flashing as he looks at me. "Your temper is going to get the both of you killed, especially if the whispers of your... quest... are true."

"I have no idea what you're talking about," I reply as I look at my nails. "Don't be a drama queen, Dezi."

He mutters something in a language I've never heard before, pinching the bridge of his nose. When he opens his eyes, I can feel the truth in his words and the pull of his gaze trying to get me to listen. "I want you to wear this for protection. It will ward off many things you're not even aware of because my old friend is correct—

you are very young and have not been taught the truth of the world."

Bristling, I shake my head. "I don't need charity or pity and I *especially* don't need condescension."

"La Magra, help me," he mumbles as he fishes something out of his pocket and holds it up. Tilting my head, I study the thin leather collar with a new version of my dog tag hanging from it. It has my safe word stamped on it and a new, ruby blood drop gemstone dangling on the opposite side of the sapphire.

"Uh, I don't know about you, but I'm not putting on a collar because some rando tells me to. That's stupid *and* wrong, buddy." Crossing my arms over my chest, I give him a look that says I think he's finally taken leave of his senses.

"It doesn't mean *that*," he says in a tight voice. "This is an upgraded version of your current tag and when beings see it, they will know you are under my protection. I've been alive long enough to have a great deal of sway here and in the many places I've traveled or lived in a thousand plus years."

"Uh-huh. Why a collar?"

"Because it would be expected," he shrugs and pushes it into my hand. "Don't be stubborn, Fiadh. Put it on and listen to someone for once. I have made this offer less than five times in my long life, but it is important."

A commotion on the other side of the garten gets my attention and I sigh, taking the token and shoving it in my pocket with my brass knuckles.. "Fine. I'll think about it."

"Excellent."

Hopping the counter, I leave the brooding vamp to his own devices as I walk over to find Khol and Khal standing in front of Feray arguing. Apparently, while I was having my tantrum and interview with the vampire, they were off playing carnival games. Khal is holding a giant pink hippo with big eyes and my sister is making goo-goo eyes at him. My idiot, however, approaches with a big black bat with bloody fangs, wiggling it at me.

Must. Not. Tell. Him. It's. Cute.

"You think winning these silly things will impress me, hmm?"

Feray is squealing at Khal and Khol arches a brow at me. "Maybe?"

"His is bigger." I smirk as he looks like I've offended his ancestors.

He drops the bat on the table, taking off towards the games area with a whoop. That gets Khal moving—he kisses Fer's cheek and tears off after his brother. I'm not sure if they have some weird twin thing that lets them know what the other is thinking, but it sure as hell *looks* like he realizes Khol is headed off to top his prize.

"Do you think they realize they could have just *bought* all this shit? They definitely have the money," Tiernan says as he dances the bat over the table at Revelin.

The Fae chuckles and uses his magic to make it fly around over the table then towards the garbage can. Frowning, I walk over and snatch it out of the air, giving him a dirty look.

"And *that* is why they don't give a fuck," Torben says as he points at Fer cuddling the hippo and to my absolute humiliation, my hands curled around the bat as I hold it.

That gets another round of laughter and I stomp away, going behind the bar and praying for real customers to get their asses here before I kill everyone in the vicinity.

"Is this…always… like this?" Easton says hesitantly. He's sitting with Torben at the table on the left and the bear laughs heartily.

"No, sometimes it's worse. But that's family, doc."

Family?

Panic sets in as I clutch the bat, feeling anxiety crash over me. Outside of Feray and Philly, I haven't had family since our parents died and those words are making this very, very real. I bite my lip, looking around at the guys and my sister, all chatting and looking so at ease and comfortable. That isn't even remotely how I feel now, because fear is flooding my veins.

I reach into my pocket, pulling the damn necklace Dezi gave me out. Grumbling under my breath, I sit the stuffed animal down and put his gift on reluctantly.

I have too many people to protect to take chances now.

Just as I click the clasp closed, the twins come running back, damn near tripping over one another to get to us first. Khal has a wolf the size of fucking Great Dane in his arms and Khol is carrying something behind his back, grinning triumphantly as he approaches.

"Oh, Khal, it's beautiful!" Feray squeals as she shoves the hippo at Torben. As soon as he gets close, he hands her the wolf that's almost as big as she is, leaning in to whisper in her ear. "Of course we can go out again!"

The basilisk beams and the men at Feray's table look at one another knowingly.

I don't blame them—she's definitely mating with that dude on that date.

I walk over to where Tiernan and Rev seem to be arguing with Khol, arching a brow at them all. "What is going on over here?"

That's when I see the tiny bat sitting in the middle of the table— except this one is real.

"Torben's going to murder you," Tiernan groans low as I walk over and pick up the tiny little thing and cradle it in my hands.

Remembering the meme I saw online, I whisper in a scary voice, "I am the darkness. But first, I want cuddles."

Revelin's eyes widen and he rubs his hand over his face. "That does it. Now we've got a fucking pet bat in a house full of predators, you fanged moron."

Khol grins and shrugs, clearly not giving a single fuck as he walks up to me. "But I win, right?"

"You win," I agree as I push up and place a kiss on his jaw. "Torben is definitely going to kill you, though."

"Um, I hate to interrupt, but does anyone know who this ghost deer belongs to?"

Easton's words make everyone turn to look at the feystag standing in front of Dezi's biergarten with a haughty look. Revelin shrugs at me, clearly not knowing how it got here, either.

~You must do a full moon ritual to scry for the missing object. My horde is too large and I have too many hiding places. Visualize it and find me when you know where it is located.~

I nod and it disappears into thin air, leaving me holding a bat and the bag in its wake.

"So there's this creature from the Faerie stalking me apparently…"

FERAY

The warm summer sun beats down on the front porch as I wait for Khal to arrive.

It feels like the forest is alive with the sounds of all different manners of animals and birds singing their happy songs. He told me to be hungry since a hungry wolf hunts best. After the club incident with Fi and Khol, we know it's safe to mate, especially if I bite him first. The drive to seal the bond with this sweet man is at the forefront of my mind. Torben has been reaping the benefits of my frustration when I've been in close quarters with Khal for too long.

I hear the crunching of rocks at the bottom end of the driveway and my heart rate accelerates. I've been anticipating this hunt since the first time he mentioned it weeks ago. Double checking my small duffel, I make sure I packed spare clothing in case I shift prematurely.

Khal's sleek black sports car pulls up in front of the house as Torben steps out onto the porch.

"Be safe and have fun." He kisses my cheek softly then pats me on my ass, sending me toward Khal. Khal closes the distance between them and they shake hands. "Keep an eye on her, she's light on her feet and swift as the wind."

"Thanks for the advice." He returns the firm handshake then motions to the trail leading to the big field. "We're heading to the switchgrass field to shift and hunt."

"I'll call the others and tell them to stay clear." Torben says with a smirk.

I swear I see something pass between them; if they are having a quiet conversation without me, I'm going to kick someone in the shin.

"Can we go now? My wolf feels like she's going to claw her way out of me any moment." A soft whine escapes my lips and Torben's demeanor changes. He's not a fan of when I whine—as an overprotective mate he gets angry when he thinks I'm hurt or upset.

"Yes, get going and enjoy your time together." He waves at us as Khal throws my bag over his shoulder and takes my hand to lead me to the path.

"Thank you for taking me hunting today." Bumping his shoulder, I can't help but smile excited over getting to hunt with him. "I've hunted with Tiernan when Torben wasn't available, but this feels different." As I gaze at the trail ahead, I feel him watching me.

"It's always different with a mate. Other than my brother, I have never hunted with anyone else." Khal's tone betrays his nervousness —it has a slight waver, so I squeeze his hand.

"I haven't been hunting very long, especially with everything that's happened." My voice softens when I realize that actually being hunted has sucked the fun out of running through the woods.

Khal stops short and comes to stand before me. "I will turn an entire army to stone to protect you. Once you've had my bite, my stone gaze and venom will no longer be an issue for you." Looking into his eyes, I can see the nictating membrane adding a haze to the color of his eyes.

"I know you will." Standing on my tip toes, I press my lips to his before we start walking again.

Along the trail, Khal distracts me by explaining the different medicinal qualities of the plants and flowers we find. Fi taught me about some of these plants, but Khal has alternate knowledge of their uses. The trail opens up at the end to a huge field of golden switchgrass.

When the wind shifts, I smell dozens of rabbits in the field. Torben rarely takes me here without his sleuth because there's too much field and bears don't move quickly. He's always worried a shifter faster than he is will cross the field and hurt me. I pause, looking around hesitantly for danger. I feel like a doe stepping out during hunting season; death can lurk around any corner and there's no place to hide.

"You're safe, Precious. I won't let anything get you." Khal walks me out to a small patch of green grass in the field. "You already know how my eyes and the lenses work, so that's helpful."

He looks around briefly before turning to face me again. "Think of my shift as if a dragon and an anaconda had a love child. I have teeth and heavily armored scales. Unlike your shift, I have six eyes instead of two." Khal is so calm as he explains his beast to me though it sounds like a nightmare made into flesh.

"Is there anything I should or shouldn't do?" If his prey drive is like mine, running isn't a smart idea.

"Keep your eyes closed until I tap you with my tail. I need time to get my membranes over my eyes. The things that would trigger your wolf to attack are the same for me. Whatever you do, don't show fear. I am aware of everything, but like your wolf, sometimes instinct overrides reason." He smiles as he starts to unbutton his shirt and tosses it over my duffel bag.

"Okay, easy enough." Khal pulls his shirt over his head, exposing his toned body. He's lean, but defined with enough muscle to give him those sexy lines that disappear into his jeans. I watch as he kicks his shoes off and peels off his socks. He hesitates at the button of his jeans before he pulls them down.

Why did he hesitate...

"Oh my." He literally has two dicks—one is a normal human dick and the other is a snake that's moving around like it has a mind of its own. "Wow. I knew different species had unusual appendages, but this is amazing." I bend down to get a better look at them curiously.

"You are definitely taking this better than I thought you would." He watches me in amazement..

A giggle escapes my lips. "Are they supposed to scare me? Wolves have knots that you get stuck together, you know. It's quite painful, I hear. I'm not an omega, so I'm not built for an alpha's knot." Shrugging, I keep staring at his members thinking this is going to be a hell of a ride.

"Eyes up here, Precious. I'm going to shift; close your eyes until I tap you with my tail," Khal instructs.

Slamming my eyes shut, I put my hands over them to be extra safe. The snout of his basilisk nudges my arm and I lower my hands. Long jagged teeth fill his mouth at odd intervals. The only sense of order I find is they are all curved backwards to keep his prey from escaping. There are heavy bone plates on his forehead adorned in sharp spikes that point backwards like a porcupine. The membrane on the spikes tells me they might have venom in them, too.

Three yellow-green serpentine eyes are located under a boney eyeridge— the smallest is closest to his nose and the largest is in the normal position. There's a fin on the side of his head that might be to funnel sound to his ear hole.

I circle him, estimating he's about thirty to forty feet long. "I'm going to shift now, Khal."

Moving away from his basilisk, I change to my white and cream colored wolf. Remembering his warning, I approach his animal with my head held high. His tongue flickers over my fur and it tickles. My wolf sniffs him, memorizing his scent before he takes off, slithering ahead of me. I trot alongside him until I scent a deer off to the left.

Bumping his body, I motion with my head before taking off after the deer. I chase the herd back towards Khal. Next thing I know, his basilisk rises up from the grass and strikes, snatching the deer and swallowing it whole. Seeing that he's been fed, I hunt down a rabbit before we turn and head back to where we stripped earlier.

The moment of truth is upon us.

I shift back, waiting patiently for Khal to join me. Watching him shift back is utterly amazing. *How does such a huge beast fit into his human frame? I guess it's the miracle of shifter magic.* My shift doesn't outweigh my human form by much, so it makes sense how she fits into me.

Khal lets a relieved sigh escape his lips as he looks at me with pure hunger in his eyes. He reaches out and takes a hold of my hands and gives them a squeeze. "I was worried that my shift would scare you."

"It's still you, no matter what skin you wear." No sooner are the words out of my mouth, he descends on me, kissing my lips roughly. Reaching up, I wrap my arms around his neck and hold on tight.

I want to climb him like a tree.

"Remember to bite me first," he pants out as he breaks the kiss for a moment. His snake slithers along my lower abdomen until it finds my clit and starts rubbing itself against me.

"Cheater," I moan as I writhe against him, feeling my knees start to buckle.

He smiles against my lips hearing me call him a cheater. "You like it," the wise ass responds as he reaches down and picks me up by my thighs.

Memories of our time together after the piercing flood my mind and I feel my greedy core pulse in anticipation. His snake is the first to find my wet sex, slipping his way in. The width of its head stretches me unexpectedly and I wiggle, tightening my thighs around his waist.

"Someone is wet." His tone holds dark promise and he arches his chest to make his skin rub tease my piercings. It sends jolts of pleasure to my core. He moans into my mouth when I pulse around his snake before he positions himself to slide his human dick deep within me as well.

Arching my back, I push up, shocked at the intrusion. My eyes flair as my wolf rises to the surface.

Khal's eyes are every bit his beast and its serpentine slits stare back at me hungrier than before. "Trussst meee." His hissing voice makes the hairs on the back of my neck stand on end.

My wolf is concerned about the size and power of his basilisk. Fight or flight instincts want me to run—flee to save ourselves. The woman in me knows my sweet Khal would never harm me. "I trust you."

Leaning forward, I allow my words to wash over his lips before I kiss him again. Gently, he guides me down onto his entwined length, seating him deep within me. I relax and adjust to the girth of both members then get the urge to move. As soon as I move, his eyes glow and his grip on my hips changes as he thrusts up into me. I hold on for dear life as he slams me down onto his length. The snake starts to slither, sliding side to side with every thrust. As odd as it feels, he's hitting all of my most sensitive spots. The early flutters of my core make me whine as I feel my canines elongate.

Bite him… my wolf demands.

I make eye contact with Khal and he rolls his head to the side. "Do it, make me yours. Claim me."

Kissing down to his shoulder, I find the meaty muscle extending from his neck. Slowly, I drag my canines over his shoulder and his thrusts become erratic with every drag. My mouth waters thinking of the copper tang of his blood filling my mouth. When I can't take anymore and I feel myself about to tip over the edge into oblivion, I bite him hard, growling as the burst of blood fills my mouth.

Khal thrusts harder just before he sinks his fangs into my shoulder. The sharp sting sets my blood on fire and triggers my orgasm. My greedy core crushes down on his length, milking him for all he's worth. I feel a sharp pain as if his snake bit me as well. A strange euphoria fills me as every touch and slide of his length is magnified. Gripping the back of his neck, I buck harder against him, chasing a second orgasm riding on the back of the first.

Never in my life have I experienced a multiple orgasm, but it seems all I needed was a Basilisk to work his magic. Just as I feel stuck right on the edge, his snake starts to move independently from the other dick. Khal wobbles slightly, lowering us to the ground to lay flat on our backs.

As he lies down, I release his shoulder at the same time he releases mine. Blood runs down my chest as I sit up with my hands flat on his pecs. This is one of my favorite positions, so I grind down hard to tip myself over the edge. I grab his hands and place them on my breasts. Recognition flairs in his eyes and he teases my piercings until I scream his name. The second orgasm hits me like a freight train and Khal takes that as his cue to flip me onto my back and thrust into me hard until I see stars.

If this is what heaven is like, I sure as fuck don't want to come back.

My core spasms around his length until Khal comes. The duel pulsing of his cocks spurs my orgasm on, making it last longer. He stops moving, both of us breathing heavy and drenched in sweat. I am sore, but in the best way possible; I wouldn't change a thing.

Khal gently nuzzles my cheek and kisses my lips gently. He whispers next to my ear, "Mate."

"Mate." I reach up and caress his cheek, staring up into his eyes. I'm not sure how it is humans mating with a shifter but for us, it's so much more than sex. It's an eternal pledge until death and beyond. We would die to protect our mate and children. I look into Khal's eyes and like with Torben, I see a male that would do anything for me.

We doze off for a while and when I awaken, I find myself in the coils of Khal's Basilisk. The sandpaper armored scales of his beast feel as though they are the strongest armor ever made. When he feels me move, he lowers his head so I can look him in the eye.

"Let's go home," I say softly and he uncoils from around me. When my feet hit the ground, he stretches out and grips my bag in his teeth, then uses his tail to push me towards his body.

"You want me to ride on your back?" I'm not sure what he's trying to signal, but that's what I take the pushing of his tail to mean.

Khal nods his gigantic head, then lowers it to the ground. There's a spot behind his head where there are several large flat scales that look like a seat. Using the spikes on the side of his head, I climb onto his back, sitting on the concave scales.

"I'm ready," I say as I grip two of the bare spikes in front of me. He rises up and starts slithering home.

Fi is going to have a fucking cow seeing me riding a basilisk home. I can only imagine what she's going to say.

62

Dezi

Looking around my club, I curl my lip as the cleaning staff move about the rooms, getting everything done before the staff arrive to set up for the night. I've spent the better part of two centuries building this safe haven for my kind and those who enjoy the darker delights, but lately, it isn't enough. We are at capacity most evenings, and sometimes, we even have lines wrapping around the block, even on weekdays. *Cocktails & Screams* is so successful that I've been fending off other ancients and business owners offering to purchase it—something that has never happened before.

It's all because of those two girls turning everything on its head since they arrived at the door.

Scoffing under my breath, I walk through the room, noting all of the improvements the witch has suggested. Re-arranging furniture to make more cozy alcoves and create a more prominent space for the crowd watching shows was a rousing success. The sister suggested we hire larger bouncers on a contract basis only for full moon weeks—the orcs are stupid, but their presence cut down fights by a landslide. Barring that vulpine moron from the private and VIP rooms has increased bookings and tips exponentially.

Though, if I'm honest with myself, I would have fired the weasely little shit a long time ago if his laziness didn't rile the witchling up so nicely.

Apparently, I'm not nearly as mature as my millennia of life would suggest because I can't stop myself from sneering at their ideas when presented, then implementing them in secret later on. Something about the way the witchling's blood sings to me when she's angry has awakened parts of me I thought were long dead. I have to consciously avoid her once I've set things in motion because the hotter her blood boils, the more I ache to sink my fangs into her and claim what I know is mine.

Shaking my head, I stride past the pixies and brownies working on the main bar, intent on pouring myself a calming drink. To my surprise, Louie is behind the bar dressed in... normal clothing? *What sorcery is this?* I frown as I open the blood cooler, selecting a particular vintage to stir into the Eye of the Dragon vodka that only I have access to. I finally give in, looking at the blonde vampire I've employed since the Victorian era. "Might I inquire as to what finally caused you to enter this century?"

He shrugs and I note the faint scent of embarrassment coming from him as his eyes flash red. "The mutt keeps giving me hell about the wardrobe. I thought I might attempt to try something new."

My eyes widen and I tilt my head. "And?"

"I quite enjoy not having sleeves that get dirty while I work. I am considering expanding my repertoire to include more modern pieces."

He hasn't updated his wardrobe since the fucking French Revolution, so that's shocking.

"Interesting," I murmur as I stir the AB+ into the ridiculously expensive alcohol. "This is quite unexpected, old friend."

Louie shrugs and gives me a fangy grin. "No one is immune to their *joie de vivre*[1], *mon amie*—not even you."

I open my mouth to protest, but he walks away, heading for the stairs to the VIP area. He's usually more obedient and less mouthy, but since checking the supplies upstairs is part of his opening routine, I can't complain. Leaning against the sidebar, I sigh as I contemplate the chaos that will accompany the arrival of the sisters, especially during the moon week. Their mates will show up, as well as whatever hangers on they have with them, and that's likely to set the stage for trouble.

However, the witchling's companions are wealthy, and their entourages spend money like it's fashionable.

"They could draw worse crowds, I suppose," I murmur to myself. "At least they haven't brought more uptight magical assholes."

Thinking about Fiadh makes the demon inside of me twitch in irritation. I haven't felt that fucker this keenly since the early twentieth century and I'm not excited about him rearing his head now. My time with Dinah and Fitz ended in absolute disaster; it's something I'm not at all eager to recount or repeat. It took the humans over a decade to stop talking about that blasted baby and I had to flee to my sire's nest in Briarvale to escape the media of the time.

Why they decided to get high and kidnap a famous goddamn kid, I'll never know, but it was sloppy.

Growling under my breath, I remember escaping in the middle of night without my companions to hide under the protection of the sire I wanted nothing to do with. Aurelius was all too pleased to have me under his thumb again—he even orchestrated the human patsy to keep Fitz and Dinah out of the newspapers. They begged me to come back to the east coast with them once the human patsy was executed, but I couldn't do it.

I washed my hands of their nonsense for good when they threatened my existence for a drugged up lark. Those of my kind who survive as long as Aurelius and I do it by *not* making messes like that. Dinah and Fitz were no different than any of the other five companions I'd taken over my long life span—expendable if they threatened my ability to stay concealed and alive. I suppose that's one thing Aurelius managed to teach me that stuck.

Slamming back my martini, I wipe my mouth with a black silk handkerchief as I recall how long it took to get Aurelius to fuck off back to Europe. A few more of his misbehaving children ended up helping my cause and I settled into this mid-sized town of supernaturals determined to spend the rest of my years happily unattached.

Until now.

The call of her blood has not only entranced me, but three other powerful beings from varied parts of our society. Giving into the whims of my demon means I will have to learn to play nice with the haughty royal, the steadfast cat, and the prickish basilisk. Sighing, I consider the options, noting that the amount of power within her budding polycule is more immense than the witchling realizes.

An heir to Daybreak Court mating with her means she is now the Queen in waiting, while her criminal twin is awaiting the death of that bastard Krystos to take over the narcotics trade for half the eastern seaboard. The leopard may not seem to have much status, but the company he is part owner in is amassing wealthy clients from all over the country and has thirty satellite offices. He's no slouch, either.

Of course, both Diaval and I have fingers in so many pies worldwide that it would shock the sisters into a coma—we've been alive so long we'd have to be morons not to be immeasurably well off.

"Yoo-hoo! Where's Louie Louie? I had to open the door with my badge!" The wolf calls out as she and her sister arrive for the night, interrupting my grumpy musings.

Turning my head, I watch as they strut in, clad in tiny matching playsuits made of patent leather. A dull ache starts behind one eye as I notice the witch is wearing the token I gave her. The collar is prominently displayed above the cleavage showing above the zipper in front and I pinch the bridge of my nose in frustration. I have a deep desire to both reward and punish Clementine for the new pieces she's added to their work uniform selections.

"Oh, color me *shocked*! Señor Pissypants is drinking in the dark again, waiting to glare at us from the minute we arrive," the witchling snarks as she pulls the ponytail on the top of her head tighter.

High ponytail, ass hugging shorts, fishnets, and a zipper... I need to get far, far away.

But I don't disappear; instead I arch a brow and pour myself another drink as they come up to the bar. "Perhaps if you two could go one evening without causing chaos, I would be more amenable."

Bubbles tilts her head, studying me for a moment as she taps her fingers on the wood. "Mmm. I don't know if I believe that, but if you want to tragically lie to yourself..."

Hasn't she grown a pair since mating the bear and... I sniff for a moment then smirk. *...now the snake.*

"It might be less volatile if you two didn't always have your fan club baby-sitting you," I reply with a dark smile. "One would think they believe you can't take care of yourselves."

That gets Fiadh's attention and it's not long before she's over the bar and in my face. "Interesting opinion from a guy who *swore* I needed more protection from things I was too sheltered to know about."

"Yet, here you are, wearing it all the same," I counter.

A loud sigh of frustration comes from the direction of the wolf, but I don't pay attention as she huffs off. She's much less confrontational than her sister and I know she's used to the witch losing her temper.

"Hey, fang face! Maybe I just don't want to risk the people I love because I was too busy stroking my own ego. It has *nothing* to do with you," Fiadh shoots back at me.

I can't fault that logic, but I also can't resist taunting her.

Standing close to her, I lean in and murmur softly, "If you thought they could protect you, you wouldn't need me." Luckily, I have vampiric speed or the right hook she throws would have rang my bell. My lips curve up and I chuckle. "I assume you only play this rough with the snake. The others don't seem like the type."

"None of your fucking business, *boss*," she spits as she yanks her fist out of my hand. "But if you want to go another round, I'll kick it up a notch."

I shake my head, looking at her fondly. Not one of the companions I've had in my entire existence has dared to confront me so boldly, much less an employee. This is why I can't get her out of my mind, even when I work to suppress the call of her blood to my demon. "That's not necessary."

She rolls her eyes and backs off, turning on her heel to stomp off towards the staff rooms.

Fiadh Morgenstern has bewitched me in every way and I have no idea what to do about it.

---

1. Joy of life, my friend

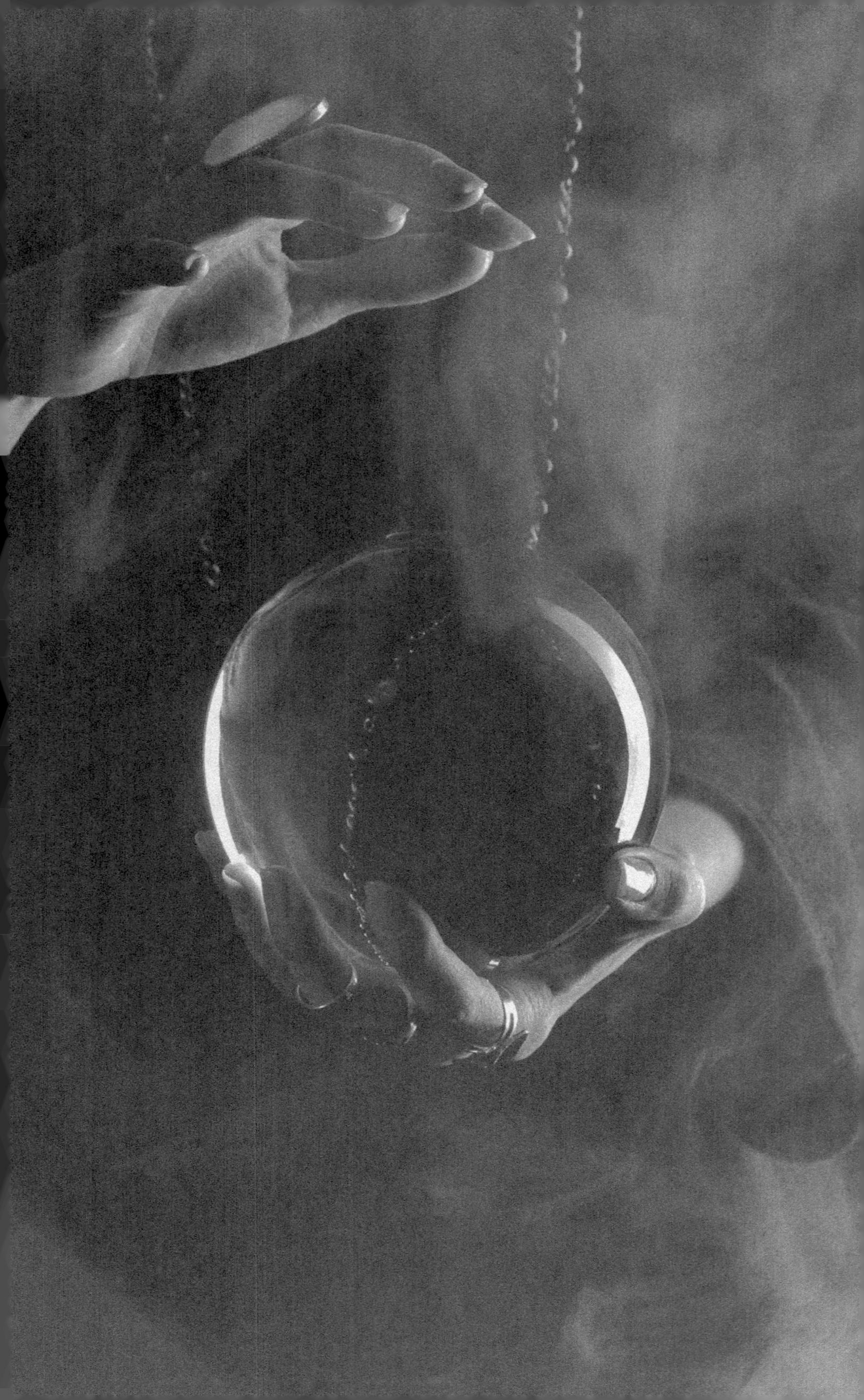

63

FIADH

THAT MOTHERFUCKER IS BEGGING ME TO FIND OUT IF I CAN PIT MY NEW powers against an ancient vampire.

Stalking into the changing room, I shove my bag into it, slamming the door with a clang. My sister looks at me, clearly trying to suppress laughter as I rage. I scowl at her as I tuck my phone in my cleavage, leaving my tiny pockets free to hold Petty and Betty. "What?"

"Nothing," she chirps as she stows her phone in the same way. Her hair is twisted in a fancy braid and the emerald green of her playsuit makes her hair look like flames. Unlike me, she's wearing blocky heels that make her look even more voluptuous.

I huff an annoyed sigh, knowing she's not trying to piss me off. "That damn blood sucker lives to piss me off. He acts all weird about the broken glass, then he seems fine, then he's mad again, then he gives me this *thing*, and now he's blathering on about protection. If he hates me so much, he should just *fire* me!"

"Oh, he won't do that." Feray smirks at me, walking by as she heads for the floor. "Not even if you actually manage to punch him."

What the fuck is that supposed to mean?!

Irritated by all the half-truths floating around prickling the magic in my head, I head out to check the stock behind the bar. The voices aren't as loud as they were when it started because Rev worked on shielding with me, but when things get emotional, I definitely hear it. Walking to the glassware stacks, I check to make certain they were switched to the unbreakable kind Dezi purchased after the festival. Limiting the amount of broken glass to clean up when the moon drunk shifters get wild this week will help immensely.

"Are there any parties in the private room tonight?" Feray asks as I grab the prep lists Louie leaves at the far end.

Scanning the details, I shake my head. "No private parties and the VIP room is fully stocked in case we get high roller parties."

"Like your mate and his roving band of asskissers?" Fer grins, bobbing her brows.

Frowning, I look up at the lounge, remembering how it used to look when he came in with all his fans. "Revelin doesn't seem to bring them around much anymore."

"Gee, I wonder why." My sister gives me a look like I'm a complete fool and I roll my eyes at her.

"I did *not* ask him to ditch his groupies," I grumble as I take the drink she offers me. "I am not so fragile that I can't allow him to do what he needs to for the band."

She laughs softly and rests her hand on mine. "Fiadh, you may not be ready to hear this, but your mates are so in love with you they'd kick Angelina Jolie to the curb."

My eyes widen and I hold my hands up. "What? No. No one is in love. Don't be ridiculous, Fer!"

"Oh, Fi…" She chuckles and shakes her head, rubbing her hand over her face. "I don't know how they deal with you, but never let go of them."

Snorting, I stand and salute her before I walk away to check the host stand and the guest list.

Maybe when I get back, my sister won't be spouting nonsense.

After all, no one said anything about love.

MY EYES ROAM around the room, watching the groups that concern me carefully. The new bouncers crack heads just fine if you point them towards trouble, but identifying possible issues isn't their forte. Then again, orcs aren't known for their superior strategizing skills, so I guess it's not surprising. There's a group of lions from the town pride who have been rowdy, a few vamps trying to skirt the house rules on feeding, and a posse of Fae who convinced Louie to let them into the private room without a reservation. I didn't see them, but Feray was pretty pissed when Dezi told her.

It's hard to keep track of how much people are drinking when they're hiding in a closed room.

The guys haven't arrived yet, which is weird. Diaval is in his usual place at the end of the bar watching my sister, but other than that, not even Torben has shown his face yet. Something about that makes my ass clench and I hope like hell they're not all planning some mischief together. I don't know if this place can handle all our men banding together with the energy floating in the air tonight.

Suddenly, I hear a shout by the door to the private room and it tears my gaze away from the troublemakers I'm eyeing as I serve drinks. I drop the round in front of the group of Cubi and stalk across the floor to see what the hell is going on. When I get there, I see a clash of gargoyles pushing their way towards the entrance, snarling at the vampire guarding it.

"Hey, block head! If he says the room is full, it's full!" I shout as they advance towards him menacingly.

This is why we don't let randos in this room; it should be fully staffed and reserved to keep the riffraff out. I'm cursing Louie's heritage virulently when I feel freakishly strong hands grab me from behind, restraining my arms as he growls.

"You will look lovely on the rack begging me while I punish you, little witch."

Is this guy fucking for real? Is he new here?

Struggling in his iron grip, I let my magic build inside as I consider what to do. This stone faced asshole is stronger than me and I can't use electricity, water, or fire to take him down. He's not undefeatable, but I have to think this through. With my hands pinned, I can't even grab my brass knuckles and risk breaking my hands to punch him.

"I bow for no one, you overgrown planter. And I sure as *fuck* don't beg." I try smashing my boot on his foot, but that only makes my heel throb. *Note to self: the steel is in the toe, idiot.* "Now, let me *go*, pebbles for brains!"

It only makes the fucker laugh harder when I continue fighting him and I have to push the panic down. I'm not usually in this position and there's no one around to help. In all the years I worked at Philly's, I never once got into a situation like this and I wouldn't have expected it here. The rules are very clear and enforced without mercy—where did this gravel sucker and his friends come from?

"Enough!"

The dark voice booms through the entire club as if it's going to shatter the lights and everything made of glass. Time stops as every single person freezes in place, looking terrified at the rage filling the air and sucking up all the oxygen. My eyes dart around until I see Dezi leap over the bar like a fucking *gazelle*, his form moving so quickly I think I might have imagined it until he's standing in front of us.

His red eyes bore into the stony shifter and he immediately turns human, wings and tail disappearing under the vampire's furious stare. He reaches out and snatches the moron by the throat until he lets go of me, then lifts him into the air like the burly dude weighs less than a feather. Sharp claws extend from his fingers and dig into his skin, leaving blood trails running from the wounds.

"You dare to harm someone marked by my protection in my own house?" Chest heaving, Dezi lifts the guy higher, watching him gurgle and struggle helplessly in his grasp.

The guy's face turns red, then an ugly purple as he tries to breathe and I watch in awe. I wouldn't have believed Dezi had this kind of strength or the level of compulsion that would allow him to restrict the entire club without batting a lash. But here he is, fucking everyone up like he's the hot guy version of the *Queen of the Damned.*

Did I just say hot guy? I really need to work out why violence turns me on so much; I have issues.

Louie walks up with two orc bouncers, tapping Dezi on the shoulder with an amused expression. "Allow our staff to handle this, eh, *mon amie?*"

He turns, snarling at the other vamp for a second before he seems to recognize him. Letting out a low growl, Dezi chucks the gargoyle at the green Hulk-like bouncers before pointing to his friends. "All of them... out. *Banned for life.*"

I watch them drag the clash out, then look down at myself. The asshole's grip was far too tight; I'm bruised and bleeding from marks on my wrists. Goddamn claws are gonna leave scars if I'm not careful. My lip curls and I wince as the adrenaline starts wearing off and the sting sets in. "Shit."

"You're hurt." Scary ancient vampire boss whirls around, looking at me as I hold my hands to my chest so I don't bleed on the floor. "Come with me."

"Uh, I'm not sure that—"

Dezi ignores me, putting his hand at the small of my back and pushing me towards the bar insistently. When we're out of the public eye, he takes my hands in his, lifting them up to examine. Before I can say anything, his head dips and he licks over the wounds, running his tongue over them slowly. I suck in a breath, feeling electricity speed through my veins like lightning.

"What in the name of Titania happened here?"

Peeling my eyes away from the vampire lapping at my blood, I see Tiernan, a smirking Rev, two smug looking snakes, and a grinning bear approaching. I shake my head, finally breaking the spell between Dezi and I. Pulling my hands loose, I give him a shy smile as I mumble, "Thanks."

His crimson gaze pins me for a moment and then falls to the skin on my wrists. I follow it, frowning when I notice the bruises starting to fade already. Dezi almost looks like he's going to have a panic attack himself, then he looks at the guys for a moment. No one speaks and I have no idea why, but I don't get to ask because the vampire takes off with that unnatural speed, leaving me hanging.

Again.

I give the crowd of men a sheepish look and raise my hand, wiggling my fingers. "Hi, guys. Super glad to see you. It's a bit rowdy here tonight."

Revelin snorts, arching his brow. "You don't say."

I'm never going to live this shit down.

Tiernan walks over, looking into my eyes with his icy blue ones. I feel his leopard prowling under his skin; something I've never felt before. He leans in to brush my cheek with his, murmuring low, "Are you still hurt, Knuckles?"

"I'm okay," I whisper. My eyes find Khol and Revelin, surprised when they both walk over and surround me on the sides opposite Tiernan. I give Rev a look and I know he understands I want him to use his special power. I feel that magic, too, and once it's in place, I bite my lip before I say softly, "It was scary, though."

That earns me three completely gobsmacked expressions and two rumbling growls. Almost as if they're in sync, they turn to face the others as one, leaving me in the middle of a *lot* of testosterone.

"She's done for the night," Khol says as he looks at his twin. "Stay with your mate."

Tiernan takes that as his cue to haul me over his shoulder, looking at Fer behind the bar. "Bring her stuff home?"

My sister nods, looking worried, especially when I'm not fighting being carried like a sack of potatoes.

"See you at Chez Furry, cats and kittens," Revelin says as he motions for the other two to follow him. "Thank the bloodsucker for us."

For once, I don't even feel like protesting their male bullshit—I just want them to take me home.

64

FERAY

I know it haunts her, too. She hasn't been the same since that night —she's more quiet and withdrawn than I've ever seen her. I miss Fi picking on me for various things, like when I leave my tail out. Hell, I've been leaving my tail out on purpose, hoping to get her to make a snarky remark. The other day I used my tail as a feather duster in front of her and nothing—not a damn thing.

Tiernan said it would take time, especially since Fi is not used to feeling like a victim. When she was napping the other day, I saw her wrists and there's not even a bruise remaining. But it's not the visible marks I'm concerned about; it's the emotional ones she's going to bury deep inside. Her mates are taking care of her, but I've known her longer than they have. My sister will hide shit until you force it out of her and when it finally comes out, you have to prepare for war.

Philly found out what happened and has taken to blowing up our phones up bright and early. To Fi's dismay, he's decided seven am is the best time to torment the fuck out of her. I don't know why, except maybe he's trying to make sure she doesn't stay in bed all day to avoid life. This morning is no different, and my phone buzzes promptly at seven. Torben and I are back from our morning run, waiting for Fi to rise and shine when her ringer goes off.

The shine part hasn't happened in awhile—it's more like rage—but I'll take anger over moping.

Realistically, she's still processing the gargoyle incident and Dezi's reaction. It was like an epic romance seeing an antihero leap in to save the day. *Maybe she's leaning on the guys like everyone has been waiting for her to do?* Sighing, I lean against Torben trying to figure out how to help Fi.

"Little Wolf, we both know she will deal with this in her own time. Poking her won't help. If her mates can't get her to talk eventually you will." He leans over and kisses my temple as I stare down at the bottom of my coffee mug watching the last drops roll around.

"I have awakened," Fi grumbles as a trail of purple glitter and dark orchids sprout up behind her.

Even her magic looks pissy.

Jumping up, I grab her three different flavors of her favorite elvish energy drinks that Revelin left for her. I pause, adding a mug of dark roast coffee as well. "Pick your poison."

Her blood shot eyes glide from drink to drink before she grabs the blue one. She cracks the top and chugs probably half the can in one go. "Bottoms up."

Within seconds, she's more alert than she was earlier. Her disposition visibly changes as well. I wonder if there's antidepressants in that drink because she seems better than yesterday.

"I'll be ready to go in fifteen minutes, Fer," she mumbles as she heads back to her room. After almost twenty minutes, Fi comes back, ready to make the trip to the hospital.

Torben sits at the end of the table getting the last of his estimates in order. When he notices Fi approaching, he looks up and says, "I can drop you off at the hospital then pick you up to take Philly home when I'm done."

We head out to Torben's truck quietly. I'm thankful my mate offered to give us a ride to save us the long walk from the cabin, but I'm squished in the middle. My sister is staring blankly out the window. He glances at Fiadh and gives me a knowing look—neither of us know what to do to help her.

When we arrive at the hospital, Fi slides out and I give Torben a kiss before I chase after her. The walk through the halls of the hospital is slow and the silence is killing me.

"I enlisted Miss Flo to help out with Philly," I offer, trying to break my sister out of the funk she's in.

"I'm sure he'll be thrilled." My sister's snark is lackluster at best, but at least she's talking.

The scent of bergamot drifts to me and I pause, looking around the hallway to see where Easton is. When I don't see him immediately, I follow Fi into Philly's room. The good doctor is at Philly's bedside going over discharge instructions. I smile to myself, happy to see him.

"I'm saved!" Philly cries dramatically as he motions in our direction. "My favorite girls are here to bail my ass out."

Fi stifles a laugh. "Philly, what did I tell you about making the doctor's job harder than it needs to be?"

Philly rolls his eyes and shakes his head. "Yes, *Mom*."

His retort elicits an unexpected growl from me. Easton moves away from him, inching closer to me, then stops to fuss with his tie. *What is it with the ancients fiddling with their clothes when they don't know what to do?* I shake my head and look at our friend. "Philly."

"Okay, okay. Sorry, Doc; please proceed." He motions for the doctor to continue, but part of me is still angry about how flippant he's being.

"As I was saying before, your skin grafts are still in their delicate stage. Don't scratch at the grafts, no matter how bad they itch, because they could tear."

Easton digs in the white bag at the end of the bed then offers me a tube of cream. The minute our fingers brush against each other, an electrical current races up my arm. Narrowing my eyes, I stare at Easton— his scent has changed. He's gone from soft bergamot scent to a sharp tang in the air, almost as if something is making him nervous.

"How do I get refills?" The tag has the amount on it, but not where to fill it.

Easton plucks the bottle out of my hand and writes a phone number on it. "This is the direct line to the pharmacy. Call them when there's one tube left and they will refill it. Each refill is four tubes." He gives it back to me, then shows me the other three tubes.

"Thank you." I tear my eyes away from the doctor to see Fi helping Philly get dressed for the ride home.

"How are you getting him home?" Easton repacks the bag, throwing in some other random medical supplies left over in the room from his stay.

Biting my bottom lip, I avert my eyes then force a smile. "Torben is picking Fi and Philly up. He has to drop off a few estimates and then he'll be here to get them. I'm going to shift and run to the bar; it'll feel nice to stretch my legs." I stumble over my words as I look at him.

Why does the doctor have to look so damn good and smell so nice?

"How about I drive the three of you to the bar so I can make sure everything is set up correctly?" His voice sounds smooth as silk and his eyes roam over me, refusing to make direct eye contact.

"You don't have to—"

"That would be fantastic, Doc," Fi cuts me off, giving me her best 'fuck with me and die' glare.

Arching a brow, I look over at Easton. "Thank you for offering to help us."

Why do I feel like there's butterflies in my stomach looking at him?

Easton makes the mistake of making eye contact as he steps closer to me; it feels like he's drawing me in like a moth to a flame. The rasp in his voice makes my greedy core clench as he says, "You're welcome."

My mouth pops open as I stare, shocked at my body's immediate reaction.

Fi steps between the two of us, watching us carefully. "I think we're ready to leave."

Trying to break the spell Easton has over me, I glance over his shoulder. That's when I notice our old goat in a wheelchair grumping at the nurse pushing him into the hallway. "Which way?"

I want to kick myself for how breathy that question came out.

Easton spins, looking like he's fighting with himself before meeting the nurse in the hallway. He leads us to the employee parking area where a blacked out, luxury SUV is waiting. Looking at the nurse, he opens the back door and assists her with loading Philly. Before I get the chance to slide into the back, Fi runs to the other side and gets in.

I'm left to take the passenger seat up front with Easton and it makes my gut tighten. The minute he sits in the driver's seat, he plugs his phone in. Looking for something to distract me, I bring up his navigation on the screen. It only takes me a few seconds to program in the optimum route to Philly's bar.

"How did you do that so quickly?" Easton asks in amazement.

"My sister is a fucking genius." Fiadh crosses her arms, glaring at Easton in the rearview mirror as if daring him to contradict her.

I guess the old Fi is in full effect now.

"I believe it; wolves are one of the more intelligent shifters. They excel in math and sciences because being an apex predator means they have to solve problems on the fly."

The way Easton explains my species' skills rings true. It's probably why I was able to survive in witch school science to simulate magic.

"That explains a lot actually," I say as I look out the window while he pulls out onto the street.

"You could be so much more than a bartender if you wanted to," he says in a low voice. He probably thought it was too low for me to hear, but it wasn't. I heard both the judgment of my job and his faith in what I'm capable of.

My phone pings in my pocket, so I pull it out. Answering Torben, I let him know we don't need a ride because the doctor is driving us. He texts me back when I express my frustration with that last statement, telling me not to be too hard on him. My bear thinks Easton is fighting his true nature which knocks me for a loop.

Why would he be fighting his true nature?

"We're here," Fi calls from the back seat.

Lifting my gaze from my phone, I marvel at what a beautiful job my mate and his sleuth did restoring the bar. They perfectly reconstructed the bar as I remember it with a few upgrades.

Elijah steps out the front door when he hears us arrive, ushering us inside with a smile. "Welcome to the resurrected *Dionysian Delights*, home of the crabbiest satyr in Briarvale." The bear motions to the bar behind him and opens the double doors wide. "Take a tour with me."

Fiadh jumps at the chance, leaving me behind with Philly and Easton. I swear, she's trying to force Easton and me into close proximity. I'm not clueless; I know what I feel when he touches me, but he's not admitting I have any effect on him so I'm ignoring the tingle.

"Let's get Philly up to his new and improved home." Glancing over at Easton, I help Philly stand. He leans on me and I guide him through the bar to the back stairs.

When we get to the stairs, I lead Philly up slowly. Easton puts his hand on my lower back to help support me and I swear to the Morrigan, my skin is on fire from his touch. Once we get to the second floor, he lets his hand linger for a moment before he snatches it away.

"Welcome home, Philly." Leaning in, I nuzzle his cheek before I walk with him to a recliner similar to the one he had before the fire.

"You girls did an amazing job. Thank you." The satyr's eyes roam around the room, taking in the details. The guys salvaged some of the original signage from outside to make wall decorations—his 'Established in' sign now hangs in the living room.

"It was all Fi and Torben. I rooted through the wreckage to salvage what I could." Shrugging, I watch Easton as he writes more detailed care instructions.

"Feray told me she has someone coming to help you."

Before Easton even finishes, Philly's head whips to face me. "You didn't."

"I did. Get over it, you stubborn old goat. You need help and I can't babysit your crabby ass every day." Pulling a Fi, I cross my arms over my chest, allowing a growl to escape in agitation.

Easton rests his hand on my forearm as if trying to calm me, not even paying attention to what he's doing. At that moment, I know he's one of mine. We both stare at the hand on my arm, feeling the current between us increase.

Until now, I convinced myself I was imagining it.

His silence scares me. He's just staring at where his hand is touching my arm. But I can't stay quiet like that—not when it's this important.

"I get it; I'm not a mythic like you." I pull my arm away and turn to face the window. The tightness in my chest is making it hard to breathe. He hasn't rejected me, but he also hasn't accepted me, either. Making up my mind, I move past Easton and run down the stairs, calling behind me. "I need to go."

"Feray!" he yells.

I hear him pursue me, but I can't deal with it. Shifting my hands to my claws, I shred my clothing as I run. By the time I hit the ground floor, my wolf rips free and I'm off. Fi will grab my belongings and call the guys.

She may also kick Easton's ass simply on premise.

Tor and Khal were so easy; we melded together seamlessly. But this? I need to process what happened just now.

Why is Easton so difficult?

65

EASTON

I SCREWED UP MASSIVELY.

Pacing the interior of my office, I stare out the window of my office. I'm drawn to the direction of the bar my flame works in.

Of course I know what she is to me.

If I had been her first mate, she wouldn't have needed the others. Shaking my head, I clear that illogical thought from my head. It's obvious there's a bigger force at play—magical attacks, mystical murder and a plot so heinous I can't fathom it.

I know two things for certain: I can't get my head around my mate having multiple mates and every fiber of my being is saying I should pursue what is meant to be mine. However, I'm not one to flaunt societal rules, so I will have to follow several things for my moral compass to be satisfied. First, I must seek out her bear since he was the first mate.

What am I going to say? 'Hi, I'm Easton. I upset your mate, but I'm prepared to grovel for her forgiveness?'

Apollo willing, he'll engage with me so we can discuss things civilly. He might kick my ass for upsetting his mate—after all, bears can be protective.

After I speak with him, I need to find a way to make up for making my mate feel like I didn't want her. Her sister flat out schooled me on how badly I screwed up by beating my ass while yelling at me for hurting her sister. Being a phoenix, I heal almost instantly which only pissed Fiadh off more. By the time she wore herself out, I learned her self preservation instinct is non-existent when it comes to Feray. When she finally calmed down, she explained how I could attempt to get in Feray's good graces again.

She told me to do something meaningful and unique to me that would make her sister's heart melt.

Wolves are one of the shifters who have long life spans, but they can't outlive a phoenix. To die and be reborn dozens of times is a lonely existence at times. Reaching into the top drawer of my desk, I take out an amulet crafted by a phoenix artisan. One of my feathers is captured inside and if I give this to her, it will be a symbol of my devotion. For phoenixes, sharing a feather is similar to humans getting engaged. If we cement our bond, I will implant my feather into her flesh to share my lifespan with her.

Of course, she can't resurrect like I can. If she gets killed, I'll die along with her—which is why we don't give these out lightly.

Shoving the amulet in my inner jacket pocket, I decide I'm done working for the day. Sixteen hours is quite enough, especially after Fi's method of teaching me a lesson earlier.

I ride the elevator to the ground floor, but I don't head for my car. Instead, I decide to take a walk. The humid air is finally losing some of its oppressive qualities as summer wanes. I marvel at the colors streaking the sky as I wander. For the first time today, my head is clear and my flame isn't setting fire to my thoughts. Little things along my path catch my attention that I haven't noticed before.

There's a quaint glass blower shop that has a mug that looks like my flames. I make a mental note to return during business hours and purchase it.

Continuing on my walk more, I watch the sky more than where I am. When I take a good look around, I've made my way across town and into the Night District. Right now, I'm standing before the red door of *Cocktails and Screams*.

Apollo help me, I've shown up at her work like a stalker.

Knocking on the door, I wait. The vampire they call Louie slides the slot open, not saying anything as he glares at me. Finally, he gives up and opens the door. There are advantages to being a mythic sometimes, especially when it's well known you can spontaneously combust.

The grumpy vamp gives me a nod before motioning for me to enter. A chill runs up my spine as I walk deeper into the club. Everyone knows this is the resting place of the ancient Dezi Ruby as well as a large coven of his children and employees. Walking in uninvited, during off hours, isn't the brightest plan I've ever conceived.

That's the least of my concern at the moment. What I'm worried about is the wolf that's become the hyper-fixation of my fickle bird. Heading directly to the bar where she works, I sit at the opposite end so I can see her arrive. I'd prefer not to have her sneak up on me —the last time someone snuck up on me, Rome burned during a fiddle concert.

A fox I think is named Mo approaches and takes my order. He brings me the double shot of fireball and a coke without a word. I down the shot then sip at the coke, still debating whether I should take off before she arrives.

In all honesty, I shouldn't be here until we talk. I didn't explain about my stupid hang-ups even though the words were on the tip of my tongue. She ran before I had the nerve to speak. It's been three days since I watched her wolf take over when pain flashed in her eyes. Being as old as I am, I know her fur color puts her in great danger, let alone adding a phoenix to her family group.

Sighing, I people watch as the employees set up for the day. For a BDSM club, the level of cleanliness and organization displayed is impressive. I understand now why the girls got upset when I called the bar dirty.

"Oxpecker!" Feray's voice carries into the bar and everything inside of me tightens.

The high pitched cackle from the doorman follows her declaration. "What the hell is an oxpecker?"

Louie's question amuses the hell out of me. Apparently, he's not as educated as my flame is.

"Come on. Louie! It's a bird from South Africa that picks blood sucking parasites off host animals. It also drinks the blood of the host when water is scarce." She looks positively radiant as she walks in, explaining her insult to the elder vampire.

"Good one, Mutt. You win this round." He smiles, patting her on the head before walking away.

I check my pulse then look around to make sure I'm not imagining this during a resurrection. It seems highly suspect that the infamous door guard for this place is being so nice to a wolf.

"Thanks! I like the suit you picked for tonight. Is it one I helped you order?" Feray adjusts his collar and straightens out his tie, fussing over him like a mother hen.

I'm jealous of a tie and a vampire. There's no going back for me now.

Somehow, I've become irrevocably devoted to the little wolf that stole my heart. Like the moon, the gravitational pull towards her cannot be denied.

A large, heavy hand lands on my shoulder and I damn near combust accidentally. "Settle down, Doc."

Ah, the bear mate, Torben, is here; I can tell by the timbre of his growl.

"Sorry. I was lost in thought and didn't notice you approaching." Extending my hand to him, we shake and he smiles.

"I appreciate what you've done for the girls' friend. It means a lot to the two of them, especially Feray. She felt horrible every time she had to leave him in the hospital. The only way I could get her to leave was if she saw you on shift." He gives me a 'you'd better not fuck up' look after he finishes.

"It was touch and go for a bit. I'm lucky to have a top notch team. The burn unit here has the best of the best employed. Philly received the most skilled care possible through the grant that covered his expenses." Mentioning the bills being covered makes Torben smile from ear to ear.

It's terrifying to see that many teeth on a Kodiak all at once.

"We still appreciate it, so thanks again."

Torben picks up his stein and slides down to Feray's side of the bar, leaving me with the overly dramatic fox. Eventually, Mo drops a drink menu in front of me and there's a much larger selection than I remember from my last visit. Waving him down, I order a 'Flaming Death.'

"I don't make that one—only the Princess does." There's a slight, whiney growl on lips as he turns his head to sneer in Feray's direction. Somehow, he accidentally catches on fire when a candle on the bar fires up and ignites his sleeve while I stare at him.

What a shame.

He runs from the bar and I can't help but laugh at the sight. A deep, hearty laugh draws my attention back to the bar and I see Torben has returned.

"The resident asshole had a little accident, huh?" A knowing smile creeps over his face as he looks at me.

"I don't know what you're talking about. He called Feray a princess and it wasn't in a nice way. I don't know *what* made the flame from the candle jump and set him on fire." I feign innocence, but I have zero regrets.

Torben nods, then looks to see where Feray is. "My Little Wolf told me about driving him into submission in front of a crowd. That had to be a sight."

As if Torben speaking her name summoned her, Feray appears before me with the drink I had ordered in her hand. "Sorry about the vermin. I'll handle him later."

Her eyes flashed to her wolf and her canines were visible when she smiled at me. I believe when my flame barks she has a bite to back it up. I watch her walk down the bar unable to take my eyes off of her.

"I see the way you watch her. Why not talk to her? Tell her what she means to you," Torben says as he sips his beer.

"That ship has sailed, I think. I messed up by hesitating when she stared at me. I was lost in her gaze and my damn bird was squawking in my head so loud I couldn't think straight. She took my silence as rejection." Looking down in shame, I stare at the drink she made me. I blow out the fire when I pick it up, slamming it back.

I can't actually get drunk, but I can sure as hell try.

"It's a once in a lifetime thing for a mythic to find their mate," the bear chides as he watches me. "Trust me, you should talk to her. My people and Khal's live in poly family groups. Wolves have poly families in their dens. None of us will stop you from trying." The calm way he speaks about the males in their bond sharing their mate with each other blows my mind.

"You're both fine with me pursuing her romantically?"

Torben smiles and nods as Feray switches his stein for a fresh one and replaces my drink without being asked. I swear, she steals my breath every time she gets close to me. Sighing, I blow out the flames on my drink, enjoying the blend of the flavors as I sip it.

"I have centuries of opposing beliefs to wade through."

"Tell me about them." Torben seems invested in accepting me as one of his mate's intendeds, so I nod.

"Phoenixes mate for life; they don't share because it's rare to even find one." My eyes drop my drink before I look back at him.

His jovial expression falls and a sadness mars his rugged features. He nods before sipping again and I can tell this smile is forced. "I understand. Do yourself a favor and explain it to her. She may surprise you."

Picking up the drink, I finish off the contents and place a fifty under the glass. "I appreciate everything you've told me tonight. There are a lot of pros to living in a poly family, but the big con is the years of conditioning I've had teaching me that's not the right way to live. However, you've given me a lot to think about. Thank you."

Reaching into my suit jacket, I pull out the phoenix feather amulet. I take his hand and drop the amulet into it. He closes his huge hand around it with a quizzical expression."Please give this to her as a token of my affection."

"I will. Have a good night, Easton." He gets up, walking to the other end of the bar.

He's a good mate; he only wants the best for his female.

I watch as Khal, the other mate, arrives and Feray rounds the bar to jump into his waiting arms. He spins her around as she giggles. Using their joyous reunion as a distraction, I leave the bar without fanfare. Standing in the hallway, I move into the shadows to watch her for a few moments. She looks to where I was sitting and says something to Torben.

He holds up the amulet, dangling it before her. The minute her hand extends to touch the glass, my feather blazes to life. Her blood and life force sing to it, causing it to radiate light as her heart beats. If I had any doubt before, my feather igniting for her proves beyond a shadow of a doubt she's mine.

The only thing standing in my way is me.

66

FIADH

"Are you sure you want to do this with me? Witches and Fae practice magic *very* differently from what I've been taught." My eyes find Rev's, feeling nervous as hell that I'll look silly. Witches may have powers, but the Fae have been wielding the gifts of the universe for eons.

Hell, they don't use any of the focal objects or tools we do; they just draw runes or think things.

Revelin tilts his head as he looks at me in amusement. "I know you're still feeling a bit off because of what happened at the club and it's making you doubt everything about yourself. Fortunately, I've seen and felt your power, lass. I know it's real and I know we've only brushed the surface of what you may be capable of."

Wrinkling my nose, I mutter something about asskissing and turn away from him to hide the flush on my cheeks. He's not wrong that I'm sensitive—the one thing I've *always* been able to do, even without magic, is defend myself. That fucking gargoyle stole my confidence and despite everyone in my makeshift family trying to make me feel better, I'm still smarting. Now I have to use magic to find this damn object for the forgetful feystag and that's never been dependable. It's like the universe is conspiring to knock me off balance as payment for the good shit that's happened recently.

What did I do to piss someone off? Can I sacrifice something and get my mojo back? I'd be happy to slice Mo up for an offering.

That makes me snicker and Rev beams. "There it is! I've been waiting for a smile for hours. Whatever made you happy brought the glow back."

I'm not sure I should tell him it was contemplating murder.

"Okay, okay." I sigh and plant myself on the big blanket he insisted I bring. "If you don't want me to mix anything in the caldron, then I think we have all the corners marked and the candles and herbs in place. What comes next?"

His lips curve up and he hands me a fluffy pillow. "I'm going to give you some of my mother's dream tea. It seemed like blending your rituals and mine might pry loose your tight hold on your consciousness. You'll have to let go so you can transcend realities."

Squinting at him, I tilt my head. "So you're giving me tea to get high so I'll be more pliant? Sounds illegal as hell."

"It is if you do it without consent. But you, lass, are most certainly consenting to drink this so we can find the object that persnickety creature has lost. We need it to help us solve the mystery around your parents' death." The gorgeous Fae I mated gives me a pointed look and I groan. He knows logic will trump fear as long as I'm not angry.

I flop back onto the blanket, handing him the lighter for the candles and incense. He watches me lie down, wiggling until I get comfortable. I'm not used to anyone but my sister watching me while I practice, but I suppose I'll have to get used to Revelin being part of my sacred space. Feray doesn't like the reminder of her past trauma and I don't have other witches, so his presence is better than having to do everything solitary.

"Take this and sip *slowly*," Rev says. He hands me a large mug of floral scented tea and goes back to fiddling with all of my witchy tools. "Don't chug it or you might end up on a Magical Mystery Tour."

I pause with the cup halfway to my mouth, muttering, "Good to know."

The meadow is quiet as I drink and my mate sits next to me with his legs stretched out. His fingers are tangled with mine as I sip the drink as instructed and I close my eyes. Having his quiet support is nice, though I like when he's giving me hell more. In fact, I like when Khol does it, too. Tiernan's the calm one and it makes him very lickable. Although, now I have these stupid dreams about...

"About what, lass?"

His question makes my eyes pop open and I turn my head to look at him. "Am I... talking... out loud?"

The belly laughs he lets out tells me I have been and I feel straight fire flood my face. Slamming my eyes closed, I go back to drinking the tea. Obviously, it works quickly and I have zero control over what the fuck I'm saying, so I definitely shouldn't think about anything I don't want him to know.

Like how I have all of his albums and always liked his music, even when he was being a douche.

"A douche, huh?"

Dammit! Stop talking, Fi!

"That was out loud, too."

I clamp my lips together, scrunching my face up as I try not to die of embarrassment on the spot.

"Don't worry; you're going to fall asleep soon. Once you do, you're not in danger of telling me just how much you've always wanted to bang me."

I'm going to stab myself in the eye.

"None of that, lass, or I'll have to restrain you. We both know you'll like it and we have other things to do before pleasure."

That makes my body wake up and I press my thighs together with a screech of frustration.

The last thing I hear before I drop off is his laughter.

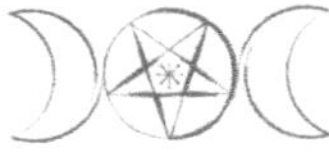

WHEN MY EYES OPEN, I look around me in amazement.

"This is definitely the dream land or whatever," I murmur.

I know that because I'm in the Faerie—which I wasn't before—and everything is sort of…transparent? It's like I can see everything normally but it's not solid. When I look out in front of me, my vision starts to stretch and it pushes farther than I could ever see when awake. I'm seeing images and scenery that are unfamiliar, including places I know I haven't ever been before.

The dark spot on the map before me is probably the Midnight Court lands, which means the blazing section is the Harvest Court kingdom. I feel a chill as I continue looking and I know that section is the Court of Reaping. It's dark and frozen, filling me with foreboding as I struggle to pull my gaze away. The last part is the Daybreak Court and it feels like sunshine embodied.

But what do I do to find this damned thing? I don't even know what 'it' is!

Growling to myself, I consider how I'm going to figure out where a mythical Fae creature would hide their shit. *Maybe I just need to ask?* As dumb as that sounds, I concentrate on the feystag, asking this dreamscape to help me find where it keeps its secret attics full of junk. To my surprise, blotches that look like heat signatures pop up all over the map, highlighting areas of the different courts like infrared.

"It can't be this easy," I whisper to myself.

Suddenly, my vision zooms and my stomach flips as I zero in on one spot at time. *I was right; this isn't easy, it's bullshit.* Every spot was the size of a half-dollar when I looked at the map as a whole, but zoomed in, it's clear the damn things are enormous. Some of them look to be above ground and some below, while others are set in forests and mountains. The biggest one is in the Court of Reaping and I'm not entirely sure it's not in a frozen lava pit.

How is frozen lava even possible?

"Revelin has a lot of 'splainin to do," I grumble. "His home land is worse than the fucking beautiful lands of Gilder. If we run into giant goddamn rats, I'm going to murder him."

Slowly, I examine the areas around every single spot in each kingdom, committing their location in relation to memorable landmarks. I have a damn good memory, but there are easily fifty treasure troves scattered around the Faerie. That damn feystag needs to be on an episode of *Hoarders*.

I don't think telling the creature I'm bartering with that I found all her secret hiding places will narrow down the options. Now, I have to discern which places might be the ones to search or she'll tell me to get bent. After all, it's not like she's forgotten where all stashes are, right?

Pondering that for a moment, I decide not to rule it out, but I still think I need to get this list trimmed somehow. If it were as simple as imagining the icon from the wreck, I believe the feystag would have found the item on her own. I'll have to get creative.

I close my eyes until the map goes back to worldview so I don't toss my dreamscape cookies, then study it carefully. Since I have no idea if there's any organization to the horde, I'll have to focus on something besides time frames or symbols. Given the size of some of the spots, the object could be tiny or enormous, so size isn't going to get me there.

Emotions. That's what I need to focus on.

Whatever she saw this symbol on, it was likely powerful and possibly dark. Any magic can be used for good or evil, but since this symbol was used by something no one has been willing or able to identify, it's probably quite old. I need to search for the oldest items that feel extremely powerful and capable of ill intent if used that way.

"Show me the ancient energy. Magic not used for so long it may be forgotten or exiled. Only highlight the places where truly forbidden objects are housed."

I have no idea if muttering commands to myself will work, but I have to convince this place to help find what I need.

A sharp pain hits me and a flash of light illuminates the map for a moment, then it starts to change. One by one, splotches disappear until there are half as many glowing dots, then a few less, until my list shrinks to sixteen places.

Four in each kingdom—how very considerate.

Going through my memory tricks yet again, I place the spots in my mind palace so when I awaken, I won't forget. The ones in the Daybreak Court don't look too awful, nor do the spots in the Harvest Court. Unfortunately, the places left in the Midnight and

Court of Reaping all look impenetrable or dangerous as fuck—which means that's almost certainly the here this goddamn thing will be located.

"Fucking Fae," I mutter in irritation. "Everything about them is difficult; why would this be any different?"

I let my mind settle, closing my eyes again as I will the transparent dream place to fuck off so I'll wake up. All I want to do now is tell Revelin what a load of crap this quest is and maybe have dinner before I get laid.

But I don't wake up and it makes me panic. Am I stuck?

Before I can have a full blown attack, the damn feystag appears and tosses her head at me.

"What are *you* doing in *my* dreams?" I ask.

~Our deal will be complete when you hunt down the object. I had forgotten many of the treasure storage I set up over the millennia. Your dreams allowed me to remember; I will take that as payment. But the quest for your answers is your own.~

I blink, looking at her in shock. "I have to go dig it out,too?"

~Yes. Truth requires work and you must earn the answers you wish for. Good luck, child of the moon. Use your gifts and those of your companions well. You will need all of it to complete this journey.~

The feystag disappears again and I'm about to lose my temper when I awaken, gasping for breath as I lay on the blanket in the meadow.

Revelin is looking down at me in concern. "Did it work? Do you know what she wants?"

Lifting my hand to my eyes, I nod and groan. "Yes. Yet another person has decided to fuck with me in the most inconvenient way possible."

"What does *that* mean?"

I look him dead in the eye, my expression furious. "It means we have to go on a fucking quest to the four courts of the Faerie."

Feray

We waited two months to get an appointment with the Shifter Council and to my dismay, our appointment fell on the Blue Moon.

Shaking my head, I walk around my room trying to find something acceptable to wear. I decide on a pair of loose fitting slacks and a fitted oxford. For some reason, dressing in more professional attire seems like the best choice. Instead of letting my hair flow down my back, I pull it into a low bun and pin it in place. Before leaving my room, I stop at my dresser and put on the glowing necklace from Easton.

I know the feather is his now; he told me during our many conversations at the bar since that night. He's still trying to show me how sorry he is for not handling our situation well. It made more sense when he explained his people and their traditions, but we're taking it slow. He even offered to come with us today in case the snooty council members wouldn't allow us everywhere we need to get to.

Oddly enough, Torben and Khal have told me many times how great a guy Easton is. There seems to be a budding bromance, which makes me think he will make a good addition to our family.

I take one last look in the mirror before I head to the living room. My collar from work is tight on my neck and the amulet Easton gave me hangs just above my cleavage. It pulses in time with my heart, making me smile softly. I look neat and presentable, but a nagging feeling stops me before I reach the door.

Turning around, I head over to my bed and stick my hand under my pillow. I pull out the talon marked doubloon Diaval had Dezi give me a few weeks ago. When I questioned the dragon why he didn't give it to me himself, he said he didn't think I would accept it from him. I was shocked; we had a rocky start, but he's grown on me. I even chastised him for being late the other night. He immediately apologized for his tardiness, leaving Dezi completely speechless.

That was a win if I've ever seen one.

Diaval also wanted to come with us. He offered to threaten roasting the council if they didn't assist me. As much as I appreciated the sentiment, they have information I need. Killing them won't help me get it.

Staring at the gold doubloon, the gears turn in my head. Diaval keeps popping up during times of trouble or family meetings at the bar. He even apologized ahead of time for having a meeting tonight that will make him late again. *It's not like he's my mate... is he?* I blink, realizing I'll have to unpack that later or I'll be late to one of the most important meetings of my life.

My heels click on the wood floor as I walk out to the living room. Two whistles and a low toned '*damn*' greet me. "Good to know you all approve. I wanted to look like I have my shit together so they'll take me seriously."

I walk over to the bierstein display case Torben built into the wall and press on the right side. It pops open, revealing our new secret room. The guys follow me in and Khal closes the case behind him. All the research my sister and I compiled since the Ascension is stored here. The family tree that I got from the Sphynx is spread out on the desk in the corner. It's still pulsing where my parents' names and my surname should be. Feeling the heat of their gazes behind me, I turn to show Easton our progress.

He takes the parchment from me carefully, looking it over. Positioning it on the desk, he passes his hand over the blackened mass. Nothing happens—it doesn't even flinch at his magic. "Whoever did this is quite powerful."

Sliding my family tree into the leather tube that Khal had made for it, I sigh in acceptance. If a phoenix can't pass through this magic, then it will take far stronger beings working together to reveal its secrets. Luckily, the tree will be safe while we wait for that day. The tube is made from Khal's last shed and he guarantees nothing will be able to get through his hide.

"We should get going. It's a long drive up the mountain to the citadel," Torben says as he looks down at his watch.

Glancing from Khal to Easton, I fall in behind Torben as I nod. "It's time."

The air is full of electricity because of the full blue moon tonight. Khal is a bit more on edge and Torben is allowing more of his bear's mass to be present in his human form. It seems only Easton and I are unaffected, which means we should be the level headed ones.

"We'll take my SUV up the mountain. It will seat the four of us comfortably and has four wheel drive."

The doctor tosses his keys to Torben who gives him a grin. The SUV is top of the line, and I can see the gears turning in Torben's head. With as smug as Easton can be, I assume Torben has something potentially wicked in mind for later. Once we load up, Easton takes the passenger seat next to Torben, leaving me to sit with Khal.

"Are you nervous?" Khal reaches out and gives my hand a gentle squeeze.

"If I'm honest? Yes. I spent my first twenty years thinking I was a failure at being a witch, no matter how hard I tried. Then I failed at Ascension, only to find out it was all because I'm a wolf." Shrugging my shoulders, I avert my gaze as we leave the forest I've come to know and love.

"Why are you nervous?" Easton asks curiously as he turns in his seat to look back at me.

"I'm afraid to find out why my parents didn't want me. Why would they give me to a family of witches who bound my wolf like that?" I feel tears trying to surface and sniffle, fighting them back.

"They had to have a good reason," Torben says as he reaches back for me. I touch his hand and give it a squeeze before he returns it to the wheel.

Easton frowns, looking thoughtful before he speaks again. "As long as I've lived in Briarvale, I've never seen wolves with your color. I've seen them in Blackmore and Dunnum, but not here. There are larger packs south of the tundra that are all white, but they are very secretive." Easton confirms one place we already had on our list to visit, but I'm pleased when he adds two more without even trying.

"Visiting them today feels like it might not be a safe idea." I fiddle with Easton's amulet and the doubloon that Diaval gave me, not sure why my gut is clenching.

"Are you worried about the moon phase?" Khal asks.

Nodding my head, I sigh. "Not everyone has the control as I seem to and I don't know why. The moon doesn't bother me like it does most other shifters."

"Looking at your bloodline, it seems to have a lot of Lunas and pack mothers. From what I learned, Luna's job is to maintain stability in the pack, so she can't be affected by the moon," Torben says as he touches the navigation screen. "The pack would be in utter chaos if the Luna couldn't maintain control." Remember what you did to Roman when he told you to go to him?"

"I got mad and said no." I still don't think what I did was that impressive.

"His knees almost buckled from the force of you saying 'no.' You resisted an Alpha's bark and put him in his place—that's a Luna move."

The pride in Torben's voice makes me sit up a little straighter. I mull over everything that's happened since I've shifted. Obviously, I've been using this Luna power without even knowing it. Tilting my head to look out the window, I see a gothic style castle come in view. The guys did a wonderful job of distracting me during the drive; I didn't even notice how close we were. "Is that where we are going?"

"Yes. It's been quite some time since I was last here," Easton says wistfully.

"Do you know the council members well?" My curiosity gets the better of me and I look at him pleadingly.

"Yes. That's one of the reasons I asked to accompany you. They won't deny me anything." His tone is haughty and I roll my eyes.

When he goes into pompous ass mode, I really want to slap the asshole out of him.

Khal looks at me, mocking him out of his view, and I have to bite my lip to keep from laughing.

If what Easton says is true, this trip may not be as horrible as I thought it would be. Snooty shifters are much better than killy ones.

Torben pulls through the wrought iron gates and parks near the white marble stairs. "This looks more like a vampire's castle than the Council headquarters."

I slip out the door and accept Torben's hand. We follow Easton up the stairs and through the open front door. *I suppose a Council of shifters doesn't need to worry about security.*

"Easton!" A voice booms out as we walk in and my wolf bristles at their tone.

"Agnar, old friend. How are you?" They embrace briefly before we get a good look at the newcomer. He's a weathered old man with a hunched back and arthritis twisted fingers.

"Not all of us can resurrect and be a young man again." A huff escapes his lips as he looks around Easton to me. "Greetings, young one. I know you have been waiting for this meeting, so let's get on with it." He turns and heads back in the direction he came from.

I study the building as we follow him. It predates medieval times, that much I gather by the tool marks on the stones making up the walls. Before I finish my assessment, we're led into the Council chambers. Agnar heads up onto the dias, taking the seventh seat to make their group complete.

"We are aware of your plight, pup," the man in the center seat says. "I am Grisom, representative of the lions. For us, family is everything. Therefore, I vote to grant you access to the pack archives."

My heart jumps in my chest as I look at the rest of them.

Agnar stands, looking down the row of his brethren. The way he looks at two of the members tells me they may be an issue. "As representative of the dragons, our nests and flights are valuable to us. I vote to grant you access to the pack archives."

Two votes out of seven so far, so good.

A little man with beady eyes stands, sneering at the others. "I am Cornelius, representative of the foxes. Our dens and safety are of utmost importance. There must have been a reason they cast you out, wolf. I vote against allowing you into the archives."

A tall skinny man stands up next and looks down the line, then back at me. "I am Aster, representative of the storks. I agree with Cornelius. What's done is done, so I vote against giving you access to the pack records."

"I am known as Barron, representative of the bears. Our sleuths are our priority—we put family first. As much as I see both sides, I believe you deserve the truth. I vote to grant you access to the archives." The heavy, muscled man smiles a tiny bit as he looks at me and I wonder if he's related to Torben somehow.

I'd bet anything that asshole fox is related to our asshole Mo.

"I'm against it. We have no idea why they sent her away." The man doesn't even introduce himself before he votes, but I can tell by the crazed look in his eyes that he's not quite all there.

"He's a hyena; they're always paranoid and vicious," Easton whispers in my ear.

The last member is a wolf like me. He's studying the reactions of the others and my reaction to them closely. "Come forward, child." There is no force behind his request, so I approach him. "Roman told me you almost put him to the ground when he commanded you. When I did so, you listened. Why?"

I ponder his question. "He used his Alpha power on me. My wolf refused to give in to force and when I said 'no,' she taught him a lesson." I maintain respectful eye contact with the elder Alpha, letting him know he doesn't scare me.

A soft chuckle escapes his lips. He doesn't break eye contact with me; instead, he smiles. "A natural born Luna! Only three bloodlines have ever been able to birth one. For that alone, I grant you access to the archives. I would like to see the family tree you were given."

He extends his hand and I take the scroll out of its case and hand it to him. "Hmmm. I believe I may know who your parents were, but you should discover that yourself." The Alpha rolls up the scroll and hands it back to me. "You and your mates are welcome to stay for the Blue Moon Celebration after you're done in the archives."

"Thank you for your kindness. I just want to see what happened to my family," I say softly.

The wolf comes down, ignoring the protests of my detractors as he leads us to the archives. "My name is Marcus. If you need anything, all you have to do is howl." He pats my cheek tenderly then leaves us to our tasks.

The guys and I search everywhere within the four walls for a hint of the names we've seen on the scroll. Several long, dusty hours pass before we hear Khal hissing in excitement.

"I found something!" He drags the ancient tome over to the table, putting it where we can all see it.

We compare the names on the scroll with the names listed on my family tree. Khal found mentions of my ancestors as far as four generations back in his book. As we go further into the history, we discover the pack originated in Briarvale, then moved to Blackmore, then moved to the Crescent Valley on the edge of the tundra. They are the main producers of magical charms for mages because stone mines are on the pack's lands.

I move away from the table, frantically searching for a book on the Crescent Valley pack. There are four books, but instead of looking at the first three, I go straight to the last one. The beginning details the familial line just before my parents and explains how several families were known to birth natural Alphas and Lunas. After their twenty-first birthdays, they would be allowed to meet so they could find their matches. Usually, the Lunas were born in the Crescent Valley but the Alphas came from either Blackmore or Dunnum. Since they could only have one Alpha per pack, the new Alpha would travel to meet the new Luna.

My heart is in my throat as I get to the page that reveals my parents' names. My hand shakes as I point at the page. There in black and white are my parents' names with my surname. "Guys, look."

Easton looks around, then leans in close to us. "Do not speak their names here. Write it down and we'll tell the others when we get back to your house."

I do as he suggests, stuffing the paper in Khal's pocket for safe keeping.

We read further into the history of the town, but the Alpha and Luna seem to disappear. There's no mention of my birth anywhere. Within months of their disappearance, there was an all out war to choose the new Alpha for the pack.

Staring down at the complete family tree, I commit it to memory.

Claridon and Lyra Joküll are my parents.

It doesn't look like they abandoned me. Whatever happened to them, I ended up with Fiadh's family for safekeeping.

My heart aches as the emotions hit me. Tears roll down my cheeks and Torben yanks me away from the table to crush me to his chest. He runs his fingers through my hair as his bear rumbles, trying to soothe me. "You're safe, Little Wolf. We've got you."

Khal presses himself to my back and kisses my cheek. Heat radiates from his body as he rubs my sides trying to calm me. "I would turn the world to stone if I thought it would make you smile."

Easton approaches and I reach my hand out to him. He takes it, kissing my knuckles. "Whatever you need me to be, however you want me—I'm here."

His eyes blaze to life with the fire of his phoenix and I know his bird doesn't have the hang-ups the man does. The fact he's offering me comfort when I need it is a big step for him. I squeeze his hand and force a smile as I remain sandwiched between Khal and Torben. "I know you need time. Thank you for being here."

"Anything for you, my Flame." His soft tone makes my heart ache in a different way.

"Can I hug you?" The minute the question is out of my mouth Khal and Torben release me.

"Yes, you may." He wraps me up in his arms as soon as I get close. His body runs much hotter than the others. I thought Torben was warm, but Easton has him beat by a mile. The warmth is so soothing that it melts away the tension in my body. Maybe it's part of the phoenix's magic because the stress leaves my body and I become sleepy almost immediately.

The next thing I know, I feel him scoop me up in his arms as my eyes close.

68

REVELIN

FIADH WOULD KILL ME IF I SAID THIS NEAR HER, BUT I BLOODY HATE commoner work.

It sounds ridiculous and like my head is straight up my ass—which it may well be—but digging around in the archives of the Daybreak Court library is not part of my skill set. Elitist or not, I'm a firm believer in assigning tasks based on who has the necessary abilities to complete them in the most accurate and efficient manner. Sending a rock star prince to comb over dusty old books full of tedious Fae history is neither efficient nor likely to produce accurate results.

As evidenced by the four times I fell asleep at this damn table.

"Felicity!" I yell over the rows of shelves and stinky scrolls. "Come to the geography section."

The short earth elemental Fae comes dashing through the aisle with a bright, eager look on her face. Her mother is the head librarian and about a zillion years old—with a temper to match her tenure. Asking Dianthia to help me search would likely get my pointed ears boxed—despite my royal upbringing—but asking Felicity will get me the help I desperately need.

"Felicity, you know I'm hopeless with this kind of shit. I need your help." Smiling my most megawatt, 'adoring fans are looking' smile, I wait to see if I've hooked her.

Her big brown eyes are understanding as she nods. "Oh, Prince Revelin. I understand this isn't suited to you. The dust alone might injure your throat. With your tour coming up, I'd *hate* for you to get sick and have to cancel! May I help you with your research? I can scan everything and email it when I'm done!"

Bingo.

I nod, my expression overly grateful as I hand her the list of places, maps, myths, and books I'm looking for. It's huge, but based on the lass's dream walk, I think most of this will be helpful. Before I came in, though, I added a bunch of other random things just in case someone snuck a peek at what I'm checking into. That means Felicity will be doing a few unnecessary tasks, but she won't know that. Knowing her, she'll enjoy this shit anyway. "Thank you, Felicity. *Darkness Falls* owes you a great debt."

She practically melts into the floor, and I wait until I'm far enough away to chuckle. I'm a bit chuffed that I gave away the most tedious job ever without even making someone mad. *That should earn me brownie points with the lass, eh?* I frown, pondering for a moment as I consider her reaction to giving the list to someone she doesn't know. *Best not bring that part up, I think.*

But I did free up some time, which means I can go back to the other realm to gather the rest of our crew. We need to figure out our next moves. Despite all of our progress, we're still pretty far away from finding anything out about who killed the girls' parents and why. The other mystery is becoming clearer, I hear, though.

My mate's sister went to the shifter council last weekend. We haven't all met to discuss what she found, but I assume it's significant. Fiadh said the wolf's been quiet and withdrawn, clinging to the men in her little group when she's not at work.

None of that will do, of course. The two of them won't be able to survive this mystery if they lose each other.

On that note, I pull my phone out, texting our group. Despite his pain in the ass behavior, I know for a fact Khol will tell his brother and that will lead to my message spreading to the others. The twins may be night and day in personality, but they're as fiercely loyal to one another as Fi and her sister are. It makes for one hell of a family grapevine and I take advantage of it every chance I get.

Whistling to myself, I wait for all the dings from the chat before I head down the hallway to say good-bye to my mother. I could give a shit less about Oliver, but I never portal out without seeing her. When I walk into her drawing room, my eyes widen as I realize I've made a *grave* error.

There sits my mother with a delighted, yet cunningly calculated look on her face—and she's surrounded by all *seven* of my fucking sisters.

What did that squid guy say? It's a trap?

BY THE TIME I extricate myself from the grasp of my mother and sisters, I'm exhausted. They had so many questions about Fiadh, her sister, and all of the people I've been associating with lately that I almost called my agent for a press release. It would have been a hell of a lot easier than facing that firing squad. I love all of them, but growing up squished between toxic masculinity in a crown and a sea of Fae feminists in crowns was no joke.

It's probably why I'm such a good performer—I was always pretending for one group or another to keep my head above water.

Walking into *Cocktails & Screams,* I make my way to the main room. Tiernan texted that Fi and Fer were off tonight, but we could meet upstairs so there'd be plenty of alcohol for our strategy session. I didn't believe him, by the way. My old friend is good at many things, but subterfuge is *not* one of them. I believe he and the bear are trying to get the last two puzzle pieces to slide into place by very carefully arranging things.

Not that I mind, to be honest, but their attempts at being subtle make me chuckle.

I see Fi's sort of friend Jaz at the bar with her nemesis and steer very clear of it. Their whole war has gotten a bit out of hand and I'm not in the mood to find a big loogie in my *Dusty Rose* tonight. As I walk over to the VIP staircase, I notice the snakes slithering in. I shake my head as Khol gets in a brief tussle with one of the cockatrices then backs off when the vampire's new orc bouncers step in. I have to be honest—as much as I love watching the lass fight, having brawny muscle back up for her makes my ass clench less.

She was a mess for a solid week after the gargoyle incident and I never want to see her look like that again.

Once I'm in the lounge, I drop into my favorite chair, propping my feet on the overstuffed ottoman. A waitress I don't recognize comes up and takes my order, making me curious. *Has Dezi brought in more people to make sure the girls actually take time off?* It doesn't seem like something he'd do, but considering he's so damn besotted with my mate, I guess anything is possible.

"Rev!"

I sigh in relief when not only the twins crest the top of the stairs, but the lass and Tiernan bring up the rear. Right behind them are the bear and the snooty phoenix, who I'm not quite sure about yet. He seemed like a git after he made Fluffy upset and I'm far less forgiving than she is. That's something Fi and I share in common— we both squint at him as we're waiting for him to fuck up again.

Of course, I have no idea what the fuck we'd do against a phoenix, but I'm fairly sure we'd have a good time trying.

"Aye, lass. Come sit with me; I've earned it." I wink at the others as they fill in the various chairs and loungers around the table in the middle. Fiadh rolls her eyes, but she drops onto my lap, pulling Tiernan down next to her. The snake flanks my other side and I arch a brow at him. "Fae usually prefer felines, but a sneaky snake'll do in a pinch."

"Stop picking at each other," Fiadh chides as she elbows my ribs. "We have more important shit to discuss."

"Like his impending tour?" Tiernan offers with an innocent expression.

Damn him. I wanted to weave that into this plan so she wouldn't—

"*Tour?*" Torben almost spits his beer out when she elbows me again hard enough to make me double over. "When were you going to tell me about a *tour?* Where is this tour?"

"I know, I know!"

We all turn to look at Feray and she gives me an evil look. "It's in the Faerie."

"Traitor!"

Tiernan snorts and shakes his head. "Man, just tell us what we need to know. I can always tell when you're working up to something. What's going on?"

Sighing, I rub the back of my neck before I look at the lass. "Honestly, I'm going to sound like a tool, but with everything going on, I forgot about this damn thing until a bit ago. However, when you did the giggly tea high, I realized something."

"That I should never let your mother drug me again?" she snarks.

"Uh… maybe. Yes. No. Not what I meant!" I shake my head, clearing the sarcastic responses out so I can think. "I realized you told me there are four feystag hiding spots in all four kingdoms. If we go running into the Faerie and have to negotiate diplomatic entry into the other courts, we'll draw attention we don't want."

Khol blinks and then grins broadly. "But if they invite you to their kingdom because you're on tour, we can go wherever we want without anyone asking questions."

"Exactly!" I shoot a finger gun at him, grinning broadly. "It's the perfect cover."

"Wait a minute." Feray looks at me, then at her sister, frowning. "Are you saying Fi's going with you?"

My mate snorts and looks at me. "I think if I don't he'll do nothing but party and end up getting his ass kicked when he gets home. Plus, I made the deal, so I sort of have to go."

"You're not going without me," Khol cuts in. "I'll find coverage from someone I trust not to fuck everything up while I'm gone."

I pinch the bridge of my nose as suddenly, a cacophony of 'then I'm going!' type remarks echo around the room. Obviously, I could have as big an entourage as I'd like, but too many non-royal Fae ass kissers will definitely catch the attention of the media. I'm not sure I can hide a dude like Torben without assigning him to the stage crew or something. He just doesn't look like one of my fans.

A loud whistle breaks up the noise and I look up to see the bear in question holding his fingers to his lips. "Hold up!"

Seven pairs of eyes land on the big guy as he stands in front of us with a serious expression. "As much as we'd all like to make sure *both* girls are protected, my Little Wolf has a lead to pursue as well. Don't you?"

The wolf's mouth is hanging open, but she shuts it quickly, giving Torben an adoring look. "Yes, I do. When we went to the Shifter Council, they were able to give me access to records that gave me the names I was looking for. There are three places we need to go and do some digging to see if we can find out what happened."

"Then you can't go on tour, Fer. You *have* to go find out about your… history," Fiadh says carefully. "If Torben, Khal, and Easton go along, I'll feel like you're protected. Then I won't worry so much."

The redhead frowns, wrinkling her nose as she looks at me. "I don't know if I think you guys have enough firepower. I mean, you and Fi have magic, but the Faerie is *full* of magic users. Khol and Tiernan might not be able to help as much unless they get close up."

Tiernan gives me a very smug look as he nods at Feray. "I feel the same about you, Feray. Fiadh will do nothing but worry if you go to these places and your options are two shifters and a walking atom bomb." He turns to Easton, looking sheepish. "No offense."

"None taken," the doctor says wryly.

Oh, I see what this kitty is doing. I just wonder if my darling lass can see it, too.

69

FIADH

"WHAT ABOUT THIS THING YE OLDE BLOODSUCKER GAVE ME FOR protection?" I point to the collar with my tag and the charms, wondering if Revelin knows what the hell it means. None of the guys have said anything about it, so it obviously doesn't *bother* them, but I have no idea why.

It bothers the hell out of me, just like its previous owner.

"That will help, but more on this side of the portal than Rev's, I think."

"I wouldn't be so sure of that, cat."

Another collective noise rises up and I glare at every predatory shifter in our group. "How the *hell* does he keep sneaking up on all of us? You're all like…animals… and shit!"

Easton gives me a perplexed look. "He's a *vampire*."

Oh, gee, thanks, Professor. That cleared it up for me.

"So?"

Dezi smirks as he walks over and my eyes widen when I see he has Mr. Fancy Drinks in tow. "My kind are able to do many things to disguise ourselves when we hunt. Even the shifters have trouble scenting, hearing, or locating us if the vampire is old and skilled enough to mask well. I do it to your people because it amuses me."

"Me, too." The dragon behind him looks just as smug and I wonder yet again if it'd be worth it to punch him in the snout.

Phoenixes can heal burns. I saw Easton do it for Philly.

Suddenly, the doc in question narrows his eyes at me. "Don't even think about it."

"I've tried to tell her," Dezi says with faux concern. "Alas, the witchling's temper always gets the best of her."

That gets a murmur of agreement and I see red. Jumping off Rev's lap, I hop onto the table and look at all of the people gathered. When I'm up this high, it occurs to me that we have an *enormous* amount of firepower, knowledge, and wealth standing around with their thumbs up their asses. Feray and I have never had this many resources to work with in our entire adult lives. This is how we're going to find the fuckers that killed my parents and locate Feray's pack—our family.

"Hey, dipshits!" I cup my hands around my mouth and yell. "Listen up."

Rev grins at me, his eyes dancing as he leans back into the couch. "I *love* Bossy Lass. Do go on."

"Gross," Feray mutters as she walks over to Torben and waits for him to sit. "But I'm listening."

One by one, they make their little comments and I watch them fall into line, taking seats in the exact configuration I would have expected. That makes this a *lot* easier and I won't even have to be sneaky.

"Obviously, we have two paths we need to follow and lucky for us, we have two pretty strong groups who can run with those leads," I say confidently. "All we have to do is make some arrangement here and within the two weeks we have left, we can be ready to go."

Diaval and Dezi look at one another, then stare at me as if willing me to continue. When I don't, the vampire finally gives in. "Okay. I'll bite."

"I bet you will," Khol shoots back.

The vamp gives him an amused look and shrugs. "Only if you consent, snakeling. But what I meant to ask is *where are you going and why?*"

Smoke comes out of the dragon's nose as he snorts, giving me a wry look. "You must have had part of this conversation in your head."

"Wrong-o, buddy. We had it before you two crashed our party like twenty-five year olds at a high school kegger, but nice try. It's none of your business." Dezi arches a brow and I roll my eyes. "Okay, it's *some* of his business because he'll need temps for while Fer and I are gone."

"I don't know, Fi. Maybe we should tell them," my sister says softly as she looks at the dragon.

Oh, for fuck's sake.

But I'm unable to resist her and she knows it. Rev winks at me when I look over, and both Khol and Tiernan nod. They must think it's okay, too. My gaze drifts, noting Torben and Khal look fine, but Easton is neutral. *Guess I can't ask the new guy to take sides, right?* "Fine, fine. Okay!"

Dezi walks over and finds a seat, waiting until the banker does the same. "Tell us, witchling. Where is the grand adventure taking place?"

"Revelin and I have to go hunt some cereal box toy down in the Faerie for a ghost deer I'm gonna start calling Chilly Willy. Meanwhile, sis and her gang have to go to the haunted village and pull the mask off some dude pretending to be a werewolf—sort of."

The ancients look at me in confusion and that sends the guys into peels of laughter. Torben laughs so hard he almost drops Fer and she giggles in spite of it. Revelin gives me two thumbs up, obviously thrilled with my taste for chaos tonight. Finally, the noise dies down and I'm left with two angry looking assholes tapping their fingers on their chairs.

"Don't get your thongs in a bunch, guys. I was just trying to lighten the mood." They don't smile and I sigh heavily. "I have to find an object in Faerie that relates to that mystery symbol from the magic store, Dezi. Feray has to follow some leads about her family tree in a couple wolf enclaves. The guys are going with us, it seems."

"I know," Revelin interrupts as he snaps his fingers. "Why don't they both join one of the groups? Both of them are older than all of us put together and have lots of power. Plus, if we're lucky, they'll give us senior discounts everywhere."

Tiernan reaches over and smacks the Prince in the back of the head, making actual giggles fall from my mouth. That seems to shock everyone into silence and when Rev pouts, I have to cover my mouth.

"That does seem like it would be a safer plan. If it's amenable," Diaval says begrudgingly.

I blink, not expecting Mr. Picky Whiskey to agree first. *Honestly, I didn't expect either one to agree which is why I'm glad Rev said it. Now it's his fault when it goes sideways.*

"Excellent!" The Fae stands, hopping up on the table next to me with a grin. "So that means the dragon will go with the wolf's men and the sneaky blood bag can come with us, and it's all decided. After all, they should go with the girl they're mates for, right?"

And then all the shouting starts again.

Finally, my sister closes her eyes, putting her hands out in the air as she says, "*Stop.*"

I'll be a son of a beer swilling satyr, that's exactly what everyone does. The shifters all find their seats again and the two ancients give her amused expressions, but calm down as well. I'm still standing on the table with Rev, and I'm pretty sure that's because neither of us are pack animals, so we get to be fucking clowns if we want.

Another dangerous thought for another day.

"Feray's right. We need to figure out how to work together so we can solve this mystery. It's unlikely there aren't more people out there looking for us or waiting for us to drop our guard. Philly being attacked multiple times was a message and traveling to other lands won't stop people who have been putting their plans in motion for decades."

"Besides, the more mates the merrier, right?" Revelin adds. When I give him a dirty look, he shrugs. "I don't know why you're pretending he's not. The idiot's been following you like a hound dog since you started working here. You're not the daft, lass."

All the color drains from my face as I look at him, then all the other people stare at me. *Definitely going to hurl.*

"What? Both of you are taking your merry men on trips—Fluffy's going to Crescent Valley and you're going on tour with a rockstar. Won't it be grand?"

I'm seriously considering getting 'fucking Fae' tattooed on my ass, but I think he'd enjoy it too much.

"Seriously, guys. If we're going to split up, we have to make a bunch of plans in a very short time. We'll need everything from new phones to housesitters and…"

That's when I start tuning my sister out as I look at the red eyed vampire and the golden eyed dragon. They're communicating without words over there as Feray outlines all the things we'll have to get together before we leave. I don't know why, but their smug know-it-all shit makes me want to scream.

Honestly, I don't even know if all of us are going to survive these journeys, much less find out the truth.

But there's only one way to find out…

FIND out in Waxing Crescent (Book Two of Children of the Moon)

REVIEWS

If you have enjoyed this book, please leave reviews!
It helps other readers find our work,
which helps us as indie authors.

Thank you!

**You can add reviews for New Moon Rising on the following
platforms:**

Amazon
Goodreads
Bookbub

SNEAK PEEK: SECRETS OF STATE U

HONORIS. VERITAS. POTENTIA.

The Society tried to punish me by sending me to State U to reign in the corruption, but I have news for them.

Fighting with my ex's loyal toadies and fending off five men who are determined to get under my skin wasn't on my bucket list, but Morgana LeCiel never backs down from a challenge.

Nothing is going to stop me from securing my freedom--not even the dead bodies that keep turning up.

Read the first three episodes free on Kindle Vella: https://hi.switchy.io/bloodontheice

Episodes drop on Tuesdays and Fridays!

- University in the South
- FMC that takes no sh!t
- Hockey playing polar bear shifter
- Grad student Siren
- Magic professor
- Dragon Prince & Bodyguard
- Secret Society
- Mûrdér
- K!nk, BD$M & Steam
- Why Choose
- Wings, Fur, and Scales

QUEEN BEE

They dim the lights in the club, and the spots click on as the curtain slides open.

It's a full house tonight in the little burlesque club off the Rue Pierre Montaine.

Chez Arc En Ciel is not well known compared to the *Moulin Rouge* or *Le Lido*, but the wealthy from both sides of the Seine gather here for shows four nights a week. If you pass the various layers of security checks to even be permitted to book a reservation, you also have to be able to afford the two thousand Euro per guest cover charge. If you don't eat or drink anything, that's all it will cost; however, that would get you blacklisted.

Intro music pumps through the speakers and I stand on my mark in the opening position. My cane is resting on the wooden boards of the stage by my front foot as I pretend to lean on it. Roars of applause echo through the room as our troupe of dancers catch the lights, sequins sparkling like diamonds when the stage lights rise. We're dressed in pinstriped black pant suits and fedoras to match the big band style opening to the song. As soon as the horn-filled intro finishes, the dance begins.

I follow the routine with precision, snapping and popping my hips to the beat as we spread out across the stage. You wouldn't know by the fake smile on my face that I'm scanning the crowd. Two fan kicks later, I've rotated past the proscenium, and I think I've found my mark. Twirling, I stop in the place I need to be for the bridge, singing along as if my life depends on it. It might, to be honest, because I need to sell my cover tonight, so no one notices me.

The Guillotine moves in the shadows, but tonight, she's in the spotlight.

My ass shakes as I dance my way through the song, swinging the prop cane I'd replaced with one of my design. You wouldn't know by looking at it, but it's not the painted balsa the other dancers have for a very specific reason. I need it to complete the mission that forced me to spend two months in Paris working my way into this job at *Chez Arc En Ciel*. If I can't strike tonight, the surveillance, counterintelligence, and time spent building this cover are wasted because my mark is leaving for Asia tomorrow.

Tonight, the Cobra dies for his sins.

The break of the song slows the music and the dancers pour into the crowd to wiggle around the rich assholes. It's choreographed, but it's also to advertise each girl for private dances in the lounges upstairs. We're not strippers—not that there's a damned thing wrong with a woman using her body to support herself—but we do bare more skin in the closed rooms. The *laissez-faire* attitude of the owners means as long as we kick them thirty percent of the fees for those dances, they don't care what any of the girls do in the rooms. I'd find it sleazy, but the girls who work here are highly skilled performers who choose to make thousands of dollars a night rather than peanuts in some ballet troupe or chorus line.

By the time I've flirted my way to the VIP tables, the Cobra is staring intently at all of us. Spotlights pin each one of us on the floor at the bass hits, and I swivel my hips as my free hand slides down to the secret spot on my jacket. In unison, we tear the jackets off to reveal rhinestone studded bras with straps crisscrossing our waists like shibari ropes. A lift of the fedora and pop of my hip, along with the beat, draws the fierce-looking brawler's eyes directly to me. I pout prettily and stalk towards his table with the swagger of a tiny dicked asshole that owns a monster truck.

His thin lips pull back over the famed curving fangs he had implanted. Dark, glittering eyes follow every move I make as I approach, and I pretend to whip my hair from side to side as I check for his guards. They're here somewhere, but I need them to be far away so I can beat my escape before they notice. When I get within inches, I tap his leg with my cane and spin around to shake my ass in his face. The grunt of approval makes me want to heave, but I turn, holding onto the prop with both hands. My feet click on the floor in a soft shoe step as I make 'fuck me' eyes at the dirty bastard. He leans back, his pants tented as he gestures towards his lap.

Fucking gross.

I don't care about his weapons trade or what happens when people get the shit he moves. I have no clue why I have to take him out. The reason they have sentenced him to death isn't part of my contract, and I'm nothing if not a dispassionate observer of the darkest parts of human desires. Twelve years at *l'Academie* ensured I care very little about anything that isn't directly related to my ability to complete my jobs.

Sighing, I dance closer and drop onto his rather unimpressive erection and wiggle. There's plenty of cloth between us to prevent him from doing anything I'd make a scene over, so I focus on the task at hand. I slip the cane behind his head, resting the wood against his neck as I tug him forward. The move reads as playfully bringing his face to my breasts, but at the last second, I click the release built into the custom weapon. One end slides open to reveal the razor sharp garotte and before he can say a word, I yank it through.

Faint gurgling is the only noise besides the end of the song, and I carefully slide the sides of the cane together. Climbing off the nasty fucker, I put my hands on his cheeks so I can pretend to flirt with him while I arrange the head so it looks as if he's leaning back in the booth. It needs to look realistic to allow me to return to the stage with the others. When I have it settled, I back away from the booth, blowing fake kisses as I walk backwards through the crowd. I almost collide with a dark-haired guy with his collar pulled high as I head for the stage, and I roll my eyes. Whatever celeb that is trying to keep their face away from the paps is doing a shitty job of it.

The entire troupe takes a few bows and shuffles off of stage left to the wings. I exhale a sigh of relief when the next group enters on the opposite side. I haven't heard shouting yet, so I don't think the

Cobra's men realize he's down. Now I take this emetic pill, have a vomiting episode, and I'll get sent home.

That's when Arabella Montaigne, the burlesque dancer, will cease to exist, and Remy Arsine Benoit will re-emerge.

I smile to myself as I chew on the tablet that will have me retching my guts out in a few moments. This is a more complex extermination than I usually prefer, and I can't leave my normal calling card behind. The Cobra's head had to remain in the booth rather than get delivered to his home in a basket.

Such a shame, that. I quite enjoy the reactions my little gifts engender when they're discovered.

Walking into the dressing room, I carefully strip my costume off, putting all the pieces in my bag. Every item in the locker room that belongs to gets placed in the duffel carefully as I wait for the effects to hit me. It won't do to leave loose ends, even if my prints have never touched a single surface in this place. My gut roils and I turn, facing one of the other dancers as the vomit finally comes. Gracelia screams like she's being skinned when I hurl on her and it's every-thing I can do *not* to smirk through the chunks.

"C'est la merde!" she shouts, running for the showers as if she's on fire.

It takes less than a minute for the owner to send me home for the night. I walk out the back door of the building with everything just as the sirens scream.

Perfect timing, as always.

I jump into the first cab I can hail, directing him to the *Hôtel de Crillon*. Their suites are the ritziest in Paris, and it's my go-to hideout when I'm here. I used to only stay in the Bernstein Suite, but some rich fuckwad purchased it six months ago. If I could track them down and beat the hell out of them, I would, but I booked my schedule until late 2025. Assassins with my skill set and accuracy are getting harder to find. They forced the old guard into retirement because they refuse to adapt to the digital age. Too many cameras, crime labs, and hackers running about to do everything Cold War style.

The future of murder for hire is millennial, people. We're old enough to be stable, but young enough to be agile with new technology. Plus, most of them are broke AF from crooked ass student loans.

It's not an issue I have, but I've been in the business since I hit double digits. You don't survive *l'Academie des Invisibles* if you haven't killed someone before the end of primary school. It's unheard of.

I was eight the first time I used the weapon that would become my signature.

Shivering, I tap on the window of the cab and bitch the driver out. He's taking a longer route than necessary to raise my fare, and I'll have his guts for garters if he doesn't knock it the fuck off. A string of curses in French erupt from him when I voice the accusation, and I slam my palm on the window with enough force to crack the plexiglass barrier. He almost drives into another car, but when he regains control, he makes the requested adjustments to our route.

We arrived at the front entrance after a few more arguments and a traffic jam around the *Champs*. I throw the euros at him in disgust, memorizing the medallion number for later. He's not worth my time, but I have quite a few contacts who might be interested in blackmailing a cabbie in town. Getaway cars are cliche in the crime world now. Most ne'er-do-wells like myself find greater comfort in anonymous taxis or ride-share accounts hacked through the deep web accessed on burner phones. If your ride doesn't know you're a villain, there's no one to flip if law enforcement comes looking.

I never look the same for any job—ever.

I will not use Arabella Montaigne as a cover in the future, and once I move to the location of my next job, I'll ensure that she meets with a terrible fate. It's a lot more work to slowly kill off my alters once I've used them, but it's also why I've never even come close to being caught. The dancer with long wavy red hair, freckles, and big green eyes will never grace the streets of Paris again after I hop a plane. She will, however, get a minor story in the paper and an obituary when I decide how she tragically dies.

The Guillotine will rise from her ashes and be reborn.

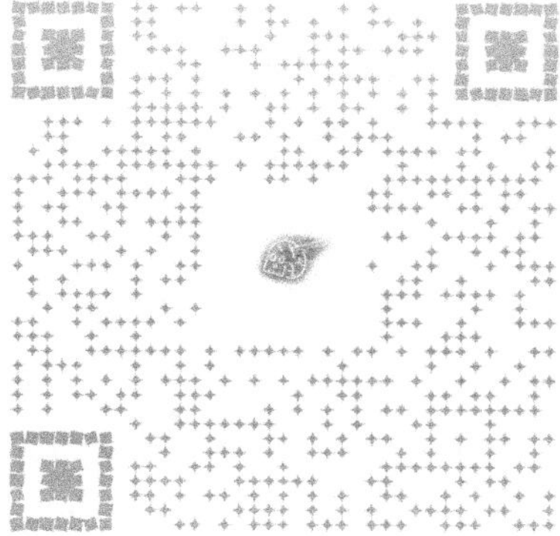

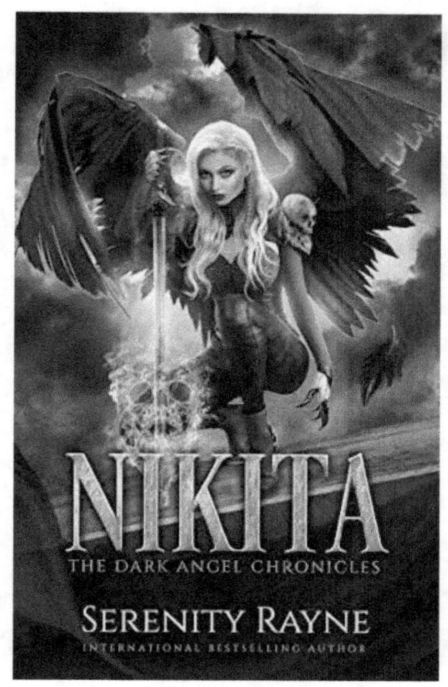

I am my mother's savage daughter...

My darkness comes with hell-fire and an impossibly sharp sword—all the better to rule when I take over my Grandfather's throne.

The elders insist the dark days are behind us, but something is stirring in the Underworld. I can feel its sinister tendrils like the blood in my veins, but the source remains hidden. Whatever this festering mass in the Wraith is, I vow to lead the hunt to destroy it and protect my people.

That is until my mother presents me with the worst five inches I've ever received—my invitation to society and the key to ascending to the throne.

Being the Death Incarnate *and* a queen isn't easy, but if I want to rule, I have to balance my thirst for vengeance and my royal persona.

Hell won't know what hit them...

Get it now!

As I watch the procession carrying my brother's casket pass by, I know the world as I knew it is over.

The Gentleman's meeting should have been safe—two families celebrating the arranged marriage that would align the Veneto's and Romanov's in their fight to rule the streets. An unwelcome guest rained down bullets killing Tony and wounding several others in the process.

My brother's death left a void in the family and now I have no choice but to marry the Romanov Don's eldest son Viktor—a man I blame for my brother's death.

No arranged marriage could ever make me let go of the anger I have for the man I hold responsible for my brother's death. I realize Viktor will go to any length to protect his prize—but who will be there to protect me when I fall for the man with a heart of ice?

Get it now!

ABOUT SERENITY RAYNE

Serenity Rayne spends most of her time either howling at the moon or creating cheeky crafts in her lair. Since she published the first book in the bestselling Aurora Marelup series, she's released sixteen more books while surviving being a nurse during the COVID-19 pandemic.

Serenity writes strong women who find their way in the world through blood and fire, learning to love and trust the men who adore them. Her books also feature positive LGBTQ representation, loss, and all the emotions that transcend species. Though her catalog has been focused on paranormal why choose and horror, she is now branching out to write contemporary why choose as well. She lives on a farm with dogs, chickens, peacocks, a one-eyed horse, and her son, who is way more like her than he wants to admit.

ALSO BY SERENITY RAYNE

Pre-orders:

Claimed by the Alpha Pack

Daughters of the Destroyer - Nikita

His to Protect

Luna Found

Children of the Moon: New Moon Rising

Shifters:

Her Elemental Mates

The Aurora Marelup Saga

Ascend

Hunt

Fight

Attack

Welcome Home

Klaus Christmas

Princess Lost

Destiny Found

Tiamat

The Dark Angel Chronicles:

Discovered

Innate

Balance

Destroyer

Omnibus with Bonus content

Stand alones:

Heart Shaped Box

Blood Moon Pack

Once Upon the a Raven

ABOUT CASSANDRA FEATHERSTONE

Cassandra Featherstone has been writing since she could hold a pencil.

She wrote her first story about a girl picking strawberries when she was three and has been creating worlds in her head ever since. After winning multiple awards for essays, poems, short stories and a very cheesy academy romance novel in high school, they selected her to attend the prestigious Governors School for the Arts in high school.

Her love of the arts is vast: she plays three instruments and marched flute/piccolo for six years), took ten years of tap/jazz/ballet/tumbling, and sang/acted major roles in many musicals and plays. She auditioned for a slew of colleges, but selected NYU for musical theater and lived in NYC for several years while she was in the studio.

After meeting her husband, she moved back to the Midwest and eventually spawned her mini-me, affectionately known as the goblin.

She has worked in many industries, from banking to retail management and, most recently, a decade in multiple positions at an indie bookstore until COVID-19 permanently closed her educational services department.

Cassandra is passionate about literacy, but when she picked up her laptop to write her first published novel in March 2020, she focused on subjects that not only spoke to her soul, but affected many of the women she'd met throughout her twisty life path.

Bullying, PTSD, body dysmorphia, mental illness, reinvention, and claiming your space are frequent themes in her books, as well as respectful, non-fetishized representation of LGBTQIA+ relationships. Her expansion of the reverse harem genre to include various types of polycules and diverse characters with three-dimensional personalities, hopes, and dreams was less common when she first published, but to her delight, becoming a standard reader request in the current atmosphere.

Because of her personal experiences in middle and high school, Cassandra is a staunch defender of those who get targeted by those with actual or perceived power that attack those who don't.

She's also affectionately known as the Muppet for her outrageous, extroverted personality and her wacky brand of theater kid social media posts and videos.

Cassandra lives in the Midwest/South with her computer geek husband, artsy college goblin, an author dog, and five cats that Loki himself spawned. Her works include sci-fi fantasy/urban fantasy, paranormal, humorous, contemporary, and academy whychoose/polyam romances with characters over eighteen. Her books never include non-consensual elements, but feature accurate, safe depictions of BDSM and kink lifestyles.

READ MORE AT CASSANDRA'S WEBSITE OR HER FACEBOOK PAGE. SIGN UP FOR EXCLUSIVE CONTENT AND UPDATES HERE.

TRIANGLES & TRIBULATIONS

Hoist the Flag (PQ)

Yo-Ho Holes (Book One)

COVEN OF THE SERPENT

Daughters of Hecate (Book One)

CHILDREN OF THE MOON- WITH SERENITY RAYNE

New Moon Rising (Book One)

THE APEX SOCIETY CAPERS

Come Out and Prey

Let Us Prey

In Prey We Trust (Pre-order now!)

ANTHOLOGIES

Unwritten

Shifters Unleashed

Jingle My Balls

Love is in the Air

(Featuring 'Reunion in the Hollow' with Serenity Rayne)

Of Seas and Storms (2024)

CODENAME: THE RIFT SERIES

Special Edition of Codename: The Rift

Special Edition of A New World Order

The Alpha & The Omega

Trials of the Beast (Winter 2024)

Book Five (Winter 2025)

Book Six (Tentative Fall 2026)

Book Seven (Tentative Spring 2027)

Book Eight (Tentative Fall 2028)

THE EARLY YEARS PREQUELS

An Investigative Tour of 'The Company' Starring Delilah L. O'Hara, Part One
*(Only available in the Special Edition of Codename: The Rift)***

An Investigative Tour of 'The Company' Starring Delilah L. O'Hara, Part Two
*(Only available in the Special Edition of A New World Order)***

The Caravan (Coming Winter 2023)

Into the Wilde

The Escape Plan (Newsletter Sign-up Exclusive)**

Hubris (Coming Winter 2024)

The Old Switcheroo (Coming Summer 2024)

Baby Steps (Coming Fall 2025)

Situation F.U.B.A.R (Coming Winter 2024)

The Beast Speaks (Coming Winter 2025)

THE WINTER PREQUELS

The Beast Rising: The Riftverse Prequels Boxed Set

(Contains: Diary of Genesis, Delilah, Forgiveness, A Twisted Path, and The
Beginning)

THE CLAW ENFORCEMENT CHRONICLES

Call the Magickal Midwife

All in the Family (Coming Spring 2024)

THE SIDE QUESTS

Hallelujah

Trial by Fire (Coming Winter 2025)

The Kitty Does Halloween

The Beast, The Maiden, and The Perfect Present